THE WIFE SITUATION

THE BILLIONAIRE SITUATION SERIES

LYRA PARISH

The Wife Situation
Billionaire Situation Series, #1

Editor: Jovana Shirley
Unforeseen Editing
http://www.unforeseenediting.com

Proofreader: David Michael
Encompass Press
https://www.encompasspress.com

CONTENT WARNING

This book includes "on-page" adult content and language that is not suitable for minors. Infertility is also mentioned.

OFFICIAL PLAYLIST

Serotonia - Highly Suspect
NDA - Billie Eilish
the 1 - Taylor Swift
My Own Worst Enemy - LIT
You Put a Spell On Me - Austin Giorgio
FU in my Head - Cloudy June
intro (end of the world) - Ariana Grande
Jokes On You - Charlotte Lawrence
I GUESS I'M IN LOVE - Clinton Kane
Call It What You Want - Taylor Swift
Like I'm Gonna Lose You, Meghan Trainer
this is what falling in love feels like, JVKE
Lover, Taylor Swift

LISTEN TO THIS PLAYLIST:
https://bit.ly/thewifesituationplaylist

To the girlies who love a tattooed baddie
with German shepherd energy.

Easton Calloway is waiting for you, darling.

Now be a very bad girl and spread those pages.

I want to wear his initial
on a chain 'round my neck.
Not because he owns me.
But 'cause he really knows me.

-Taylor Swift, Call It What You Want

1

LEXI

"Housekeeping." I lightly tap my knuckles against the door and wait for movement on the other side.

When I receive no response, I hold my key card above the reader and push it open while balancing a stack of towels with one hand. Who says I'm not talented?

I flick on the light and am startled by an older man wrapped in a towel. As I begin my apology, he chuckles and reveals his *Tootsie Roll* as if it were a magic trick. All that is missing is a *voilà*. Shock takes over, and I gasp, drop the clean towels onto the floor, and rush out of the room. It's the second time this has happened today.

"*Shit*," I whisper with my hand over my heart.

New York is *nothing* like my hometown that's located in western Texas. But the city isn't new for me either. It's where I called home while attending New York University. A lifetime has passed since then.

Two months ago, when my life spiraled out of control, I packed a suitcase and returned to this concrete jungle. Needless to say, I'm still adjusting.

"Lexi," Carlee says as the service elevator doors open behind me. Her dark hair is twisted into a neat bun, and her uniform is pristine.

I stalk toward my best friend and temporary roommate. We can add coworkers to that list too.

Her mouth transforms into a smile. "Let me guess … you saw another dick?"

"Yes! It was tiny, and his balls looked like … raisins."

"The visual you created in my brain—disgusting." She fishes her phone from her pocket and unlocks it. "Did you see this audition?"

I lean over, knowing we're not supposed to have our devices out, and speed-read the listing.

Carlee stays informed with theater news and celebrity gossip. She even has a blog where she posts about it, hoping to one day become a journalist. If I need to know anything, she's my go-to.

"*A lead*," I whisper, meeting her eyes.

It's only a preview, but it could be significant if the show does well. *Broadway huge.*

It's the type of role that could change my life, something I dreamed of landing before I moved back to Texas eight years ago to be with Beau, my ex. So much has happened, but it's like nothing has changed.

Carlee playfully elbows me as I get lost in my thoughts. "Anyway, it's tonight, and you *have* to go. You're exactly what they're looking for."

"I *have* to work until seven," I remind her, my hands moving down the crisp apron tied around my waist. "And I need *this* job, remember? Mr. Martin will fire me if I leave early."

I'm still in my ninety-day probation period at the W, one of the most elite hotels in the city. It's so luxurious that the name is one letter. No others are needed.

Celebrities, royalty, and even billionaires frequent these walls, and if I have one slip-up or missed shift, I'll be terminated with no questions asked. So, until I find my dream job, this one will have to do. Other than the romance books I consume, working here is the only form of entertainment I have. Often, my shifts are the only reason I leave our tiny apartment.

"You once told me the risk is worth the reward," she reminds me.

I meet her brown eyes. "Sometimes, it is. And when it came to you starting your blog, I was right, wasn't I?"

"You were," she says.

"But this?" I hesitate, glancing down at her phone. I read the requirements again. I'm indifferent, but lately, I've felt that way about life in general, so maybe it's a *me* problem. "I dunno."

"Look, I got approval to stay over to cover for you. Before you decline the offer, it's a selfish request. There are a lot of suits here because of the diamond convention tomorrow, and you know how I feel about a well-dressed man. Staying over gives me more time to admire, listen for hot new gossip, or find a weekend fling." She gives me a mischievous smirk.

Gorgeous men in thousand-dollar suits frequent the W, and while they're Carlee's type, none ever fraternize with hired help. We're invisible to the rich, so it's a lost cause. She's being kind.

"You're sure?"

"Fuck yes."

I smile and wrap my arms around her. Since my return, she's taken on the role of a mother bird, trying to shoo me out of my nest. Carlee wants to see me fly. Hell, I do too.

Recently, I've asked myself why I should even bother anymore. I'm tired of auditioning and not getting callbacks, but quitting isn't an option. The truth is, I have too much to prove, so I'll keep going. I'm either resilient or stubborn. However you'd like to spin it.

"Thank you," I tell her, wanting to be excited.

"Remember, when you're rich and fam—"

"I know; I know. Private jet to Paris with expensive champagne and strawberries."

"Damn straight. Something good is coming," she says, waggling her brows. "Hopefully, it will be me."

I snort. "For your sake, I hope so too."

Carlee can find the bright side in anything. It's something we *had* in common before the shit with my ex changed me. Now, I'm more of a realist and no longer see the world through rose-colored glasses. When someone shows me who they are, I believe them.

She pushes the cart forward. "How was your date last night?"

"Awful." I follow beside her. "He talked about Bitcoin for three hours straight. I barely said a word."

She makes a face. "Oh, Bitcoin bros are the worst. They love the sound of their own voice."

"Yeah, and he asked the server to split the bill to show how alpha he was."

"Eww," Carlee says with a snicker.

Since I've forced myself back into the dating scene, not one of the thirty-seven men I've gone on a first date with has gotten a kiss good night or a second chance. Everyone is so … boring or self-centered or has too much baggage for me to handle.

"I'm officially giving up. I'm broken. The hopeless romantic who's anti-love. Ironic, isn't it?"

She snickers. "You just haven't found the perfect man yet."

"Oh, I have, but he only exists between the pages."

"Maybe the books you've been reading are creating unrealistic expectations?"

Laughter bursts out of me. "Maybe men should do better."

"Okay, you have a point." She shoots me a wink.

When we reach the end of the hall, I realize how much we have to do, especially if I'm leaving early. "Want to divide and conquer?"

"Let's do it."

She wheels the cart out of the way, and we get to it. I handle the beds and restock everything while she wipes flat surfaces and vacuums. We might talk a lot, but we're efficient, so our boss pairs us together often. I'm lucky to have her as a friend.

I snatch the dirty towels from the bathroom floor and remove the linens, wondering how I missed that open-call notice. But after I learned Beau is now public with his side chick, my head has been in the clouds. Oh, and she's pregnant. Forgot about that one. *The big one.*

I let the intrusive thoughts settle deep inside me, allowing them to fuel my determination.

When Carlee enters behind me and sprays the mirrors, I move to the next suite, trashed with wine bottles and takeout containers from the five-star restaurant downstairs. Empty oyster shells and caviar spoons are scattered across the table, along with shards of broken glass. I shake my head.

"Rich people," I mutter.

After two hours, we ride the elevator to the Tower Penthouse, and excitement rushes through me. It's twenty thousand dollars a night; it spans over two stories, four thousand square feet, and has two private bedrooms, an office, and a bathroom with a waterfall shower and Jacuzzi tub. This place for a weekend costs more than I get paid to scrub the porcelain sides of the golden-handled toilets for a year.

"One last spot check before *Mr. Calloway* arrives later today," Carlee says, grabbing a rag and a bottle of cleaner.

She said his name like he's important because those who stay at the Tower Penthouse are. It's not only their ego that tells them that though; it's reality. I couldn't pick out one of them from a lineup and explain what they do. That's how much I *don't* care about their lives. I've got my own problems.

"So, what makes Mr. Calloway so special?" I glance at her.

"Oh, he's drop-dead gorgeous. Total *asshole*. Serial dater. Hates *everyone*. Never smiles."

I turn to her.

"But you didn't ask that. He's a nepo baby. Billionaire, generational wealth out the ass. His family owns diamond mines and jewelry stores."

"Impressive," I say, rolling my eyes.

We arrive at the dark oak doorway that towers over us. The anticipation nearly takes over as I slide my key card across the scanner and push open the heavy door.

The place smells like lavender and luxury with fresh, colorful flowers in vases on every flat surface. The sun shines through the windows. The only thing that would make it better was if it were closer to Central Park.

"Can you imagine staying here?" Carlee asks.

"No," I tell her with a laugh. "It's beautiful but a waste of money."

"But if you've got it to spend, why the hell not?" She looks up at the tall ceiling.

When high-profile clients rent the Penthouse, immaculacy is required. If anything is out of place, it could hurt the W's prestige. The customer is always right because most have enough liquid assets to buy the business outright.

Carlee follows behind me, and when her cell buzzes in her pocket, she stops walking.

"I gotta take this," she says.

If I had to guess by her tone shift, I'd say it's the bartender she called it off with last weekend.

"No personal phone calls," I say, mocking our boss's voice.

"Yeah, yeah. I'll check the kitchen and dining room while I chat. Focus on flecks of dust or fingerprints on the windows and mirrors. That's what Mr. Calloway complained about previously."

"I'll start on the top floor and meet you back here." I keep my tone low.

She quickly answers, her voice rising an octave, like she's

surprised. Her shift is supposed to end in thirty minutes, and it makes me wonder if she's staying over to avoid him. With her, it's about the chase. She collects men like Pokémon, but once they're captured and they say I love you, she's over it. It's a part of her relationship cycle. This guy lasted three weeks.

She walks toward the dining room, throwing a cleaning cloth over her shoulder.

I take the stairs to the top floor, my hand gliding over the smooth railing. On one side of the area is a gigantic bedroom surrounded by windows, and across the hall is the bathroom. I take in the gorgeous room that looks like it fell straight out of a magazine. The vase of flowers isn't quite centered, so I move it over one inch.

The king-size bed overlooks the city, and I can almost imagine rolling around in the silk sheets. When I turn my head, I see the comforter is wrinkled on the edge, so I slide my hand against the material, pulling it tight, and tuck the corner. My eyes land on the gold watch on the table.

I breathe in and pick it up, studying it. In the middle, where the big and small hands connect, there is a symbol, but I don't recognize it. I flip it, and on the back, there's something engraved.

I tilt it, allowing it to shine in the sunlight, and read the words, *LOVE IS ALWAYS ON TIME*.

It's a nice thought, but also cheesy. *Love. Pfft.*

An heiress previously occupied this room, so it could belong to her husband … or *lover*. I smirk, dropping it into the front pocket of my apron to take it to my manager when we finish our final walk-through.

I check each window from different angles, ensuring there are no fingerprints or smudges. After moving to the bathroom, I push open the door. I immediately stop breathing.

The shower is running, and at first, I think Carlee's pranking me, but then I notice a man with thick, messy, dark hair standing under the waterfall stream. Muscles cascade down his tattooed back and arms. A strangled breath releases from me as the water falls over his carved body. This is beautiful torture and will probably haunt my fantasies until the end of time.

When he reaches for the soap, I stumble back and quietly slip out of the bathroom. I take the stairs as fast as I can without falling, which is a miracle because I'm clumsy when I'm nervous.

My thoughts are a discombobulated mess, a ball of yarn tangled together, and all I can think is, *We have to leave* right fucking now.

I stalk through the living room and find Carlee sitting on the dining room table, swinging her legs, laughing. I grab the phone from her hand, end the call, then yank her up. She snatches the cleaning supplies as I pull her toward the door.

"What's going on?" Her brows furrow, and she's using her full inside voice.

"Shh." I search her face, pointing up. "There's a man upstairs, showering," I whisper, panicked with a racing heart.

"*Shit*," she hisses, picking up her pace. She looks as horrified as I feel. "They must've let *Mr. Calloway* check in early."

"The asshole?" I ask when we're finally in the hallway.

"*Yes*." She pushes the cart forward, glancing over her shoulder every few seconds, like he'll swing the door open and catch us.

When we step into the elevator, she lets out a sigh of relief. We're tense and breathing rapidly.

"Did he see you?" I hear the stress in her voice.

"*No*. No, he didn't. Thank God." I recall his muscles and tattoos and swallow hard.

"Good. He'd have had us both fired if he'd found us in his room. He's a recluse. Stays to himself. The memo we received last week? It was about him and his space being off-limits."

"What do we do?" I say.

"I think we're safe," she says.

The elevator stops, the doors open, and no one gets in. Then, we continue down to the bottom.

"When he's in public, does a fan club follow him everywhere? He's a *wet* dream."

She chuckles. "You have no idea. He's also New York's most eligible bachelor."

I reach inside my pocket for some lip balm, and my fingers brush against cool metal.

No. The world is closing in on me.

"That look on your face is *scaring* me." She's too good at reading me.

I slide the watch out and hold it in my palm. We stare at it like it's a bomb that will explode at any second, and it's as dangerous as one.

"When I entered the bedroom, it was sitting on the nightstand. I picked it up, thinking Helen had left it behind." I cover my mouth, realization hitting me like a ton of bricks.

Carlee stares down at it, and I don't think I see her blink once.

"What do I do?" I try not to hyperventilate. "I *have* to return it."

"Lexi, you can't, but you can't keep it either. You should give it to Mr. Martin and explain what happened before Calloway does. Let our boss get ahead of it first, put out fires instead of fighting them."

The double doors slide open, and she pushes the cart out. We stare at one another.

"I've always learned that it's better to ask for forgiveness when it comes to things like this. We know I'll be fired on the spot."

One of the security guards passes us in the hallway and I shove the watch back into my pocket.

"What if I ran up there quickly, rang the doorbell, and gave it back? I could explain to him what happened."

She shakes her head. "You don't understand. There is no *explaining* anything to that man."

"Okay, what if I snuck in, put it right back where he'd left it, then bolt out?"

"Both are *terrible* options. Go tell Mr. Martin."

"You know I'm fired either way." I tuck the loose strands of hair that fell from my bun behind my ears and dig deep inside for courage because I'm scared of what could happen.

"He's one of the biggest assholes I've *ever* had the opportunity to meet."

"You've *met* him?"

"Once. And trust me when I say, it was one time too many. He's not liked by many. There's a reason he's considered the asshole of billionaires."

"I don't have to like him. I only need him to be understanding."

"He won't be," she says. It's nearly a plea.

"The risk is worth the reward," I tell her. "I have to try."

Before the elevator doors slide closed, I rush inside, knowing I don't have a lot of time to execute this ridiculous plan. He was washing his hair. I might have five minutes to spare.

"Lexi!" Carlee rushes forward to stop me, but she can't move around the cart fast enough.

A minute passes before I reach the top floor. Adrenaline pumps through me, and I count to ten, sliding my hand into my pocket. My thumb glides across the smooth surface of the face of his dumb watch that I stupidly took. I have the worst timing in the world. Had I gone to the bathroom first, I'd have never seen it, and I wouldn't be in this situation.

The elevator stops, and I grow nervous with every step forward. I'll put the watch back, go downstairs, change into my street clothes, and leave for the audition. Everything will work out fine. I continue with my pep talk and almost believe it as I wipe my sweaty palms on my apron. When I glance at the doorbell, I consider ringing it. Could this man have an adult conversation with a housemaid who has his property?

I hear Carlee's voice in my head. My personality doesn't get along with assholes because I'm not intimidated by anyone. I might have a shake in my words, but I still rise and speak my truth. *Always.*

The thought of talking to him sounds like a living nightmare, so I'll take my chances and James Bond his watch back to that table. It's a quick sneak up the stairs and back down them. Less than one hundred steps.

My heart throbs in my chest. I realize this is the first adventure I've had since my heartbreak, and as sad as it is, it makes me smile.

I whisper a prayer up to whoever is listening. "Please let my timing be perfect. *Just this once.*"

I wait a few seconds as if someone will answer, then press my key card against the scanner and push open the door.

2

EASTON

Birthday Countdown: 46 Days

I grab a towel and move through the bedroom to the oversized closet. My clothes for the next three days, while I'm staying at the W, are neatly hung, as instructed. I slide on a freshly pressed pair of black slacks and a white button-up, then I adjust a black tie around my neck. Before going downstairs to meet with my bodyguard, Brody, I sit on the edge of the bed to put on my shoes. As I instinctively reach for my watch on the nightstand, my hand stops midair.

"What the *fuck*?" I whisper, standing, certain where I placed it.

Right there. Right fucking there.

My eyes scan the floor, but I know it couldn't have fallen because I'm not reckless. I take care of the things I cherish.

As I glance around the room, everything is the same, except for a vase on an accent table. I stand in front of it, staring at it, swearing it was a smidgen to the left, but I also know that's impossible. I've been the only person up here since I arrived exactly thirty minutes ago.

I return to the bathroom and reach inside the pockets of the clothes I was previously wearing. *Empty,* as I predicted. Shit *doesn't* disappear ... it *walks* off. And while I could buy a million other fucking watches, *that* one is irreplaceable.

Shaking my head, I decide to go downstairs. When I take the bottom step, I barely have enough time to realize there's someone in the room, and she's about to crash into me. I brace myself for the collision, and she stumbles backward, losing her balance. Before she can fall, I grab on to her tightly, pulling her into my chest, and steady us.

That was close.

Her pouty red lips part as I meet her emerald-green eyes. The faint hint of her perfume lingers, and her mere presence causes me to take pause. Everything freezes, maybe even time itself. My mouth opens and closes as I tower over her small frame. I realize I'm still holding her as our warm breaths mix together, so I drop my hands to my sides, step away, and create much-needed space.

"Hi," she says.

It's hard for me to place her expression, but there's a twinkle of something as she visibly eye-fucks me.

"Hello." My gaze scans down the gray dress with the W logo embroidered in the corner. It falls gently below her knees. The crisp white apron cinches tightly around her small waist.

She's not wearing any jewelry—no earrings, necklace, *or* wedding ring. Not even a bracelet. A woman as beautiful as her deserves to be spoiled, showered in riches. The immediate attraction is undeniable, but also insufferable and not what I need.

A hint of a blush hits her cheeks, and she chews on her lip.

The silent but *dangerous* conversation continues. How can

this woman steal my breath in such a profound way that it leaves me puzzled? Nearly speechless.

"*Hi*," she says again.

"You already said that," I tell her with a brow popped. "But you can leave now. I arrived earlier than planned, and they must've forgotten to inform you."

I'm usually not so forgiving, but this *has* to be a misunderstanding. Everyone at the W is aware I'm not to be disturbed while I'm here. I've made it crystal fucking clear. It's been talked about in the gossip magazines, the ones that have covered my family, right alongside the Vanderbilts, Astors, and Rockefellers. Thanks to them, the goddamn world knows I prefer to be alone. Except *her*.

So, I'll do this one act of kindness. When she's about to say something else, I catch the glint of gold held tight in her balled fist. My body tenses when I see it and my jaw clenches.

"What's in your hand?" The question comes out steady but with frustration. And people wonder why I'm not kinder. It always bites me in the ass.

Her dark brows crease as she glances down at *my* property and swallows hard.

She shouldn't be in here, not like this, and seeing my grandfather's watch in her possession is a cruel joke. A gorgeous *thief*, the only woman who's ever had the ability to steal my breath away with a single glance, is my karma. I nearly laugh at the severity of the situation, but keep it tucked deep inside for me to focus on in the middle of the night.

I step forward, holding out my palm, but I don't take my intense gaze from her. My nostrils flare as she gently returns what she took.

"What's your name?" I roll the shirtsleeve to my forearm before sliding the cool metal onto my wrist. I adjust it, glancing at the logo of my family's business on the clock face. It's past four, and in a few hours, I'll be schmoozing investors while closing multimillion-dollar deals.

I tuck my hands into my pockets, glaring back at her. When her pretty face saddens, my heart almost stops beating. But I need to know who she is and why she's here.

"*Your name*?" I breathe out, growing impatient with every passing second. The words come out harsher than I intended, but I'm fucking pissed and disappointed. "Did someone send you?"

I've never met anyone who dared to take *anything* from me. There has to be a better explanation for this. *No one* keeps me waiting, but here I am, with bated breath, desperate for this woman to tell me who the fuck she is.

"Mr. Calloway," she kindly says, clearing her throat.

"That's *my* name. Now, I'd like *yours*. And please don't make me ask again." It comes out like a growl as I continue to grow impatient.

"No one *sent* me. I'm Alexis, but I prefer to be called Le—" Her voice is sweet with a hint of a Southern drawl.

She's charming, but I've never met a criminal who wasn't. Especially in the business I'm in.

"I don't give a fuck, *Alexis*. Why are you here?" I glare at her, scratching my finger down the scruff on my cheek.

"It's *Lexi*," she corrects.

"Why did you have my watch?" I cross my arms over my chest.

"I'm sorry. I was cleaning and saw it on the nightstand, and that was it. No one sent me. I—"

"You took it." I'm unamused as my care meter begins to lower.

"Yes. But you're unwilling to let me explain myself, so I guess this conversation is over, isn't it?"

"Correct." I need her out of my space.

"Ugh."

She groans *at* me, and the ghost of a smile plays on my lips.

I'm not used to anyone being so fearless around me, or maybe it's carelessness. Most are too intimidated, afraid I'll be the man they've been warned about. But it's obvious Alexis doesn't care about who I am or what it is I do. If I didn't know better, I'd say she believes *I'm* the inconvenience.

"You can leave now," I state, wanting to be alone.

She glances away, and I can see the anger building behind her eyes. I shouldn't find her reaction adorable.

"You've already wasted enough of my time today."

"Wow. For a second, I thought you'd be different from the rest of them."

Her words shouldn't affect me, but they fucking wound me.

"You thought wrong."

And when her perfect mouth moves into a firm line, I think she knows she struck a nerve.

"I hope you have the day you deserve, Mr. Calloway." She mockingly curtsies me, then turns toward the exit.

"Goodbye, *Alexis*." It's the last thing I say before the door slams closed.

I try to relax, feeling the metal on my wrist, the reason for this entire encounter.

I immediately call the concierge. "I'd like to speak to Mr. Martin, please."

He's the manager of the hotel, the only man I deal with when on these premises. Because my family's company is hosting the world's largest diamond convention at this location, I was compensated for a weekend stay at the Tower Penthouse.

"Yes, *Mr. Calloway*, one moment."

I'm placed on hold.

I exclusively stay at this hotel chain when I travel, and considering who I am, I thought my requests during this visit would be taken seriously. The only reason I'm staying on-site instead of at my penthouse is so I didn't have to travel. It also gives me an escape if the conference grows too overwhelming. As an introvert, I can only handle so much peopling.

While I patiently wait for Mr. Martin, the door opens again. This time, it's Brody, and he's carrying a bag of food.

"Special delivery," he says, holding it up.

When he looks in my direction, he tilts his head. He's my cousin, and he's worked for me for fifteen years. He almost knows me better than my identical twin brother, Weston.

I glance at the time; a minute has passed.

Mr. Martin finally answers. He's lucky; I don't wait longer than sixty seconds for anyone.

"Mr. Calloway. How may I be of service, sir?"

He's breathless.

"I'd like an explanation for why your housekeeper—*Alexis*—entered my room and stole my watch."

Brody's jaw drops to the floor.

"Excuse me? Alexis Matthews?" Mr. Martin's voice rises an octave, which is surprising. He's usually calm and collected.

He's concerned. Hell, so am I. But now, I have her *full name.*

Alexis Matthews.

"I've mentioned countless times that I don't want to be disturbed in the Tower while I reside here. Over the years, the W has complied with my request without issues. However, what happened today is *unacceptable,* and I hope you take care of it *immediately.*"

There's a long pause, and I don't have to threaten to take my business elsewhere. He can read the invisible writing on the wall and already knows what's on the line. I will move every convention my company hosts for the next two decades to a competitor who doesn't hire beautiful little thieves who sneak into guests' rooms and steal family heirlooms.

"Yes, sir. Please accept my sincerest apologies. This will *never* happen again. Guaranteed."

"Thank you." I end the call, then walk to the door and turn

the deadbolt. The last thing I need is another person entering without permission.

Brody turns to me. "Easton, I was gone for thirty minutes. What the fuck happened?"

"I *almost* found my conscience," I say.

Her green eyes already haunt me.

"Damn," he says with a laugh. "Now, that would've been a miracle."

I return upstairs to grab my suit jacket, wanting to erase Alexis Matthews from my mind. The sooner I can forget those pouty lips and how loose strands of dark hair fell around her face as she looked up at me, the better.

Today, I met the woman I'd eat a poisoned apple for. Thank fuck I won't *ever* have to see her again.

3

LEXI

With my heart trying to escape my chest, I rush to the laundry facility to search for Carlee. As soon as I spot her, I drag her toward the storage lockers so we can have more privacy. Adrenaline bursts through me, and my knees are shaking. Me being flustered is the first indicator that things didn't go as planned.

"What happened?" She searches my face.

I might be sick as I breathe in. I lock my fingers together and raise them over my head, hoping to calm down.

"Blow in my face," I tell her, flapping my hands to cool off my hot cheeks. I might combust.

You know how I know Carlee is one of my besties? She doesn't even hesitate and blows her cinnamon breath in my face. I close my eyes tight.

When I get too overwhelmed, it's weirdly the only thing that helps.

"You were right." I wish I could go back in time and do things differently. "I should've reported it to Mr. Martin. Ugh. I'm so mad at myself. And my entire body is on fire!"

"Let me guess. Your timing was shit, like always, and he caught you?"

"*Yes*," I whine, remembering how I crashed into him because I wasn't paying attention. I was too focused on the plan, the same plan that went to Hell in a handbasket as soon as our eyes locked. "He had the audacity to accuse me of stealing. I've never stolen anything in my life. Never had the temptation, want, or need!"

"You, a thief?" Her head falls back on her shoulders, and she laughs. "Did he yell? He seems like he'd throw tantrums. Little nepo baby."

"He didn't raise his voice once. He was eerily calm and somehow, that was worse." I hesitate. "It felt like the entire world was collapsing around me when he saw his watch in my hand. I swear he damned me to Hell, Carlee. I'm so fired."

She continues giggling and blowing on my face. "You're being dramatic."

"It's not funny," I cry out as I have an existential crisis.

Mortification takes me under. I grab my hot cheeks. I've never experienced embarrassment quite like this.

I won't survive this.

I won't survive *him*.

Knowing a man like him exists …

"I'm sorry for laughing," she says, squeezing my shoulder. "What else happened?"

"I could barely speak. And you know that *never* happens. I said hi *twice*. Twice!" I mock myself. "*Hi*. He says hello in his deep, booming voice. Then, I stupidly said *hi—again*. And now, he probably thinks I'm an *idiot*."

She searches my face and smirks. "You act like you fell in love with him. I mean, *fuck*, I would. Plus, he's single."

"At first sight? Impossible." I wave her off, imagining his naked body and tattoos, not wanting to forget how damn good he smelled after that shower. Mahogany and mint mixed together. "I'm anti-love. It's not even an option."

"They say you fall hard when you least expect it," she singsongs.

"Who is this *they*? Because they don't know what they're talking about. Also, isn't he *old*?" I cross my arms over my chest.

Keeping up with billionaires has *never* been my thing unless they're fictional. I'm sure a quick internet search would give me more information than I want.

"I think he's thirty-nine. That's only ten years older than yo—"

"It doesn't matter," I interrupt, holding up my hand before dropping it back to my side.

I won't even entertain this idea. It's ridiculous. A stupid fairy tale, a fantasy. But I know when I looked into his blue eyes, I felt a shift. Something happened before it turned into a horrible disaster. And I don't want to admit that to anyone, not even myself.

"It will work out," she urges. "It always does."

"Yeah, maybe he'll forget it," I tell Carlee, trying to reason with logic. "Who knows? It could be my lucky day. He was going to let me leave."

"Alexis Matthews."

I freeze when I recognize my *boss's* voice. As my eyes slam shut, I wish I could disappear and wake up from this nightmare. Carlee's smile falters, and she tenses. My back is to him, so he can't see my reaction, thankfully, because shit just got *very* serious.

"To my office, please," he snaps.

"I'm fucked," I mutter, my heart rate galloping in my chest. "So entirely fucked."

"Explain your truth," she whispers as I turn and follow Mr. Martin to his dungeon.

I stare at the back of his black, perfectly pressed suit. There's not a wrinkle or a piece of loose lint in sight. He exudes excellence and luxury, everything the W represents. Everything I'm not.

When I step inside the cold room, I'm asked to sit. His desk has a hand-carved W in the front, along with the hotel crest. The same one that's embroidered into my uniform.

"Do you know why I've called you into my office?" He interlocks his fingers and stares me down.

He's stern, but I guess when you're forced to kiss the feet of rich people all day, it wears a person down to this.

I calmly exhale. "Yes, sir. I can expla—"

"*Ms. Matthews.*"

"Lexi," I correct.

"Mr. Calloway stated you were in his quarters and had taken his watch. Did you?"

"It was an accident."

He tilts his head.

"I know that sounds ridiculous, but it's the truth. I didn't know he'd arrived early, and I thought it was left behind. I planned to turn it into lost and found."

"But you didn't," he says. "You went back to the Tower Penthouse instead."

"Yes," I whisper, knowing I shouldn't have done that. There's only one punishment for a thief—*even though I'm not one*—so I prepare myself for the inevitable.

"I don't understand. When you returned, did you know he was in his room?"

This question catches me off guard.

"I did." It's the truth. I have no reason to lie about that. He stunned me stupid.

"But you still entered when all employees have been notified not to enter the Tower while he's on-site."

"Yes," I admit, knowing now that it's not the watch that's getting me fired, but my inability to follow company policy.

"Over the years, we've had plenty of women obsessed with Mr. Calloway. If this was an attempt to meet—"

"It wasn't," I snap, not allowing him to finish that thought as my cheeks burn hot.

I disassociate halfway through his explanation. He discusses the optics, the business they'd lose, and the gossip that would spread around elite circles that continue to support the W.

Meanwhile, I'm only concerned about how I'll pay my bills. Our rent is due next Friday, and I won't have enough money to cover it if I get fired. I want to believe it will be okay, but I'm living to work and working to live. It's a vicious cycle, the rat race we're all participating in. Right now, I feel like I'm stuck in a hamster wheel as I wait for something good to happen. Unfortunately, I've only had bad luck.

"Because of the reasons discussed, I have no choice but to terminate you, effective immediately. News that our housekeeper took a *family heirloom* of the Calloway dynasty could destroy our reputation, and you know that's what the W was built upon."

"Reputation or the Calloways?" I ask. I'm already fired. It doesn't matter anymore.

I meet his cold gaze, telling myself I won't show any emotion. It's a replaceable job, one of a million, but it doesn't stop the emotions from rushing through me. The tears I've held back for months threaten to spill, but I won't give this man the satisfaction of seeing me cry. I'm an actress, for fuck's sake, and I put on the performance of a lifetime as I tuck my emotions and lock them away.

"Please turn in your uniform and return your badge."

"Yes, sir."

There is no reason to argue. I knew when I left the Tower floor, I was fired. I hoped I was wrong.

He clears his throat. "You have fifteen minutes before you're escorted from the premises."

I stand. My heart might burst out of my chest as I go to my locker and grab my bag. After changing into my street clothes, I go to security. I wish I had never taken that watch, but I also wish the beautiful bastard had a conscience. It's too bad. Perfect man, shitty personality.

As I round the corner, I nearly crash into Carlee. She sees the gray dress and white apron neatly folded in a stack in my hand.

"They're firing you?" She's as pissed as me. "What the fuck?"

"Yeah. Text me when you get a chance. Otherwise, I'll see you at home." I don't want to cause a scene, and I know I have three minutes until I'm trespassing and escorted out. I need to disappear.

"Okay, I will. I'm so sorry, Lexi," she says. "We'll fix it."

"It will be fine," I say, but it's more for myself than for her.

I slide everything across the counter and leave without telling any of my other coworkers goodbye. This wasn't on my bingo card today.

When I'm outside, I stare into the street as people pass me. The warm summer breeze surrounds me, and I'm at a loss as to what I should do. I'm twenty-nine, and I have never been fired, not even from the shitty jobs I half-assed as a teenager. This is an experience I will never be able to put on my résumé.

The pessimistic internal dialogue begins and I question if I can do this or if I need to get over my pipe dream and find a real career. Like the dead-end teaching job I held back in Valentine for a few years. While it was respectable, each day I walked into that classroom, I died a little inside.

When someone bumps into me on the sidewalk, I'm jerked back to my reality. I'll pick myself up off the ground and try again, like always, even when life has beaten me down. If I can make it here, I can make it anywhere. Or at least that's the lie I eat daily.

I fall into the crowd and follow the direction of traffic, needing to shake the funk. I almost don't feel my phone buzzing in my pocket.

CARLEE

I can't believe this.

LEXI

You should. Calloway contacted Mr. Martin about his watch, and, well, the rest is history.

CARLEE

I'm in shock!

LEXI

I'm pissed.

CARLEE

I can help you get another job. I've got a few favors to call in. So, don't worry about it. Tonight, focus on your audition. Break a leg!

I forgot about the audition. I'm not in the right headspace.

LEXI

Thank you. Appreciate it.

CARLEE

You're still going, right? Don't let this asshole ruin this for you!

LEXI

I won't. I'm heading there now.

I wait to cross the street at the edge of the sidewalk. I'm a little over two miles away, so I walk, hoping it clears my mind. Returning to Texas with my tail between my legs isn't an option. I refuse to let the naysayers win. Right now, I desperately want something to work out for once. Maybe this audition is my shining light.

When I arrive at the small theater, I see a big, bright cancellation notice on the door. I stand in front of it, staring at the sign, and shake my head.

"This is my luck," I whisper, take a picture, and text it to Carlee.

She immediately calls me. "When one door closes, a window opens."

"I think I want to write a screenplay," I say, forcing myself to walk away. It wasn't meant to be.

"I support this amazing idea! You totally should."

As I leave the theater and take the stairs down to the subway, she gives me a pep talk. I can tell she's trying to pump me up, encouraging me, but I zone out. I feel lost.

"Did you hear me?" she finally asks.

I shake my head. "Sorry. No. Was lost in my head."

"I asked if you're quitting on life."

"No. Absolutely not," I confirm. "I'm just tired of being down on my luck."

As I wait for the next train, I see an advertisement for Calloway Diamonds on the wall. I recognize the symbol that was in the center of that fucking watch. A diamond with a triangle.

I groan and turn my back toward the poster. If *only* I'd recognized it before I shoved it into my pocket.

Carlee continues, "Chin up. This is a new beginning, baby. And maybe one day, you'll be able to look back on this moment and realize it's the one that changed your life."

"Who knows?" I tell her.

Then, we say our goodbyes, and the line falls silent.

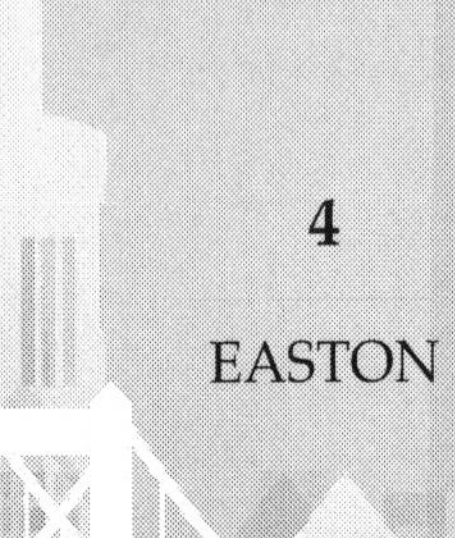

4

EASTON

Birthday countdown: 44 days
Since meeting her: 2 days

After I finish my closing remarks, the diamond convention ends without any issues. Thousands of manufacturers, miners, and other industry leaders are in attendance. I'm given a standing ovation by a room full of people, most of whom want to be me. I'm told I should run for president. I am handed so many business cards that my once-empty pocket is now full.

Being an introvert doesn't mean I can't snap on the charm and charisma when needed. I'm damn good at my job even if it's exhausting.

As of this morning, I've confirmed half a billion dollars' worth of investments, and the wire transfers have already begun. The networking I've done over the last six months, traveling around the country, worked. Because of my willingness to sacrifice my time for the good of the company, we will have the most successful fiscal year to date. I know that.

So does everyone who expects me to take over the position of chief executive officer when my father retires.

I might be the quiet Calloway, but I can make *any* deal happen, and I *always* get what I want.

I stalk down the center aisle and the crowd parts for me like the Red Sea. Brody falls in line beside me, stopping anyone from getting too close.

Once Weston and I were old enough to legally be sexualized by the media, we gained celebrity-level attention. Weston dating A-list actresses didn't help and my father's affair with a supermodel, only added fuel to the fire. It's always been difficult to be in public situations and stay under the radar.

Some people wish for fame. I don't give a fuck about it.

I don't care about the ego shit. I want to run a successful company that takes mining ethics seriously without a spectacle. Is that too much to ask?

Our demand always increases when the paparazzi and tabloids take our personal lives into their own hands. Weston says it's good for business. The numbers prove it is. So, I've learned to deal with it and navigate it the best I can, even when they turn me into a thirst trap, disrespect me, and sexualize anything I do. Over the years, I've been particular about what I show the world, and I try to write the narrative as I see fit. Oftentimes, it works. Sometimes, it backfires. It's a risk I'm willing to take as I strive for a somewhat-private life.

"Where are you going?" Brody asks when we're in the foyer of the W.

My eyes are zeroed in on the exit. I want to leave.

He crosses his broad arms over his chest. He's ex-military, and he used to work for the Secret Service before joining me. The man takes zero shit. I might be scared of him if he wasn't family and hired to protect me.

"I called for the car," I explain, pulling off my suit coat and tie and handing them to him.

He passes them to one of the interns who is following behind him, not too close though. "Do something with this," he tells him. "We'll be back."

Some heads turn as I approach the double doors, but I'm a master at ignoring everyone. I pretend no one exists because it's easier.

After I remove my cufflinks and drop them in my pocket with my tiny sketchbook and pen, I roll my sleeves up to my forearms.

Three feet away from the exit, I'm stopped by Mr. Martin.

He's smiling. I'm not.

"I assume the issue was handled?" It comes out cold.

"Yes, sir."

I give him a firm handshake, and he glances down at the watch on my wrist. That tinge of guilt flares again, but I push the thoughts away.

Why does it matter? She took what was mine *first*. She was in *my* space. I didn't ask for this. I didn't search for trouble. No, trouble fucking found *me*.

When I step outside, I let out a relieved breath. Brody stands beside me, his eyes scanning the perimeter.

"Mr. Calloway," a voice says at my side, grabbing my attention. She's wearing a W housekeeper uniform, like the one Alexis wore.

I look at her, raising my brows, aware she has something to say.

"My best friend isn't a thief," she states. "She's one of the most trustworthy people I've ever met. You're wrong for getting her fired."

"I beg to differ," I tell her as Brody rushes forward, moving me toward the limo.

She fades into the crowd as I slide across the leather seats, thankful for an escape. Brody takes the front passenger seat.

"Where are we headed, Mr. Calloway? Home?" Nash asks. He's been my driver since I was sixteen.

The car pushes down the narrow street. It's not the first time I've asked him to pick me up after a conference this size to decompress. I do have a limit to how much I can socialize, and today, I nearly met it.

"Central Park. Do you have an extra pair of my sunglasses?"

"Yes, sir," he says.

Seconds later, the car stops. Brody opens the back door, handing me some Ray-Bans and a Yankees baseball hat. I happily put them on as we zoom away from it all. I've been traveling for six months, and nothing has changed except the season. However, being in New York during the summer is my favorite, so right now, I'm happy. Even if it's temporary.

I look out the windows at the puffy white fluffs of cumuli drifting in the blue sky. It's a beautiful day, one that shouldn't be wasted. As we turn onto another street, my cell vibrates, pulling my attention away. I see my brother's name and answer.

"Did you survive today?" Weston asks.

"You know I did." I'm being short, but I *hate* talking on the phone. I prefer text unless it's something serious, and if that's the case, I want the news delivered to my face. Weston doesn't care though.

"Sorry I couldn't be there with you." I hear a cheeky smile in his tone.

"You're not," I state.

"I'll happily let you stand in for me and deal with Lena any day of the week."

That's his soon-to-be ex-wife. They've been publicly fighting in divorce court for months.

"Next time."

When we were younger, we'd switch places weekly because very few people could tell us apart. Even now, when we're bored as fuck or I need air, he'll tap in for me.

"Snap your fingers, and we can trade lives, little brother." He's fifty-five seconds older than me, and he'll never let me live it down.

"Had I been standing in your shoes, you'd have been divorced last year."

"She could use some of the asshole cold shoulder you've perfected over the years."

We might laugh, but it's true.

"So, I know your schedule is your life, but are you free tonight?" he asks.

"No. Are you free on Friday night?" I ask.

It's only six days away. Gives me some time to decompress from nonstop travel.

He chuckles. "Considering I'm no longer shackled to the wicked witch, I have no definite plans until the end of time. I'll put something together."

"Somewhere with no dress code." I'm tired of entertaining. I want to sit at a shitty bar and drink cheap whiskey out of a dirty glass and pretend like the paparazzi aren't following me around the city. I noticed them as soon as I landed in the city.

"I've got the perfect place in mind. I've missed you," he tells me.

"Yeah, yeah." The truth is, I've missed him too.

Weston is my best friend, and we're thick as thieves. Always have been. In our profession, they call us *double trouble;* because we fucking are. He's the chief operating officer, and he's been waiting for me to assume the CEO role. Together, we'll rule Calloway Diamonds as it was always intended.

My father will retire within the next few months, and I'll be promoted as long as *every* condition is met.

I attended several Ivy Leagues, studied abroad, befriended world leaders, and sold billions in investments.

Only one requirement remains unfulfilled—marriage before forty. Now, I'm currently the world's most *eligible* bachelor with *zero* prospects. And the only people who know that are on the inside.

"Are you thrilled to be back?" he asks.

"No." It's the truth. I need a vacation because I'm teetering on the edge of burnout. "I demanded someone at the W be fired."

The line is silent for a few seconds.

"Because?"

"She took my watch."

He chuckles. "Was it returned?"

"Yes, but I think I was a bit irrational."

"When are you *not*?"

"Point taken."

It grows quiet again.

"Is the Grinch growing a heart three sizes too big?"

"She was ..." I think about the words I'd use to describe her. My brother takes any opportunity that presents itself to give me shit, so I stop mid-sentence.

"What?" he asks. "She was *what?*"

Stunning. Breathtaking. She thought I'd be different.

"I have to go. Text me about our plans on Friday."

"*Easton,*" he urges, but I end the call.

I turn it on silent and shove my phone into my pocket. Eventually, the limo slows, and the door opens. Sunlight rushes in, and I leave the car, ignoring lingering glances.

I've visited Central Park a million times to clear my mind. It's one of my favorite escapes.

I shove my hand into my pocket, ensuring the miniature notebook the size of my palm and the fine-nib fountain pen are there. I never leave home without it because I never know when inspiration will call.

Since I was nine years old, I've captured moments of my life just like this, however exciting or boring they may be. The daily sketches started when I was a young, introverted boy in speech therapy. Sketching became my escape when I was frustrated about not being able to properly articulate my thoughts or needs.

Every day was a living Hell, and I'd force myself to draw one thing that would pull my mind away from reality. When my pen was gliding across the smooth paper, nothing mattered, not the words stuck in my throat or the room of people who stared while I froze in place. It helped me disappear and transported me to somewhere else, somewhere deep within my mind, and calmed me.

When I was on the verge of a meltdown, Weston always saved me. He used his voice for me when I couldn't. Sometimes, I still see the disappointment on my father's face when he learned the future of our family's company rested in the hands of a boy with a genius-level IQ who couldn't read out loud or properly articulate his thoughts.

How would I ever be able to hold a meeting, regardless of running a billion dollar company? How would I make deals happen if my words were like bricks in my mouth? That was when Weston and I became a packaged deal, and he refused to do anything without me. My father chose us both or lost us both. It was Weston's boundary; one he's stayed firm with.

Years of speech therapy and determination helped me. Now, I can command a fucking room without issue, even if it's mentally exhausting. That time in my life may be nothing more than a faded memory now, but I never stopped documenting my life in fine lines.

Over the years, I've sketched anything and everything, from animals to clouds to strangers. Each day, I draw at least one scene, a tiny but significant moment in my life, so I'll never forget the time that's always passing by.

Maybe when I'm retired and gray, I'll look back at these sketches and smile, knowing the moments I'm living in right now were the best damn days of my life.

When I'm in the park, just existing as everyone else, it's easy to pretend I can blend in and be invisible. Normalcy, it's something I desperately crave. That and true love, but I know that doesn't exist. At least not for me.

As I move onto the walking path, I glance up and see my penthouse waiting for me up above with its blue-tinted glass windows. It's one of my favorite homes when I'm in the city.

A green Frisbee zooms by in my peripheral, and when I turn my head, I see her.

I stop in my tracks.

I'll never forget those high cheekbones, pouty lips, or long eyelashes. She's wearing bright pink athletic shorts and a T-shirt with something written across the front. It says, *My Book Boyfriend Is Better Than Yours*. The thought makes me laugh. She commands my attention in the same manner as she did the first time I saw her.

Alexis reads with her legs crisscrossed and next to her is a water bottle and a tote bag. It's incredible how she can look so unbothered and at peace, as if nothing or no one could disturb her.

I move my hat farther down my head, knowing sunglasses were a good call. It gives me the opportunity to freely watch her. As I'm cast under her spell for the second time in two days, the world moves around me.

Brody falls in line beside me. His eyes scan across the park, and he spots her too. He's aware of what happened between us, but he has no idea what she looks like.

"Shit, is that her?" he asks, noticing I'm in a trance.

"Yes," I whisper.

"Did you plan this?"

He doesn't glance at me, but keeps his eyes forward.

"Don't follow me," I state, not wanting to be hovered over.

I spot an empty bench behind me and sit. Then I pull the notebook from my pocket, along with my pen, and sketch the scene. Seeing her in a crowd of people is undoubtedly my highlight, but I don't focus solely on her, making sure to take in the entire scene.

I add in the Frisbee players, the branches of the trees that sway in the breeze, and the long wisps of clouds that float above the surrounding buildings. It's almost like a *Where's Waldo?* inspired scene, but if I were to name it, it would be called *Where's the Woman Who Nearly Stopped Time?* I glance at the edge of the page, spotting her in my drawing, and smile. There she is.

The odds of seeing her today are astronomical. Some might even call it fate. Her long hair blows in the wind and whatever she's reading has her smiling. When she looks up again, her gaze is zeroed in on me. I keep my head down, but my eyes are on her. Seconds later, she brings her eyes back to whatever she's reading.

I should get in the limo and pretend I didn't see her. The man I was before she crashed into me head-on would. But she's caught my attention *twice*. That doesn't happen.

5

LEXI

Carlee was right about me needing to touch grass today. I promised her I'd relax while she was at work. Plus, I haven't had a Saturday off since I moved back to the city.

I reach over and run my fingers through the short green blades, so now I can say I *literally* touched the grass. The sun shines bright and I love how warm it is on my skin. As I continue reading, a shadow covers the cream pages of my book. It's not the clouds. It's a person.

I glance at the designer dress shoes and my eyes trail up the black slacks. I continue up the stark white button-up and the tattooed arms and see that *smirk*.

Fuck.

He removes his glasses, revealing his blue eyes, and I scowl.

"You've gotta be kidding me," I whisper.

He lifts the Yankees hat from his head and runs his fingers through his messy hair before replacing it.

"Hello, Alexis." My name falls from his mouth in a deep gruff.

I don't like being called that, but at least he remembered it.

He shoves his hands into his pockets and towers over me like a Greek god, glancing at my book—*Fifty Shades of Grey*. It's a comfort read, the first novel that introduced me to the world of cliterature. It's my version of doomscrolling.

A devilish smirk plays on his pouty lips. "Billionaire kink?"

I nearly choke. He's the *last* man on Earth I want to see right now. "Are you *stalking* me?"

"Sadly, no."

He sits beside me on the ground and I sit up and scoot over, creating space between us. I'm still buzzing where his hands touched me before. After he checks his watch, he leans back onto his elbows, smelling like mahogany and sweet peppermints.

"Good, because if you were, I'd tell you to wear a mask next time," I mutter. "Makes it hotter because this billionaire thing is overdone."

He holds back a smile and successfully pulls it off. Men like him don't get to where they are without being a master at the game though. Charismatic, charming, *attractive;* but I won't get sucked into him. I can't.

With those eyes and lips, this man is the type who breaks hearts for sport. I'm already broken enough.

The silence draws on.

I'm not over what he did.

"Are you always like this?" He looks up at the clouds, and I can't help but steal a glance.

"Like what? Myself?" I'm not sure what he's talking about. He shouldn't be here.

He nods. "Authenticity—that's what it is."

I make a face at him. "You must hang out with fake people."

"I do. And most are kissing my ass."

"One thing you won't have to ever worry about from me." I wait for him to say something. "I won't worship you like all the other normies."

He smirks. "It's preferred."

I sigh, wanting to return to Christian and Anastasia. I'm still at the beginning, where she sits down to give him the famous interview that starts it all.

He chuckles, and the sound grabs my attention. It's … *carefree*.

"You know how to laugh?" I ask.

"Yes, and I've got other tricks up my sleeve too."

"Wow," I say, pretending to be impressed as the pages of my book flutter in the breeze.

He turns to me. "I'm not one to believe in serendipitous events, but this one presented itself, so here I am." He breathes in deeply. "I want to apologize about what happened. I hope you can forgive my behavior."

I shake my head, blinking at him in disbelief. "*No*."

"*No*?" His brows crease.

"I'm sure it's a word you're not used to hearing, but it's a complete sentence, *Mr. Calloway*."

"*Easton*."

"You had me fired. And in the twenty-nine years I've been alive, I have *never* been terminated from *anything*, especially not for theft. I *desperately* needed that job, but you wouldn't know what that's like." I slide my book and water bottle inside my bag and stand.

I grab the corner of my blanket and wrap it around my fist before pulling it from under his ass. After I throw it over my arm, I turn to him.

"I hope you have the day you deserve, *Easton*," I say, as I did before.

I grew up with two older brothers on a ranch and can hold my own. And right now, I have nothing to lose. This man is no one to me.

As I walk away from him, I shake my head, and laughter echoes from behind me. He's laughing at me, and that only enrages me more. Being around Easton is too intense, and it sets me on fire. I twist my hair into a messy bun as I strut away.

Seconds later, I hear him say, "Alexis."

I turn to say something to him, but he's closer than I thought, and I crash into him again. I slam into his chest, and he carefully steadies me, and I'm frozen in time with him. I'm having déjà vu.

"Can you stop running into me?" I ask, meeting his eyes.

"Alexis, let me make it up to you." His voice is velvety. "All of it."

This is a dangerous game. One I don't want to play. Right now, the chessboard is full of pieces, and there have been no casualties of war. We're on neutral ground, and we can both go about our lives like we never met.

"Learn to call me Lexi, or don't say my name. I won't answer to anything else."

"*Lexi*." His tone is an entire octave lower, almost a growl. He licks his perfect lips. On the bottom one, there's a slight crease, a kissable one. "Please allow me to make it up to you," he says.

Being this close to him is dizzying, nearly rocking me off my axis.

"Why does it matter? I'm a random person you had fired. A complete stranger."

He straightens his stance. "Maybe you won't be, going forward."

I swallow hard.

"What do you need?"

"A job so I can pay my rent next week. Are you hiring?" I sarcastically ask. There's no way I'd work for a man like him.

"How much is it?" He's acting polite.

I take a step away from him so I can breathe without being encapsulated by his intoxicating scent.

"Actually, it doesn't matter. I'll take care of it. Consider the next year paid for," he says. "Anything else?"

I meet his gaze. "You're serious?"

A grin takes up residence on his sculptured face. "I am."

"I'm sorry, but you can't buy my forgiveness. That's not how this works."

"Well aware. I look forward to *earning* it."

"Why?" I question.

In a heartbeat, Easton removes the space between us, leaning over to whisper in my ear, "Because I *love* a challenge."

His hot breath is on my skin, and my body temperature rises ... *again*.

"I won't make this easy for you, *Easton*."

"I don't ever take the easy way out. Let me give you my number."

He holds out his palm, and I don't know *why* I hand him my phone, but I do.

It doesn't take long before he's placing it back in my hand. I glance down at the contact he added, noticing he programmed himself as ASSHOLE.

"Call or text me if you need *anything*," he says.

"I've got to go," I whisper. My ability to speak nearly vanishes, and I'm convinced I'm still asleep, that this is a weird dream that I haven't woken up from.

"Well, I hope you have the day you deserve, Lexi." He repeats the words I've said to him twice now. "Maybe I'll *crash* into you again."

I walk away, annoyed that he's so fucking attractive. When I look over my shoulder to steal one last glance, he hasn't moved. Instead, he's watching me with his arms crossed over his chest, wearing that delicious smirk.

It's then I realize I'm dancing with the devil; after all, he did damn me to Hell the day we met.

6

EASTON

Birthday countdown: 38 days
Since meeting her: 8 days

It's been eight days since I returned to the city, met Lexi Matthews, and had her fired. And a week has passed since I saw her last.

I spent Monday and Tuesday catching up on emails. Wednesday and Thursday, I was forced to attend meetings from dawn until dusk. Now, it's Friday, and I've barely been able to piss in peace without talking to someone.

After our mid-month board meeting, I follow Weston and my father to the large corner office, the one that will be mine if a miracle happens.

"Welcome back," my dad tells me as I sit opposite him and beside my brother. My father's hair is grayer than I remember, and he looks tired. "Apologies for not having the chance to welcome you home yet."

I look past him out the window, enjoying the view of the

Empire State Building. I can see tiny specks of people walking around the top, viewing the city from above. It's the perfect time of day because, in the late afternoon, the sun and sky reflect off the windows of the surrounding buildings, casting rays of silver and gold. There's nothing like it.

In moments like this, I want to pull out my notebook and sketch, but I don't.

"Any updates I should be aware of?"

I return my attention back to my father.

I know what he's asking—if I've found a potential bride—and I don't know how to deliver the disappointing news. After six months of traveling around the world, I'm still painfully single. I've given women chances, but not one lasted past the fourteen-day mark. I've tried.

"Not yet," Weston says. "He'll figure it out."

"I can talk," I snap out with frustration.

When I was younger, if I hesitated too long like I must've done, my brother would speak for me, to protect me however he can. When I've needed him the most, he's been there. I have his back, and he has mine, no matter what.

But right now, I need to use my voice. Otherwise, I'll be in a loveless marriage, just like the ones every man in this room has gotten himself into.

"Son, the lawyers reviewed the contract your grandfather created. The requirements are clear, with zero loopholes. It's locked tight."

I lean across the desk. "Don't you find this ridiculous? I was born to run this company. I'm the best there is."

"Well, the *second* best." Weston laughs.

"Not now," I tell him. I'm not in the mood.

Dad glares at me. "If you *aren't* married before your fortieth birthday, I'll have no choice but to promote Derrick to CEO when I retire. You have thirty-seven days, son."

My brother tenses beside me. "That *cannot* fucking happen. He's not family."

"Do *you* want to step up?"

My father stares him down and the room grows frigid. The tension is so thick; I could cut it with a knife.

Weston has enough experience to take over the company, and he would be incredible. But last year, he was promoted to the chief operating officer. Finding a replacement for him would be nearly impossible. He's the *best* there is, and he can charm a *snake,* which is why he was married to one.

"That's what I thought," my father says, unamused. He's stern. Always has been.

"It was never my dream. You know that," Weston tells him.

Since we were children, we were encouraged and trained to take on these roles.

CEO is *mine*. He wouldn't take that from me.

Weston interlocks his fingers. "If Derrick takes over, you will receive my resignation."

Our dad stares him down, but Weston doesn't flinch. He can be a bigger asshole than me when he wants. Most people don't realize he's *just* like me.

I clear my throat. "Father, there has to be some—"

Before I can continue, the door swings open, and it's Derrick, the man who has been my father's shadow since we were teenagers. He's tall with jet-black hair and a permanent scowl, and he has a voice like he's smoked a pack a day for the last twenty years. Weston and I are convinced he has a Death Eater tattoo on his arm because he's pure *Slytherin*.

While he does have executive experience and the board of directors respects him, he's a *terrible* choice, and he makes awful business decisions. I've never liked him because he puts profit over people. He can disrespectfully get fucked.

"Apologies for being late," Derrick says, sliding into the chair on the other side of Weston.

I pretend he doesn't exist.

Over the years, he's tried to destroy my credibility and reputation, but I've always recovered.

I don't like how his beady eyes dart around when I speak or how he inserts himself into situations, giving opinions when not asked. My father might trust him, but it doesn't mean I have to.

Never have. *Never fucking will.*

"Perfect. The three of you are here," my father says, interrupting the argument Weston would've successfully started had we sat in silence for any longer. "I've chosen my retirement date. Forty-five days from today."

My hard expression doesn't change. I have thirty-seven days to find a wife if I want to become CEO in six weeks. And I can't have one without the other.

"Great." I glance down at my watch, knowing this meeting could've been an email or something we quickly discussed over dinner, but my father is forcing us to be in the same room as Derrick. He's studying our interactions to see if this would even be possible. It wouldn't. Weston and I would both walk away from this. I don't want to do that, but if my hand is forced, I will. "Anything else?"

"Have you chosen your successor?" Derrick asks. He knows my father will choose between the two of us, but I don't believe he's aware of the clause in our family contract.

Weston tenses beside me and balls his hand into a fist. I wish he would beat Derrick to a pulp right here. There have been plenty of times when I wanted to.

"No," my father says in his rough tone, the one that says this conversation is over.

I stand, and my father doesn't look at me again. He's disappointed in me. That much is certain.

Weston follows me to my office, and neither of us speaks as we move toward the opposite side of the building. I didn't notice the file folder in his hand until he sits in front of my desk.

This space is foreign to me. The only thing that makes it mine is my business cards sitting on the edge of the desk. I've never settled in this space because I know it isn't where I belong. The corner office should be mine, along with the fucking title.

"This is bullshit." I seethe as I pace. I lift my fingers to the racing pulse in my neck to feel my heart rapidly beating. It's anger that pumps through me.

"It is. But I don't think it's the end. Not yet. Tell me about this woman you met."

I stop pacing and give him a dirty look. "Who?"

I move to my desk and sit, recalling the few dates I've gone on this year. Each one was a disaster, and the tabloids *never* got it right. There is no one; if there were, he'd have been the first to know.

"Don't be coy." He tosses a pen, catches it, and twirls it between his fingers, grinning like the Cheshire cat.

He's acting like a cocky fuck, and it frustrates me when he gets like this.

"I don't know what you're talking about." I glare at him, growing impatient with each passing second.

I've been gone for months, and nothing has changed here either. Derrick is still being a rat and my brother isn't taking any of this seriously. And then there's me, stuck in the middle of want and need, watching my dreams and everything I've worked so fucking hard for fade before my eyes. All because I refuse to marry for any reason other than love. I'd rather stay single.

"I'd love for you to tell me about the woman you got fired a week ago. She was ..." His voice trails off, exactly like mine did when we spoke on the phone.

I narrow my eyes. "Don't you think we have more important things to concern ourselves with right now?"

He opens the file folder and pulls out a stack of pictures and printed articles from gossip sites. Weston proudly spreads them across the desk. There are *hundreds*. "Now, I know for a goddamn fact this wasn't me with this beautiful woman."

"Shit," I whisper, picking one up.

I hoped the paps hadn't followed me, but in New York, the photographers are sly. They watch from a distance, always lurking with a telephoto lens instead of getting in your face. They want their targets to feel comfortable so they can capture the natural shots and sell them for thousands.

This is my fault. I should've remembered that no public space is safe. I went against my own rules ... because of her.

My eyes scan over the images. Our conversation is displayed in snapshots, and I almost smile, recalling it. There is one of us standing on the sidewalk that catches my eye. She's smirking at me as I hand her phone back. It's fucking adorable.

"*New York's Most Eligible Bachelor's New Lover.*" I read the title out loud before glancing at my brother. "This is a lie."

"Maybe it is. But I haven't seen you smile like that in over fifteen years. Maybe *never*," he says with a raised brow. "So, I want to know who she is."

I inhale sharply. "Please mind your damn business, okay? It's a lost cause. *Trust me*."

"Being in your business allows me to do what's best for the company, so hell no. The time *is* ticking." He looks down at his wristwatch—another priceless family heirloom.

When my grandfather passed away, our inheritance included these watches, accompanied by a staggering amount of stock in the company. They have different inscriptions engraved on the bottom. I like to think my grandfather chose each one for a reason, although when I think of mine, it's brutal—*LOVE IS*

ALWAYS ON TIME—for the grandson who can't and won't find it. But it's not from a lack of trying.

"I'm aware of my situation." My words drip with sarcasm.

"So, why not her? The tabloids have already started writing the story. I can see the sparks." He snaps his fingers and points to the word *lover*. "Plausible. Believable as fuck."

"You know I said I wouldn't get married unless I was in love."

"So, fall in love," he says like it's easy. "Or maybe it's time to take some chances. Do you want to lose everything, Easton? For a version of love that *doesn't* exist?"

I clench my jaw. "Just because you haven't experienced it doesn't mean shit. You perpetually choose the wrong women, like it's your hobby."

"And you've chosen *no one* in over a decade," he quips. He leans forward, lowering his voice. "All you have to do is get married and make it believable. That's it."

Weston is like a devil on my shoulder, whispering terrible things in my ear. The promise I made to myself—to marry for love only—sits on the other shoulder while my future hangs by a single thread that's quickly unraveling.

My grandfather created this contractual obligation for his bloodline only. He once told me he never wanted us imprisoned in the business. This requirement was his way of pushing us to find love, to take risks, to start a family. It will also be the number one reason why the Calloway dynasty will be destroyed from the inside and thousands of people will lose their jobs. The thought of it makes me sick.

Weston has my undivided attention and knows it.

"Okay, so what if I meet the love of my life while I'm fake married?"

"Oh, it should be a *real* marriage on paper and in public. Scandals are wonderful for business too."

I groan. "This is fucking ridiculous."

"You only have to stay married for one year. Pretend to be the happiest, in-love couple in the world, and no one will question anything. And if you find *the one,* wait to pursue her until you've divorced your temporary wife. After three hundred sixty-five days, you'll be free to do the same thing you're doing right now, and you can continue your toxic affair with the company."

"Is that what you and Lena did?"

"No. It was very real and by far the biggest mistake of my life, but I met the qualifications. I genuinely tried. It didn't work out. There is nothing anyone can do. I did what our grandfather had asked."

He shrugs, but I've witnessed how difficult it was for him. Weston loved a horrible person, the real kind of love that I've searched for my entire life. When it ended, he was broken. She'd nearly destroyed my brother.

"But—"

Before I can finish my thought, there's a tap on my door, and our shared secretary enters.

"The information you requested," Taelor says and hands me the file.

As she turns and walks away, Weston snatches it from my hand.

"Alexis Marie Matthews. Texan. Twenty-nine years old. New York University performing arts graduate. Excellent GPA. No criminal record. Not a felon."

I yank it from his hands. "*Bastard.*"

"So, this is her. *Alexis Matthews.* She's perfect. No one knows her. And she's a performer, so she can *easily* pretend to be in love with you. Plus, the housekeeper thing could work in your favor. Make us seem down-to-Earth."

"There is no *us* when it comes to this." I glare at him, my eyes scanning over the rest of the information.

I'm aware that our reputations are intertwined. If Weston

pisses off the masses, then they're upset with me too. We rise and fall together. It's a part of the game.

He smirks. "She must've made an impression on you if you ran a full background check. Admit it."

"*No*. She has a *bad* attitude."

"You do too." He sits back in the chair. "She's way too pretty for you though. Maybe I should date her? Would make a *great* rebound."

He knows he's getting under my skin and he's doing everything he can to dig deeper.

"Don't worry. Brody shared how you two hit it off at the park."

My face contorts. "I'm firing my bodyguard."

"Wow." Weston chuckles. "You already have a *thing* for her."

"I've known her for a week. We've spoken twice, and each time ended with her walking away from me like she couldn't escape fast enough. That doesn't qualify as a *thing*."

He knocks his knuckles against the desk. "Shit. This might be the greatest story of all time. Easton Calloway finds a wife and *actually* falls in love. Maybe you'll get the best of both worlds, little brother."

I shake my head. "Get the fuck out of my office. You're pissing me off."

"Not even a please?"

"Now!" I point toward the door, and he stands.

He smooths his hands over the front of his charcoal-colored three-piece suit that's identical to what I'm wearing, down to the black silk tie. If I turned it around, it would most likely be the same brand.

"You *encourage* the twin jokes."

"*Love them*." He smirks, but doesn't say anything else.

I suspect he has a closet of suits in his office and changes once he sees me, but I haven't confirmed that. He swears it's a lucky twin guess, but I don't trust him. It happens *too* often to be coincidental. I believe he's texting my stylist and tailor.

"The only reason I'm leaving is because I have shit to do, not because it's what you want. Are we still on for tonight?"

"Yeah, I'll be there," I confirm.

He reaches for the door, but stops and turns to me. "I hope you have the day you deserve."

"Brody's fired."

7

LEXI

Carlee slides on her high heels, holding the back of the couch for balance. Over the last five days, I've applied for a handful of jobs, and I'm waiting for interviews. Carlee graciously offered to cover the portion of rent that I didn't have, and I promised to pay her back as soon as I could. But tonight, she insisted that we go out, her treat. I think she senses I've not been feeling like myself lately. To be honest, I haven't been myself since I learned my ex was a cheating bastard.

"Have you thought any more about your screenplay?" Carlee asks, flipping her straight brown hair over her shoulders.

"Yeah, a little. I think I want to write about a tragedy. Something that's like a modern-day *Romeo and Juliet*. Everyone dies in the end."

"That sounds depressing as fuck." She grabs a pair of earrings and puts them on. "So, are you not going to tell me about you being with Calloway at Central Park?"

My cheeks immediately burn. "How did you know?"

"Lexi, there are pictures of you two together splashed all over the internet! What were you even talking about?"

"It was a normal conversation about authentic people and

how I won't kiss his ass." I stand up and stretch. "Trust me, we weren't hanging out. I was reading, and he interrupted me."

"Damn, girl, you look hot," she says, nodding her head. "Tonight, I'm using you as bait to reel in the gorgeous men, and then I'll go in for the kill."

This makes me laugh as I look down at my outfit. I'm wearing black slacks, dark red heels, and a black V-neck shirt that shows enough cleavage to tease. My hair is down, and my lips match my shoes. I do feel pretty for the first time in a while, and I appreciate the compliment.

"Thank you. I'm happy to help."

I reach for my phone to check the time, and Carlee's rings.

Her face contorts after she answers. "What do you mean?"

"What?" I whisper, not liking how her demeanor has shifted.

"Who did?" She's staring at me. "You didn't get his name?"

The conversation continues.

"Okay. Well, thanks. Yeah, no problem."

She shoves her phone in her back pocket. "Someone paid our rent for the year."

"Wow," I say, trying to act surprised. Guess he wasn't joking.

"This has your scent all over it. What did you do?" she asks.

I hold back a smile. "Easton Calloway offered to pay it if I forgave him for having me fired."

She shakes her head, not believing it. "Oh my God! Tell me you forgave him?"

"No, I didn't. He can't buy me, Carlee. The man walks through life, getting whatever he wants. It stops here."

I explain how I was reading and how he magically appeared. I keep some of our conversation to myself, but I don't know why. I have no reason to protect this man.

"Don't tell anyone."

"I won't. It's safe with me, even though I'd blow my blog up if I released a firsthand account."

"Please. I don't want to draw any more attention to myself. If it's on your radar, it's already an issue," I say. Not wanting any of this.

"I promise. It's for my entertainment only. Wait, did you say you have his number?"

"Yeah." I unlock my phone and turn the screen around to show her.

"You programmed him in as ASSHOLE?"

This makes me laugh. "No, he did that."

She snorts. "So, he has a personality. Girl, what are you doing? Call that man *right now*. Give him a *proper* thank-you."

Just thinking about talking to him has me ready to combust. "And say what? *Thank you for following through after nearly ruining my life?*"

"That's a start. Or you can offer your sincere appreciation and ask him to join us tonight. It might be fun."

I meet her eyes, knowing she can't be serious. "That wouldn't happen. He'd deny the invitation. We're not his crowd, Carlee. Trust me. He's filthy rich, and he probably eats placentas for breakfast or something *super* evil."

I think about that boyish smirk and how it felt to hear him chuckle.

She lifts a brow and places her hand on her hip. "Want to put some money down on it?"

I shake my head. "I'm not betting you. I'm already broke enough, and I owe you so much."

She pulls a one-hundred-dollar bill from her bra and straightens it. "Mr. Franklin could be going home with you tonight. All it takes is *one* phone call. And if he denies the invitation, I will never mention him to you again. We'll pretend like none of it happened."

The thought of speaking to him makes my throat dry. "You're making me want to drink. I'm sorry, I can't call him."

"I should contact your mama right now and tell her how

rude you're being. Not even a *thank you* to a man who spent eighteen thousand dollars on you like it was nothing?"

"On us," I say with a groan. "Sometimes, you're really annoying."

"Only when I'm right. Show me those Southern manners."

I slowly take in a deep breath and look down at his contact. ASSHOLE. My phone is heavy in my hand, like I'll drop it. Calling him feels personal, but he deserves a thank-you, even if that's where this ends. I'll quickly make the call, get it over with, and put my protective walls back up.

"You can use my room," she says, lifting her hand toward it.

"Do I *have* to do this?" The thought gives me hives.

"Yes."

She pushes me down the short hallway and into her room. There's only enough space for her bed, a small table, and a standing mirror. I look down at my phone as she clicks the door closed. It's the most privacy I'll get.

"I can do this," I whisper and click on his number.

It immediately rings, and after the fourth one, I hang up and meet her in the living room.

She grins. "Well?"

"He didn't answer," I explain with a shrug. "Ready to go?"

Her brows furrow. "Did you leave a message?"

"No, that wasn't part of the deal. If he calls me back, I'll pick up."

We take the stairs down the four flights of our building. The evening chill hits my cheeks when I push open the door.

As I look out to the street, I stop mid-stride.

There *he* is, standing in a gray three-piece suit with a black tie. He's leaning against a white Mustang Shelby GT500 with black racing stripes down the hood—1967, if I had to guess, and I think I'd be right. Pure muscle and Americana. He's holding a bouquet of yellow roses as the ghost of a smile plays on his luscious lips.

As my foot hits the bottom step, he moves forward and hands them to me.

"For you," he says.

I look at him like he's lost his mind.

Carlee looks over at me. "I think I forgot something upstairs. I'll be right back."

"Carlee," I say between clenched teeth, not wanting her to leave me alone with him.

She's out of sight before I can say anything else.

I turn back to Easton. "What are you doing here?"

"Didn't you call me?"

My mouth falls open and closes. He has a point.

"I did. I wanted to say thank you. Also, thanks for the roses. We're heading out for the night."

The roses smell incredible, and I can't remember the last time anyone bought me flowers.

I meet his gaze. "I thought I told you the next time you decide to stalk me, wear a mask?"

This makes him chuckle. "I wasn't stalking you. Was in the neighborhood."

"Really? You hang out in Harlem often?"

I know he paid our rent, so it's more than likely true.

His deep blue eyes scan my body from head to toe, then he gives me a boyish grin. His hair is a wild mess on his head, messier than usual. "Join me tonight."

Before I can answer, my phone buzzes. It's a text from Carlee.

CARLEE

GO OUT WITH HIM NOW!

CARLEE

NOW! I WILL SURVIVE.

I look over my shoulder and see her standing at her

bedroom window, shooing me away. I glance back at him. He's patiently waiting, looking so damn sexy, as the sun sets in the distance.

"Are you denying me?" he asks, his voice a deep husk.

"Yes," I whisper, nearly drowning in his eyes, knowing I can't do this.

His smile widens as he takes a step forward. "Do you want me to beg?"

"You don't seem like the kind of man who's ever begged anyone for anything."

He lifts a brow. "I'm *not*. But I'd make an exception for you."

"After this, will you promise to leave me alone?" I ask, resting a hand on my hip.

"I don't make promises I can't keep." He looks down at his watch. "Trust me when I say, we can't be late."

"That coming from your mouth doesn't surprise me."

"Alexis Matthews, I'd be honored to be in your presence tonight," he says, opening the car door and presenting my carriage.

Inside are red leather seats, the dashboard, and the steering wheel. It's a standard, and I can't deny that shiny Cobra logo in the middle.

I bring my attention back to him. "I'll make a deal with you."

"Oh, so you're into negotiating. I fucking love it. Continue," he says, returning to the smart-ass I know.

"I'll join you *if* you let me drive."

"Mmm," he growls. "I don't let *anyone* drive my vehicle."

I hold out my palm, waiting for the keys. I want and need this. "That's my condition. Agree, or good night, Mr. Calloway."

"Hardball. *Fuck*," he whispers. "*You're perfect.*"

Easton pulls the keys from his pocket and holds them above my hand, meeting my eyes before dropping them into my palm, which is exactly how I handed him his watch. "You'd better make it worth my while."

"I'm thinking the same damn thing." I go around the back, my fingers sliding over the slick white paint, and climb inside behind the steering wheel. I set the flowers in the back and adjust the position of the leather bucket seat.

As he buckles in, I bend over, remove my heels, and place them next to the flowers. After I push in the clutch, I turn the key and listen to the car roar to life. It's ferocious.

The steering wheel in my grasp makes me smile as I rub my hands across the smooth leather. "Wow."

"I guess we're on the same brain wave tonight," he says. "Want directions to where I'm taking you?"

I nod, glancing down at the stick of the four-speed. I shift into first gear and it lurches forward. I didn't expect that much power, though I should've. It's a GT.

He gives me a look of concern, but he doesn't question my ability to drive as I get acquainted with this beast. With any vintage car, you have to learn it. They all have a sweet spot in gears.

"We're going to a bar called The Garage. It's not that far from here," he says, glancing out the window.

"I know where that is," I tell him. "They have a Chevelle hanging from the ceiling. I've been there a few times. Doesn't seem like your type of place."

"There's *a lot* about me that would surprise you."

I glance away from him.

"I take it you know a lot about vintage cars," he says. "Most people wouldn't give two fucks what kind of car is hanging in that restaurant."

I coast in neutral to the stop sign as the engine purrs. I want to take her up on the highway and drive ninety with the windows down.

Before pulling away, I turn to him. "Kinda. My dad was into restoration. He had a 1927 Model T. We rebuilt it together when I was a teenager and drove it to vintage car shows. I've been around muscle cars all my life."

"That's impressive." His eyes scan the street as I turn right.

We're about twelve blocks away.

The sun sets over the distant buildings, and the sky transforms from orange to purple and eventually nightfall.

"I've never met a woman who can drive a standard," he admits.

"That doesn't surprise me. But you know, I've never met a guy like you who has a driver's license."

"Ouch. You *are* feisty." He shakes his head. "It makes perfect sense."

"What's that?" I ask.

"Nothing." He laughs.

"*Now* you're quiet?" I'm confused.

He's hot, then he's cold. I don't know how to read him.

"You'll figure it out soon enough."

The conversation comes to a lull, and my heart rate increases. It takes everything I have not to laugh because this is ridiculous. However, anytime I've been around this man, it's been an unpredictable situation.

I place my left hand out the window, allowing the air to blow through my fingers.

"So, you're from Texas?" he asks.

"Yeah, but how did you know that?" I glance over at him.

"I've made knowing everything about you my job," he says. "You've become my new hobby."

I shake my head. "For some reason, that doesn't surprise me."

"Do you miss it?" His tone is sincere.

"Sometimes." I think about the circumstances that made me leave. "Like right now, I miss being unable to hit an open road and drive this car as fast as possible. I love New York, but … there's no place like home. Valentine is special."

He nods and turns back to me. "I think you belong here."

For a moment, it's like a dream.

"You seem different today."

"Do I? Much better than acting like a cold asshole, right?"

"It's night and day," I admit.

"Thanks. I'll take that as a compliment. Oh, there is one tiny thing. I need to apologize in advance, but so far, it's been a delight."

"Wh—"

He quickly interrupts me, "Take this parking spot. Can you parallel park?"

"You love offending me, don't you?"

"I'm sure I say all the right things at the wrong time."

He chuckles as I reach my arm across the back of the seat. I look into his eyes before glancing behind me as I inch the car into the tight place. After I engage the parking brake and turn the engine off. He holds out his palm, just like the first day we met, and I return his keys.

"Ready for the time of your life?" he asks.

"As ready as you are," I tell him.

"A little secret: I was born ready," he says, getting out of the car as I slide on my high heels.

He walks to the driver's side and opens the door with his hand held out. I take it, and we walk toward the entrance. He's close to me, and I wonder if photographers are snapping photos of this.

After we enter, I turn to him. "I need to quickly stop by the ladies' room."

"I'll meet you at the bar?" He points over toward it.

"Five minutes," I tell him, knowing he has a thing with time.

I smile and move toward the restroom as excitement and adrenaline rush through me. I go inside the stall, ignore all texts, and call Carlee. I explain everything as fast as I can because it's quicker than texting.

"Holy shit," she says, and I can tell she's smiling. "You're on a date with Easton Calloway."

"It's not a date," I explain.

"Call it whatever you want. If a man picked me up in that car, wearing that suit and giving me flowers ... well, let your imagination wander."

"I'll leave and meet up with you so we can go out," I tell her because I feel guilty.

"Don't you dare! If the roles were reversed, I wouldn't."

I laugh. "Okay. That's true. I'm sorry."

"Stop apologizing," she says. "Go have fun!"

"Thanks. I'll keep you updated," I whisper.

"And don't forget to say thank you to him."

"I already did. Thank you for everything. I'll make it up to you, I promise."

I end the call and lean my back against the stall of the bathroom door. Once my heart rate has settled, I wash my hands and walk to the bar area. On the way there, I pass the same guy I saw in the park last weekend. This must be his bodyguard. I wonder where he's been all night. Following us?

I shake my head at him. "You're good at hiding."

He looks at me like I've lost my mind, but he doesn't say anything. I move through the crowd and find Easton sitting at the bar with a drink.

I place my hand on his back as I climb onto the stool beside him. "Sorry. I'm back. Hopefully, I wasn't a second over five minutes."

He does a double take. The small notebook he was writing in is snapped shut, and he places a pen on top. His mouth opens and closes as he searches my face like I'm a ghost. "Alexis?"

"Remember when I mentioned you were being weird as fuck?" I don't even address him using my full name.

He lifts a brow. "No, I don't recall that one. Please, enlighten me."

"Okay, well, you're doing it again. And it's giving me whiplash."

"I'm not sure wha—"

"Thanks for saving me a seat," a deep, familiar voice says behind us.

My eyes nearly bulge out of my head as I see two Eastons standing in front of me, wearing the same exact thing.

"You're so rich that you have a fucking *clone*?" I gasp.

"Weston, *you didn't*," the one sitting beside me says.

"*Weston*?" I turn and look up at him, grinning. "You're *twins*?"

Easton glances at me. "You didn't know?"

"I didn't care enough to learn every detail about you. I'm not obsessed," I harshly whisper.

"Not yet," he whispers, placing the glass to his lips.

I've tried to forget he exists since I crashed into him at the W. Somehow, here I am, with this man for a third time. And I was tricked into it.

Weston takes my hand, stealing my attention away as he places his lips on my knuckles. "Nice to meet you, Lexi. I told you I was sorry already, and I have had a pleasure hanging out with you. Now, you two have some chatting to do," he says with a wink.

My mouth falls open as Weston turns and walks out of the building. He waves at me as he makes his way in front of the windows until he's out of sight. Then, I awkwardly sit next to Easton, the man I thought I'd been with for the last thirty minutes. The man I thought I'd somewhat warmed up to. But no, we're actually still at *square one*.

Moments later, Weston returns with the bouquet of yellow roses. "A pretty girl should *always* have flowers on a date."

"Date?" I ask, confused.

"Perfection." He laughs, squeezing Easton's shoulder. "You're welcome."

The bartender comes over and takes my order—single malt whiskey.

I don't say a word for a few minutes, and it grows awkward. The conversation in the Mustang makes more sense. When I'm handed my drink, I take a sip and glance at Easton. I think he's as shocked as me.

"Anything else I should know?" I ask.

This man is a bag of surprises.

"Sorry, he's very charming and flirty."

"I'm confused how he knew anything about me." I try to put the pieces together, but it doesn't make sense.

"The photos in the park started this," he says. "And now, my brother is trying very hard to play matchmaker—to his own demise." He rolls the ice around in his glass. "I'm not sure what's more unbelievable—him creating an elaborate scheme to take you out, or that you fell for it."

He glances over at me, but I see the smile threatening to emerge.

I scoff. "Oh, I can't believe I fell for it either. You, *that* charming?"

"Actually"—he tilts his drink toward me—"I'm charming when I want to be. I could easily be the man to sweep you off your feet and have you begging for more of me—*if* I wanted. Don't get it twisted, darling."

When he looks at me, it's as if he peels off my mask and sees the raw me. "Well then, kinda glad you don't want to."

"Oh, I *never* said that." He breaks eye contact. "I can tell you were blindsided, and I apologize for that. I'll take care of him first thing on Monday morning. It will never happen again."

I don't know what wrath Easton will throw his way.

"It's fine. He meant well, and he's not hard to be around."

"I know," he says.

I realize how different they are. Easton is all business, the mastermind.

Calculative. Intelligent. *Dangerous.*

"I called you," I say, not sure if he knew it was me or not. I never gave him my number.

"I don't like to talk on the phone," he mutters. "To *anyone*."

I nod, making a mental note of that. "That's too bad. I was reaching out to thank you and was extending an invite for you to hang out with me and my best friend tonight."

"Really?"

"She kinda bet me I wouldn't ask you. I explained you wouldn't have joined us anyway."

"You'd have lost," he mumbles.

My heart rate upticks. "Oh?"

"You intrigue me, Alexis," he admits.

"Like a toy?"

Easton shakes his head and gives me his undivided attention. "Like an inferno."

His words catch me off guard, and I smile. "I *love* playing with fire."

He narrows his eyes before licking his lips. "You are the fire."

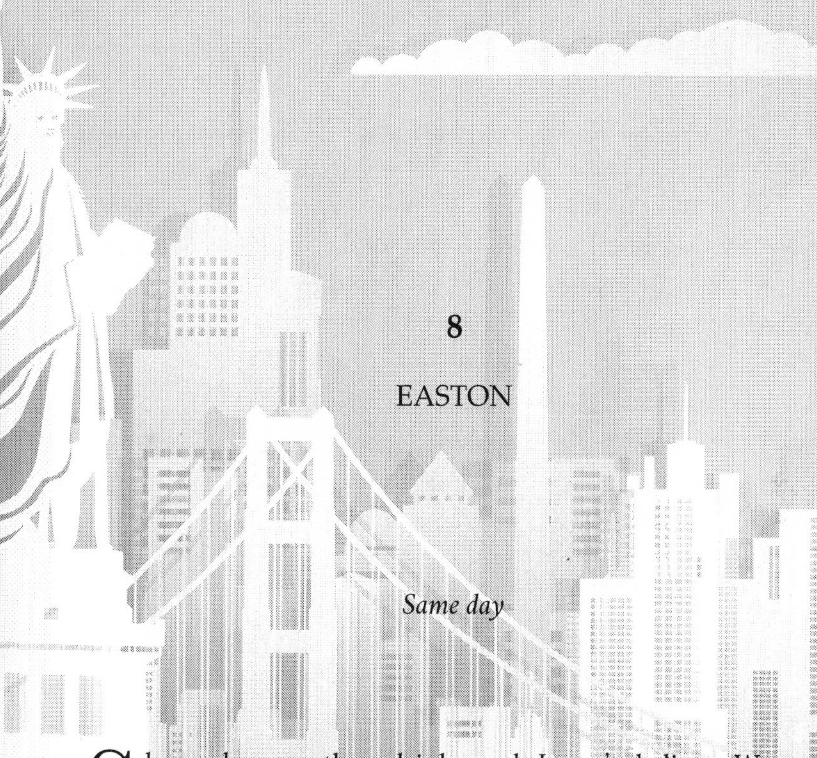

8

EASTON

Same day

She orders another drink, and I can't believe Weston convinced her to join *him*.

How?

I can only imagine what he did, what he made me do. When I gave her my number, I decided she'd have to cross the line first. I'm not desperate for attention. I chase *no one*.

But here she is, eight days later, having a drink with me at a bar. I don't give a fuck how she got here. I only care that she hasn't left. Lexi wants to stay because she's intrigued by me.

It's a dangerous game to play, but when I meet her green eyes, it's like the entire world melts away. It's like the rules don't apply to us, and I'd heavily consider rewriting them if it meant getting to know her.

"Earlier, after you called, I texted you back," I admit. "You didn't reply."

She unlocks her phone. My text is there, as I said, and she smiles.

"I'm sorry, I didn't see it. Your brother kinda had me occupied."

"Did you have fun with him?" I ask, knowing he probably picked her up after I texted him that she'd called me. Bastard.

"Actually, yeah." She pauses. "I was thinking about how I needed to thank you for what you had done, and then you were magically standing outside of my apartment. Well, Weston was, but I thought it was you."

"*So,* you were thinking about me?"

A smile plays on her lips. "I guess you could say that."

The bartender picks up our empty glasses. He gives Alexis another drink before helping someone at the other end of the bar.

"Curious. *How* did Weston get you to join him?"

She laughs. "Had he not shown up in that white 1967 Mustang Shelby GT500, I *wouldn't* be here."

My jaw clenches. "*Son of a bitch.*"

"Oh, so that *is* yours?" she asks like she's impressed.

"Yeah, I have a *thing* for muscle cars," I admit.

She stares at me for a few seconds too long. "It's a beautiful car. The clutch felt great. Lots of power. I was cheated though because I couldn't open her up on the highway and cruise."

I hold up my hand. "Wait. Wait a second. He let you *drive*?"

"He mentioned he never lets *anyone* drive his vehicles. So, I made it my stipulation, and he *happily* handed me the keys," she says. "That should've been a dead giveaway that something was up. I have a feeling you wouldn't have fallen for that and would've renegotiated somehow."

"I'm sure he thought that was fucking hilarious." I glance over at her. "And you're right. No one drives my cars. I would've renegotiated."

"You said … cars. As in plural."

"Yeah. Lots," I admit. "But I'm impressed."

Alexis turns to me with her eyebrows raised. "Why? Didn't think I could drive a standard?"

"Mainly because you knew the year, make, and model—355 horsepower, V8. It was when the Shelby GT was introduced to the Mustang line. The introduction and birth to all muscle cars, dare I say."

"Mmm. I don't think I realized that," she says. "Makes it even more special then."

Her smile falters for a split second, but she pushes it away.

"What were you just thinking about?" I ask because curiosity takes hold.

She takes a sip of her drink. "You're good at reading people."

"Paying attention is one of my best qualities. You'll learn that." I pause for a few seconds, capturing her gaze. "When I was younger, I was shy and didn't talk much. I watched how people interacted for years. Because of that, it's easy for me to pick up on subtle nuances, like nervous tics and tells. When people's energy shifts. And I have an impeccable judgment of character."

"And you still got me fired," she says, shaking her head.

"Yeah, I think that's why I felt—and still feel—guilty. Because I realized I'd overreacted."

"Mr. Calloway, do you actually have a heart?" Her voice has a hint of sarcasm, but she's playful. And she sounds like my damn brother.

"Don't tell anyone," I say with a smirk. "Might ruin my reputation."

The jukebox in the corner plays an old rock song and chatter fills the space. It's a Friday night in June, and the place is growing more crowded. I was supposed to be catching up with my brother, but instead, I'm here with Alexis, sharing my truths. I'm not complaining.

"What do you see when you look at me?" she asks.

"Do you want the truth or a lie?" It's an honest question. Some people can't handle the truth. I believe Alexis can.

She doesn't act like anyone I've met, and she sure as fuck doesn't care about me, my life, or who I am. Being unfazed by me is her best quality.

"The truth," she whispers.

"I think you're confident, good at masking your emotions, gorgeous, but also insecure. I want to figure out why."

She swallows hard, studying me as she licks her lips.

I'm right though. I know I am, and so does she.

"I just wish you could see what I see. That's all." I take a sip of my whiskey.

"What do you see?" she asks.

"Someone who has the ability to make all of their dreams come true."

Her breath hitches. "You mean that?"

"Raw truths, Alexis. Now, it's your turn."

She twirls the ice in her glass before finishing her drink. "Truth or lie?"

"I'm curious about the lie, but I want the truth. *Always.*"

She studies me. "Hmm. I see a man searching for something that money can't buy."

"And what would that be?"

"If I had to guess … companionship. *Love.*" We fall into silence for a few seconds. "But … I don't believe love exists. So you could be wasting your time searching for it."

I wait for the punchline, but one doesn't come. "You're serious."

"Dead serious." She nods.

"I'm shocked." I regroup my thoughts.

She reaches over and lightly pinches me. "Hi. I'm the anti-love, hopeless romantic. It's *very* nice to meet you."

"I'm sorry," I tell her, noticing her mood shift.

The mask she wears when placed in an uncomfortable

situation makes an appearance. She's a professional at blocking her emotions, but I see it in her eyes. There's no fooling me.

"No need to apologize." She covers her pain flawlessly.

"If you stopped believing in love, someone in a past relationship hurt you, and that shouldn't have happened. It's okay to have feelings about that."

She doesn't confirm, but she doesn't have to. I see right through her.

"So, what about you? What's your deal? You obviously have one."

Her arm brushes against mine, and I can smell the strawberry scent of her shampoo. I try to think back to the women I thought might've been the one, but weren't.

"I've never met anyone who's kept my interest for over two weeks," I say with a single sigh.

Her face scrunches. "*Ever*?"

"It's been nearly two decades. I grow bored easily, and it's a turnoff when people try too hard. I want something more than the superficial shit. Otherwise, I'd have had a thousand relationships, and none would've counted. So, after fourteen days, if I'm not interested, I end it. I've been waiting around for the right woman. Haven't found her yet."

"Does she exist?" she asks with a smirk.

"Probably not," I tell her, glancing at my watch.

We've been here for an hour, but it feels like five minutes have passed.

"Got somewhere to be?" She lifts her brows.

"Right here."

She orders another round of drinks and I move to water. Her leg presses against mine, and she's warm. I'm tempted to place my hand firmly on her thigh, but I don't. No lines will be crossed.

"I have a feeling you've never gotten caught up in a moment," she says.

My eyes glaze over as I try to recall my life in a snapshot of memories, of sketches. "Not really. And I'm never late. It's my number one pet peeve."

Her face softens, and I think I see … *pity*? "That's … *really* depressing. It's not the flex you think, unless you're eighty."

"First time anyone has ever told me that. Being punctual is an *excellent* quality to have."

"If you're a nerd or an ass-kisser." She shrugs. "I'm on time to work but late everywhere else, especially to parties. Sometimes, it's about arriving once the room is warmed up and everyone has moved past the awkward stage of the night. I can remember the very first time I nearly missed something important."

"Really?" My brain can't comprehend the carelessness.

"It was my thirteenth birthday party. My mother almost canceled because they couldn't find me."

"Where were you?" I ask, intrigued.

She snickers. "Lying in the rain. I stayed there while the mountain drops stung my skin. My parents were *pissed,* but it was an experience, one that I'll never forget. When I think back on my life, I've got a lot of adventures like that."

"Sounds like something that'd never happen to me."

"Have you ever howled at the moon in your underwear until you were hoarse, or hiked part of the Appalachian Trail until you had no idea what day it was anymore?"

"No. I've done other things though. Like raising over a billion dollars and enriching people's lives."

She frowns. "Okay, that's great. Incredible. The world needs more philanthropists. But what about *your* life, Easton? You have no idea what it's like to be purposely lost." She shakes her head. "I wouldn't trade places with you. No way."

I think about days and times and my schedule for the next year, realizing none of it includes spontaneity. I'm by the book; I follow the rules and do the right thing. Weston is right; maybe I need to take more chances.

A flash in my peripheral vision catches my attention, and I glance out the front windows. There's a man across the street with a long lens, and I think Brody spots him at the same time I do. He points to the exit and I nod.

I turn back to Lexi. "Do you want to get out of here?"

"Because you have somewhere to be?" she counters.

"Because I want to be *somewhere else* with you."

I close out our tab and set hundreds on the bar top. She grabs her flowers and we approach the door.

Brody shoves something cool into my hand. "Weston told me to give you these."

I look down at the keys to the Mustang and shake my head at his car choice.

Clever bastard.

"Did you know about this?" I ask Brody, but as he opens his mouth, I interrupt, "We'll talk about it later."

Lexi follows me, and when she's closer, I place my hand on her shoulder, leading her toward the exit. When we step outside, I stand in front of her, blocking her from the view of the camera across the street.

"What are you doing?" she asks, looking up into my eyes.

"I'm sorry, paparazzi. I want to protect you from the rumors," I tell her.

"Are you embarrassed by me?"

"Absolutely not," I say, the spark igniting deep inside, but I also know how this goes.

It's *always* the chase. It's always the first fourteen days, the prospect of falling in love. But then it ends when they show their true colors.

"Okay." She reaches forward and takes my hand.

Her touch makes me tense. It's the electricity, the undeniable attraction, that's almost too much.

I narrow my eyes at her and swallow hard. "You shouldn't start something you don't intend on finishing."

"Why not live in the moment?" She interlocks her fingers with mine, and I surprisingly relax. "You should make them eat from the palm of your hand, Easton. Give them something to talk about."

I tilt my head at her. *"You're perfect."*

She laughs. "Now, that's officially the second time you've told me that tonight. Oh, wait, that was your brother. Guess it's true then?"

I make a mental note to ask Weston why he said that. Maybe he sees the same thing I do—determination, mixed with a dash of defiance. My favorite combination in a woman. And the only type who can handle me.

"One hundred percent true. Now, do you remember where you parked?" I turn my body, loving how small her warm hand feels in mine and how soft her skin is as I rub my thumb across the top of hers.

"At the end of this block," she whispers, smiling at me as we stroll down the sidewalk. It's almost easy to pretend with her, especially when she looks at me the way she does.

A silent conversation streams as we arrive at the car that's parked perfectly between two others.

I let go of her hand and face her. "You're not like anyone I've ever met."

"I'm one of a kind. Now, gonna give me those keys?" She holds out her palm.

"Hell no. I'm okay to drive. You're not." I unlock the passenger door and open it for her.

"I'm having déjà vu from when I got picked up," she says, tugging on my black tie and sliding her hand down the length of it. I notice how her gaze meets my mouth, and how she licks her plump, kissable lips.

"You can try all the tricks in the book, but you're *not* getting the keys this time. I've got a little secret." I lean in and whisper, "I'm much harder to crack than my brother."

"Great. Because I love challenges too," she whispers, holding back a smile as she gets inside and buckles.

"You play dirty as fuck." I close the door and hear her laugh as I walk to the driver's side.

I get behind the steering wheel and crank the engine, loving the way it roars to life. I haven't driven this car in so fucking long. There was no reason to.

"Parking brake engaged," I say with a brow lifted. "Good girl."

She tucks her lips into her mouth. Mmm, maybe it's not a billionaire kink she has, but a praise one.

I hold down the clutch carefully moving the stick into first gear as I slowly inch onto the road. As we speed off, leaving Brody and the paps here, I know hundreds of pictures of us were taken together in that short amount of time. The tabloids will run with this story.

"Do you like the yellow roses?" I ask.

"Yeah, they're beautiful," she admits.

"If I had to guess, I'd say white ones are more your style."

She grins. "It's almost like you know me."

9

LEXI

As he stops at the intersection, I notice he's on edge.

I clear my throat. "Does it bother you, being watched and followed like that?"

"It comes with the territory," he says. "You learn to get used to it."

"I understand, but that wasn't my question."

He nods. "Do you have plans tomorrow?"

I turn to him, watching how his hair blows in the breeze. He loosens his tie and has that old-money, James Dean vibe going. I realize I'm staring.

"Funny story. This asshole got me fired, so I don't have anywhere to be until I find another job."

This makes him smile as we head toward the city's outskirts. "I want to take you somewhere."

"Luckily for you, I *love* surprises," I admit.

He glances at me. "Truth?"

"Yes. The more surprised I am, the better, because I'm usually two steps ahead of everyone or I have really shitty timing. I've lost count of how many times I ruined Christmas."

"Interesting. So, I'm curious, when was the last time you were caught off guard and shocked?" he asks.

"Easy. The moment I crashed into you at the Tower. And you?"

"Same for me."

I swallow down the lump that formed in my throat. Before that … I don't want to talk about it. Some things are better left unsaid, and some skeletons deserve to stay in the closet.

The engine revs, and we're cruising over a bridge after a few more blocks. I place my hand out the window and look up into the sky to see two stars and the moon. At home, there would be an ocean of them.

"I think I skipped timelines or something," I say, grinning. It's genuine, the kind that hurts. I don't remember the last time I felt this way. "How old are you?"

He glances at me, and I'm frozen in place. "I turn forty in thirty-eight days."

"An elder millennial. Yikes."

"What was the *yikes* for?" He makes a face.

"Your generation is a different breed," I tell him.

"I'd argue my generation is full of the *coolest* people in the world. Britney. Channing. Serena. Beyoncé. Prince Harry." He scoffs. "We're the G.O.A.T. generation."

This has me laughing. "You call them by their first names like you know them."

"I do," he says like it's nothing. "Do you date older?"

"I don't date *anyone*," I explain. "Anti-love, remember?"

"Ah, right."

The engine echoes off the buildings, and I try to make mental notes of different landmarks that might give away where he's taking me. I realize we're close to Central Park. We turn into a private garage, where he scans a card to enter. My eyes wander as we drive down to the basement level of a building.

"You live here?" I ask, feeling like we're entering Batman's cave. I have to hold back laughter.

"Sometimes," he says. "Depends on my mood."

I shake my head—him and that damn mood.

"What?" he asks, scanning again.

"Nothing," I say.

We drive into a storage area that's the size of the building. He gets out of the car and opens the door for me, and my jaw hits the floor when I see handfuls of vintage cars in every color —some with racing stripes, others not.

I run my hand across the hood of a black Chevelle SS. "A 454?"

He nods. "Impressed."

I walk around to the back of it, and all the emblems are shiny, not a smudge on them. "Four hundred fifty horsepower. Why didn't your brother choose this one?"

He chuckles. "He chose correctly."

I know that means something. "Do you name them? Is that what it is?"

"No, and you're not driving it," he says, leaning against a vintage Aston Martin. Next to him is a Mercedes-Benz 300SLR. All of this is unbelievable, especially being here with him like this.

I bend over, peeking inside to see the Benz with light-tan leather and wood grain accents. "I told your clone this earlier, but my dad was into restoring old cars. We used to go to car shows on the weekends. It was a good time."

"You said *was*," he says.

"Yeah, he passed away four years ago," I explain, checking out the Aston Martin he's modeling for me with his arms crossed.

"I'm sorry." He gives me a sad smile, not taking his eyes off me.

"Thanks." I don't know why I feel the emotions begin to

bubble, so I change the subject. "You've never let *anyone* drive these?"

"Only me and my mechanics. Well, I can now add Weston and you to that list." His mouth tilts into a sideways grin.

I walk back over to him. "This was great. You have anything newer than a 1970?"

"Ah," he says.

Then, he clicks on the lights in the other half of the building. Motorcycles galore. Half looks like a vintage museum, and the other half looks like a luxury car lot.

My mouth falls open when I see several Lamborghinis and Rolls-Royces parked beside one another. The only difference is the color. "Are you kidding me? One wasn't enough?"

"Depends on my mood," he says, and I notice he smiles.

I give him my full attention. "Really? So, what mood do you have to be in to drive the Mustang?"

A smile lingers on his lips. "Do you play chess?"

"Not since my dad died," I admit. "But I used to be pretty good."

"Well, I look forward to learning how strategic you are," Easton quips, leading me to the private elevator.

He scans his phone across it and the doors slide open. We get inside and I lean against the wall with my thumbs tucked into my pockets, focusing on the floor numbers and how fast we zoom upward.

I feel him watching me, so I glance at him, and he shakes his head.

"You're too trusting, Alexis."

I don't correct him because he expects me to. "And why would you say that? Do you plan on luring me to your billion-dollar dungeon?"

He chuckles. "The one located inside the Red Room."

"Wait, you've read *Fifty Shades*?" I do a quick memory scan through scenes and snort, covering my mouth.

He can't deny it. The look on his face gives him away. *Guilty.*

"Oh my God, you *did*. Why? Don't you have better things to do?"

He shrugs and relaxes. "A while ago, I had to learn about the guy the tabloids kept comparing me to." The elevator grows silent for a few seconds. "I hate to be a disappointment, but there's no sex room."

"Any room can be a sex room with enough creativity," I say. "Do you read a lot?"

"Yeah. I do," he admits. "And I'm aware of book boyfriends."

"You're referring to my shirt at the park. And what about them?" I lick my lips, knowing this man *almost* has me believing love might exist.

"They're fictional." He pushes off the wall as the elevator doors open, and the hallway is nothing but windows, like we're suspended in the air.

"So is love, but I have a feeling you still think it exists," I say.

"An anti-love, hopeless romantic, a pessimist, and an extrovert. What a fucking combination I've found."

"I'm a realist, not a pessimist. Get my list right." I grin, then stop and admire the city's golden glow.

It's a triplex penthouse with a multimillion-dollar view. I walk to the end of the hallway, and my eyes can't scan over the area fast enough.

"Gorgeous," I whisper, knowing only the lucky can experience this view and this adventure.

"Agreed," he says, his deep blue eyes locked on me. "It gets better though."

"How is that possible?"

He grabs my hand and my heart lurches forward. Easton Calloway might be my *biggest* mistake.

I move beside him as he unlocks a door. He steps aside, allowing me to enter first. A winding staircase greets the entrance and leads to the top floor.

I move forward and run my fingers across the grand piano keys. They ring out in tune. I follow him past the formal dining and living rooms, and he pushes the door open. We're standing on a glass-paned balcony overlooking Central Park.

"Wow," I whisper. "Okay, I'm shocked. Next time someone asks me when a moment blew me away, I'll say this one."

"This place has a three-hundred-sixty-degree view from above. But from the ground, if you look up, the balcony hangs over, and the blue windows make it shine—"

"Like a diamond in the sky." I smile. "I'll have to look up the next time I'm in the park after the sun sets."

I stare out into the night, and so does he.

"To answer your earlier question … it does bother me, always being tracked and watched," he tells me, and I know it took being vulnerable to share that.

"I noticed," I say.

"Only my brother knows that," he admits, moving his gaze from me because it grows too intense. "How did you know?"

I smile and interlock my fingers. "I saw it in your eyes. The window to your soul. But don't worry; your secret is safe with me. Along with having a heart—oh, and being a Christian Grey fanboy."

He chuckles. It's a nice sound, one that he should share more often. "Thanks for hanging out with me."

"You should be thanking your brother."

"Do you prefer that version?" he asks, but I see how his jaw clenches tight.

"No," I admit, turning my attention toward him. "*Truth,*" I confirm so he knows I'm serious.

He glances away.

I chuckle. "Too much of a good thing, ya know? I can't be out here, falling in love. Like right now, I'm not worried about you and me."

That laugh returns, but it's sarcastic, like he doesn't believe me.

I make a face. "I'm *not,* especially not with your inability to date anyone longer than two-weeks."

Easton shoves his hands in his pockets and turns to me. He leans his head against the glass. I can't help but smile as I tuck hair behind my ear.

He studies my lips. "You should marry me."

I look at him like he's lost his mind. "What?! Are you feeling *okay*?"

"Better than ever." He places his hand on my shoulder. His hot breath is on my skin.

"I don't understand," I say, knowing I'm being pranked.

"I can explain everything, but I need you to sign something first."

Then, I realize what he said. "Are you seriously asking me to sign an NDA?"

His beautiful face cracks into a smile. "Yes, I am."

"You're playing dirty, Mr. Calloway."

"You set the standard, *Alexis*. That's how you got the keys to my car." He crosses his arms over his chest and smirks. "And if you want to know more, you'll sign on the dotted line. And if not, well, goodbye, *Ms. Matthews*."

"I'm amazed at how quickly you can turn the asshole on," I say, thankful for the reminder.

"I'm a pro," he tells me.

It's confirmed that I've met my match. Extremes, willing to fight, and loves a game, otherwise we wouldn't be here right now. But there is no way I'm walking away without more information. Curiosity will eat me alive.

"I'll give you some time to think about it, but one thing you should know: I always protect *my* assets." He walks inside, leaving me to myself as he goes upstairs.

He wasn't joking about the glass windows. From this

vantage point, I can see all three stories of his penthouse. I watch him climb the stairs, loving how he moves, pure muscles and man. When he glances over, our eyes meet, and I turn around as if I wasn't staring. We both know I was.

I inhale the fresh air and close my eyes for a few seconds. We're suspended so high that I can see the lights from the city reflecting off the water, and I look up at the moon. The hint of his cologne still lingers, and I pinch myself to confirm I'm not dreaming.

I pull my phone from my back pocket and unlock it. After I open my camera, I snap a selfie with the skyline behind me. I'm tempted to post it online, but it's a moment I want to keep to myself.

Movement in the kitchen grabs my attention.

Easton changed into black joggers that sit low on his hips, and he's shirtless, grabbing a glass from the cabinet. With his back toward me, I admire the tattoos across his body. My temperature increases when he turns around, removing a cork from a bottle. If I could stare at him all night, I would. He's artwork.

More ink is etched across his chest, and it all perfectly connects. The tattoos stop where a suit would no longer cover them. Everything about Easton Calloway screams professional on the streets, bad boy in the sheets. The man looks like a rock star with a *V* that points down to his package.

Pulling myself from my thoughts, I realize he's staring back at me with a smile. When I snap out of it, he waves me inside.

I grin, giving myself the biggest pep talk of a lifetime as I make my way to the double doors.

He's right; I want to know the secrets he wants to share. But at this point, it might be a need.

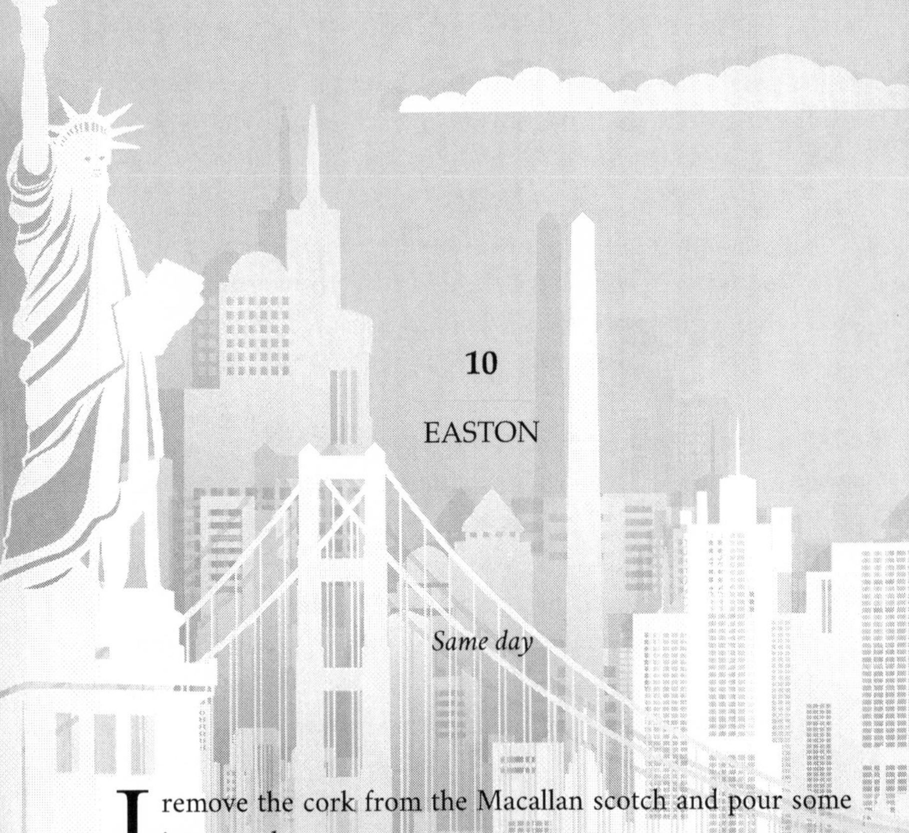

10

EASTON

Same day

I remove the cork from the Macallan scotch and pour some into my glass.

When Alexis enters, I hold up the bottle. "Would you like to try this?"

She glides through the living room, past the grand piano, like a figment of my imagination. When she's closer, I notice how her eyes scan across the label and then up my body. She's eye-fucking me again. That much is obvious. But I welcome it.

"Sure."

I scoot my glass toward her and grab another. "This is strong. You have to be careful," I warn.

"Fill it up because I have a feeling I'll need it for our chat." That twang in her voice is there.

Instead, I give her the bottle, and she pours it until the glass is halfway full.

"Damn, girl," I whisper, shaking my head. "You might be fucked tomorrow."

"I hope I am," she says, swirling it around and taking a sip, not flinching. "Smooth."

"You're going to give me a run for my money, aren't you?"

She sits. "You have no idea. I've already warned you once that I won't make this easy for you."

"I look forward to it," I tell her, scooting the contract and pen across the marble countertop that stretches the length of the kitchen.

The yellow of the overhead lights makes her look like she's glowing golden.

Her eyes are locked on me for a few seconds, almost as if she's contemplating her life choices. But I can tell by the expression on her face that she won't leave here tonight without signing because it would eat her alive.

Tonight, the two of us connected on a deeper level, a raw one, and I know she felt it. Weston is right. She is perfect. Knowing he said that to her was the confirmation I needed.

She flips to the back page and signs it.

"Alexis, you *never* sign a legal document without reading it. You could've just signed your soul over to me."

"Well, *Mr. Calloway*," she says, folding the packet back to the front page. "Did I?"

"Don't be reckless, *Lexi*."

"I know how an NDA works, *Easton*. Keep my mouth shut and don't tell anyone about this."

"You can't tell any family members, not even your best friend."

"It goes to the grave. I understand how to keep a secret. A Texan's word is their life."

Like a champ, she shoots back the scotch in one gigantic gulp, placing the glass back on the counter before filling it again. I shake my head and she smirks as I flick off the lights.

I turn on a lamp in the living room and move to the couch, staring at the city lights. I've missed the comfort of the diamond in the sky.

Alexis kicks off her red heels and sits beside me, facing me, with her legs crisscrossed. I stare forward, and she stares *at* me, but I don't mind. I like being under her microscope.

As I lean back, I take a sip of my scotch, savoring it.

"Easton, seriously, are you going to edge me all night with this?" she whispers, leaning sideways against the cushions, impatiently waiting for me to speak.

I glance at her. "Edging is my *favorite*. But if I recall, you're the one who likes to get lost in the moment. This *is* a *moment*."

"You're an asshole," she mutters with a laugh.

"But you find it endearing for some reason," I say.

She looks out at the city and empties her glass again. "I do."

When she drinks, the little filter she has falls away. They say a drunk man's truths are a sober man's secrets. What secrets does she keep?

We fall into silence, and Alexis moves her hand forward, tracing the outline of the compass tattoo on my arm.

"This is beautiful," she says. Her eyes scan over my ink, like she's memorizing them.

I watch her, and when her eyes finally meet mine again, I speak. "I need a wife," I mutter.

"*Need* is an odd word choice. Shouldn't it be *want*?"

"No. Not in this circumstance. I don't know how to say this … to fulfill the requirements of becoming CEO, I must get married before my fortieth birthday."

"You mentioned your birthday was in thirty-eight days," she says. "I was listening. Did you know that's beekeeping age?"

"Not sure what that means," I admit.

"It's a good thing." Her lips slightly part. "Being forced to wed is old-fashioned though."

I suck in a deep breath. "That's one of the many

requirements my grandfather established when the company was formed. An invisible clock has been ticking down since I was old enough to get married. It was supposed to encourage us to start a family early and not be obsessed with our job."

"Like how you are now?"

"Yes," I admit.

"And he's not Southern?"

"No. French."

"Right, because then the expectation would've been eighteen with a baby on the way."

Her finger continues tracing the outline of the compass. Her touch is intoxicating, but I try not to act affected by her closeness, even though she intrigues the fuck out of me.

"I don't have any other options. The odds of finding someone to spend the rest of my life with within six weeks is astronomical."

"A fake marriage is dishonest," she says.

"Oh, see, it'd be a *real* marriage—at least on paper and in public," I confirm, remembering what my brother said. "But I agree. It's dishonest. However, thousands of people will lose their jobs in the next six months if I don't take over the company. My brother will quit, and I'll lose everything I've worked for. My hand is being forced. And I'll do whatever I can for my employees, even go against my wants."

"Which is?" she asks.

I've never told this to anyone I dated. "Over the years, I've refused to get married unless I was in love."

That sad expression I saw in the Tower Penthouse meets her pretty face again.

"So, you're making the ultimate sacrifice for your employees. And you say *I'm* a hopeless romantic."

Our faces are close, and I melt under her as she continues to touch me. As if she notices, she pulls her hand away and clears her throat.

"So, let me make sure I've got this straight. You've refused to get married until you found true love, and now that you've got a month and a half, you're like, *Fuck it all. Let me marry this woman I've known for weeks.*"

"Eight days," I correct. "It's only been a week."

"I haven't been counting, Easton, but you have," she says. "I don't know why you're choosing me. There are a thousand women who would happily marry you right now and try to be the perfect wife for you."

"And that's the problem. I don't want someone falling in love with me in the process. You don't believe in love, and I need to marry someone whose heart I won't break with this situationship."

"And the expectation is?"

"Be my date to all social events, where you act like you're in love with me while *not* falling in love."

"That sounds easy. For how long? A month?"

"That's *cute*. At a minimum, a year."

Her mouth falls open.

"And after three hundred sixty-five days, I'll present divorce papers and write you a check for a million dollars. Afterward, we can go our separate ways."

"You want me to put my entire life on pause for a million dollars? I'm worth more than that, Easton." She laughs, but she's not joking.

"You're negotiating?" I grin, but it wasn't unexpected, considering she got the keys to one of my prized possessions.

"You're a billionaire, and you're *lowballing*."

I rub my finger across the scruff on my chin, utterly impressed by her honesty.

"Oh, I almost forgot. You'll also have to live here with me, and I'll give you a hefty allowance to buy whatever you'd like. You'll be wined, dined, and treated like royalty as your social life grows exponentially. Knowing that, name your price, *darling*."

"So, I'll have to act like you're my everything in front of people, be presentable on your level of prestige, put my acting career on hold for another year because of you, and potentially hang out with a bunch of snobs at boring social events, where there'll be too many leaders and not enough followers, right? And I'm sure that means celibacy because there is no way a man like you will let his wife fuck around. Not to mention the spotlight on me anytime I'm in a public space. Did I get that right?"

"Yeah. And you can't fall in love with me. That's the most important one because it will make things awkward."

"Don't worry about that," she says.

"Oh, and about the spotlight ..." I hesitate. "I think that's already a thing."

"Shit," she whispers. "You're right."

"I'm sorry. I shouldn't have approached you at th—"

"Don't you dare apologize for talking to me—unless you regret it?"

"I don't *ever* regret anything with you. I'm apologizing because it wasn't a moment kept between us only. Just promise me when you leave here tonight, you'll research me. Naïvety is cute, but you need to learn what you can about me first before you commit to this."

"One second."

She lifts upward, taking her phone from her back pocket. After she types my name into the search bar, the articles of us immediately load. When she sees the photos, she gasps and zooms in.

"Well, no wonder you came up with this idea. Look at this." She quickly scrolls through the pictures and reads a few gossip articles. "They're convincing *me* that I'm in love, and I know I'm not."

"The story is writing itself." I repeat what Weston said. He was right.

"Are you sure you won't feel guilty about this and regret it later? You can only get married once."

I think about her question. "I'll consider it a practice run with my *temporary wife*. A lot of people are depending on me right now. What about you?"

"I'm always up for an adventure, Easton." I can tell she's lost in her thoughts. "My price is fifteen million."

"Eight," I counter, holding out my hand, ready to close the deal.

"Twelve. Million." She keeps her focus on me. "But I need to think about it."

"I'll give you three days." I look down at my watch, thinking about those stupid chain letters that used to spread around when I was in boarding school. This does somewhat feel like a curse.

"Okay," she whispers. "Also, you were right. This is a *moment*."

We both bring our attention to the city lights. Her breathing slows beside me, and I'm lost in my thoughts. I don't remember the last time I *talked* to someone.

"I think that scotch is starting to kick in, or maybe it's the excitement from the day," she mutters with a yawn.

"I can have my driver take you home," I offer.

"Most guys would try to get me between the sheets," she says.

"I'm not most guys, Alexis."

"I've noticed." She grins.

For a brief second, I think I see our future in her eyes, and that's when I wonder if this is a bad fucking idea.

"A driver would be great," she tells me with another yawn.

I stand and move to the kitchen to grab my phone from the counter. I call the transportation service to send a limo for her.

"Your ride will be here in ten minutes."

"Or you could let me borrow one of the nine hundred cars you have downstairs. The Chevelle."

"I could," I mutter.

"But you won't."

"No," I say. "It's late and—"

"You protect your assets."

"Always."

"I wouldn't let anything happen to your car."

"I'm not worried about the car, Alexis." My phone buzzes, letting me know the driver has left. I stand and hold out my hand, helping her up. "I'll walk you down. Let me grab a shirt and some shoes."

She nods and wanders over to the built-in bookshelf that ranges the height of two stories. There's a ladder attached to a railing. I glance back at her as I take the stairs to my bedroom where I slide on a T-shirt and some sandals.

When I return, her eyes soften.

"You've got a nice collection of first-edition, signed books." She turns toward me, her eyes sliding up and down my body. "The way you can transform your entire look, you're like a magician."

I chuckle. "Look like a crypto bro?"

"Oh God!" She huffs. "Gross."

"Yeah, I agree."

"Question: do you like the theater?"

"Yes, quite a lot."

She shakes her head. "Watch out, Easton. You're checking boxes off my Dream Man list."

"That's the scotch talking."

"You're right," she says.

We take the elevator to the foyer and pass several security checkpoints. It's hard to break into Park Towers because of the extra security measures they have in place. It was one of the reasons I bought the diamond in the sky and why Weston purchased a penthouse on a different floor. He doesn't stay often though.

"If your answer is yes, expect me to take you on many dates," I mutter.

"Really?" She lifts a brow.

"Yes, I will spoil you with adventures for helping me. The world will fall in love with you, darling. My only regret will be not keeping you to myself."

"Pick a truth or lie." She meets my eyes with defiance.

"Truth, always."

"Don't *try* to break me when it comes to love. You'll lose."

Her words come out as a warning … or a *challenge*. But it's a moment of clarity, raw truth. She feels whatever this is bubbling between us. It's the only confirmation I need to know this isn't one-sided.

"And don't smirk at me like that," she warns.

I keep the expression firmly planted on my face.

The doors slide open. We step outside and wait for my driver, but my eyes scan around the perimeter, and I spot several paps.

"Will you text me when you arrive home?" I ask, tucking hair behind her ear.

"I will. They're watching, aren't they?"

I lean and whisper in her ear, "Yes. Have a good night, Lexi."

"Good night," she mutters and pulls away.

"I'll be waiting for your answer."

She nods, meeting my eyes, then gently wraps her hand behind my neck and slides her lips against mine. I wrap my arms around her waist as her tongue slides into my mouth.

My body sings with pleasure as I taste the scotch on her tongue, mixed with her strawberry lip balm. The kiss deepens and we lose control, slipping into the abyss and losing ourselves in one another's touch. It's only a kiss, one that shouldn't stir desire deep within me, but it does. Alexis moans into my mouth, grabbing my shirt in her fist, and I don't want it to stop. The intensity of it, of her, nearly destroys me on this side wall as the inferno inside me rages.

"Alexis," I desperately whisper against her mouth as she releases a ragged breath.

"I'm *not* sorry," she says as the limo stops before her.

I open the door with swollen lips and a racing heart, unable to articulate my thoughts.

My mouth and body are on fire as I watch her move inside.

When she turns to look at me, she gives me a mischievous grin. "Three days. I'll have my answer."

I shut the door and stand with my arms crossed over my chest. The car speeds down the road, and I watch until it's out of sight before I shake my head and laugh. If that was her putting on a show, unpredictably predictable, then I should guard myself.

Thirty minutes later, I'm sitting in the same spot I shared with Alexis on the couch, sketching the view. I flip the page and see the previous drawing was at the bar before she arrived. And a few pages before that, her reading at the park and the Tower Penthouse. Moments with her are already displayed in my artwork. Multiple in a week? This is moving quickly, almost too fast.

Afterward, I go upstairs and lie in bed, staring at the ceiling, wondering if this is a mistake. Suppose I get in too deep and end up being destroyed, like my brother.

A handful of moving pieces have to come together for this to work; above everything, it must be believable.

My phone vibrates and lights up on the nightstand. I grab it, laughing at how I saved her in my Contacts earlier.

MY WIFE

I'm home. Thanks for a fun night.

EASTON

Anytime. Just know, I don't wait for anyone.

MY WIFE

Love that I can teach an old dog new tricks.
Next up, begging.

EASTON

I don't beg anyone either.

MY WIFE

Your brother told me.

Of course he did.

EASTON

Good night, Alexis.

She reads my text message, but doesn't reply.

I'm more than ready to play this game with this woman. I have been since the moment we crashed together at the W.

One year with Alexis Matthews as my temporary wife would be *priceless*.

She wants twelve million, but I'd pay twenty-four.

She's the *only one* who can do this.

11

LEXI

Couch springs shove into my back, and I roll over while Carlee brews a coffee pod in the kitchen. The rich scent of caffeine wafts through the air, but I focus on pretending to be asleep. After last night, she'll have a million questions I won't be able to answer because of the NDA.

"Is Sleeping Beauty awake?" she asks from the end of the couch, and it takes every acting skill I have not to answer or smile.

Nearly ten minutes later, the front door opens and closes. Once she's gone, I sit up and run my fingers through my hair before twisting it into a top bun.

I glance at the heels on the floor and my clothes that are in a small pile. Then, I recall last night.

I kissed him. I lost control.

And he did too.

I snatch my phone from the coffee table, open my Internet app, and type his name into the search bar, just like I did last night. Pictures of us kissing were taken from all angles, three hundred sixty degrees. Combined are pictures of Weston picking me up in the Mustang, and they think it's Easton. They have no idea.

My eyes scan over the fresh articles that were written this morning. Easton is right; the tabloids are constructing the story about us.

I reread our convo from last night and chuckle at my bluntness, but I can't deny the dash of flirting too.

He texted me good night, but when I saw he used Alexis, I didn't respond. I'm a gangster, and I keep my read receipts on so people know I'm *purposely* ignoring them.

He knows I read it and ignored him. My energy is expensive and exclusive, something money can't buy. Well, that's not true. *The price tag is twelve million dollars.*

The thought of being his temporary wife almost sounds too good to be true. However, I think we could be good friends.

As I'm doomscrolling gossip sites, the door swings open, scaring the shit out of me. I almost scream, but when I see Carlee, my brows crease.

"Why are you grinning like that? Like you're daydreaming."

"Why are you home?"

"I forgot something." She sounds breathless, like she ran back to the apartment. "What's with the guilty look?"

I cover my face. "I signed an NDA and can't talk about it. But I really, *really* want to talk about it."

This makes her laugh as she plops down beside me on the couch. "Is this about *Mr. Calloway*?"

"He told me to call him Easton," I say.

She's smiling. "Already on a first-name basis. Nice."

I clear my throat, knowing I need to watch what I say because this has to be locked tight if it will work. "Well, he also wants to date me."

"*Now* I have a million questions. What the hell?" She stands and paces. "The answer is yes. Right?"

"I've known him for a week."

"So what? Dating is the first step to forever, Lexi!" she squeals, and I see happiness radiating over her.

I almost feel guilty, knowing it's a sham that I have to set up perfectly for everyone to believe.

"You do know he has a twin brother, right?" I ask.

She tilts her head at me. "Oh yeah, but isn't he divorced or going through one? That's a lot of baggage and *other woman* drama. No thanks!"

I burst out laughing. "I have no idea. But I *did* meet him."

Her mouth falls open. "Meeting the family too? Damn, girl. Wait, did you tell him you're anti-love? Like, he's aware?"

"Yeah," I admit. It's the truth. "He understands and doesn't care."

She laughs loudly. "He'll break you of that."

"What? No! *No*, he won't. It's not like that, trust me." I wish I could tell her everything.

"It's *exactly* like that. Men like Easton Calloway don't date just anyone. Especially him. This is a huge fucking deal."

I shake my head, because she's being serious and that scares the shit out of me more than anything. "You act like I'm going to fall in love with him."

She pulls her phone from her pocket and pulls up photos of us. "Are you sure you haven't? Look at how you're kissing him. Totally into it. No shame. I would be too."

She continues, "Not to mention the day you tried to *Mission Impossible* a watch return. You couldn't even *speak*. Now, he's picking you up in a vintage car with flowers and sends you home in a limo after an open-mouthed tongue kiss?"

"Actually …" I shake my head, not wanting to go deeper into it because the optics are on point and she's confirmed that for me. Weston picking me up in Easton's car was more calculated than initially intended, especially seeing the photos. Weston knew what he was doing—sneaky bastard. "Okay, you got me. You're right."

"Do you plan on seeing him tonight?"

I lick my lips. "No. Why? Do you want to do something?"

"Nah. I think I'll come home, shower, and watch *Bridgerton* in my pajamas." She checks her phone. "Shit, I gotta get going. If you call it quits with Easton because you're too scared of falling in love with a gorgeous-as-fuck billionaire, tell him you know someone."

I snort. "You're terrible."

"My body is ready." She chuckles, walking past me. "I still want my trip to France, okay?"

She moves toward the door.

"Wait, I thought you forgot something?" I ask.

"Oh." She pulls her subway card from her pocket and smirks. "It's right here. *Sometimes, the risk is worth the reward,* Lexi."

The door closes and I try to figure out why she's acting weird.

My phone is unlocked next to me on the couch. I want to live in the moment as my fingers fly over the keyboard.

LEXI

Mr. Calloway, I'd love to continue our conversation at your earliest convenience.

Then, I see a read receipt without an immediate reply. He's a savage too.

When he doesn't respond, I know I've met my match.

Carlee is right; he will try to break me—I know that. I can see it in his eyes and hear it in his raw truths, but that road goes both ways.

After I shower to clear my mind, I tighten my ponytail and leave our apartment.

It takes over half an hour to get across town, but I feel like the main character when I arrive at one of the largest independent bookstores in the world, with over eighteen glorious miles of books. It's an escape.

The red and white sign stretches around the block, and inside awaits several stories of shelves so tall that I need a stool to reach the top. It also has that old-library smell that only a book lover understands. It's one of the things I missed most when I moved back to Texas. Although we have a small bookstore in my hometown, the selection is limited.

I stroll down the aisles and read the back of each pink-and-purple romance book I find. Some make me smile, and others intrigue me, so I can't decide what to buy. My TBR list is already a mile long, but I settle on another billionaire romance. I find it hilarious as I carry it to the front and push the book across the dark wooden counter.

The lady scans the barcode with a grin. "This is a great one."

Our eyes meet, and I know we're both smut queens. *Proudly.*

"I bet I know how it ends," I tell her.

"I bet you *don't,*" she says, and I'm intrigued all over again.

After I leave, I stare up at the sky, smiling as fast-moving clouds cast shadows on the ground, casting parts of the sidewalk in splotches of darkness. Sounds of cars zoom in the distance while classic music streams from businesses on book row. I overhear phone conversations of passersby on the street.

I smile, remembering why I love being here—I can be no one and someone, all at the same time.

Instead of getting on the subway, I purchase an iced coffee I can't afford and walk to the park to read. I find a place under a tree that casts shade and look up at the *diamond in the sky,* wondering if Easton is there right now, looking down at me.

I chew on the corner of my lip and snap a picture with my phone from my current vantage point in the grass. The last photo in my phone is a selfie from up there.

I go back to my book, losing time while devouring the pages. The heroine and hero are on a helicopter above Seattle, and he kisses her mid-flight. While I don't want to stop here, I head to the subway before the five-o'clock rush, or it will take me double the time to get home. I glance back at the diamond in the sky before rounding the corner.

After a train change and another twenty-minute ride, I walk into my apartment, open the windows, and return to the pages. I know they're about to have hot, dirty sex for the very first time, and I'm giddy with excitement until I hear the loud revving of an engine.

The noise echoes off the surrounding buildings and pulls me away. I groan, annoyed, wanting to concentrate on the spice. The constant roaring goes on for thirty more seconds before I lose my shit. I grab the receipt and place it between the pages. I can't be bothered with a bookmark.

I get up and search the street for the nuisance as I place my hands on the windowsill.

Immediately, I spot the jerk and scowl as I give the asshole a *what the fuck* shrug.

The guy removes the helmet, and I'm preparing to get cursed out. But that's when I realize it's *him* in rider gear.

Easton.

I shake my head. My heart rate ticks up. He waves me downstairs, and the smile on his beautiful face makes me want to risk it all.

Every alarm bell screams that I should walk away while I can, but he's my ultimate temptation. And like he said, we could have fun in the process. It would be the adventure of a lifetime, wouldn't it?

I take the four flights downstairs, and he unstraps a pink helmet from the back of his bike.

"Join me," he mutters, holding it out toward me.

"You're Easton, right?" I ask, looking down at the helmet, my favorite color, wondering how he knew.

He nods and smiles. "This time."

"Are you sure this is safe?" I ask, taking a mental snapshot of him leaning against that cherry-red bike.

"I won't let anything happen to you," he promises, his blue eyes shining like diamonds before he closes his visor. All I see is my reflection staring back at me.

I take the helmet and slide it over my head. It's a perfect fit. Easton snaps the kickstand up and mounts it. I lift my leg, sliding behind him, scooting forward until my breasts press against his back.

"This is un-fucking-believable," I mutter, shaking my head as I carefully snake my hands around his strong body.

Then, I hear him audibly chuckle from a speaker in my helmet. "Agreed. Hang on."

He wasn't supposed to hear that.

Excitement takes over as we zoom away.

"Of course they're linked together."

"Yeah. So we can chat if needed."

I can hear the smile in his voice. I can already imagine the look on his face.

He slows at a stop sign, and his firm hand grips my thigh as he looks both ways. My heart pounds so fast that I swear I can hear it inside the quietness of my helmet.

Experiencing the city like this in the late afternoon is incredible. I look up at the buildings, taking it all in as we cruise by. I hold him a little tighter, wanting to get lost with him and live in the make-believe, even if it's only for a year. I have nothing to lose and *everything* to gain.

"What book are you currently reading?" he asks.

"*Fifty Shades*," I tell him.

"Lie," he says.

"Stalker."

He chuckles, but doesn't deny it.

"Well, joke's on you. I'm *into* that shit," I tell him with a laugh. "I'd be the worst person to try to kidnap. I read too much."

"What am I going to do with you?" he asks.

"I think you're gonna make me your wife."

"Mmm. I think that's still to be determined."

His words come out in a deep rasp, and I can only imagine that devilish smirk on his bastard face. I'm only sad I don't get to experience it.

12

EASTON

Birthday countdown: 37 days
Since meeting her: 9 days
Company takeover: 44 days

We arrive at the small Italian restaurant my grandfather and I frequented when I was a boy. The idea to start the company that changed my family's life came to fruition inside these walls; sharing this place with her is fitting.

Alexis flawlessly dismounts the bike and removes her helmet, shaking her long brown hair out before tucking it behind her ears. I watch her from behind my visor, hidden from her gaze. She's naturally beautiful, a woman who doesn't have to try to steal my breath away, but somehow manages to.

Will this fire that's threatening to ignite last more than two weeks? I guess we'll fucking see.

I take off my helmet and strap them both to the back of the bike before I look around, knowing we're safe from the paparazzi—at least for now. I spot Brody across the street, keeping watch. He nods when I glance in his direction.

When we're close to the entrance, I open the door for her, moving my hand to the small of her back. I guide her to the booth across the room, tucked in the corner. It has more privacy than any other seat, and the paparazzi can't capture a good image because of the tinted windows.

A red and white checkered tablecloth covers the scratched tabletop. If anyone peeked under it, they'd find my and Weston's initials carved into the wood. We did it before we left for university. That was the first and only time we went our separate ways in life. It was hard because, before that time, we were inseparable. He knows everything about me, and vice versa. It's a requirement when you wear the same face.

Once I received Alexis's text this morning, I called my brother, and we had a long discussion about this. About her. About the company.

Weston invited me to join him in his *fuck it* era. I think I might.

As I sit in front of this woman, recognizing the undeniable attraction that streams between us, it's a yes.

Alexis leans back and reads the laminated menu as I try to read *her*. The restaurant has served the same items longer than I've been alive. I've got it memorized at this point.

"The usual?" the owner, Giana, asks with a smile.

I pull my attention from Alexis and meet her warm brown eyes. "For me, *yes*."

Giana glances at Alexis and gives a slight nod of approval, but I don't miss it. I've never brought a woman here in the years I've visited. This is a first.

Alexis scans the front and back again and sets the menu down. "I'll have what he's having."

"Excellent choice."

Moments later, a bottle of red is brought to the table with

two glasses. Two cups of water are placed next to a pile of napkins and two forks. When we're left to ourselves again, Alexis fills her glass and moves to mine.

I hold up my hand. "I'm okay."

She nods, taking a sip. "I never thought you'd step inside a place like this."

"Why?" I ask.

"You seem more like a *caviar and champagne* kind of guy." The sunshine reflects through the windows, making her brown hair shine.

"But do I?" I ask, lifting my brows, knowing she's being facetious. "Truth."

She glances away, unable to handle the eye contact as she sucks in a ragged breath. "*No*. It's hard to believe you're somewhat *normal*."

"It's hard to believe you're somewhat *not*."

This plan might work better than I *ever* expected it could.

"So, if I read the intentions behind your text, you've made your decision?"

A hint of a smile plays on her beautiful face. "I've decided to give you my answer after this date."

"*Date*?" I interlock my fingers on the table, smirking. I know more than she thinks I do.

"What else would you call this?" she asks.

"A meeting." I tilt my head, keeping my voice low enough for only her to hear. "You can't play games with me, *darling*. After the performance you gave last night, I *know* you're all in."

She shakes her head. "For once in your life, be patient."

"*No*. It's a complete sentence."

That twinkle in her eye, the one I recognized in the photos of us posted online, returns. This time, I don't miss it.

"Why are you smiling like that?" she asks as our spaghetti and giant meatballs are slid in front of us.

"No reason." I offer a thank you to the guy who delivers our meal. We both reach for the silverware. "So, *Alexis,* what did you do today?"

Her lip twitches, and she lets out a humph, but it's adorable.

"Why do I have a sneaking suspicion that you know what I did today?"

"I have a bodyguard watching you for your protection."

She grins mischievously. "Really? Did your guard dog tell you I went to my fuck buddy's place?"

"Never thought I'd meet an actress who's a terrible liar." I lift a brow. "But you *should* know, I'm *very* jealous about what's *mine,* and soon, that might include you."

I know this dance; it's a classic, and we're already spinning together—something we shouldn't do—but the temptation and her willingness to bust my balls every chance she gets encourage it.

"We might have more in common than we think," she says, twirling the spaghetti around her fork as she takes a bite.

I check my watch; it's the first time I've looked since I picked her up. "I have an engagement party to attend at seven thirty."

She unlocks her phone, glancing at the time. "That's in *two* hours."

"I know," I admit. "I need a plus-one. Do you have plans?"

"It sounds like I do now."

A sly grin touches my lips. "It's your decision, but I'd love to introduce you to my friends."

"Wait, you have *friends*?" The sarcasm drips from her tone. "I heard you were a recluse."

I nod. "Soon, you'll learn that people see what I allow. I try to protect those I care about as much as possible. A lot of my life stays private."

She twirls the spaghetti noodles on her fork and takes another bite. "So, tell me about tonight."

"It's a test to see if my closest friends believe our façade. If they don't, we should call it quits before we waste any more time."

She smiles. "Luckily for you, I'm *always* audition ready."

"Lucky me," I say.

Eventually, she'll be able to read me like a book, like those fictional billionaires she's obsessed with.

"That was a truth," she mutters, and I tilt my head at her. Maybe she already can.

I nod and glance down at my wrist, knowing my grandfather's watch is the only reason we met. The thought encapsulates me.

"Love is always on time," I mutter with a huff.

"Yeah. I read that on the back of your watch when I *stole* it," she says with a playful eye roll.

"But what if it is?" I question, wishing I knew the answer.

We stare at each other for a few seconds too long.

"When you look at me like that, it's like you're reading my mind," she says.

The temperature rises in the room. I remove my rider jacket and set it next to me.

Her eyes slide over the tattoos on my arms. "I don't need mind-reading abilities when you eye-fuck me like that."

"Is that against the rules?" She picks up the wineglass, swirling the dark liquid in the bottom, but she doesn't deny it.

"It's welcome. Without attraction, this would *never* work. I'm good at pretending, but not *that* good, Alexis."

"Lexi."

"So, that's Lexi or nothing?" I wait for the confirmation.

"Eventually, you'll catch on," she says.

After we finish eating, we return to the bike, and I glance at Brody. He points north and holds up two fingers, which means we're being watched. I hand her the helmet as I put mine on and turn to her. Her eyes slide over me before she puts her helmet on.

"Paps to the right," I tell her over the voice-activated intercom system.

"Let me drive." She holds out her hand.

"See, now, I don't know if you're kidding." I cross my arms over my chest.

"I grew up on a ranch, Easton. I can ride *anything*. I thought you said to do your research." She scoffs.

I place my hand on her hip. "Get your ass on the back of my bike and pretend like you don't want to let go."

"Funny."

I crank the engine and she lifts her leg, scooting forward until her body is against mine. She lets out a contented sigh, wrapping her arms tightly around my waist, and we take off. We ride in silence as I take it in. The smile that's found residence on my lips since meeting Alexis lingers.

"What if your friends don't like me?" she eventually asks.

"I'm afraid they'll like you too much," I admit.

"Is that a problem?"

I hesitate. "One for future me to deal with."

"Mmm." I can feel her shaking her head. "When you play with fire, Mr. Calloway, you risk getting burned."

"I fight fire with fire, Alexis, so try not to get scorched." I give the bike more power as the sun hangs lazily in the sky.

She chuckles. "If we successfully pull this off at the end of three hundred sixty-five days, you might not want to let me go."

"And now, you've discovered what I'm afraid of," I admit, knowing what the possibilities are.

The silence draws on, but I notice she holds me tighter.

"About tonight," she whispers, "I don't have anything to wear."

"I've already taken care of everything, darling."

13

LEXI

Easton drives us to the diamond in the sky, and I'd be lying if I said I wasn't anxious about tonight. The elevator shoots up to the penthouse like a speeding bullet.

"I want to make a great first impression," I say, a lump forming in my throat.

"Wait, are you nervous?" he asks.

I pause, finding it easy to tell him the truth. "A tad."

"You should be. They're intense, but you got along with my brother fine. And now, he's your biggest fan."

Laughter bursts out of me. "He's an *asshole*."

"Can't deny that. I know first impressions aren't your forte, but I have faith in you. Otherwise, we would not have made it this far. And Weston wouldn't be on board."

At first, I want to deny it, but then I remember how I met Carlee. And my best friend Remi back in Texas. We can add Easton to the list too. All disasters.

"Shit. You're *right*. I do suck at first impressions."

He chuckles. "We'll stay for one hour; if everything goes okay, you can sign the contract."

"I don't recall giving my answer. Tonight isn't just a practice run for me, but it's also *your* audition. I could change my mind."

"You *could*. But you *won't*."

"Keep saying things like that, and I'll refuse, just to defy you."

He smirks. "And that's why you're the perfect match. That defiant, snap-back attitude is *impossible* to fake. Everyone knows I wouldn't be with someone who wasn't strong-willed."

I laugh. "And to think, we're just getting started."

"Joke's on *you*. I'm into it," he says back to me, repeating the words I told him earlier, but I know he's not kidding. He doesn't want anyone to worship him. He's searching for his equal.

The lights are low when we enter the triplex penthouse, but sunlight leaks in from the surrounding windows.

"Would you like an official tour?" he asks as we climb the stairs to the second floor.

"Uh, *yes*. I found it quite rude that you didn't offer last night."

"If I forget my manners, please let me know. But I think this will be your favorite room," he admits.

"Your Red Room?"

"Better," he says, pushing open the door, and my mouth falls open.

I never expected a massive library with a wall of books from floor to ceiling. A ladder that's even taller than the one downstairs swings from one full side to the other.

"Holy shit. Are those ten-foot bookshelves?"

"Fifteen," he says as I notice the reading nook with big, fluffy pillows.

"You're kidding, right?" I ask, my eyes scanning the books. I'm tempted to climb the ladder and swing across it like Belle. "You've read all of these?"

"Yes." He leans against the doorframe as he watches me.

I'm searching for *Fifty Shades*. I know it's in here somewhere.

"If I decide to marry you, I'll read one of your favorite books, and you can read one of mine."

"If you fool my friends, I'll read whatever the fuck you want."

He checks his watch, and I know the time is ticking.

I turn to him. "Do I need to get that in writing?"

I love hearing him laugh; it's low and sexy, and his smile suits him. It's the type that can light up a whole town. "You have my word."

"*Great.* Now, about tonight … can we show up thirty minutes after it begins?" I ask, following him through the rest of the second floor, knowing if I looked up the word *punctual* in the dictionary, I'd see a picture of his nerdy but sexy ass.

"I'm never late," he restates, opening the door to his home office that overlooks the park.

I remember, and I'll never forget the conversations we've had.

I can tell the idea makes him sweat, almost as if it's too much. Maybe it is.

As I glance around the gigantic space, it's easy to imagine him sitting behind that desk, staring outside as he works. His desk faces the view, not the door.

"You always arriving early is the reason we should be late. *Everyone* will notice us entering after they assumed you weren't attending. It would be out of character for you, but so is getting married. That's the point. If you want to properly fool them into believing you've found the *love of your life,* do it right. Don't be cheap."

He studies me, contemplates it, and calculates the outcome. I can literally see the cogs spinning behind his gorgeous eyes.

"Okay. Fine. We'll do it your way. However, I'll warn you … when you ask for attention in the public eye, you always receive it, especially when attached to me."

"Babe, I was made under pressure."

"Just like a diamond," he says with a smirk, leading me to the second flight of stairs that leads to the third floor.

I move in front of him and climb them. After I push open the door, a hushed gasp releases from my lips.

"So, this is where the magic happens," I say, studying his gigantic four-poster bed with the fluffy comforter on top. It looks comfortable, like I'd float away in it because it's made of literal clouds.

"No one sleeps in here but me."

The silence draws on.

"Ever?"

"You're the only woman who's visited the diamond in the sky. *Ever."*

My heart rate increases, but I don't dare meet his gaze, so I turn my attention to the three-hundred-sixty-degree view of the city. This room's vantage point is better than the balcony overlook, especially in the late afternoon.

I walk the perimeter of the space, taking it all in. "People dream about this."

"They do," he says.

When I turn to face him, his focus is on me. I enjoy how he looks at me, like he's trying to solve an equation he can't figure out. At least I'll keep him on his toes.

This would be much easier for me if he didn't have that perfect scruff on his chiseled jaw or a tattooed body that looks like it's chiseled from stone. It would almost be easy to fall in love with this man. Thankfully, he's incapable, and I'm unwilling. We're the perfect combination of fucked up. He can't, and I won't.

He breaks eye contact and walks to his closet that's the size of Carlee's apartment. A minute later, he returns with a black suit and tie in one hand and a garment bag in the other. "This is for you."

"How do you know my size?" I ask, taking it from him.

He places his clothes on the bed, then shrugs his rider jacket off. He's wearing a black T-shirt that hugs him in all the right places and motorcycle pants that squeeze against his quads. It's impossible not to stare.

"I wish I could say I guessed, but I asked your roommate," he admits. "I handpicked it though."

"Hopefully, you're not dressing me like a hooker." I suck in a breath. "Wait. *You spoke to Carlee?*" I think my voice goes up an entire octave.

"I *conveniently* ran into her this morning and had her sign an NDA before I asked her several questions about you, actually," he says nonchalantly.

This is why she was acting so strange earlier. She'd just spoken to *him*.

"You're *ridiculous*."

"I think you meant to say *cunning*. I wanted to surprise you. I think I accomplished that." He's close enough to me that I can smell his sweat, mixed with cologne. It's all man, all Easton, entirely intoxicating.

"She's no better than your brother. She's already playing matchmaker. I know my best friend better than anyone, and you getting intel from her adds fuel to the fire."

"Mmm, as long as it's to my advantage, I don't give a fuck." He chuckles. "She did warn me about *you* though."

My face contorts. "What? Why?"

"If I recall, it was right before she threatened to cut off my dick and shove it down my throat."

I can't hold back the laughter. "I guess you won't be sharing what else she said?"

"I won't. And neither will she." He checks his watch and opens the bathroom door, allowing me to enter. "Everything you need should be in there."

"How much time do I have?" I ask, glancing over at him, looking like a bad boy.

"An hour and *a half*. If you need anything, let me know."

"Thanks," I say, knowing we're arriving late. I smile, loving that he's not too egotistical to listen to logic.

The door clicks closed, and once I'm alone, I hang the garment bag on the back door. Luxury makeup and every tool I might need for my hair are on the counter. I run my finger across the countertops, which look like they have flecks of gold in them.

This space is him. Everything about it drips luxury—from the waterfall shower and Jacuzzi bathtub with jets, to the marble floor with a big *C* in the center.

"This tub is wild!" I yell, and I think I hear him laugh.

When I turn back around, I move to the bag and move the zipper down, revealing the black cocktail dress. The price tag is still attached—Valentino, $12,000.

I cover my mouth with my hand so he doesn't hear me. This is too much for one night. For one hour. That's what he said, right?

I remove my clothes, slide the soft material from the hanger, and step inside of it. It fits like it was tailored for me, hugging my curves. It's elegant, but it reveals enough skin to keep it sexy.

My collarbone pops, and I spin, seeing how great it fits, accentuating my breasts and ass. I can tell he picked this out. This is his vibe; hell, it could be mine too.

I pull my phone from my jeans pocket and text Carlee because she's in trouble. Big trouble.

LEXI

Enjoy your Bridgerton.

CARLEE

Enjoy your DATE.

LEXI

It's not a date.

CARLEE

Whatever you say. He's already outlasted your record.

LEXI

Please tell me you didn't share THAT with anyone.

I'm choosing my words wisely, and while I want to ask her what she shared with him, I'll respect it. Carlee would never throw me under the bus. She's a vault, and she knows everything about me from when we met until now. *Everything.* She'll do whatever it takes to help me believe love exists, so I can only imagine what she shared purposely with Easton. I have to hand it to him though; approaching her was smart.

CARLEE

Anyway, have fun!

I send her an eye-roll emoji, and she sends one right back. I lock my phone, knowing we can't talk about this because there can be no receipts. But, damn, it's tempting.

A bottle of perfume in a sparkly gold bottle grabs my attention. The glass is heavy in my hand, and I remove the lid, spraying it on my wrists and neck. It has a light hint of citrus, and the smell compliments my skin. I wonder if he picked this out too.

Once I finish my hair and makeup, I realize I don't have any shoes. The trainers I sported won't work.

I take one final look at myself, wondering if this is what Easton wants, then I push open the door and step into his bedroom, barefoot.

He's dressed in his black suit, staring out the window with one hand in his pocket. I focus past him, noticing the cloudless sky.

"Wow," I whisper, only sad that I won't be here to witness the sunset.

The sound is enough to grab his attention, and he turns toward me. That's when I notice the pair of heels in his other hand. A smile plays on his lips as his eyes slide up and down my body. I walk toward him, eliminating the space between us.

When I'm close, he drops to one knee and holds one of the high heels out for me. I point my toe and my foot slides into the black patent heel like a glass slipper.

"Louboutins," I gasp, and he looks up at me with a smile.

I almost feel like Cinderella as he offers the other. Gently, he grabs the back of my heel, guiding me into it. Having this man bow before me to put on my shoes isn't something I ever expected. It feels too intimate as I glance down at him on his knee for me.

"You don't have to start acting yet."

He zeroes in on me. "It's called having manners, Alexis. I'm sorry you've not been around many men with them."

Easton stands tall, like a statue. He's every bit of six-two, but with these three-inch heels, I'm only five inches shorter than him. I'm aware of how close our mouths are.

"I got you something else." His voice is husky.

I study his bottom lip, watching how the edge of his straight teeth grazes it.

He puts some space between us by walking over to the oak nightstand. He slides a velvety black box from the top drawer and moves back toward me.

He hands me the jewelry box. It's heavy in my hand, and I hesitate to open it. When I do, I hand it back to him, but he doesn't take it from me.

Inside is a black diamond pendant and matching earrings.

"Easton, I *can't* accept this." I shake my head.

It's too much.

"It's a gift from me to you."

It's still in my hands as he leads me to the full-length mirror.

He reaches forward, removes the necklace from the box, and stands behind me. "It's a pear-shaped black diamond pendant."

His fingertips lightly brush against my collarbone as he places the necklace on me. Goosebumps coat my arms, and I try to push them away, keeping my breathing steady. The cold metal presses against my chest as he clasps it.

"You can't wear a necklace without earrings. They go together," he says, dropping them into my palm.

"Easton," I whisper.

"Please," he urges, but it's more of a plea.

I can't deny him, so I place them in my ears.

My hand magnetizes toward the pendant, and I glance at myself in the mirror, then back at him.

He's still standing behind me. "The rose gold complements your skin tone," he says.

"Thank you," I whisper. "No one has ever …"

His brow lifts. "I'm not no one, Alexis."

The silence draws out between us.

"I'm going to have a lot of fun spoiling you," he mutters, giving me that damn smirk.

I scan over the man my arm will be hooked to all night, maybe for a year. "I assume it's a black-tie affair?"

He nods.

"What would you have done had I said no? After you went through all this trouble?"

"I knew you'd join me," he admits.

"*Cocky.*"

"It's my middle name."

When I meet his eyes in the reflection, I can see he's nervous too. It's barely there, but I spot it. He doesn't know if we'll actually pull this off. He has doubts.

"I'm glad you're joining me because, had you declined, I'd have considered skipping. Truth," he says without hesitation.

I turn to face him, taking a few steps forward, closing the space. "Why?"

"I prefer the quiet. It takes a lot for me to be in large crowds, but I adapt when needed."

"I had no idea," I say. "But I get it."

"It's why a lot of people think I'm a coldhearted bastard," he admits.

"Wait … you're not?" I crack a smile.

"I guess that's still to be determined." His eyes slide over me. "That dress suits you."

"Thanks. My stalker picked it out," I say in a light tone, spinning around for him.

"It looks exactly how I imagined. *Fucking gorgeous.*"

I think my heart flutters as unspoken words linger.

"So, does this officially count as day one?" I jokingly ask, hoping he can't hear my racing heart.

I remember what he said about only being able to date someone for a total of two weeks before it's over, but when does the counter start? Not that he's interested in me. This is a business transaction *only*. I'm curious as to when he'll grow tired of me, and if he changes, how he acts on day fifteen.

"Technically, we're on *eight*," he confirms, adjusting his cufflink.

"So, it starts the day you meet someone?" I ask, walking past him.

"No, it starts when I can't get the person out of my fucking head."

I look directly into his eyes, knowing it's one of his truths. One that I understand, but also one that I can't fully unpack right now so I don't.

"So, tonight is about reassurance, to make sure you're not making a mistake, correct?" I quickly change the subject and bring the conversation back on track.

"Yes," he sighs. "I don't like performing like a puppet. I *have* to."

I see him, see his sadness.

"I'm so sorry. I haven't considered how this might affect you. Are you sure about this? We can stop right now," I tell him.

What if this is a gigantic mistake?

Easton straightens his shoulders and smooths his hand down his suit. "I'm *more* sure about this than anything I've done in a long fucking time."

"Okay. I'm along for the ride."

"We should probably get going." His voice is soft, caring even.

I carefully descend the stairs, holding on to the railing until we're on the bottom floor. My heels click across the marble. I've put on my costume and makeup, and the show will start soon.

He leads me to the door, which locks automatically when he closes it.

"Is there anything I should know before we arrive?" I ask.

Anxiousness bubbles in the pit of my stomach as we leave the penthouse.

"Just be yourself. You're endearing. They'll love you how you are."

We enter the elevator, and he continues, "Weston will be there. He attends every social event, twinning with me. Considering the theme, you should expect us to be dressed the same."

My head falls back in laughter. "So, let's come up with a sign or saying that only we'll know. That way, if I have any doubts, you can confirm it for me."

"I like the way you think," he says.

When I was a kid, my childhood friends and I used to have secret handshakes.

"What if I interlock my fingers with yours and squeeze your hand three times? Kinda like me saying, *Is that you?* You'll return it with two squeezes—*It's me*. If it's Weston trying to trick me, he'll have to be a good guesser. But if he's smart, he will *never* try to deceive me again, especially regarding you."

"He won't. Now." He holds out his hand for me. "We have an engagement party to attend."

"We're crashing it," I say, and he chuckles.

"I do feel guilty, knowing all eyes will be on you tonight," he admits.

"They'll be watching *us*. We're in this together," I say, and I feel him relax into me.

We walk through the first security clearance for his private garage and board another elevator.

"How *in love* am I supposed to be?"

"Just *act* like you're considering spending forever with me," he says with a smirk.

"Oof, that'll be *hard*." My voice drips with playful sarcasm.

"On a serious note, they're very good at spotting a fake. One hundred percent of the women I've introduced to my friends, it's been an instant no."

"One hundred percent?"

He nods. "They don't even have the decency to wait until the next day. I will be pulled away and told to break up with you if you're not liked. If it happens, don't be offended, okay?"

"Uh …" I gulp. This might be harder than I expected. "So, you're actually feeding me to the sharks?"

"Yes, and you'll either sink or swim." He meets my eyes. "But if we can fool them, we'll fool the world."

14

EASTON

Same day

Once we're on the garage level, I flick on the lights and move to the safe. I press my thumb against the pad and it unlocks, revealing the glittering keys to the cars. There are almost too many to choose from.

"How about the Charger tonight?" she asks, running her hand across the freshly waxed black paint.

"I'm a mood driver. And that one is …" I pause, knowing what it represents as I glance back at her. "*Fitting*."

I laugh and walk toward her, twirling the key ring around my finger. She holds out her palm.

"That's a no."

"You're smart for saying no. I'd have driven it like I'd stolen it."

"I know you would've," I tell her, knowing she wouldn't go easy. It's not in her nature.

I unlock the car and open the passenger door, and she struts over, sliding against the smooth black leather seat. The hint of citrus on her skin drives me fucking crazy as I shut the door.

When inside, I insert the key into the ignition and turn. The engine growls, and I love the feel of the thick steering wheel under my grip.

I turn to her. "Are you ready?"

Alexis nods and I push in the clutch, revving the engine, warming it up, and slipping it into first gear. It feels like butter.

She laughs. The smile on her face is so damn genuine, and I love to see it. "This is a *fuck around and find out* kind of car."

"I only drive it when I'm searching for trouble."

"Mmm. That explains *a lot*." Her brow arches. "I think I chose wisely."

"Absolutely."

I scan my card and the garage door opens to the paparazzi standing at the end of the street, snapping photos of us as we leave. In the rearview, Brody pulls up behind me in his blacked-out Range Rover. I burn off into the street, peeling out, leaving rubber and smoke behind. I almost forgot how powerful this car is.

"They've been waiting since we arrived on the bike?" Lexi asks, glancing behind us in the side mirror.

"Yes. They never tire. Twenty-four hours a day, they're ready to follow me wherever I go."

"Why?" she asks, not understanding.

"The general public has been obsessed with my family since before I existed. We're considered American royalty."

"And you hate it," she says.

She knows I do. It's clear.

I glance over at her. "You're now being followed after that show you gave them last night."

She doesn't meet my eyes, but I notice the smile playing on her lips. "It was a *stage kiss*."

My hand rests on the knob of the shifter as I move into

second gear. "Do you slide your tongue into all of your costars' mouths?"

"A job is a job."

"When we're married, that stops immediately," I say, meaning every word. No way in hell will I allow that with anyone else. Pretend or not.

"If," she corrects. "*If.*"

As we turn onto another street, Lexi rolls down the window, holding her hair in her hand so it doesn't blow around the car.

"Earlier, Carlee told me you'd break my heart without any fucks given and that I should be prepared."

"That's true," she says, but I see her pulse quicken in her neck.

Is she concerned about what I know?

"I believe her. You're a goddamn tiger. You look sweet and innocent, but"—I shake my head—"fierce."

She looks pleased. "Guess you have me figured out."

"Carlee also mentioned that you've been speed-dating people and dumping them after one date. So, I guess I've already beaten *your* record."

She groans. "I'm seriously having a long conversation with her when I get home. But technically, by my count, *this* is our first date. Yesterday, I was tricked. Tonight, I chose to be here. I warned you earlier that you'd better make it good. I meant it."

"I know you did."

When we're twenty minutes from the venue, I can tell she wants to say something. "What's on your mind?"

"Won't people recognize I don't know shit about you?"

I shake my head. "No, they're used to the new flings trying to chase clout."

"Ahh." She nods and smiles. "So, they'll think I'm disposable?"

"Yes. Most of the conversations will be surface level. If you last past the expiration date, they'll know we're serious. They all know about my two-week rule. It's like Fight Club—no one talks about it, but everyone knows."

She looks horrified. "And how many hearts have you broken?"

"Too many to count. I'm not proud of what I've done; I'm just determined to find what I'm searching for. Maybe you're right though. Maybe love doesn't exist."

The car grows silent again.

"I did date someone long-term," I offer. It's the reason this began. "She was a princess."

Her mouth falls open. "*Actual* royalty?"

"Yes," I admit. "Our parents fabricated it, and I didn't realize it was fake until I caught her with someone else."

"Is ... is that why you thought someone sent me to your room?"

I grip the steering wheel a little tighter. I was hoping she'd forgotten about that.

"Yes. I was the main character of a gigantic publicity stunt when I started dating Adela. Millions of women became interested in my love life overnight, and it hasn't stopped. I fell in love with her, and it was used against me. It's why I have trust issues and avoid relationships. I never know if what I have with someone is a setup or if I'm being chased because of what I can give them. No one wants *me,* only the things that come from being with me."

Lexi keeps her gaze locked in on me and her brows pinch together. "I'm really sorry that happened to you. It's not fair, and I can't imagine going through that. I'd have trust issues too."

"Thank you," I say. "So, now I'm known as a serial dater. Honestly, removing that title is welcome," I admit. "But what about you, Little Miss Anti-Love? What happened?"

She glances out the window for a brief moment, almost like she's replaying the memories. I can tell they're painful.

"I learned he had another life with another woman in the

town over. We had been high school sweethearts. I'd thought I loved him." I hear the sadness in her voice.

"I'm sorry," I offer.

"To me, him doing that to me—the woman he was supposed to be madly in love with—was proof that true love didn't exist. It just didn't make any sense how I could care so deeply for someone and believe they felt the same while living a lie. Or maybe I was the one who was lost in the make-believe? Love might have blinded me, but my eyes are wide open now. And don't even get me started on trust issues."

This saddens but also angers me. I wonder what she was like before that experience hardened her. Probably happy.

"I look forward to sending him a wedding invitation … *if* the auditions go well."

"That would be petty."

I smirk. "You're right. But I don't give a fuck either."

This makes her smile. "Without that breakup, I wouldn't be back in New York."

"Hey, Siri," I say.

"Yes, *sir*?"

Lexi chews on the corner of her lip as I continue, but I see her face soften.

"Please add a reminder to my to-do list. Send Lexi's ex-boyfriend a *thank you* and *get fucked* card in two weeks." I shoot her a wink.

"You have your Siri call you *sir*? That's very *Mr. Grey* of you."

"It's easier than having her blast my name to whoever is listening. I don't need my phone name-dropping me—ever."

We enter the valet area and I turn to her. "Are you ready?"

"As I'll ever be," she says.

The car rolls to a stop, and the doors are opened for us. We take one last glance at one another and nod.

It's showtime.

I walk around the front and meet up with her, wrapping my

arm around her waist and resting my hand on her hip. She leans into me, her body melting against mine, and I feel her warmth.

"New York's most eligible bachelor," she whispers, and I know she's done some research. "Let's show them what you've got and get rid of that ridiculous title."

We move up the steps of the venue's entrance, and it's almost like a red-carpet event. Tomorrow, I can only imagine what the headlines will say because I can hear the cameras clicking as we enter like we own the fucking place. Her head is held as high as mine.

She was right. Everyone is watching, and while the attention is focused on us, we're too focused on one another. When I meet her gaze, it's like no one else exists. The crowd and wandering eyes fade away, and I relax—something that never happens in public.

We're led to the outdoor area with Bermuda grass and hanging lights that glow yellow. It's easy to imagine we're somewhere in the countryside as a pianist and string quartet play popular music. I remove my arm from Lexi, grab her hand, and scan the outdoor area until I find my brother. He lifts his champagne glass from across the room. He's impressed; everyone is.

I lean in and whisper close to her ear, "Weston is at our twelve o'clock. He's talking to our mutual friends Jaxon and his brother, Anthony. Their family found success in software—Silicon Valley and all that. By the firepit are my best friend, Samuel, and his soon-to-be wife, Heather. At our three, the tall guy chatting with the redhead, wearing a gray suit, that's Charlie. His real name is Chance; we call him Charlie to give him shit because it's his father's name, who he hates."

She nods. "Jaxon. Anthony. Both are in software. And Charlie with his daddy issues. Got it."

A laugh escapes me, and when I turn my head, I see Weston stalking toward us, wearing a smirk.

"Hello, Lexi," he says, taking her hand and kissing her knuckles. "Nice to see you *again*."

"Tone it down." I cross my arms over my chest.

"You chose the Charger tonight *and* arrived late?" Weston shoves his hands in his pockets and glances back at Lexi. "What have you done to my brother? The car though …" He meets my eyes. "Can't get over that one."

"I know what it means." She places her arm around my waist and grins.

"Of course you do." He chuckles. "What else do you know about my little brother?"

He's getting under my skin and he knows it.

"A lot." Lexi blinks up at me before turning her attention back to him. "But I think you should tell me what that Mustang represents. You kinda owe me for tricking me."

His head falls back with laughter. "No can do. Bros before hos."

I expect Lexi to be offended, but she joins in on the joke. "I'll find out why *you* chose that car, Weston. That's a promise."

My brother's eyes flick toward me, and Lexi's ruby-red lips tilt into a smile.

He gives her a playful purr. "Feisty little firecracker. You two are more than *perfect* together. I almost didn't believe it, but seeing you two like this is … wow. *Explosive.* I want a special thank-you for playing matchmaker."

"Okay, okay," I tell him, trying to reel him back. "You're going overboard."

He pats me on my back and leans in until only I can hear him. "She's the one. Bet me."

I meet his eyes, even more confused. "*What?*"

Someone bumps into Weston and he almost spills his champagne.

"Billie!" he yells.

"Billie?" I turn around, wrapping my arms around her. She

turned thirty last month and launched a clothing line, so she's been occupied. Being a part of the family business was the last thing she wanted in life, so she created her own. "I didn't expect to see you here."

"I didn't either. Decided to fly at the last minute to support Heather and Samuel."

"I'm so glad to see you. I want to introduce you to someone. This is Alexis, but she prefers to be called Lexi."

Billie holds out her hand, and a diamond bangle hangs from her wrist. "Hello. I'm Billie Calloway."

Lexi immediately relaxes. Weston notices, too, but I try to ignore him.

"Jesus." She places her hand over her heart. "I thought you were *royalty*."

Lexi glances in my direction, but I'm already locked on her. She's mesmerizing.

She continues, "*These* are your brothers? I'm *so* sorry. How did you manage it, growing up?"

Billie bursts into laughter. "Okay, I like her a lot."

I nod.

"Well, Alexis, Lexi, I hope you stick around. What day are we on?" Billie asks, looking between me and Weston.

My sister knows about my cycle, so it's become a joke between the three of us.

"Nine days, apparently," Lexi says.

Billie's eyes widen as a cocky smile meets my lips.

"You told her about your *commitment issues*?" Her voice lowers.

"I did," I say, looking between Billie and Weston.

They're giving me the same expression.

"Those are Fight Club rules. You don't share that with anyone," Billie whispers.

"Lexi isn't just *anyone*," I say, wrapping my arm around this beautiful woman.

She grins up at me like I *could* be her world. She's so good at this, almost too good.

"Well, tonight has been interesting," Billie says to Weston, and they turn their attention to me.

"Please stop doing whatever it is you're doing right now," I say, noticing how they're each grinning like the Cheshire cat.

Lexi chuckles as a few colleagues interrupt us.

"We'll see you around," I say to everyone, and I take Lexi's hand.

I don't want to get wrapped up in a business conversation, not tonight. We pass one of my old friends, Chase, on the way to see Heather and Samuel. Our parents were friends and attended the same social events growing up.

"Easton! I didn't think you were coming," he says, then notices Alexis.

"Yeah, I got tied up," I say.

He lifts a brow.

"I'm Lexi. Sorry, Easton must've forgotten his manners at home." Her Southern drawl is charming.

"Nice to meet you, Lexi. Are you two …"

"*Dating.* I'm trying to figure out if I want to give him a chance." Her soft gaze meets mine, but I know she's telling the truth.

"Oh, so you've finally met your match," Chase says to me.

"What can I say? I've been unable to get her off my mind since we bumped into each other," I say. Another truth spilled, even though she already knew that one.

"We're on day nine," Lexi happily shares.

Shock spreads over his face. He gives me the same expression that Billie had.

I find it amusing, and so does Lexi. It's a punch line to a joke.

"She knows. It's all out in the open," I say.

"All of it?" Chase asks. "Even …"

"The princess?" Lexi finishes. "Yes. But I think Easton's currently searching for his queen. Right?"

"Hot damn, this is … *speechless*," Chase says. "Do you have a sister?"

"No, just two older brothers," Lexi tells him. "But I have friends. *Lots* of them."

Before this conversation can go any further, I give him a smile and a handshake. "Okay, okay. We need to visit Sammy and Heather and give our congratulations."

I cannot leave this party until that happens, so it needs to be next on our list. Not that I want to leave, not yet. I'm actually having a good time.

"Maybe I'll be giving congrats to you two next," he says, glancing between us. "Nice to meet you, Lexi. Hope to see you past fourteen."

"Me too," she says sweetly, *perfectly*.

I interlock my fingers with hers and lean in. My mouth brushes the shell of her ear. "You're amazing."

"You make it easy," she admits, squeezing three times, and I grin, giving her two pulses.

"Need to your A game," I tell her, hoping she understands.

Sammy and I went to the same boarding school. Both of us are stone-cold when it comes to business. For years, neither of us thought we'd find our person. He did.

I greet him with a grin and a tight side hug before turning toward Heather.

"He's been on his best behavior?" I ask her.

"Yes," she says. "I wouldn't be marrying him otherwise."

"I'm happy for both of you," I admit, glancing between them, seeing the spark they share. "I'd like to introduce you to Lexi. My girlfriend."

When the words leave my mouth, her face softens.

"Hello. It's so lovely to meet you both. Congratulations on

the engagement. The venue is gorgeous. You two look great together."

Samuel's eyes meet mine, and he nods like it's an approval.

Lexi and Heather quickly fall into a conversation about the flowers and her dress. No matter where Lexi goes, she makes everyone feel like they're her bestie. She's genuine, and it radiates from her like sunshine.

Samuel turns to me. "I'm trying to recall the last time you brought someone around I didn't immediately dislike."

"Never," I admit. "But it's different this time."

"I can tell."

As I cross my arms over my chest, I grow concerned because this is too simple. "What do you mean?"

"The way you look at her, it's different."

"Huh?" Now, I'm confused.

"You look at her like you found what you'd been searching a lifetime for," he says.

My mouth slightly parts. This plan is working too well, almost like Weston told everyone and they're in on the joke.

"You mean that?" I ask, knowing he wouldn't lie.

"Yes," he says. "When you know, you know. And so does everyone else."

I search his face, and as soon as I open my mouth to say something else, Heather walks over, laughing.

"You'd better marry her," she says, and Lexi moves next to me.

"I think I might." I look directly at Lexi, who beams, and I love to fucking see it.

As other people walk over to chat with the happy couple, we move to the side.

"Would you like to dance?"

"Thought you'd never ask," she says as we get lost in the crowd.

She wraps her arms around my neck and I place my hands

firmly on her waist. My eyes wander around the room, and I spot different friends and colleagues chatting.

"Well?" she asks in a whisper.

"This is effortless," I tell her, aware people are watching us.

"What do you mean?" She creates enough space so she can look up into my eyes.

"You might've broken my record," I tell her. "They love you."

Somehow, I knew they would though.

She laughs. "That's a good thing, isn't it?"

"Yes. But it's *suspicious*."

"Maybe they don't want to have the *drop that ho* convo while I'm around? I'll grab some champagne and mingle. Maybe they're being polite since you're being a helicopter *boyfriend*?"

My brows furrow. "What does that mean?"

"It means you're being overprotective, like you're afraid I'll run away." She smiles. "I'm not going anywhere, I promise. I'm not your hostage ... *yet*."

"I like to have my eyes on you at all times," I admit, meaning every word.

That twinkle in her eye reappears. "I've noticed."

The song ends and she gives me a devilish grin.

"I'll get some champagne and slowly make my way around the room. Twenty minutes, then we'll report back," she says, and I glance down at my watch, giving her a nod.

Lexi turns and struts across the room like a fucking queen. Her chin doesn't drop once, and the invisible crown stays put. I shove my hands in my pockets, utterly mesmerized as she works the room like it's her stage. She steals a glance at me over her shoulder and licks her lips. *Flirty as fuck.*

I shake my head and she barely hides the smile before bringing her focus back forward. Lexi is the main character. *All* eyes are on her, especially mine.

It takes all my strength to pull my attention away, and as soon as Weston ends his conversation with someone, I join him.

Across the room, I spot Lexi chatting with our sister. They're laughing about something and it warms my heart. Billie has never once clicked with any woman I introduced to her.

Another first.

My brother clears his throat, keeping his voice low. "I know that look."

"Not sure what you're talking about."

He chuckles at me, taking a sip of his champagne. "This will be the greatest show of the fucking century. I'm ready for this season, little brother."

My jaw clenches. "Did you tell anyone?"

I don't have to finish. He knows what I'm referring to.

"No. Absolutely not." He gives me his firm tone, the one we use when we're not fucking around.

He's a *vault*. But then that means ...

"Stop overanalyzing shit and have fun. You still have five days. Make it count." He pats me on the shoulder.

Billie and Lexi look like they're friends, and maybe they will be.

"I can't believe you told her about the car and your *issue*."

"I have *nothing* to worry about. In thirteen months, everything will go back to normal."

"You sure about that?" he asks.

"Absolutely," I confirm, knowing Lexi is emotionally unavailable.

Even though we're twinning, she finds me in the crowded room and lifts her glass to me. I nod and Weston laughs.

"Do you have something else to say?" I ask, glancing at him.

He smirks. "The chase. The *falling in love* part is the fun and games. I'm almost jealous."

I shake my head at him. "That's not happening."

"Deny, deflect, distract. I know the tactics."

I'm trying to ignore him because I don't have answers. When a man approaches Lexi and Billie, my jaw clenches. I don't like how he looks at her or how he reaches his hand out to take hers. I don't fucking like it at all.

"Excuse me," I mutter, my brows furrowing.

Weston grabs my arm and stops me. "Already jealous?"

"Kindly fuck off." I pull my arm from his grip, straightening my jacket, and stalk across the room.

When I'm close, Lexi politely excuses herself from him and places her hand on my chest. "I still had ten minutes," she whispers.

I glance over her shoulder and watch Billie shoo the guy away. She's a pro at that.

"It's fine. I kinda missed you," she says, pulling my attention back to her with a smile.

"Truth?" I ask, tilting my head.

"Yes," she whispers. "In a room of strangers, you're the only person I know."

I lean into her, close to her ear. "Want to get out of here?"

"Thought you'd never ask," she says.

My hand finds its way to the small of her back as I lead her across the room. Weston watches from the perimeter and shakes his head with a smile, because he knows.

When we're away from everyone, I slightly relax. The jealousy that reared its ugly head was almost too much. I don't like seeing anyone too close to her, looking at her like she's the whole damn meal. A buffet for anyone to enjoy. She's not. Alexis is mine.

The valet area is busy; cars are driving in and out, and there's a small crowd waiting. I'm instantly approached and I hand over the ticket.

"I'll have this right out to you, Mr. Calloway," the man says.

I say, "Thank you," with a nod.

Then, I pull Lexi away from everyone, aware that eyes are still on us and the cameras probably are too.

"What happened back there?" She doesn't sound mad or upset. Her tone is neutral and curious.

"I didn't like how he was looking at you," I admit.

I brush my thumb against her cheek and she smiles at me.

"It's kinda hot when you go feral like that. The jealousy act—it was a perfect touch," she says.

"It *wasn't* an act," I growl.

I can smell the sweet champagne on her breath.

"Oh." Her eyes darken. "That was *real*."

"I don't want anyone touching you or disrespecting you or looking at you the way he was."

"Thank you." Her breath slightly hitches, but it's there.

"It's different with you. I don't know why," I tell her.

She grabs my tie, running her hand down it. "It's because I don't desperately want you. You've only ever surrounded yourself with women who do."

I rest my hands on her waist as she stands before me, her mouth inches from mine. "You're my karma."

"I like the thought of that, but I'm more like your lifeline."

I study her lips, contemplating kissing her but knowing that line shouldn't be crossed too much. Especially in moments like this, when I'm drunk on her perfume and presence. I'm not setting myself up for heartbreak.

"Maybe I'm *yours*," I mutter, and her breaths grow ragged.

"Maybe you are," she admits. "Truth."

The engine of the car revs and the driver gets out, opening the passenger door for Lexi. I pull away from her.

When we're inside and the doors are closed, I drive us away from it all.

She removes bobby pins from her hair, allowing it to fall loosely around her face. "I hope it wasn't too much tonight."

"It's easy to be with a social butterfly," I say, appreciating that she cares.

"The extrovert to your introvert. I think we did okay."

"Better than okay. Better than I ever imagined."

She rolls down the window and I do the same.

"Woohoo!" she yells outside with a laugh.

The engine growl echoes off the buildings and I can't help but smile. This almost feels like happiness, an emotion I've missed.

"Do you truly believe we can pull this off?" she asks.

There's no hesitation in my answer. "After tonight, *yes*. But my new concern is everyone getting attached to you. Especially Billie and Weston."

"As long as *you* don't, there shouldn't be a problem," she reminds me. "Who knows? Maybe you'll be the one to change my mind about love."

"Maybe." *Hopefully.*

Fifteen minutes later, I pull into the marina and park.

"This one of your secret make-out spots?"

"I can never predict what will come from your mouth."

"Like to keep ya on your toes," she says, pushing open the door and getting out. I follow her as she looks out at the calm water.

I slide my hand into hers, and she takes it without hesitation.

"They're watching," I whisper.

"Of course they are," she says, but she's smiling, unfazed by the cameras or me.

I lead her down the pier to my yacht.

"Wow," she whispers as we board.

I unlock the door and we escape inside.

I turn to her. "They were sitting on the bench at the end of the dock. Did you spot them?"

"No," she admits. "But after all the photos, I always assume someone is watching if we're in public."

"As you should, because that's reality." I move to the bar, grab a bottle of whiskey, and place it on top. "Would you like a drink?"

"Maybe the entire bottle," she says, grabbing it and removing the lid.

She presses her ruby-red lips to the opening and takes a long pull. I follow her lead, desperately needing to relax and decompress.

My friends and my sister had nothing to say. They would've taken me to the side and told me to end this now or had some sort of smart ass remark about how we weren't compatible.

Is Alexis Matthews *the one*?

I shake the thoughts out of my head. That's *impossible.*

When I glance back at her, she's turned around, focusing on the space.

"So, this is one of your hideouts?"

"Only when I want to disappear."

"Cars. Now, boating. Wow." She laughs. "Is there anything you can't do?"

"Fall in love, apparently."

15

LEXI

Easton shrugs off his suit jacket and sets it on a coat hook on the wall. My eyes glide down his body as he rolls up his sleeves, revealing those delicious tattoos. I'm staring, and when he notices, those beautiful lips tilt upward. I don't glance away, regardless of how intense it is to be in his presence sometimes. This man is the king of intimidation, and I understand why people say what they do about him, even if I don't believe most of it.

I reach for the bottle, needing another drink.

"Did I pass *your* test?" he questions.

"Was that a date? Because they usually end with an attempted kiss." I smirk, meeting his blue eyes.

"Really?" he mutters, stepping forward. His fingertips trail up my shoulder, causing goosebumps to form, before his fingers gently thread through my windblown hair.

I search his eyes, not sure what I'll find. Easton leans down until his mouth is dangerously close to mine.

My lips part in anticipation of tasting him. The temptation has me in a choke hold as we're suspended in time, neither of us making the next move. But my eyes flutter closed as need and want and deeply rooted desire take over. I feel as if I'm holding my breath, desperately waiting for him to kiss me, knowing no one else I've dated has made it this far. No, just him.

Easton whispers across my mouth, "Consider this an attempt, Alexis."

The overwhelming need to move forward half an inch nearly takes control, but I don't. It's sweet, agonizing torture, and when I think I might be able to feel his lips against mine again, he pulls away.

I swallow hard, wishing my body weren't on fire, feeling the deep ache between my thighs.

Easton Calloway will destroy me. I know this to be true.

"Why didn't you kiss me?" I finally ask, my heart still thumping, the butterflies fluttering as the rejection onsets.

"Because I can't," he admits.

It's a power move.

The control this man exudes is impressive.

My brows furrow and he notices my frustration.

He releases a breath, his jaw clenching as he tucks hair behind my ear. It's gentle. "You're emotionally unavailable, and after tonight, this isn't a game to me."

"Okay," I whisper, knowing he's right. He's always right.

Easton gives me a sweet smile; his gaze lingers a few seconds longer. "I want to take you somewhere."

I nod, needing and wanting the distraction to pull me away from the realization that I *wanted* him to kiss me.

"I'll be right back." He turns and climbs the stairs.

Being alone gives me time to think. I drink more whiskey, my cheeks tingling with each sip. However, I'm not sure if it's the booze or Easton's lingering touch.

The boat glides forward as I give myself a tour of the bottom floor. A long, leather couch fills a wall, and all the light fixtures look as if they're coated in gold.

I follow a hallway to the other side and find a mini library. I scan all of the books on the shelves. There are some about sailing and boating, several thrillers, and business books. At the end are the sleeping quarters, with lamps hanging over the bed. It's easy to imagine him in here, reading by the soft light, hiding on the waterfront, away from it all. A bathroom connects to his bedroom, and I'm actually surprised by how large it is—it has an actual tub.

I pass a kitchen that's larger than the one in Carlee's apartment and a dining room area too. It would be easy to live here, comfortable even.

Once I'm back in the living area, which also has a minibar, I grab the bottle of whiskey and step outside for some fresh air. I walk the perimeter of the deck as the boat soars across glassy, smooth water. At the front of the boat, there's a leather couch, and I sit, looking out at the moon casting reflections on the water's surface.

I close my eyes, leaning my head against the cushion as I replay tonight. I had a great time. The pendant still hangs around my neck as I sit on a yacht in a $12,000 dress. All of this is unbelievable, and I'm waiting for the bottom to fall from the paper bag. It will, won't it?

It always does.

The engines stop, and we slow to a halt. I open my eyes to see the glittering skyline shining bright in front of me. I sit up straighter, taking it in, never once seeing it from this vantage point. I've experienced the city so differently since I met Easton.

The door opens and closes, and I focus on the view as he joins me, leaving plenty of space between us.

"This is beautiful," I admit, taking a drink and handing him the bottle, but he declines.

"So, now that my friends are fully on board, what have you decided? Are we moving forward?"

I turn to him. "I think we should flip a coin to determine the outcome."

"Ah, so not only are you reckless and sign documents without reading them, but you also aren't afraid to gamble away life-changing decisions." He shakes his head. "What am I going to do with you?"

"Do you have any pocket change?"

"No." He gives me a look, tilting his head. "I might have something, but if I don't, then what?"

"We'll play Rock, Paper, Scissors."

A roar of laughter escapes him. "You're unbelievable. But I'll go with it."

Easton walks inside, and five minutes later, he returns. He drops a golden coin into my hand. There's an eagle on one side and a woman on the other. I've never seen anything like it.

"What is this?"

"It's a Saint-Gaudens gold coin. It belonged to my grandfather. It's named after its designer, the sculptor Augustus Saint-Gaudens. It's often considered to be one of the most beautiful coins in the history of the United States."

I hand it back to him. "Nope, I'm *not* flipping that into the water. This is all on you. I can't be responsible for that."

He chuckles. "You call it."

"I'm choosing the woman. If it lands on her, it's a yes."

With a flick of his wrist, the golden coin flips and twirls in the air. Easton catches it and holds it in his palm before flipping it onto the back of his hand. He scoots closer to me, close enough that his arm brushes against mine.

"Are you ready?" he asks.

I wait with bated breath as he removes his hand, revealing the side I chose. I think I hear him sigh in relief.

"It's a done deal," I say.

I love seeing him on edge over this. I'd have moved forward regardless of what that damn coin showed, but I won't tell him that.

A smile plays on Easton's lips, and it almost feels like this is meant to be.

The two of us fall into silence, both zeroed in on the skyscape.

"Now I need to think about what book I want you to read," I mutter. "Maybe an alien romance."

He glares at me. "That would be a first, but I'll keep my word. Also, I have a contract prepared."

"Of course you do." The whiskey courses through my body. "But I'm not reading it."

"You will," he says.

"Can you give me the TL;DR version? Because I wouldn't be surprised if it was five hundred pages long."

"It's three hundred, to be exact."

"I only read smut," I tell him, grinning.

Easton gets up and returns with a manifesto and a black ink pen.

I set the stack of papers on my lap, flipping through it. "You killed an entire tree for this."

"I'd suggest you read it to understand the expectations."

"What price did you decide on?" I ask. "Probably should've negotiated that before the coin flip."

He grins. "What you requested."

"Twelve million," I whisper, then laugh. "Unreal."

"But I'd have paid double," he mutters. "A steal."

"*Asshole*." I shake my head and he chuckles.

Without reading a word, I flip to the back page and sign it. I know how to be the perfect wife and will follow my end of the bargain. After a year, we'll say our goodbyes, and I'll have enough money to do whatever I want.

"You have no idea what you agreed to. And now, you're contractually obligated." He sounds displeased.

"Sometimes, the risk is worth the reward."

Easton shakes his head at me like a parent. I smirk, close my eyes, and enjoy the wind against my skin. I hope this is the right decision. It feels like it is.

"I hope, at the end of this, we can be friends," I tell him.

"I want that," he says.

"Maybe best friends," I say. "A year is a lot of time together."

"Who knows what will happen?" he says. "But I can guarantee Carlee won't like being replaced."

"She'd track you down and kick your ass," I tell him and he chuckles.

The amber lights reflect on top of the water in ripples and a playful smirk graces his lips as his arm rests on the back of the couch. I scoot closer to him, leaning against the curve of his body, and I don't move until he relaxes against me.

"You smell good," I whisper.

"You do too," he says.

"I'm gonna have a good time getting to know you, Easton."

"I look forward to it," he says, glancing down at me. "What time will you be moving in tomorrow? Also, we have to get married within the next thirty-seven days."

"What?" I turn toward him.

"You really *should've* read the contract, darling," he quips.

I'm second-guessing myself for not doing so. "Was sex mentioned?"

"Your body isn't up for negotiation, Alexis, just your time." His words are dominant in all the right ways.

The silence takes over.

"I don't want a shitty courthouse wedding," I say. "I'd like it to be somewhat special, even if it's not legitimate."

His lip quirks up. "Whatever you want, darling. We'll make it an adventure."

Excitement soars through me. "And we'll write our vows."

He gives me all of his attention. "With truths."

"With truths," I repeat back to him.

His phone vibrates and he pulls it from his pocket, glancing at the screen. "I have to take this."

I nod before I'm left to myself again, but he's not gone for quite as long as before.

When he returns, his hair is a mess, like he ran his fingers through it a few times, and he looks tired. I can't imagine the pressure he's under with this. His family, the business, the public, and then I'm mixed in somehow. It's a lot. All I have to do is look pretty as he deals with the consequences of our actions.

"We should probably go," he says, his voice gruff.

"Sure." I grab the booze and follow him inside and up the stairs, where the steering wheel is.

As he navigates us back to the marina, I sit beside him, lost in my thoughts.

Sometimes, when I'm with him, neither of us says anything. We don't need to because the silence isn't always awkward. Words don't always have to fill the space. If being with him has taught me anything thus far, it's that.

After killing the engine, he turns off the lights and locks everything. Before we leave the cabin, Easton stops me.

"Thank you," he says, his voice smooth like chocolate. "I know you're stopping your life for this."

"For you," I correct, searching his eyes. "You have a good heart, Easton. That means something."

He wraps his arms around me and pulls me into a hug. I hold him for a few seconds before we break apart. With his hand on my shoulder, he guides me outside.

As soon as he steps foot on his private pier, he holds his hand out for me. I grab it, but my heel gets stuck in a crevice in the wood and I fall toward him, crashing into his body.

"You've got a knack for that," he whispers, catching me.

We're standing too close.

"I know. And you keep saving me," I say, noticing how he's looking at me.

My world shifts—or maybe that's the alcohol taking over.

Our fingers interlock as we walk back to the Charger. Holding his hand comes naturally.

"What are you thinking about?" he asks as he opens my door.

"What the internet will say tomorrow."

My door closes and I lean my head against the seat as he joins me.

"I can predict what they'll say. Our story will be the love story of the decade."

I chuckle. "The irony."

Easton drives across the city, and thirty minutes later, he's slowing in front of my apartment. I glance up at Carlee's room, noticing the colorful shadows from the TV dancing against the wall. She's still awake.

He parks and kills the engine.

I turn to him. "When I left Texas, I told myself I'd take more risks and try to live instead of coasting through life and wasting time. For years, when I was teaching high school kids, I wasn't living. There was no adventure. I was a shell of a person who'd talked herself into believing fairy tales were possible with a man who was never capable of loving me. I don't believe in fate or any of that, but something is going on beyond me or you. This feels *right,* doesn't it?"

Easton is patient; he listens and doesn't interrupt me as I find my words. "Yes, I can't deny that either."

I glance up at Carlee's room again and see the curtain move. I shake my head, knowing she's probably spying. Hell, I'd do the same thing.

"You have to promise me something."

"Anything." His voice is gravelly and low, and as he studies me, my body buzzes under his gaze.

"Promise that we'll get to know one other sooner rather than later. I don't want to be strangers."

The street light illuminates his sculpted face and I watch his mouth turn upward.

"I'd like that."

16

EASTON

Birthday countdown: 36 days
Since meeting her: 10 days
Company takeover: 43 days

A fuck ton of messages wake me from a dead sleep. Most of my friends ask about Alexis, wanting more info about her. The selfish part of me wants to keep *everything* to myself.

I open my brother's messages and read the last one he sent.

WESTON

Last up, Lexi meeting our parents!

I push the thought away because I'm not ready for that yet.

I stand and stretch, looking out at the taillights from the cars traveling in the distance. The sun hasn't risen, but the city is awake.

It's barely past five. The start of a new day—*a new life,* I think as I grab my watch off the nightstand and slide it on my wrist.

I go downstairs to make a shot of espresso.

Yesterday was the last day of my living here alone until Lexi and I go our separate ways. Even though I enjoy being by myself, I won't take her company for granted. It's fucking lonely at the top.

As the beans grind and the espresso pours, I watch the sun rise over the horizon. The rays reflect against surrounding buildings, and the sky transforms from dark to light blue with wisps of clouds.

My phone buzzing on the counter pulls me away from my thoughts and I glance down to see a new text from my brother.

It's screenshots of articles with photos of Lexi and me entering the party and waiting at the valet. We're close, too close, and I remember the moment clearly. I wanted to kiss her. I still fucking want to.

Easton Calloway's New Obsession.

Will Easton Calloway's new fling get a ring?

Easton Calloway, New York's most ineligible bachelor.

WESTON

Looks like you found the trouble you were searching for.

EASTON

We made it official last night.

He knows what *that* means. My phone immediately rings. We talk when we don't want things in writing. Over the years, we've become pros at covering our asses.

"Is the wedding date set?" he asks.

"No good morning or hello?"

I need the caffeine to work faster after staying up late last night. After I dropped Lexi off, I was in my head for hours before I fell asleep.

I think back to our last conversation and how she doesn't want us to be strangers. *Fuck,* I don't either.

"Our birthday is in thirty-six days. The clock is ticking."

"Thank you, Captain Obvious. It'll happen between now and then. She's aware."

"Did she read the contract?" he asks, and I can tell he's walking somewhere.

"No," I admit with a laugh. *"Painfully predictable."*

"Hopefully, you won't need it."

I hear a door open and close on his end.

"I have a feeling I will," I admit, knowing what was written inside. Needing to be two steps ahead of everyone, even Alexis.

Before the last half of my espresso cools, I take it in one gulp and brew another. The penthouse smells like a café by the time it's done.

"And you're positive she's anti-love? Like, you don't think there's a chance?"

"No," I confirm, taking her words at face value, even though an inkling of hope has bubbled. "But if anything changes, since you're the number one fan of my personal Lifetime drama, I'll keep you informed."

"Great! I'd appreciate it. The popcorn is ready and wagers have been made."

"Wagers?" I ask.

"Billie and a few others have a pool going and one of us will win a hefty jackpot," he explains. "And that's all I can say."

"The last thing I need is to fall in love with someone who can't reciprocate. Okay? It would only complicate this situation, so I'm avoiding that. At best, by the end of it, we'll be friends."

"But you're attracted to her. She's moving in with you. You'll be taking her on dates. Charming her. And you're already jealous as fuck."

"Right. We'll be glorified roommates." I'm growing frustrated with this conversation.

"That's all marriage is. Trust me, I know." He chuckles. "But I look forward to watching you eat a shit sandwich full of your words."

I sigh. "It's not even six, and you've somehow managed to piss me off. Might be a record."

"What else is new? You're a grouch. Anyway, I'm walking into the gym. We'll chat later. Want to meet up tonight?"

"I've got plans with Lexi."

"And so it begins," he says.

Before I can tell him to fuck off, he ends the call.

After I've had my caffeine for the day and get dressed, I climb the stairs two at a time and enter my office. My degrees and certificates hang proudly on the wall with photographs of my family.

Each Sunday, I spend the morning reviewing my agenda for the week and lay out every video conference I'm required to attend. My days are full of virtual and in-person meetings with investors, board members, directors, and executives.

While I was traveling around the world, doing official business, I was in different time zones, so I missed a lot. I tried to stay informed as much as possible. Playing catch-up while trying to fulfill my end of the contract to become CEO has been difficult, and I find myself growing exhausted with each passing day.

Half of the meetings should be canceled because they are a waste of my time. When I take over, if it can be said in an email, I expect one. This needs to stop.

I work until nine and find myself daydreaming as I look out at the park. It's a beautiful day without a cloud in the sky, and I need fresh air.

After I change into a pair of shorts and a T-shirt, I grab my Yankees baseball hat and sunglasses, then text Brody. When I step out, I always let him know where I'm going.

He sends me a thumbs-up emoji and I shake my head. I don't

know why one thumb can aggravate me so much, but it does. Lexi would probably say it's elder millennial rage. It is.

I grab my drawing notebook and ink pen, then leave.

Stella, the building manager, greets me by the security desk. "Good morning. I received your email, Mr. Calloway."

"Thank you," I offer.

"We'll be ready for her arrival."

I nod and continue, happy to know Lexi will be given access to everything I own. Except for the keys to my cars.

Once outside, the bright sun warms my skin as I cross the street and take the sidewalk to the paved path. People play with their dogs. Bicyclists zoom by as runners sprint past me in their gear, huffing. I glance over my shoulder, spotting Brody fifty feet away. I find a random bench and sit.

Five minutes later, Brody joins me at the same one.

"You had fun last night." His brows pop. It's a statement, not a question.

"Please remind me why I haven't fired you yet."

"Because I'd fuck you up."

"Good point," I tell him.

Plus, he's the best there is, and he's family, but we never discuss that.

"So, you two ..." He doesn't finish, but the silent question lingers.

"She's moving in today."

He doesn't react to the news, but I didn't expect him to because he's a brick wall. Brody's perfected shielding his emotions over the years, and I'm convinced he's better than I am.

It's why I tell him things though. He's a good listener, and it stays between us.

"This just got interesting," he says, and I follow his gaze.

Then, I see her.

Alexis walks with Carlee across the grass, and she's smiling. They're holding iced coffees, laughing about something.

"What does her shirt say?" I strain to read the words in the distance. *This is my improv shirt*. I burst into laughter.

"She gives no fucks," he mutters, and I don't take my eyes off her.

"I think she's making a statement," I say.

Anytime she's with me, it's improv hour.

"We should get out of here before the paps spot me."

He chuckles. "It's too late for that."

"Fuck," I hiss, knowing what I have to do so no *trouble in paradise* stories are created about us. I stand, stalking toward them, moving across the grass.

When she looks up and sees me, she grins. "Speak of the devil!"

She puts her arms around me, pulling me into a hug.

"I missed you," she says, looking up into my eyes.

"I missed you too," I tell her, and it's the truth.

"Wow," Carlee says as condensation drips from her coffee. "Okay, seeing you together? Yeah, I get it."

Lexi playfully rolls her eyes, but I keep my arm wrapped around her, unable to not touch her when she's close.

"I'm sorry. Can you stay like that for, like, five more seconds?" Carlee digs in her purse and it sounds like she's moving charms around inside it before she fishes out her phone. "Say *I'm madly in love*. I mean … cheese!"

Lexi smiles with her teeth gritted together. "Wait until we leave here."

Laughter escapes me and Carlee takes the pictures. "I cannot wait to share this on my Instagram."

"Carlee," Lexi urges.

"Sorry. Easton doesn't care. Do you?" she asks me.

"I'm not getting involved. It's up to Lexi."

Lexi's eyes soften. "Please don't."

Carlee grins, looking down at her masterpiece. "Okay, but only because you said please. Do I hear wedding bells?"

"Probably," I say.

Carlee's eyes widen and Alexis playfully slaps me in the stomach.

"What? It's *true*," I offer, stealing a glance as a blush hits her cheeks. It's cute that she gets this way.

Carlee freezes in place, searching between us. I think she knows I'm not joking.

I clear my throat. "When you find the one, you just know."

Carlee squeals so loud that I think I hear her voice reverberating through the park.

"Paris and strawberries," she says to Lexi with her finger pointed.

"Excuse us," Lexi politely says, grabbing my hand and leading us away.

"What are you doing here?" she whispers.

I sigh, placing my mouth close to her ear. "Trust me when I say, I was here first. However, once Brody spotted you, it was necessary to speak. Don't need any stupid fucking headlines discrediting us."

She nods. "Okay. You realize I'm going to have to hear how great we are together until I meet you later?"

"It's the truth, darling. Might as well get used to it."

There's a twinkle in her eye. "We're going to have a long chat later."

"I look forward to it." I hold out my arms and she falls into them. "See you in a few hours?"

She smells sweet, and I place my lips on her forehead. I don't know why I did it. It felt natural, like she needed it. A content sigh releases from her.

I'm sure the paps are snapping hundreds of pictures of this public display of affection. I shouldn't have given them that moment, but I couldn't help it.

"Do you need a ride?" I ask.

Lexi shakes her head and pulls away. "I can manage the subway."

I grab her hand, bringing her back to me. "I insist."

A defiant grin spreads across her pink-tinted lips. "See you soon, *Easton*."

She breaks away and blows me a kiss over her shoulder. I catch it and shove it into my pocket with a smirk.

I hate to see her go, but, damn, I love watching her walk away in those ripped jeans that make her ass look perfect. I don't take my eyes off her as Brody steps up beside me.

"That was interesting," he says. "Already fucking whipped."

"I'm going to make her my wife," I admit as we head toward the diamond in the sky.

He glances over at me. "I know."

"Follow her," I say, and he turns on his heel, leaving me to myself as I cross the street.

As I enter the building, I realize everyone in my life is Team Alexis.

17

LEXI

I turn and blow Easton a kiss. He looks so damn good in that black T-shirt that gives the perfect peek of his dark ink. Under his baseball hat, I know there's a head of messy brown hair. Hair that plenty of women would die for the opportunity to run their fingers through.

If I were an outsider, watching us, I'd believe we were falling in love.

I know better though.

I also know fourteen days is all it takes for him to grow bored, so being with him for a year concerns me.

What if he turns into a complete monster on day fifteen?

The thought makes me laugh. What if he turns into a beast? I snort, thinking about it.

At the end of the day, it doesn't matter; I'm getting paid, and I'll make a new friend. It's only one year, and he's promised me adventures. Easton Calloway isn't the type of man who lies.

"I didn't realize he had so many damn tattoos," Carlee mutters, pulling my attention back to her. "I wouldn't have recognized him in the wild."

"There are more than what you can see," I confide, recalling the memories of when I've seen them.

"You've seen them?" she questions.

"Yes," I say, knowing exactly what it sounds like, but I don't correct her or give any additional information.

It feels like months have passed since crashing into Easton at the Tower, but we're only on day ten. Maybe that's why most women don't last two weeks. Everything moves so quickly with him, even his relationships.

"Did you know he'd be there?" Carlee asks when we're on the sidewalk.

"No," I admit. "But he does live very close, so bumping into him doesn't surprise me."

"Which means, in a few hours, *you'll* live close."

I told her I was moving out over brunch at a cute restaurant near Central Park. Most would consider it a hole-in-the-wall, but they have the best smoked salmon bagels in the city, and their iced coffee is to die for.

I was nervous to admit I was moving in with Easton today, worried about what she'd say, but she supported it without any pushback. Sleeping on her couch in her tiny apartment was a temporary arrangement until I got back on my feet. Neither of us expected this though.

Finding a billionaire bachelor wasn't on my bingo card. It's a shock to the world.

I turn around and point to the oversized hanging balcony and the penthouse that looks like a diamond in the day too. The blue-tinted windows sparkle in the sunshine.

"That's it," I tell her.

Her brows rise. "No way."

"It's gorgeous inside, with leather furniture, fluffy rugs, high ceilings, and a view that's unheard of. And his library ..."

"Please invite me over ASAP."

"Once I'm settled, consider it done." Nervous laughter escapes me.

I'm fully committed to Easton and to being his temporary wife. The thought of being all in for a lie terrifies me, but I believe we'll pull it off. I remember why Easton is doing this—because he cares about his family's business and their employees.

We take the stairs that lead below ground and wait for our train to arrive. A small crowd of people forms around us, so we move farther down to have some privacy.

Carlee shoves her hands in her pockets and grins at me. "You're falling in love with him. I can see it on your face."

"It's been ten days," I tell her.

"And you're already moving in together," she says. "You know the rhyme."

I shake my head. "Don't start."

"First comes love, second comes ... just saying, falling in love looks good on you."

She knows me better than I know myself at times. We dated the same man in college, and she watched me fall back in love with my now ex after a summer fling. In my adult life, she'd recognize it, and she'd also notice when something was off. She believes I'm falling in love, and the thought scares me more than anything.

I *can't*. I won't. I know what it leads to—heartbreak.

This is my moment of truth, and I don't say anything. I don't confirm or deny the allegations. I sit in her words, marinate in them, so she keeps talking.

"He looks at you like he's totally obsessed. I mean, I get it. You're *hot*. The both of you just ... match. It's like ... wow."

I smile.

"I wish I had that," she says.

"You will," I tell her. "You'll find something that's real, with someone who makes you excited to wake up in the morning. I promise."

One day, years from now, I'll tell her the truth. It's a promise I make to myself as we step onto the train.

Carlee says something to me, but I'm caught off guard when I see Brody at the opposite end of the car. He doesn't make eye contact, and as soon as we step off, I stand on the platform with my arms crossed over my chest and wait for everyone to clear out.

"What are you doing?" Carlee asks, confused when I don't budge.

As soon as Brody steps off, I walk over to him. "Seriously?"

He shrugs. "It's for your protection, Alexis."

"Lexi." I narrow my eyes. "So, you *can* talk?"

"Oh, hi," Carlee says, tucking her hair behind her ear while batting her eyelashes.

I elbow her. Her flirting with Easton's bodyguard is the last thing I need.

"I talk when I have something important to say," he explains, but says it like I should know that. His voice is deeper than I expected, and it catches me off guard.

This man is tall and buff with tattooed arms, and I know he's carrying a weapon under his jacket by the holster I see strapped across his chest. He's not someone I'd want to wrongly cross. Then again, everyone in Easton's life has that *don't fuck with me* vibe. But I can't deny that there's something familiar about him too.

"Can you *not* follow me?" I ask.

He glares at me.

"Please?"

"I have orders."

Our next train arrives, and people flood on and off. I sigh, knowing my days of strolling the city without a buff shadow are over.

I glance at my best friend. "Come on. Let's go."

"You're joining us?" Carlee asks him with a smile when he follows behind us.

He doesn't answer her either.

Carlee loops her arm in mine while we walk home. We're only eight blocks from our apartment, but it's enough time for her to ask me every question under the sun. The cogs in her brain are turning as curiosity eats her alive.

"Okay, who is he?"

"Easton's bodyguard. He's been keeping tabs on me," I whisper.

"I wouldn't mind a man like that following me everywhere."

"Hush," I say with a laugh. "He's usually stealthy and I don't see him. The one day I know he followed me, I never saw him once."

"Hmm, I guess there's no reason to hide anymore though. You and Easton fucking Calloway are publicly dating. You should have expected this."

"Shh. I don't know if he's listening to our conversation."

Brody chuckles.

I turn to him. "See, you *are*."

"Not purposely. You're louder than you think."

"Pretend like we don't exist."

He shakes his head. "With that attitude, you're gonna bust Easton's balls."

A smile takes over. "You'd better believe it."

"Oh, she is," Carlee agrees and turns to me. "Now, can we walk a little faster? That coffee is making a comeback."

"Eww," I tell her.

Her eyes widen. "Oh God. Number *one*," she confirms with Brody, her hand over her heart. "I'm a lady."

I think I see him almost crack a smile, but he doesn't. The three of us continue.

"Are the paps watching us right now?" Carlee asks.

"Yes," Brody confirms. "They're always watching Alexis."

It sounds ominous when he says it.

Ten minutes later, I climb the steps of our stoop and open the main door. Carlee follows behind me.

"We can't let him stay out here," she says, glancing back at Brody, who looks like he's guarding the building entrance. "It's rude."

"What do you want to do? Invite him in?"

"Where's your Southern hospitality? You left that shit back in Texas?"

"He won't come inside," I say, turning for the stairwell. "Trust me."

"You wanna bet?"

"Sure," I tell her with a laugh. "Name your price."

"A hundred."

"Deal."

I take the four flights of stairs to our apartment and shove the key into the hole, twisting the knob before entering.

The two boxes of items I had shipped here are stacked in the corner. I grab my suitcase and place my clean clothes inside, but I wait to zip it. In the tiny kitchen, I find my favorite coffee mug with the saying *I'm not old, I'm a classic* with a cherry-red 1970 Chevrolet Camaro Z28. A coffee ring circles the inside, and I scrub it out before setting it next to my books so I don't forget it.

A minute later, Carlee walks in and rushes down the hallway to the bathroom, leaving the apartment door open. Before I can shut it, Brody enters. All six feet of him makes our place shrink —or at least, it seems that way.

"You cost me a hundred bucks," I say, shaking my head.

"I'm aware."

I hear the toilet flush, followed by the sink water running.

My mouth falls open. "You knew she bet me?"

"That's why I'm here." His brow arches.

I scoff. "You're an asshole, just like Easton."

He meets my eyes. "It runs in the family."

"Wait, you're related?"

He doesn't answer.

My eyes scan over the tattoos on his arm and I spot a symbol I recognize with the words *death before dishonor*. He's a Marine. That explains his demeanor.

Brody glances around the room. The space is Carlee's—with a collage of framed photos on her living room wall, pink pillows on her green couch, a fridge that's covered in word magnets, and souvenirs from different places she's visited.

Carlee joins us, opens the fridge, and peers inside. "Want something to drink? A beer?"

"No thanks," he says.

I shake my head at him.

When his phone rings, he fishes it from his pocket, answers with a, "Yes," and walks out the door.

"You play dirty," I tell her, shaking my head. "You told him about our bet."

"You deserved it. Now, don't let Mr. Billionaire make you forget who you are, babe. That's all. Plus, Brody the Bodyguard is total eye candy."

I remember what he said.

"It's because they're related," I say.

"I can see that."

She laughs and pours herself a glass of water. I open one of the boxes I had shipped here and look inside, trying to remember what I packed. Most of it is photos.

Carlee sets her glass on the counter. "Still can't get over you two. Pretty sure you and Easton are proof that love still exists. Kinda gives me hope."

Guilt floods through me; I know it's all fake. Maybe my idea of love has always been fake. Maybe everyone is pretending, and this is as real as it will ever be.

"Thanks," I offer, hoping this doesn't get out of hand, but the avalanche has started. There's no stopping it now. I realize that this could be the secret recipe for disaster.

She yawns. "Well, I guess I'm gonna take a nap before work. What time do you have to be ready to leave?"

I unlock my phone and glance at the time. "One hour."

Carlee walks toward me and hugs me. "If you need anything, I'm always here, okay?"

"Same," I tell her with a smile.

She moves to her room and the door closes.

It's quiet, other than the faint sound of a horn honking in the distance. I realize I have questions I want answered, and there is one person here who can help.

I let out a sigh, taking the four flights of stairs to the ground floor and stepping outside. Brody is playing a game on his phone and looks up at me before returning to what he was doing.

"You said I was going to bust Easton's balls."

"You are." He doesn't look up.

"How are you related?" I ask.

"We're cousins."

"Oh," I say. "The things you must've seen, being his bodyguard."

He clears his throat. "Can we skip the small talk?"

"Rude." I scoff. "How long have you worked for him?"

"Fifteen years."

I glance away, focusing on the cloudless sky. The sunlight reflects through the trees, and I swallow down my nerves and ask what I want to know. "Is this typical day-nine behavior?"

Brody bursts into hearty laughter. "He actually told you?"

"Yes."

"Nothing with you and Easton is typical." He crosses his arms over his chest. "He's never looked at anyone the way he looks at you. Ever."

He's being sincere, and I appreciate the honesty.

"Can you expand?" I ask.

"No."

"Expected that," I tell him. "If you wanna hang out, you can join us."

"I'm okay, thanks."

Then, I go upstairs and sit on the couch. The problem is, I don't know Easton and sure as hell don't know if his current behavior is normal or out of character. He could be reinventing himself before me and I wouldn't know.

Are we really that good at convincing our close friends, or is there something there that neither of us sees? Because I'm starting to have an existential crisis, like Easton had. I lie back on the couch with my eyes closed, but my mind is reeling.

As I drift off, I receive a text, notifying me that my car will arrive in five minutes. I get up and knock on Carlee's door. She opens it, her hair in a bun on top of her head. I give her a tight squeeze goodbye.

"How was your nap?"

"Short," she says. "Promise me we'll hang out soon."

"I still owe you one. Brunch didn't count." I glance out her window, seeing the slick black limo roll to a stop in front of the apartment. "I gotta go."

"Please don't be a stranger."

"I won't, I promise." I grab what I can carry, then go downstairs.

Once I'm outside, the driver opens the door for me and Brody moves to the front passenger seat.

Once inside, I see a bouquet of white roses, a bottle of champagne, and chocolate-covered strawberries. There's a handwritten note attached. I open it, giddy as fuck.

I meant it earlier when I said I missed you.
-E

The handwriting is neat, as if it were its own font. I read over it several times and press my fingers against the smile on my lips before I take a ragged breath.

He'll break me. He's going to do it.

I swallow hard, pouring myself a glass of champagne, trying to stop the butterflies from fluttering. This is bad. Very fucking bad.

Forty minutes later, we arrive at the diamond in the sky, and Nash opens the door for me with a smile. "Have a great day, miss."

"Thanks. You too." I nod, staring up at the luxury high-rise I will now call home. I'm thankful for the champagne because I needed to relax.

As soon as I enter, I'm greeted by security.

"Ms. Matthews," the guard says, and a woman wearing a pantsuit approaches me.

"Hi, Lexi. I'm the building manager, Stella. I was asked to give you access to Mr. Calloway's assets."

"Yes," I tell her, following her into an office. Ten minutes later, I've got cards, keycodes, my face and fingerprint scanned, and an app on my phone to allow me in and out of the building at any time. The only thing I didn't give her was a blood sample and the promise of my firstborn.

I offer a thank-you and make my way to the elevator. Once inside, I scan the reader and push the button for the top floor. The elevator bolts upward and my nerves fully take over.

When the doors slide open, I hesitate before stepping out. I don't know why I tense—maybe because none of this feels real or it's too good to be true.

I glance into the reflection of the shiny wall and get nothing more than a disoriented funhouse version of myself. The mirrors lining the ceiling show me how I really look. I'm not even trying to impress him, not in these ripped jeans and a snarky theater T-shirt.

There will be pictures of me floating around the Internet, wearing this. I have to start trying because these images might haunt me forever.

With my head high, I adjust the tote on my shoulder.

I pause to peek at the people in the park before moving toward the door. Instead of knocking, I place my thumb on the keypad, wondering if it will work.

It unlocks and I reach forward, twisting the knob with a racing heart. When I walk in, I expect to find him alone. But he's not.

On his lap is a dark-haired, blue-eyed little boy.

"Oh my God," I whisper, "You have a *kid*."

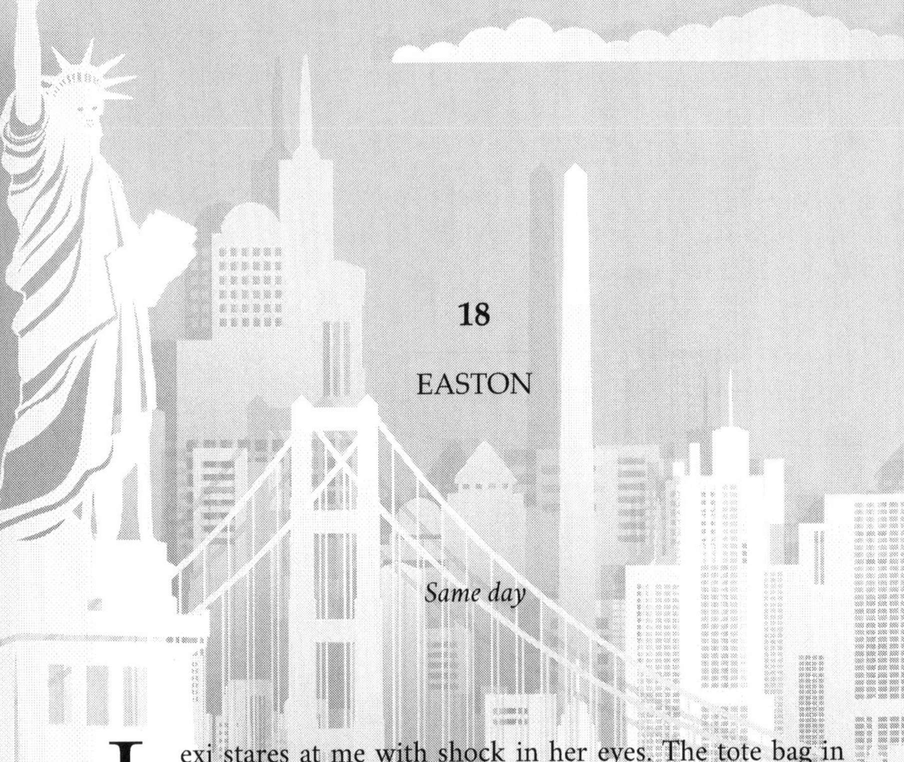

18

EASTON

Same day

Lexi stares at me with shock in her eyes. The tote bag in her hand crashes to the floor and a few books spill out.

"Uh-oh," Connor says.

I stand and hold him in my arms as I move to her.

She's frozen in place, staring between us. "I should've asked. I didn't realize …"

"It's fine; don't worry about it," I tell her, bending over to help her pick up everything. "You had no issues getting in?"

"Wee," Connor says, laughing as I hold him tight against me.

"None." Her cheeks burn bright red, and she doesn't look in my direction as I hand her the bag.

Then, I see her mentally build the brick wall, masking her emotions. She moves to the kitchen and puts something on the counter.

"Airplane!" Connor demands, and I hold him at his waist, flying him like Superman around the leather couch.

I walk around the living room as he screams and laughs, enjoying every minute. When I look up, Lexi smiles and watches us.

"This is Connor Calloway," I tell her. "And he's coming in for a landing! *Vrooooooooooom.*" I try my best with the sound effects, flying him back to the couch and swiping his belly against the cushions.

I set him down and he climbs back onto my lap.

Lexi joins us.

"Hi, I'm Lexi," she says to him, holding her hand out.

He shakes his head, tucking his face into my chest.

"Don't be shy," I whisper. "She's *very* nice."

Lexi chuckles. "He looks so much like you." Her voice is light and playful.

"Yeah, he's a dead ringer for me and Weston." I give her a smirk.

That sparkle returns to her eyes as she turns back to Connor. "How old are you?"

"Three," he says, holding up four fingers.

"He's two and a half. But his mother would say thirty months." I bend his fingers down. "*Two.*"

Mischievously, he flips me off. Weston taught him that. It takes everything I have not to laugh, and Connor points his loaded finger at her.

"Manners," I say. "A gentleman doesn't act like that toward a lady."

Lexi snorts.

I meet her eyes, leaning in to whisper, "You're encouraging him."

Connor looks up at her and pushes off of me, crawling to Lexi and plopping onto her lap.

"Uh, hi." She readjusts herself to support him better so he doesn't fall.

Connor reaches forward and runs his fingers through her

hair.

"You should be glad I just washed his hands. Otherwise, you'd have sticky fingers to deal with."

"I appreciate that," she says. "Connor Calloway, you're adorable."

"Runs in the family," I mutter, watching her be so gentle while asking him questions.

He's as mesmerized by her as I am. I lean against the couch, noticing how patient she is.

"Mine." Connor pokes her shoulder.

I laugh, placing my hand on Lexi's back. "No, she's mine."

He shakes his head. "Lex. Mine."

I chuckle when he decides to shorten her name, and she glances at me because I've tried it too.

"*Lexi*," she corrects.

"Lexi," he repeats, grinning. He nods and then looks at me. "Mine."

"Connor, she's going to be my wife. Did you know that?"

A hint of blush touches her cheeks.

"*No*," he says, pointing his finger at me sternly.

"Actually, *yes*." It takes strength not to laugh as he wiggles from her and sprints across the room toward a few toys he was dropped off with. He grabs a truck and bolts back toward us, handing it to her. "I like this."

"Oh, me too." She turns it over, studying it. "Hmm, 1950-ish Ford F1. You can tell because of the front fender." She points to the front of it.

He stares at her and gasps like she told him the most important fact of his life. "Wow."

"Wow indeed." My phone buzzes before I can say anything else, and I unlock it.

ANNA

Be there in five minutes.

EASTON

No problem.

I shove it into my pocket, bringing my attention back to them. Lexi shares more truck facts, and he listens to every word.

"Do you have a puppy?" he asks.

Lexi laughs and shakes her head. "No. Do you?"

"He doesn't because his mother won't allow it," I explain.

"Oh," she whispers.

A minute later, the doorbell rings, and I answer. I step to the side and allow Anna to enter. She smiles at me before noticing Alexis with Connor.

There's a look in her eye, but she doesn't say anything. She knows better. "How is he today?"

"In a good mood—for *once*."

"Connor," Anna singsongs, and as soon as he sees her, he latches on to Lexi and cries. "Come on, sweetie. It's time to go to your friend's birthday party."

He screams at the top of his lungs, and my ears ring. Lexi doesn't know what to do as Connor grabs on to her T-shirt and refuses to let go.

Anna struggles but eventually pulls him away and holds him in her arms as he kicks his feet and arms. "You need a nap."

"*Noooooooo*," he screams like she's hurting him. She's not.

"Lexi! Lexi!" he says with his arms outstretched.

"You'll see each other again soon," I tell him, following them to the door. "But you have to be good right now."

He blinks up at me, pouting. Elephant-sized tears run down his cheeks.

"Lexi." He points to Lexi, then shoves his fingers in his mouth. Tears that he forces streak his cheeks. The boy can turn them on in a snap.

"I'll be here," she promises.

"She's not going anywhere," I confirm.

He nods and I hug him, moving his messy hair from his face. "Be a gentleman, okay?"

"Thank you," Anna whispers, meeting my eyes before they leave.

When they're gone, I lock the door, then turn toward her. "How was your day?"

"Wait." She shakes her head. "That's the first thing you're saying to me after that?"

I smirk and lift a brow. "What are you referring to?"

"Easton, you have a *secret baby*. I did some research, and no one ever once mentioned you had a kid."

I move to the couch, sitting next to her.

"How do you feel about that?" I ask, studying her, reading her, trying to understand what she thinks.

Lexi sucks in a deep breath. "Having a child involved with something so ... *temporary* is a bad idea." She leans back against the cushion.

"He's already Team Lexi though. The kid has the memory of an elephant. I'm sure he'll be asking about you for weeks to come."

We sit in silence for a minute as she tries to process whatever it is she's thinking.

"You two have the same eyes."

"It's a Calloway thing," I admit. "My dad and grandfather. Good genes."

"He's cute. It will be fun, having him around," she finally says. "Give me someone to hang out with when you're off doing whatever you do. But ... I wish you'd told me so I could've been more *prepared*," she hurries and adds.

I can't hold it in any longer and burst into laughter.

Her brows crease and she shakes her head. "Why is that funny?"

"Connor is my brother. *Not* my kid. Anna is his nanny. My

father traded my mother in for a younger *model,* literally, and knocked her up almost immediately."

Her lips part and I think I hear a relieved sigh release from her.

"When I told you there were no other women, I fucking meant it. It's only you, Lexi. There is *no one* else."

She smiles. "I'm glad."

"You're adorable," I admit. "What were you thinking?"

"I thought how awful it would be to become the evil stepmother. I kept thinking that you'd knocked up someone in two weeks and broken it off after fourteen days." She shakes her head.

I chuckle. "I'm not *that* big of an asshole."

"That's the thing, Easton. I want to know everything about you. I'm in a constant state of guessing and gathering crumbs from the things you do share. I don't even know your favorite color or number or day of the week."

"Black. Thirteen. Saturday."

"Very emo of you." She swallows hard. "And I want to know the deeper things too. Like, do you want kids?"

"I don't know," I say on an exhale. "This world and life are so fucked up. I don't know if I'd want to subject anyone else to this. By the time I'm ready to retire, Connor will be old enough to take over the business, so it's not like I need an heir, and I'm sure Weston will have fifteen children when he finds *the one*. It's never really been an option for me, so it's not something I've ever considered."

She meets my gaze, and I can't place the sadness on her face.

"I think you'd be a wonderful dad," she whispers. "And you'd be able to give your children one of the best lives there is to live."

"With the right person," I say. "I don't want them to have the same life I did. My parents weren't in love. I realize that now."

She nods. "You'll eventually find someone. I know it."

"I hope," I say, wondering if I already have. "And what about you?"

She glances at me. "Yellow. Four. Friday. And maybe about the kids." She pauses for a long while. "I've always wanted to be a mom, but I can't get pregnant. Pretty sure I'm broken."

"You're not."

"I am, and that's okay. I've come to terms with it. When I'm no longer anti-love, maybe I'll try again or adopt." She forces a smile. "It doesn't really matter right now though, not until our agreement has expired."

I watch her intently as she shuffles through her emotions and buries the ones she doesn't want to share.

"Please don't look at me like that," she whispers.

"It's not pity, Lexi. It's admiration."

She nods, giving me a small smile.

"So, onto my next question. Do you have plans tonight?" I ask, smirking, knowing she wants to talk about anything but this.

"Actually, my calendar has been cleared for the next year."

"Love to hear it. I want to take you somewhere."

She smiles. "You know I love surprises."

19

LEXI

We ride across town in a limo and are let out in front of a small building with a faded burger on the sign hanging crooked from the brick. I think it says *Frankie's*, but I'm unsure because the sign isn't illuminated and the paint is faded. It has character. I like it.

I turn to him, and he smiles.

"We're here."

"Great. I'm starving," I admit, walking to the door.

When I'm close, he opens it and follows behind me.

Inside, there's only enough room for five two-person tables. It's cramped, and the menu is handwritten in Sharpie on faded poster board, but I can still see the three combos they offer.

A tabletop fan blows toward the cash register, fluttering pink ribbons from the center. It reminds me of my childhood and growing up in the Texas heat.

"Easton," an older man says from the kitchen, wiping his hands on a towel before coming up front.

He has a Buddy Holly vibe with dark-framed glasses and a clean-cut haircut, but his mustache sets him apart. I wouldn't be surprised if he's Easton's age with a dash of salt and pepper in his hair.

"Hey, man, long time no see."

Easton smiles, looking like a diamond in the rough, like he doesn't belong. "Frankie. I want you to meet Lexi."

He holds his hand out to me. "Hi, Lexi. Short for Alexis?"

"Actually, yes." I take his firm grip. "Pleasure to meet you."

"Where ya from?" he asks, and I wonder how Easton knows him. "Catching a hint of Southern."

"Texas," I explain with a smile. "West Texas."

"Ahh, yes. I can hear it now. So, what're you two lovebirds having?"

Easton looks at me as I stare at the menu one last time before I order. "I'll have a cheeseburger with onions, lettuce, and mayo. Seasoned fries. Bottled Coke."

Frankie looks at Easton. "You told her your order?"

"No," he says. "Pure coincidence."

"Hope you enjoy your meals," Frankie tells us, returning to the kitchen. "Two patties down," he yells over his shoulder.

As soon as the hamburger meat hits the grill, I hear the sizzle.

Easton pays with a hundred and tells him to keep the change. We move to one of the small tables with mismatched chairs.

He pulls mine out for me and I sit. Afterward, he grabs our sodas and pops off the caps, using the bottle opener bolted to the counter's edge, before joining me.

"Another place you frequented with your grandfather?" I ask as he hands me the icy-cold bottle.

He stops before placing the bottle to his perfect lips. "Not this place. Frankfort—or Frankie, as he likes to be called—and I attended Harvard together."

"Seriously?"

"Yeah." He shrugs. "Some dream of being CEO; others dream

of owning a hamburger stand. But the Italian place, yes, I frequented it with my grandfather. How'd you know?"

"The menu had a history section that mentioned what your family did to save their business."

He grins. "Ahh, so you *do* pay attention."

"More than you realize."

"Well"—he takes his drink—"Frankie's is one of my tests. I've brought *every* woman I've *ever* dated here."

I snort, glancing around, noticing the mousetrap in the corner. I've eaten at some sketchy-looking taco trucks, so I'm not concerned. However, this isn't a date location for a Calloway. I don't understand.

"Because the burgers are fab?"

"The burgers are good, but it's mainly to watch how they react."

My mouth falls open, then I burst into laughter. "That's a dick move. I can imagine the entire scenario. She dresses in an expensive cocktail dress and Louboutins, expecting a Michelin-starred meal, but you take her *here*."

He shrugs, smirking. "I can't be with someone who thinks they're too good to eat with their hands at a friend's restaurant, regardless of how it looks. I crave normalcy, Lexi. It's not about extravagant shit. I don't want to perform twenty-four/seven or have heads turn when I walk into a room. I want to eat a meal, maybe spill some ketchup on my shirt, and go home without fanfare."

I search his face. "If you keep telling me your secrets, I'll be able to make my next millions by writing a book called *How to Snag Easton Calloway*."

"So damn glad you signed that NDA," he says with a chuckle. "Guess you'll have to keep it to yourself."

"It'll go with me to the grave." And I mean that.

Easton needs someone who doesn't mold herself to be his dream woman. He needs someone who just *is*.

"So, what would happen after you walked inside? Would you judge her on her burger order? She chooses pickles, and she's out?"

He chuckles. "That's a great idea. I fucking hate pickles. But the truth is, no one ever ordered, only me, and I'd sit here and eat a cheeseburger alone while they tried to make small talk. I'd say a few words, but was unamused and disappointed."

My mouth slightly parts.

He nods. "We'd sit at this exact table on day fourteen."

Our burgers and fries are slid in front of us.

"Wow, so this is the final test."

"Yep. And everyone failed." Easton grins. "Except you."

"And that's why I'm going to be your wife," I say, meeting his eyes.

"You are," he says, causing butterflies to haunt me.

We pick up our burgers at the same time.

"Cheers," I tell him, moving mine forward, and we tap them together.

After one last glance, we take a bite simultaneously. Grease runs down our faces, and there's mayo on his cheek. We laugh, reaching for napkins.

I swallow down my first bite. "Okay, you said they were good, but this is fucking amazing."

"Right? The best I've ever had, but I like to downplay it in case you think it sucks," he says, picking up a fry and putting it in his mouth. "Five out of five, and I've eaten a lot of cheeseburgers worldwide."

"Humblebrag," I say between bites. "But, yeah, same. My dad's favorite meal was a cheeseburger with mustard and onions. I'd eat at questionable places with him over the years when we attended vintage car shows and auctions."

His expression softens. "Do you miss your dad?"

"Yep. Every day. But you learn to live with it after a while. And sometimes, when I'm reminded that he's not here anymore, it steals my breath. I tell myself he's on a road trip around the US, driving in a hot rod with his hand hanging out the window, listening to old country music." I smile and suck in a sharp breath. "At least it's a nice thought because he was the world's worst at answering his cell phone. So, in my mind, it's almost believable."

"I'm so sorry, Lexi."

"Thanks." I try to push the thoughts away. "Now, I only have to worry about my mom, but my two older brothers are around, helping her with the ranch. She dates random men, trying to find what she lost, but never commits." I shake my head. "I think I just realized I've been acting like my mother. Wow."

"Yikes," he says, and I toss a fry at him, but he catches it and pops it into his mouth.

Mom had true love with my father. I had some fucked-up version that I thought was real. Boy, was I fooled. My ex knew exactly what to say to me to appease me. I think that's why I couldn't believe he had a second life with someone else.

"I've been thinking about my past relationship and what I miss about it."

"Yeah?" He listens intently as we eat.

"Companionship. The sex was never good, so it's not even that. Years of bad sex—it sounds like a curse I got from a witch in the woods."

Easton chuckles and nearly chokes. My eyes widen, and I'm two seconds away from doing the Heimlich, but he waves me away when I stand.

"Don't go dying on me," I whisper, sitting back down. "The rumors would be awful. Everyone would think I did it!"

He catches his breath. "So, you want companionship?"

"And amazing sex," I whisper.

"That would complicate things."

I take a sip of my drink. "Would it?"

"I wouldn't want you falling in love with me, Lexi. And once that happened, you'd be a fiend, begging for more." Easton picks up a napkin, trying to hide his smirk, that one that drives the tip of Cupid's arrow straight into my heart.

"Don't flatter yourself."

He gives me a cocky-as-fuck shrug. "I've been told I'm addictive, like a drug."

I chuckle. "And I'm sure you believe it."

"Seeing is believing, darling."

He finishes his fries, and when his phone buzzes, I take the opportunity to excuse myself.

"I need to go to the ladies' room. I'll be right back."

He laughs. "Good luck in there."

I turn to him. "I'll be okay."

I move my chair under the table before walking around the corner and down the long hallway. The restroom is at the end, and when I enter, I take a deep breath and close my eyes tight.

Needing confirmation, I pull my phone from my back pocket and text one of my best friends from home, the only one who can give logical advice without emotions or matchmaking. She's a computer genius, the most intelligent person I've ever met. We've been best friends since we were kids.

LEXI

How do I tell if I'm falling in love?

Her text bubble immediately pops up.

REMI

If you could invite anyone to hop in your dad's hot rod and go on a road trip with you ... who'd that be?

LEXI

Fuck.

REMI

Falling in love is the easy part. Keeping it is when it gets complicated.

LEXI

Smart woman. Thank you.

REMI

I hope to see you soon!

LEXI

We'll see. I might have someone I want y'all to meet.

REMI

Girl, don't get my hopes up! I'll stick my boot up your ass.

I tuck my phone in my pocket and move to the mirror. I feel like I'm floating, but that happens anytime I'm around him for too long.

I will keep my end of the bargain.

I have to.

After I feel a bit calmer, I return to Easton.

"You okay?"

"Great," I say, smiling.

Easton carries our baskets to the front counter.

Frankie waves at us. "Bye! Hope to see you again, Lexi!"

"You will," I tell him.

We leave, the bell on the door clanging our departure before we get in the car that waited for us.

"My father called. I took two weeks off to be with you, Lexi," he says as we zoom off. "Ready for an adventure?"

"I'll go anywhere with you."

This pleases him, but he turns away so I can't see his reaction. However, I can see him holding back a grin in the window's reflection.

I glance at the sunroof and open it, then stand to take in the city. I wave Easton up with me, and we stand beside each other, smiling.

"Have you ever done this before?" he asks.

"No," I admit. "I saw it in a movie once."

He studies my lips, touching my cheek, and I melt into him. I swallow, noticing our breaths growing more ragged.

"Are you going to kiss me?"

"No," he says in a low voice. "Not this time."

I smile. "Too bad. Might've been magical."

My hair whips around in the wind, and when we pick up speed, Easton pulls me down with him.

Twenty minutes later, the car comes to a stop. When the door opens, I see we're at an airport, and there's a private jet waiting on the tarmac with the stairs down.

"Easton," I whisper.

He places his hand on my back and leads me to the stairs. At the top, a beautiful flight attendant eagerly awaits.

I look over my shoulder as the driver unloads suitcases from the trunk, knowing Easton had this planned. Then, I move my attention to him, and he catches me staring. I find the strength to turn away and continue up the stairs.

"Hi, Ms. Matthews. Welcome aboard," the blonde tells me.

I step inside and it's like nothing I've ever imagined—a leather sitting area, a bar, and several luxury seats. There's a door in the back, which is probably another room.

"Hi," Easton says to the flight attendant behind me.

When his hand finds its home on my back, I relax. I sit, and he takes the one next to me.

"This is too much," I tell him.

"For you, there isn't a limit."

I laugh. "You're being ridiculous. Things that impress me, money can't buy."

"That's something we can agree on," he says matter-of-factly.

Not too long later, the private jet lifts off, and I watch Manhattan's skyline fade through the large circular window.

The flight attendant brings us booze in glasses with ball-shaped ice.

"Will you tell me where we're going?" I ask, taking a sip of the smooth drink.

"Hell no," he says, checking his watch. "I'm not letting you ruin this."

I should've expected that answer. As I watch the skyline disappear, I close the window shade and turn to him.

"I want to get to know you, the real you. Away from it all. Just me and you."

"Why?" I drown in his blue eyes.

"I'm marrying you. I want to know *my wife*." His voice drops.

My eyes slide down to his mouth, and that smirk might do me in this time. I follow the buttons down his shirt, which is rolled at the elbows, showing his tattoos.

"Can I ask you anything while we're together?"

"No limits. I have nothing to hide from you."

I tilt my head. "You *might* regret saying that."

"Try me." It sounds like a dare.

The cabin lights lower and I pull my gaze away from Easton's perfect mouth, one that's assuredly broken many hearts.

I want to know him, all of his secrets, and I'll keep them until the end of time. I want to know what makes him tick, what he dreams about, and what makes him happy. Everything. Because right now, this man is an enigma.

"You should get comfortable," he tells me, lifting the armrest between us.

When he opens his arms, I hesitate.

"You think sleeping on stone is comfy?"

His laugh floats through the air, and it's contagious.

He leans in and whispers in my ear, "The flight attendant hasn't stopped watching us together."

I understand. We're not alone. *The show must go on.*

I slide my arms around him and rest my head on his chest. His heartbeat rapidly thumps; it's faster than average.

I pull away to meet his eyes and don't realize how close I am, but I can't find the strength to create space. He doesn't either.

"You good?" I whisper, searching his eyes.

He tucks loose hair behind my ear. "Better than ever."

"Your heart is racing."

"I have a secret," he says. "I *hate* flying."

For a brief second, I see a sliver of this man's vulnerable side.

"You're safe. I've got you," I whisper, moving back into position.

Easton places his arms around me, holding me tighter against him. The smell of him nearly tugs me under—mahogany with a hint of mint.

He twirls a strand of my hair around his finger as I listen to him inhale and exhale slowly. The real him, the man he hides under designer suits, hates crowds and flying and frequently does both. I don't envy the money and what he sacrifices by having it.

"You smell good," I whisper, smiling. He encapsulates me.

"You do too," he says back.

His heart rate eventually slows, and when I nuzzle into his chest, he relaxes. I'm lost in my thoughts, thinking about what Remi said. I think about my dad and if he'd have liked Easton or what he'd have said after meeting him. He always told me to find a man who appreciated vintage cars because they were the ones who still opened doors for ladies.

He was right.

My eyes grow heavy, and it doesn't take long before I drift off as we soar through the sky like a bullet.

"Lexi," I hear Easton say, lightly brushing his fingertips against the outside of my arm.

"Mmm?" For a moment, I'm not sure where I am.

"We're about to land," he mutters in a gruff tone.

I sit up, rolling my neck on my shoulders, feeling stiff.

Easton yawns and I lift the window shade. It's still dark outside, and my mouth falls open as we descend.

The moonlight illuminates the snowcaps at the top of the tall peaks.

"Are those mountains?"

"I love seeing your excitement," he says as we touch down into a valley.

We taxi to a private hangar, the flight attendant helps us deboard, and a blacked-out car waits. It's the middle of June, but there's briskness in the air.

Our suitcases are loaded into the back of the car, and then we leave. The windows are dark, so I can't see through them, and I wonder if that's by design. Maybe I won't be able to ruin his surprise.

Easton leans his head against the seat and closes his eyes. I take the opportunity to study how fucking beautiful he is.

His eyes flutter open, meeting mine, and I feel like I'm locked in place, frozen in time, knowing he caught me. Neither of us says a word as we hold a silent conversation, and I'm glad he can't hear *my* heartbeat right now.

"We're almost there," he says.

His arm brushes against me as he checks his watch. He closes his eyes again and leans his head back.

His lips turn up into a small smile. "Lexi, I can *feel* you staring."

I can't deny it. I focus my attention forward. It's nothing but a two-lane highway and headlights guiding the way. We're the only vehicle on the road.

Eventually, the car stops and Easton's door opens. He walks to my side and holds out his hand. I take it as I admire the log cabin *mansion*.

"Uh ..."

He smirks. "Come on."

The driver follows behind us with our luggage, and Easton punches the code on the front door. It opens and he leads me inside.

A wooden chandelier with lights that flicker like candles hangs from the high ceiling, and I notice the gigantic vase of white roses under it on a center table. The door clicks closed and he stands beside me, crossing his arms over his chest.

"This is one of my favorite places to be," he admits. "I can't wait for you to see the view in the morning over coffee."

He leads me into the living room, and an entire wall is windows. A stone fireplace starts at the floor and goes to the ceiling. I spot the bookshelf across the room. Behind me is a staircase that spirals to the top floor. It drips elegance and sophistication but still feels like home in a warm way.

"And where will I sleep tonight?"

"There are five bedrooms, and they've all been prepared for our arrival. It's your choice."

"How long are we staying?"

"Until Thursday, unless you'd like to stay longer," he says.

He's dressed in black from head to toe, staring at me like the devil he is.

"I can do basic math, Easton. We'll leave here on day fourteen."

"And your point?"

"What if, on day *fifteen*, you realize this was a mistake?"

He narrows his eyes. "And what if, on day fifteen, I realize I want more than a year?"

"See, when you say things like that . . ." I nervously laugh.

He shrugs. "I can't predict the future. Can you?"

"Well, no."

"You're dreading something that might not even happen," he says, leading me to the second floor. He gives me a quick tour of the house. "You can back out, but I need to know now."

"You're not getting rid of me that easily," I confirm. "At this point, I'm continuing through with this out of spite. To confirm I'm anti-love."

"And what if you bust your myth?"

I press my lips together. "I guess I will win either way. But right now, I'm not convinced it's possible."

I say those words, but do I mean them?

"To be truthful, I'm not either," he tells me.

Easton lets me choose where I'd like to stay, so I take the suite at the end of the hallway. It's at the opposite end of the house from his dark gray room, which looks like the living quarters of the vampire, Lestat. It even comes with a wooden carved bed and a Gothic chandelier.

Easton sets my suitcase beside the oak dresser and leans against the doorframe. "Do you need anything else?"

"No, thank you," I say, kicking off my shoes.

Then, I open my suitcase and pull out something to sleep in.

"I can feel you staring," I say with my back toward him.

I know he's watching me. He always is.

"The difference between me and you is, I'm not ashamed."

I glance at him over my shoulder, meeting his eyes.

Fuck. I cannot handle him looking at me like *that.*

"Good night, Easton."

"Good night, Lexi."

He lifts a brow, as if waiting for me to say something, but no words come. I turn away from him, not daring to get captured in his delicious web.

When the door closes behind him, I wiggle out of my pants and thin sweater, sliding on an old, faded T-shirt I've had for years.

I turn off the light and slip between the silk sheets, staring at the vaulted ceiling in a house tucked into the mountains. Everything about Easton fills my thoughts, and I squeeze my thighs together as my body begs for a release.

I haven't touched myself in months, but right now, as I envision his blue eyes watching me and his mouth on me, I slide my fingers between my legs. My pussy is slick, and I slam my eyes shut as I rub gently against my clit.

A whimper escapes me as I imagine him hovering above me. My heart races, and I'm already so worked up that if I don't pull away, I'll come. And I *want* to come. I *need* to come.

I think about him in the other room, grabbing his thick cock and stroking it to the thought of me, and I dip one finger inside my pussy. I'm wet, and I need more, so I give myself a second finger.

"Easton," I whisper. His name falls from my lips like a prayer.

My body tenses, and as I'm about to spill over the edge, I hear a knock on the door.

"Lexi?" Easton asks from the other side.

I try to suck in air to speak, but my breathing is so ragged that I'm nearly gasping out.

"Mmhmm?" I urge, then cover my mouth.

Every rustle of the sheet as my hand moves is enhanced, so I slow my pace. I'm about to explode, but I hold off.

"I thought I heard something. Do you need any help?"

Fuck, if he only knew what he could help me with right now, in this very moment.

The thoughts of him turning the knob and climbing into bed

with me are almost too much. I want his lips and tongue and eyes on me. The fantasy could be a reality.

"No," I pant out, slowly returning to my cunt, knowing he's on the other side of that door as I teeter on the edge to thoughts of him.

"Are you sure?" I hear something in his voice. *Desire.*

My hand falls back to my clit, rubbing torturous circles as my body begs for release. And then it happens; the orgasm takes hold, and I come so fucking hard that my vision blurs. My pussy pulses and it nearly rips me to shreds.

"Yes," I say breathlessly.

"Mmm. Good night, darling," he growls.

And I realize what he's doing to me—getting under my skin.

I fold my arm over my eyes and lick my lips, knowing I've never experienced anything quite like that.

And it's all Easton.

He's right; he *is* a goddamn drug. Even in my fantasies, he has me begging for more.

I roll over, feeling the exhaustion take over. And as I fall asleep, I think getting away will be good for us.

By the end of his two-week vacation, I'll know this man *better* than anyone else.

Hell, that might go both ways.

20

EASTON

Same day

I heard her desperate pants as I flicked off the hallway lights. At first, I thought she was crying, but I quickly realized she was pleasuring herself.

And when she said my name … fuck, she'd better be glad I didn't barge in there and do exactly what she wanted me to do to her.

The thought of Lexi in the next room, teasing her sweet pussy with my name on her lips, has my cock *begging* to be unleashed.

I move to my room, go to the shower, and step inside, washing the day away as I stroke myself to thoughts of her.

"Fuck," I groan, allowing the water to fall over my back as I press my palm against the wall.

She whispered my name.

I rub my finger across the tip, feeling the pre-cum she caused at the end. As I stroke, I think of her hot mouth begging me, her perky nipple in my mouth, and her saying my name as I slam deep inside her wet cunt.

My darling. My Lexi. My future wife. The one?

My pace increases, and my balls tighten. I come so hard that my knees nearly buckle. With panted breaths, I rest my head against the wall as the water falls over me. She makes me want to lose control. She makes me want to believe that love does exist, even if she doesn't think so.

Alexis Matthews may be the woman who finally breaks me.

Birthday countdown: 35 days
Since meeting her: 11 days
Company takeover: 42 days

I think I hear my name from the doorway and I stir, wondering if it's a dream. If Lexi has embedded herself so deep into my subconscious that I hear her while sleeping.

"*Easton*," she says again.

I sit up and turn on the lamp beside the bed, glancing at the time on my watch. It's four in the morning, which means two hours have passed since I went to sleep.

Lexi stands in an oversize T-shirt, and I see the tiny, dark circles of her hard nipples poking through. The hem falls at her upper thighs and the neck has been cut out, so it slouches on her shoulders. Her long hair surrounds her face in wavy curls.

She's like a ghost, a figment of my imagination. How is it possible this woman exists?

Then, I realize it's raining, pounding against the roof and windows. It's a mountain storm; they happen often at high altitudes. When lightning strikes, she jumps, sucking in a deep breath.

I cross the room toward her.

"Lexi?" I keep my voice soft.

When I'm close enough to touch her, she meets my eyes. "I had a nightmare."

"I'm sorry," I say as she falls into my arms.

At first, I hesitate, but I quickly cave, wrapping her into me, feeling the warmth of her thin frame against me. I think I hear her crying as I hold her.

"Do you want to talk about it?"

"No." Her voice cracks, and we stand like this for a moment too long. "I'm tired," she mutters.

My mouth parts. I don't let anyone sleep in my bed, but seeing her like this stirs something inside of me and I think back to the plane, when she had me. We both try to speak, but neither of us gets any words out.

"What were you going to say?" I place my finger under her chin, forcing her to look at me. "Do you want to stay with me?"

A small smile meets her lips. "Is that allowed?"

"Not usually, but I'll make an exception this once." I can't return her to her room when she's visibly upset. I only want to comfort her and tell her that whatever it was, it wasn't real, that it will be okay.

"Thank you. I'm sor—"

"No. Don't apologize." I place my hands on her shoulders and shake my head. "I've got you, Lexi. The same way you had me."

She nods.

I wipe a tear from her cheek and it breaks my fucking heart. "You're too pretty to cry."

She shuts her eyes tight and sucks in a deep breath. "Sometimes … I have these nightmares about my dad. And …"

"Hey," I softly whisper, wiping more tears. "Tell me later.

Okay? We don't have to talk about this right now. You're exhausted, Lexi. Let's get some sleep. Okay?"

She smiles, almost grateful. "Okay."

I lead her to the bed and pull down the sheets and blankets. She slides in and I move the covers over her, tucking her in.

"Now, you're a human burrito," I say, and she grins.

I love to see it.

Brown hair splays around her head as she blinks up at me with bright green eyes. "Do you always sleep in clothes?"

"Sometimes I choose to be naked."

She gulps and closes her eyes tight. It's the only time she's not eye-fucking me, and I know why. My little naughty girl.

I walk to my side of the bed, climb under the sheets, and realize she's in the middle of the king-size mattress. "Will you be moving to your side of the bed?"

"I like the center," she whispers, pulling the covers farther.

I shake my head, reaching over and turning off the lamp. Then, I stay on my side, making sure there is space between us so I'm not tempted. Lexi rolls in the opposite direction, and our backs face one another.

The storm continues, the rain pounding harder, and the lightning flickers outside. Ten minutes pass, and I'm staring at the raindrops falling down the windows, replaying it all.

"Easton?" she whispers into the quiet, startling me from my thoughts. I assumed she was asleep.

"Hmm?"

"I'm really glad we met."

"Me too." I chuckle. "Good night, Lexi."

"Night."

Hours later

I wake up to her arm wrapped around my waist and her body molded against mine. I'm confident I feel her lips and warm breath on my bare back. Then, I realize my palm is gripping her thigh, and my cock is rock hard.

"Mmm," she says, running her hand across my stomach and stilling.

I keep my eyes closed and focus on my breathing as she slowly pulls away from me, lifting her hand from me.

Right now, I want to laugh as she quietly inches from under the blankets. Her feet pad against the wooden floor of the bedroom and the door quietly opens.

"Good morning," I say, not letting her escape that easily.

She doesn't say a peep. We can play cat and mouse, but I'm always the cat.

I sit up and stretch, placing my feet on the floor. After I grab my watch, I attach it to my wrist.

I might not have gotten much sleep, but I'm wide awake, seeing things more clearly than I ever have before.

Only three days to go until my record has been beaten and thirty-four days before I have to be married. And I might have somehow randomly found the woman of my dreams. *No fucking way.*

Lexi's right; I am lucky.

I get dressed in a T-shirt and jeans, then grab my Yankees hat and running shoes. When I take the stairs to the kitchen, Lexi is already in there, brewing a cup of coffee. My eyes slide over her messy hair and body in that oversize T-shirt.

"Who's Beau?"

She stills. "Why?"

"Because you're wearing his clothes."

She glances down at the faded name in the corner. "It's my ex's."

My brows furrow and my jaw tightens. The thought of her wearing some other man's shirt …

"Throw it away."

Lexi licks her lips and moves before me, lifting it over her head and tossing it onto the floor. "Better?"

My eyes stay focused on hers, and I don't have to steal a glance at her bare breasts and tiny cotton panties to know she's perfect. "I prefer you with clothes *on*."

She looks offended.

I touch her elbow. "Less temptation," I mutter, and her face softens. Fuck, I'd stare at her all day if I could.

"Are you jealous?" she asks, her nearly naked body inches from mine.

"No, because you were sleeping in *my* bed last night."

She licks her lips.

"I don't like seeing you with *his* name on your chest, like you're still his. Are you?"

She crosses her arms over her breasts, covering herself, and sighs. "No."

I don't take my gaze from hers; seriousness coats my tone. "If you're wearing a man's name, going forward, it's *mine*."

"It won't happen again," she whispers, breaking eye contact and grabbing the shirt from the floor. "I'll be back."

When she moves past me, I don't turn toward her, but I speak up as she climbs the stairs.

"Wear something you're not afraid to get dirty."

The sound of her feet against the wooden floor is followed by the door clicking closed. As she's upstairs, I pull eggs and bacon from the fridge.

When I told the real estate manager I'd be arriving in Jackson Hole this week, they asked if I wanted the chef I typically hire to join me. He stays in the guest house in the back and serves breakfast, lunch, and dinner when I'm present. This time, I passed, so it would be more private for us.

I place a skillet on the burner.

"You know how to cook?" she asks, grabbing two mugs from a cabinet and filling them for us.

"Sometimes. When I'm in the mood. What about you?" I give her a nod as I hook my finger through the loop of the ceramic mug.

"Is this another test?" She smirks as she leans against the counter.

I'm happy she's not upset with me.

"No. It's not a requirement," I tell her with a chuckle.

"If by 'cook', you mean bake an incredible batch of chocolate chip cookies, then yes. But I'm known to burn toast and popcorn."

I glance over at her. "I'm sorry if I was harsh."

"You weren't. I needed the reminder and appreciate it. Always truth. I prefer it," she says. "Now, can we talk about something else?"

"Sure," I say, glad she understands.

"Check out the backyard," I tell her, flipping the bacon.

She walks in front of the wall of windows, staring at the mountains in the distance. "Wow."

"The best view," I tell her, but I'm not talking about the snowcaps.

Once breakfast is ready, I set the plates in the nook and she joins me.

"Napkin?" I offer, handing her one.

She picks up a slice of bacon and it crunches.

"Well?"

"Perfect. Just how I like it."

"It's how I like it too. So, today, I've got something fun planned …"

She turns to me and her eyes widen. "Yes?"

Excitement radiates from her.

"*Never mind.* I'll let you wait a little longer."

"You *suck*," she says. "*A lot.*"

"I *love* building anticipation."

She chuckles. "And I love being edged."

I tilt my head at her and she smirks before turning away.

"Noted," I mutter, banking that information away, wondering if that's what she was doing when she whispered my name.

21

LEXI

Easton rinses our plates and loads them into the dishwasher.

"Why are you looking at me like that?" he asks, eyes on me.

"It's odd, seeing you be … *domestic*."

This makes him laugh. "In another life, I think I was a house husband."

"*Trophy* husband, for sure." I nod, my eyes gliding over his body.

"That too," he says.

In the short-sleeved shirt, his tattoos are on full display. I lick my lips, trying very hard not to eye-fuck him but finding it difficult. Especially after he was the main character in my fantasies last night.

His blue eyes sparkle as he studies me, and it's easy to imagine him as someone else in a different scenario with a loving wife and a family.

I know that when Easton is in a relationship, he commits to it. He seems like the person who is either one hundred percent in or one hundred percent out. There's no in-between, unlike every man I've ever dated.

I push the thought away as I stand and stretch.

"How'd you sleep last night?" he asks, wiping his hands on a dish towel.

After I crawled into bed with him, I listened to the rainfall and drifted away. I dreamed of nothing.

"I think you might be my nightmare catcher."

Quickly, my mind wanders to this morning, when I woke up and I was holding him and his grip was firmly on my upper thigh. It was dominant and sexy, but I know he's not in control of what he does when he's asleep.

"Nightmare catcher. *I like it.*" Easton checks his watch.

"Sounds frightening, but it's not. Fitting, considering you're not as terrible as you want people to believe."

"Lexi, don't convince yourself the man they say I am doesn't exist. Being an asshole is *very* much a part of who I am."

I give him a small smile. "Oh, I know. I've met that version of you. Total *dickhead*."

Laughter releases from his perfect lips. "You're into it."

"We all have a type," I say matter-of-factly.

"And I'm yours?" His mouth curves up into a devious grin.

"In another lifetime," I say, knowing I cannot have this conversation with him because he knows. He sees right through me. The mask I wear is invisible to him.

"Let's play a game." Easton pulls a small notebook from his pocket, flips it to the back, and rips two sheets of paper the size of my palm from the spiral. He scribbles something on his, folds it in half, then hands me the pen. "Rate me on your *dream partner* scale from one to five, and we'll trade later."

"One being no way in Hell?" I ask, tapping the pen against my lips.

"And five being you'd whisper their name as you came," he says with that goddamn smirk.

I swallow down the words I *want* to say. If he knew, he shouldn't have been chickenshit. He should've opened the door and given me what my body was desperately begging for —*him*.

"That sounds pretty hot, doesn't it?" I meet his intense gaze.

"It's *very* fucking hot," he mutters in a deep gruff.

Yep, I might internally combust, especially when his eyes slide down to my lips and he focuses on them.

"Now who's eye-fucking who?" I call him out, trying to calm my beating heart as I scribble down my number.

"Mmm." It comes from his throat like a growl.

I fold and tuck it into my front jeans pocket.

I notice the black silk in his palm when he glances at his watch. Easton stalks toward me, crossing the space in long strides. Then, his hands are on my shoulders, turning me around, placing the material over my eyes.

"The car will be here in five minutes," he says close to my ear.

"Is the blindfold necessary?"

"Yes. Considering you ruin surprises, it's absolutely necessary." He carefully ties it behind my head, but doesn't step away. Instead, he moves directly in front of me. His body and mouth are inches from me as his voice falls to a low husk. "Now, tell me, darling, can you see me?"

I shake my head. "Unfortunately, *no*."

"Good."

I wish I could though, because I feel his eyes on me, studying me, trying to figure me out.

Easton is a work of art with straight lines and edges carved into his body. He's like a sculpture and I have to stop myself from admiring him more often than not. Something that absolutely *shouldn't* happen.

He pats my shoulder, placing both hands on me as he moves me through the living room.

"Will you let me guess what we're doing today?"

"No." He's abrupt. "And I wouldn't tell you if you somehow figured it out; which you won't. I'm too unpredictable."

Easton stops walking and I hear the door open. He leads me out onto the porch. I imagine the stairs I walked up yesterday after we arrived and slightly panic, knowing I won't make it down.

His hands slide under me as if he can read my mind, and I'm lifted into his arms. I hold on to him, not letting go as we descend the steps. Right now, I'm so damn thankful for this blindfold because I wouldn't be able to look away from him. Not when he acts like Prince Charming.

Easton continues forward, carefully setting me down, keeping his hands on me until I'm steady. "I had a feeling you wouldn't make it."

"You're right," I say, licking my lips. "You can stop staring now."

"Can you see me?" he asks, his voice low.

I shake my head. "No."

I imagine him smirking, and those stupid butterflies flutter.

No, no, no, I think, lost in my thoughts as I chew on the corner of my lip.

I *cannot* fall in love with this man.

Birds chirp in the distance as the mountain breeze whips across my cheeks. I hear gravel under tires, followed by a car door swinging open. Easton places his hand on my back, guiding me inside.

"Keep the blindfold on the entire time. No peeking. I'll meet you there."

"Wait, what?" I barely get out before the door shuts.

The car moves forward and my heart gallops.

Thirty minutes later, the car comes to a stop, and the seconds feel like minutes as I wait. I don't know how much time passes before the door opens. It feels like an hour, but it might've been ten minutes.

"Lexi," Easton says, and I relax.

"I missed you," I say, holding my hand out to him.

As soon as he has me, he interlocks his fingers with mine. I squeeze three times, and he squeezes twice.

"Sorry, it took a little longer than I anticipated."

"It's fine. Hopefully, no one got fired," I joke.

"Not this time," he tells me as we continue to walk forward.

"Can I take the blindfold off now?"

"Very soon."

I hear something in the distance and feel a whooshing of wind.

"One second," he says, and I'm being swooped up in his arms again and placed into a seat.

Hands reach across me, and I'm buckled into something before a door closes. It smells like a new car, fresh leather and plastic. Easton climbs in, but I can't place any of the sounds. They're all unfamiliar.

Something is placed over my ears—headphones?

"Are you ready?" he asks on the headset.

"For what?"

Then, I feel a different sensation like we're going straight up and levitating.

"You can take your blindfold off now."

I suck in a deep breath, removing the material from my eyes. That's when I see I'm inside a *helicopter,* and when I look over, Easton is at the controls.

"You said you were afraid of flying."

"One thing about me, Lexi: when I'm afraid of something, I go after it head-on with zero regrets. I started taking flying lessons when I was sixteen. I have a private pilot's license too. I trust myself and no one else."

I'm stunned silent.

He smiles as we soar over mountaintops, and I glance at the

rushing river down below. On the bank, elk graze in a herd, and I gasp.

"In a minute, you'll be able to see Grand Teton," he says.

The valley opens up wide and I spot the pointy peaks in the distance. It's a clear sky, and it looks like a Hollywood backdrop.

"Is that real?"

"I think that every time I see them. Gorgeous, isn't it?"

"Breathtaking. Thank you. This is *incredible*. And you're right; I wouldn't have ever guessed this." I glance over at him, smiling. "From house husband to helicopter pilot. *Impressed,*" I say.

Sunlight leaks through the windows, causing his watch to sparkle on his wrist. Easton looks down below and calls out something on the radio. It sounds like pilot jargon. Moments later, we're descending, landing in an open, grassy field.

In the distance sits a neon-green Jeep with big tires and the top off. On the back is an ice chest that's caked with mud. A twisty trail travels up the side of the mountain to the very top.

He cuts the helicopter's engine then unbuckles and reaches over to help me.

"I hope you love this," he says.

"I already do."

Our gazes linger too long before he opens the door for me.

Easton gets out and meets me on the ground. I step down and stumble into his arms.

"I'm sorry," I say with a laugh.

"I'm getting used to it," he says, letting me go.

We take the short hike to the Jeep. It's lifted, and it sits on fat, knobby tires for climbing and trail riding.

I walk around it. "This thing is a monster."

Easton opens the driver's door and steps to the side. "You can go first."

"Fuck yes," I say, clapping my hands together.

"Don't make me regret it," he tells me.

I climb up the step, pull myself inside, and buckle the harness seat belt, noticing the reinforced roll bars. I move the seat closer to the steering wheel, knowing whoever drove this thing last must've been a giant.

Easton adjusts the passenger seat, shaking his head. "We've got fifteen miles of trails to climb. When it gets rough and beats the shit out of you, we can trade. Overall, the view is worth it."

He points to a single dirt track with several switchbacks.

I lean backward, covering my eyes with my hand, and wish I'd brought a hat.

"You think you can handle it?" he questions.

"Pfft. Let's fucking go," I say.

He grabs onto the *oh shit* bar, and I kick in the clutch, popping it into first gear as we take off toward the trail.

"When do I get to start asking you questions?"

"Now."

"What were you like as a teenager?"

Easton laughs and looks at me like I grew a third eye. "You're the only person in the world who's ever been given the opportunity to ask me anything, and that's what you want to know?"

"It's my first question, not my only one. Plus, I'm curious," I explain.

The smile on my face might be permanent as I breathe in the fresh air and soak up the sunshine.

"I was a smart-ass who thought he had the world figured out."

I chuckle. "Nothing has changed."

"Touché," he says.

I position the tires to avoid the ruts and kick it into second gear. It's bumpy, and I can feel the incline as I'm pushed back into my seat.

"Have you done this a lot?" Easton asks, watching me navigate.

"Back home, there was this community on the mountainside, and it had the *shittiest* roads. Rough and bumpy. Ruts so deep that it was easy to believe you might fall into the pits of Hell. When I was sixteen, my best friend, Remi, and I stole my older brother's truck. He had a four-wheel drive, so we drove up there after a rainstorm to go mudding. I got stuck in three feet of mush and the tow truck couldn't get up there and pull it out for weeks. My mama grounded me for a month, but I have no regrets because I'm still laughing about it. When my friends and I were bored, that was where we'd go."

He laughs. "Were you rebellious?"

"No, I never got into any real trouble."

"Ah," he says. "So, you're still the same too."

"In a way, yes," I admit, focusing. "But some things have changed."

"Like what?"

He genuinely wants to know, and I want to tell him.

I think back to my childhood, and it seems like so long ago. "You won't believe this, but I used to be timid. I was *never* a rule breaker. On the first day of my senior year of high school, I told myself I'd start saying yes to things I didn't want to do. The main one was moving to New York for college. I broke up with Beau and moved away. That's when things changed for me."

He rests his arm on the door. "You dated him in high school?"

"Yep. And after college graduation, I returned home for the summer and believed we'd have our second chance." I sigh. "Going forward, if I break it off with someone, I'll never give them another chance. When it's over, it's over for a reason. Lesson learned."

"The more I hear about this stupid fuck …" Easton shakes his head.

My mouth tilts up. "But I should thank him because without that, I wouldn't be here right now."

"Is the pessimist looking on the bright side for once?"

"Pfft." But he's right.

The grade grows steeper the higher we travel. He's right about the roughness of the trail though. It's not for newbies.

"Grand Teton was a bucket list item for me."

"Yeah? What else is on that list?"

"To name a few, skinny-dipping, making love under the stars, dancing at Stonehenge, taking a train ride across America, getting my first tattoo, joining the Mile-High Club, visiting the Empire State Building at night, and ice-skating at Rockefeller Center. I never got to do the touristy things before. I also want to see aurora borealis and a penguin in the wild, *not* one at a zoo."

"Life experiences," he confirms.

"Aren't most people's?"

He shakes his head. "No. Some have materialistic items listed. Buy this, buy that, own this."

I take a switchback, rolling across a gigantic rock. I notice the straight climb upward as we kick up dust. "Do you have a bucket list?"

"I do now. I added some of yours to it."

I glance at him. "You can't have the same ones as me."

"Says who? Did you make the rules?"

"Tell me the ones you added," I urge.

"Skinny-dipping. Making love under the stars. Dancing at Stonehenge. Taking a train ride across America, joining the Mile-High Club, and visiting the Empire State Building at night."

"You do realize some of those aren't one-person tasks?"

He laughs. "Well aware."

Before we take the next switchback, I pull off to the side and place it in neutral to shake out my wrists. Off-roading can get like this sometimes.

"I know you're determined, but do you want to trade for a

while?" he asks, glancing at his GPS. We've only driven three miles.

"Fine," I playfully groan, but I'm thankful for the break. We're not even halfway up the mountainside.

We switch places and get buckled, then Easton shifts the Jeep into gear, taking it much faster. I can't help but glance at him, admiring the veins in his arms and how his tattooed biceps flex. Our eyes meet and we exchange a smile before looking away.

"Where is the most devious place you've had sex?" I ask.

He thinks about it. "On a throne."

"Wow." My mouth falls open. "Okay, I can't top that."

"You still have to share," he says.

"The church parking lot."

"I didn't think you had it in you," he says.

"I did that day. So, what's your body count? If you don't want to answer—"

"Three."

My mouth falls open. "*Three?*"

"That surprises you." He says it matter-of-factly. It's not a question.

"It does. I thought …" I can't finish.

"The relationship rumors about me are rarely true. I might date a lot, but that doesn't mean I'm fucking every woman I'm seen in public with."

"Most men who could have anyone *would*."

"I don't want just *anyone* though. Sex always complicates things, so I've never fucked around. Now, Weston is a different story."

I snort. "That doesn't surprise me after spending time with him. Totally get it."

Easton glances at me. "Yeah, he's *very* good at his game. However, it's awkward when his flings believe I'm him, especially after they've had a wild night together or a breakup."

"Oh God," I say. "I didn't even think about that."

"When he was married, life was great. But now that it's over, I'm sure he'll be back to it. Anyway, what about you?"

"Three," I say with a shrug. "Nothing to write home about either."

"That's a pity," Easton says, shaking his head.

Two hours later, we park at the top and get out. The altitude is higher than what I'm used to, but it's the best view of Grand Teton. A bright blue body of water glimmers at the bottom of the mountainside.

We take a foot trail, and in the clearing there are flat-surfaced rocks that are perfect for sitting on. I rest my hands on my hips, breathing deeply, trying to acclimate to the thin air.

Easton sits on one of the rocks and I plop beside him. Our arms and thighs touch.

"Will you take a picture with me?" I ask, pulling out my phone.

"Sure." He places his arm around me and pulls me in close.

I snap a few, then review them.

"Look at us," I say, showing him.

We look like a happy couple. We go together—that's undeniable.

"Do you think everyone sees something we don't?" I ask. It's an honest question.

He shrugs. "I don't know. It seems like they do."

"It's wonderful here. I like it a lot," I say.

"I thought you would. That body of water is a lake, and if you come early in the morning, you can sometimes catch moose down there."

"I bet it's beautiful at sunrise."

He nods. "It is. Maybe one of my favorite spots in the world."

We sit in silence for ten more minutes before Easton stands and holds out his hand.

"There's one more vantage point," he says as I take his hand.

We take a trail that leads to another overlook. Easton

carefully walks in front of me, leading the way down the path into the trees. When it opens up, it's a better view of the Tetons. The sky is clear without a single cloud, deep blue, the same color as Easton's eyes.

"It's different, seeing it here than in the sky," he says.

I cup my hands over my mouth. "Woohoo!" I yell out. My voice echoes down the valley. I bump into him. "Join me."

He shakes his head with a laugh and does; the wind carries our cheers and laughter. Right now, we're as free as the birds in the sky.

I take a few pictures and don't have to ask him to lean in this time; he just does.

"For the 'gram."

I lean in and place my lips on his cheek, snapping the picture. When I glance at it, he's smirking.

"If you post that, you'll break the Internet," he says.

"Too bad I don't have a cell signal. When we do, I will. I guess that will be my official announcement to the world?"

"It can be."

"Wait, do you have social media?" I ask.

"What elder millennial doesn't?"

I snicker. "Are you following me?"

Easton's grin doesn't falter. "I only follow the corporate account, Weston, and Billie. However, I'll rectify that now."

He pulls his phone from his pocket. "No service either. Damn." He playfully snaps his fingers.

"So, will that be your official announcement?" I lick my lips.

"Since the pictures of us together have been released, I don't have to make one. It's been done for me, but I'll follow you. Just get ready for the attention," he warns. "It's intense."

"You're serious?"

"Yes," he confirms.

"I look forward to it. Who knows, maybe they won't notice."

He chuckles. "It's too late for that, Lexi."

I shove my phone back into my pocket, but the crumpled paper stops it. I pull it out, remembering that we'd written our ratings for one another on it.

"Oh yeah," Easton says, holding his toward me. "Ready to trade?"

"Not yet," I admit. "I want it to be at the perfect moment."

"Always searching for an experience?"

"In *everything* I do," I confirm. "I don't want to live my life with regrets."

He wraps his arm over my shoulders and I rest my arm across his waist.

"I'm ready."

I laugh. "You have no idea what you're asking for."

"Oh, but I do."

22

EASTON

Same day

We stand close, staring at the tall mountain peaks. As her hair blows in the warm breeze, I can smell her strawberry shampoo and the sweetness of her skin.

Summer is my favorite season to visit Grand Teton. The wildlife is active, flowers are in bloom, and the temperatures during the day are perfect. The company makes it even better.

"What did you want to be when you grew up?" I ask.

"You first," she says.

"*CEO first.* President second," I admit.

"Your answer *doesn't* surprise me."

I snicker. "At one point, I heavily considered becoming an artist." I pause. "Now, that's something only Weston knows. Facts from the vault."

Sharing the real me with her is easy because she never judges and she's never shocked by my admissions.

"Really? Do you paint?"

"I draw." I pull the small spiral notebook from my pocket and offer it to her. "I've never let anyone see these."

She takes it, studying the worn cover, rubbing her thumb across the curled edge, but she doesn't open it immediately. "Are you sure? It's very ... *personal.*"

"It is, but I *want* to share these with you."

Lexi lifts the cover and starts at the beginning, studying each one like she's saving them to memory. They're all scribbled in black ink, beginning in January.

"This is your life in little moments." Amazement fills her tone.

"Tiny but *significant* moments," I say, and her eyes soften. "The highlight reel."

"Easton," she whispers after a few minutes, her fingers brushing over the pages as recognition meets her expression. "These are *our* moments."

It's the Tower Penthouse, her reading at the park with the flourishing scene around her, whiskey at the bar, our motorcycle ride together, the diamond in the sky, the yacht, our plane ride, and being here. It's been eleven days, but these are the moments that count. It already feels like I've known her for a lifetime.

I've always heard this happens when you *click* with someone, but it's the first time I've experienced it.

"This is ... incredible. *You're incredible,*" she softly says.

Then, she turns to the last one I drew this morning—of her lying in my bed with her back toward me. Dark hair splashes across the pillows. She makes filling the blank pages easy.

"You do this every day?"

"Yes, since I was nine years old. I have thirty years of them," I admit. "It's nearly 12,000 drawings on 3x5 inch pages just like this in the same type of notebook with the same ink pen. Some days I drew more than once."

"Easton." Amazement fills her tone. "I bet it's fascinating to see the progression of your skills and your life. It's one of the most creative daily diaries that I've ever seen."

"Maybe I'll show you the collection one day, from the very beginning to right now."

"I'd be honored," she says. "I'd love that."

I hesitate, wondering if I should share this with her, knowing I don't want any secrets between us. No secrets means no future surprises. I want to share every part of me with her, even the ones that don't shine like gold. "I started sketching because I couldn't speak freely like other kids my age."

She glances down at the page. "Really? I'd have never guessed."

I smile. "It took years of hard work and practice."

"I can't imagine how difficult it was to want to communicate and not being able to."

"It was a fucking nightmare. It felt like prison because I knew what I wanted to convey but couldn't. I was frustrated during my adolescence, but I was determined not to let that stop me. Between my daily lessons, I'd turned to drawing because it was the only thing that calmed my busy mind."

She nods and listens as I focus on the view.

"I just remember whispering a lot in my brother's ear and he'd act as my voice in social situations. Weston was the only person I trusted. Still true today."

"I understand why. He's a protector. From the little time I spent with him, I could tell he has your best interest at heart." She meets my eyes. "So what about now? Do you get nervous when you're in front of a crowd?"

"Sometimes," I say, realizing she actually cares enough to ask questions. "But I've learned to compartmentalize it, perform, if you will. More times than not, I'm uncomfortable. I learned that I can do hard things, and afterward, I sit in a quiet room and decompress. Overstimulation from social situations is very much my kryptonite."

"I get it." She bumps my shoulder. "You're a pro. I'm amazed by your resilience. Not to mention your ability to stay consistent. Most people outgrow their childhood hobbies, but you've made it your life's work."

"I've never thought about it like that." I actually feel relieved sharing that part of me with her. Lexi accepted it, accepted me and my vulnerabilities without judgment. She's...perfect.

I return the conversation back to my original question. "That's enough about me. What did you want to be?"

"Don't laugh," she says.

"I won't."

She lets it out in one breath. "I wanted to be a magician's assistant."

I hold back my laughter and keep most of it in. She bumps me with her shoulder.

"I liked the one who had knives thrown at her head and walked away, unscathed, like a standing miracle. When I was older, I wanted to be an actual magician but realized I didn't have the skill for it."

"Because you have bad timing and suck at surprises?"

She smiles. "How'd you guess? But I realized after a while, I only wanted to be the center of attention and be appreciated by an audience. Change some lives with my performance. I dunno; it meant something to me."

"You do that now," I say.

She shakes her head. "No."

"When we went to Samuel and Heather's engagement party—"

"You did that," she confirms. "When you enter a space, it's like you suck the air from the room."

"Not around my friends and colleagues. They're as unfazed by me as you are."

I can almost see the gears running in her head, but it's true. That night, eyes were on *her,* not me.

"There's a reason I chose *you,* Alexis. I hope, one day, you understand why."

"Tell me now," she pleads, her long lashes fluttering.

"I can't articulate it yet." I run my fingers through my hair. "It's just this … *feeling.*"

"Yeah, I know what you're talking about. Being around you is electric, like … you *see* me."

"I *do* see you." I stare at her, realizing the same current that's tugged me under has its grip on her too.

Her cheeks heat. "I see *you* too, Easton."

"I know. And there aren't enough words in the dictionary to describe that, whatever the fuck it is."

As a kid who barely spoke, I spent a lot of time studying people and their behaviors. It's one of the reasons I'm a good judge of character. I notice specific movements, the way someone speaks or the dart of their eyes. Everyone has a tell, it's just finding it. Cheap words don't win me over, it's a person's actions that do.

Lexi is kind and has a good heart, that much I know, and I trust her.

She flips back to the beginning, which includes countless boardrooms, plane rides, stacks of papers, and random coffee in different mugs and disposable cups. I look them over as she goes through each page again. Then, I notice the pattern in the sketches.

"What is it?" She searches my face, noticing my shift.

My 2D reality transformed into a 3D world of adventure the day I met her.

My scene blossoms with countless details, memories I never want to forget when we're together. Nothing is left out.

"It's one of my tells." I flip through the notepad, and she leans over and focuses. "Watch the progression."

"There," she says. "This is when it changed."

The Tower Penthouse.

"The day we met," I confirm. "About ten years ago, I went through each notebook because I was curious if I could learn anything from it. When my drawings became more detailed, a major shift happened in my life. I've never been able to pinpoint it until now."

"Easton, you're about to get fake married. I think *this* fits the bill for a life change."

"Oh, it's very much real," I say.

But I know it's deeper than that. It's not the marriage; it's *her*.

She studies me, her gaze lingering a few seconds too long before she looks away.

I focus on the mountains, too, trying to steady my racing heart. "I've worked beside my father for fifteen years. But I'm not the only one. A backup successor has been chosen if I can't fulfill my grandfather's wishes."

"Weston?" she asks.

This makes me laugh. "I wish. He doesn't want it. The man's name is Derrick Petersen. He's worked for the company for thirty years. My grandfather loved him. I can't stand the fucker, and the feeling is mutual. He's tried to ruin me on more than one occasion."

"Why?"

"I'm the only person standing in the way of him taking over. I'm not sure if he's aware of the marriage agreement in my family's contract, he just knows he'll be promoted if I don't meet the requirements."

She shakes her head.

"Weston told me this morning that rumors are spreading around the building that I'm on vacation with a woman. Two things that never happen, especially not in the same sentence. I'm telling you this because I need you to be prepared. The attacks will come. This man will do whatever he can to ensure he becomes CEO, and you're the *easiest* target."

"Attacks?"

"Rumors. Lies. Scandals. You being targeted is the *only* thing I don't like about this temporary marriage. Being with me will be challenging, and some days will be much harder than others."

She turns to me. "That's life, Easton. There is one thing that's bothering me, though. I want it to be known that if you meet someone you could spend the rest of your life with, you *should* pursue it."

"No." I adjust my watch. "You're my new hobby, *Alexis.* At least for a year."

She chews on the corner of her lip. "Trying to get under my skin?"

I lean back on the palms of my hands. "I'm already there."

"Cocky as fuck." A devious grin takes residence on her perfect mouth. "So, that means you're committing to me in return? Did the contract specify that?"

"You should've read it," I say, enjoying this conversation.

"I know."

"Would you like to keep me to yourself?" I lift a brow.

Lexi meets my gaze. "I don't want to share you, even if this is fake. Call me greedy if you'd like." The words come out confident, like a woman who knows exactly what she wants.

"Mmm. Consider it done. I'm all yours, Lexi."

"*Good,*" she whispers.

I stand, holding my hand out to her. She takes it, and I pull her to her feet; her chest presses against mine.

"I believe honesty is the best policy with us. I want you to know the truth about me, my life, and my family. People will try to destroy what we have—temporary or not. So, ask if you read or hear something that makes you pause. I have nothing to hide from you. The right, wrong, or indifferent. Truth always."

"I trust you, Easton. And I can handle the bullshit. I grew up in a small town. If I can survive that, I can survive a year of being your wife."

I tuck a few loose strands of dark hair behind her ear. "I don't want you to get hurt."

A breath escapes her. "And I don't want to be the one to hurt you."

"Ah, right, *my little heartbreaker*. Almost forgot you were so fierce," I say, creating space between us before I do something I shouldn't.

I lead the way back to the Jeep, then open the bear-proof ice chest bolted to the back. Inside is a fresh bottle of Fireball shoved into the ice, along with a few sandwiches and water. I'll have to thank my friend Philip for packing the essentials.

I hand a bottle of water to Lexi, and we drink. The last thing we need is to get dehydrated up here. It's easy in the mountains.

"Ready to take the trail down?" I ask, dangling the key on my finger.

"Sure, but you can drive," she tells me.

"Really?" I'm almost shocked as I open the door for her. We climb inside, buckling. Nothing happens when I press the ignition other than the dashboard lights flickering.

"Ha-ha, that's a funny joke," Lexi says, tightening her harness and repositioning her seat.

"I wish it were a joke," I say, pulling my phone from my pocket to text Philip. "Shit."

Her smile fades as she glances at her phone. The corner shows *SOS*, just like mine. She immediately turns it off, which is brilliant. She won't waste battery.

"How far is it to the bottom?"

"Fifteen miles. On foot, it's an extreme trail. We'd make it after dark, and I won't fly in the mountains after sunset. It's one of my hard rules."

I grip my useless phone. I could use the emergency satellite option, but I refuse. It should only be used in extreme emergencies out here in the Tetons.

I try to imagine the different scenarios and don't panic.

"Let's pop the hood," she says, unbuckling and hopping out.

The latch is under the steering wheel, and I pull it. The hood clicks, and Lexi stands on a metal step attached to the reinforced steel bumper.

"The battery terminals are corroded," she says, shaking her head. "Do we have a wrench? Maybe we can loosen it and try to clean it off?"

After Lexi steps down, I take her place.

"I might kill Philip."

"Me too," she says as we move to the back of the Jeep to see what we have on board.

We have a small tent, a sleeping bag, and a toolbox with an axe inside.

"Reasons why I have trust issues," I mutter.

Lexi checks the storage compartments and under the seats. "Any sodas in that ice chest?"

"No," I tell her as she leans against the Jeep.

"Well, using that to remove the corrosion was our last hope. What are our options?" she asks.

"Hike down fifteen miles, use the satellite phone in the helicopter, and call someone to pick us up. Hike to the bottom and wait in the helicopter until morning. Or wait here because Philip will return for the Jeep when the sun rises, so he'll find us."

Lexi turns to me. "You swear this isn't one of your tests?"

I hold up my hands. "This wasn't planned. I had dinner reservations made for us at one of my favorite steakhouses in town. The entire back room was supposed to be ours so we could have privacy during dinner. I handpicked our steaks."

"Aww, that would've been awesome. What time is it?"

"It's a little past five," I tell her. "Sunset is at nine. That gives us a solid four hours until dark."

"Let's not waste any time then."

I tilt my head at her. “Wait, you don’t mind camping in bear country?”

“I should be asking *you* that question, considering our backgrounds,” she says, moving to the Jeep’s back storage area. “We have a tent, a mattress pad, a sleeping bag, an axe, a flint fire starter, one foldable chair, and a can of *expired* bear spray.”

I stand behind her, looking over everything. “Add four sandwiches, water, and a bottle of Fireball.”

Lexi turns to me. “You and these serendipitous events are going to do me in.”

“You nearly begged for adventures.”

She laughs. “And so far, you haven’t disappointed.”

23

LEXI

Easton takes the expired can of bear spray and enters the trees to search for wood. I suck in a breath, wishing my body would acclimate to the altitude quicker, looking around at my surroundings.

It's a beautiful place, and I'm glad we're camping. As I walk around, I find a fire ring with some old coals and know where those who stay here usually camp.

When I dump the tent out of its bag, all I can do is laugh. I laugh so hard that a few tears stream down my cheeks because it's a one-person backpacking tent. It takes me less than ten minutes to set it up. I stand with my hands on my hips, trying to figure out how this will work.

Easton walks up behind me with an armful of wood. He sets it next to the fire ring, and his face contorts when he notices our shelter for the night.

"No, this is the fucking joke." He points at it.

"Does that look miniature to you?" I ask, covering my smile with my hand and laughing. "I don't have any words for this."

"Will we even fit?"

I shrug. "I guess we'll find out later."

He doesn't look convinced or amused as I pull the mattress pad and sleeping bag from the back seat.

I position them inside the tent and take a step back. It is what it is, and we'll make it work.

Easton makes several trips as I gather loose leaves and smaller sticks for kindling. I grab the fire starter and let out a sigh of relief when I see the striker still attached. Otherwise, this entire setup would have been useless. To be honest, that would've been the icing on the cake.

I shave off magnesium onto the kindling pile. After I flip it around onto the ferro rod side, I strike against it, and sparks fly. The magnesium instantly catches on fire and I add other smaller sticks, blowing on it to keep the flame hot.

Eventually, it catches, and I stand up, adding thicker sticks until I have a roaring fire. When it pops and cracks, I smile, proud of myself. It's been years since I started a fire using one of those, but I still have it.

Sometimes, it pays to grow up in the middle of nowhere. Situations like *this* aren't frightening.

Easton returns, drops the rest of what he gathered on the vast pile, then steps back. The fire crackles and he tilts his head, impressed.

I nod as he gives me a high five.

"Mmhmm." I brush off my shoulder.

"Southern girls." He proudly folds his arms across his broad chest. "You're made different."

"A good kind of different?"

"*Very* good."

"I'll take it as a compliment," I say.

"You should."

Easton returns with the camping chair and the bottle of Fireball.

I look down at it in his hand. "That a good idea?"

"Are you scared?" He chuckles, removing the lid.

"No, but you should be. At some point when I drink, my filter disappears."

"Wait." He tilts his head. "You have a filter?"

I narrow my eyes. "I'm glad you can dish *and* take it."

"I love to reciprocate," he says, moving the chair close to the fire.

Easton sits and pats his lap. I take his offer, and he wraps his arm around my waist, hooking his finger into the front belt loop of my jeans.

He brings the bottle to his lips before handing it to me. "Eww, that tastes like shit."

As I take a long pull, he watches me with a brow lifted, a small smile permanently planted.

"It reminds me of bad decisions," I say.

"Like what?"

"Oh, there are way too many to even name. I went to a few cast parties and kissed people I probably shouldn't have. It's why I never kissed any of the guys I went on dates with when I moved back. For some reason, when I do, guys get weirdly obsessed."

"Really? Maybe that's the problem. You cursed me when you stuck your tongue down my throat in front of the paps," he says.

I turn around and smack him. "Please. I cursed you when I stole your watch."

A howl of laughter releases from him, and it echoes through the trees. "So fucking true."

"Speaking of, what time is it?"

He checks his watch—the watch that started it all. "Almost seven thirty. An hour and a half until sunset."

"And what day are we on?" I ask, curious.

"Eleven."

I can smell the cinnamon on his breath. I lean against him, with his arm lazily wrapped around me, and glance at the low-hanging sun. Eventually, it will fall behind the mountains, and temperatures will drop. We have enough wood to last all night. The booze, as shitty as it is, will make this easier.

I try to hold back a smile and focus on the blazing fire. Some of the wood must've been wet because it pops and wheezes.

"What if this is a mistake?" I whisper, wishing I could predict the future.

"And what if it's not?"

"I guess it's the flip of a coin," I say.

"Yep."

If ever I needed a crystal ball, it's now.

I'm too lost in my thoughts, trying to predict our outcome.

Marriage for three hundred sixty-five days, divorce, and a payment.

But what if, in the end, it's not what I want?

My biggest fear is growing attached to this man, but I can't deny how he makes me feel when we're alone. This is the version of him I can see myself falling for. And right now, as he holds me, nothing else in the world matters but us, this moment, and this wild adventure we're on together.

We drink like we're running from our bubbling feelings, the ones we vehemently deny.

It's not worth discussing until day fifteen—or at least, that's what I tell myself.

Until then, we can continue our spiral down this path of denial, paved with silent conversations and stolen glances.

The flames have us transfixed, and we fall into silence, watching it, sipping the Fireball. At some point, it no longer has a taste, and that's when I know I'm on the road to Truthville. After an hour, my stomach growls so loud that Easton hears it.

"Let me grab those sandwiches," he says, patting me.

I stand, and the world shifts.

"Shit," I say, not realizing how much I had to drink until now.

His hands are on me, gently positioning me in the chair.

I reach up and run my fingers through his hair and smile. "I've been wanting to do that," I admit.

"I'll be right back. Don't go anywhere," he says, giving me a boyish grin.

The sun is setting, quickly dipping below the mountain as the sky slowly fades into night. It's gorgeous here, and the picture is perfectly shaded with bursts of color.

Moments later, Easton returns with bottles of water and food. He adds more wood to the fire, then I stand, allowing him to sit, and he pulls me down with him.

"You're like my throne. All rigid," I say, wiggling my ass against him as he hands me a sandwich.

"I like the thought of that."

I unzip the plastic baggie and bite the soft white bread and turkey with cheese and mayo. "This is so good. We'll have to thank your friend."

"After I kick his ass." Easton checks his watch. "Darkness will fall soon."

"Nighttime is my favorite. I can't wait to see the stars here. It's one thing I hate about the city. It's like the outside world doesn't exist."

"It doesn't," he says. "When you're in New York, you're *in* it."

"And when you leave, it's in you," I add. "When I moved back to Texas, I always felt like I was playing a part."

An admission that nearly takes my breath away.

"Like this?" he asks.

"No. When I'm with you like *this*, it's real. I was too busy trying to make everyone else happy instead of focusing on myself."

He nods. "I understand that more than you know."

We finish our sandwiches and Easton rests his chin on my shoulder while we enjoy the fire.

My eyes grow heavy, making me realize how tired I am. "Can we go to bed?"

"Yes," he says, grabbing our trash and picking up everything to move it away from our tent.

He locks it in the cooler on the back of the Jeep, meeting me as I stare at the comically small tent.

"Go ahead. You first," I say as he unzips the entrance.

Easton climbs inside and sits on the mattress pad, hunched over, and removes his shoes. He props himself up on one elbow, glancing at the little space left for me.

The flame lights his face perfectly, and I realize I'm staring.

"Your turn," he says, patting the pad and scooting over, giving me more room.

"Fuck it," I say, taking off my shoes, stumbling back into the tent. I fall against him, laughing.

My ass presses against his cock, and his hot breath is on my neck. He lifts the sleeping bag, covering us the best he can.

He wraps his tattooed arm around me, pulling me closer against his muscular body. "Are you comfortable?"

"Actually, yes." I tilt my head toward him, and his mouth is so damn close. That perfect smile that's just for me is so damn intoxicating. "You think this will work out?"

"It's one night. We'll survive," he admits.

"You know that's not what I'm asking, Easton." My breathing grows more ragged as his thumb brushes against my cheek.

"The only thing I'm certain of is you being the end of me," he whispers.

Temptation swirls in the air.

"Okay, trade me," I say, reaching into my pocket and struggling to find the wadded paper. "I'm ready."

"Oh, *this* is the moment?" he says, slightly repositioning himself to grab his.

My nerves get the best of me, but I can't wait any longer. I have to know what number rating this man gave me. I have to know if I have a chance in Hell.

"What if this doesn't have the answer you want?" I search his face.

"I'll accept it," he says. "No questions asked. And you?"

"Same." I suck in a deep breath, open it, and see a ONE. My heart drops, and then I see the ZERO next to it. "Asshole."

He opens mine and sees the same. *A ten.* "You are too."

I roll over onto my side so I'm facing him. His strong arm wraps around me, and we lie there as he holds me against his chest. The scents of cinnamon on our breath and campfire on our skin fill the tent.

"What does this mean for us?" I ask.

"It means we're rule breakers. But most importantly, we're *fucked.*"

I close my eyes, unable to look at him, feeling my temperature rise as the electricity pulls us together.

"Easton," I whisper.

"Lexi," he says, moving closer—honestly, I didn't know it was possible.

His lips are mere inches from mine, and I want to feel his mouth again. I hang by a thread, waiting, wanting, wishing, and needing to know if anything has changed between us from the first night until now.

He feels it too. I know he does.

"Once lines are crossed ..." he whispers. "We can't undo it."

"I know," I barely say, swallowing hard.

His nose brushes against mine, and butterflies flutter.

Is the risk worth the reward?

I inch forward, making the first move. Not giving a fuck anymore.

His soft lips and tongue capture mine as he runs his fingers through my hair, tugging. The kiss deepens, and I'm desperate for more of him. I know this man will be the one to burn me to the ground.

He growls against me, and his other hand rests on the small of my back, pushing me against him as I run my fingers through his messy hair.

"Fuck," he hisses, tugging my bottom lip into his mouth, shaking his head.

I'm lost in his need for more, feeling how hard he is against me.

Whatever is going on between us is mutual. Right now, we're damned if we do and damned if we don't.

"Mmm," I whimper, knowing I'm losing control, but it's all happening too fast.

My eyes flutter open, and so do his.

"We shouldn't," he mutters, his lips brushing across mine like butterfly wings. Fierce desperation is written on his face, the same expression I'm wearing.

"I know," I say.

"Are you *sure* you're anti-love?"

I search his eyes, falling deep into his blues. "I'll give you my official answer on day fifteen."

He smirks. "I'll be waiting. I'm sorry. This should be done with a clear conscience, so there are no regrets," he says.

He softly kisses me, and I breathe out, knowing he's right as he stole my breath away.

"I hate it when you're right," I say, his nose rubbing against mine.

He chuckles. "Good night, my little heartbreaker."

"Good night," I whisper, rolling the other way so I don't do something I'll regret.

His cock is hard against my back, and knowing I've caused that gives me too much satisfaction.

Easton holds me tight against him like our bodies were made

to be together, like if he lets go, I'll disappear. And I don't want him to let go, in case I do.

I melt into him, realizing how right he is.

I *am* fucked. But so is he.

Tonight has proven that to me.

24

EASTON

Birthday countdown: 34 days
Since meeting her: 12 days
Company takeover: 41 days

I wake up sweating in the comically small tent with Lexi's body molded to mine. My hand is on her bare stomach, and her ass is pressed against me. My arm is asleep, and my back hurts, but I'm smiling. Based on how light it is, the sun must be rising.

"What time is it?" Lexi asks, clearing her throat. "So thirsty."

"I'll get you some water," I say. "It's five after six."

"Don't go," she pleads. "You're too comfy."

Lexi wraps her warm arms around me, holding me tight.

I breathe her in. "Okay," I say, not wanting to leave her. "Just a little longer."

I'm a greedy bastard, and I don't want to pass up this opportunity. As I'm falling back asleep, I hear the revving of an engine coming up the side of the mountain.

"Philip is here," I groan.

"No. I'm so tired."

I laugh. "Sorry. You can sleep as long as you want when we get home."

She lifts her head to look at me. Her hair is a mess, but it looks cute. "Will you be joining me?"

"I might be able to arrange something," I say.

I scoot from under the folded sleeping bag that barely covered us. All night, we held each other, keeping the other warm. It had to have gotten down into the forties, and it's not much warmer now.

"I'm going to climb over you so I can meet him. You can stay here until it's time to leave. Okay?"

She nods, and I roll on top of her, holding myself above her, but I don't expect her thighs to part as I position myself between her legs. She arches up into me.

"You're a bad fucking girl." I shake my head, knowing exactly what she's doing. *Testing me.*

"You have *no* idea," she says.

I press my cock against her, bringing my mouth down to her ear. "Now, who's playing with fire?"

She wraps her arms around my neck and brings my ear to her mouth. "Still you."

"Remember, I wrote the rulebook for these games." I look into her eyes, our mouths so fucking close that I could kiss her, like last night. But so far, I've let her decide where this goes. I haven't initiated shit; it's why I don't know if she's really anti-love.

Her mouth says one thing, but her body says another.

Instead of kissing her, I keep my boundaries and use every bit of willpower I have to continue crawling over her body. I unzip the flap and check my shoes for spiders, sliding them on.

The morning air is brisk, and when I breathe, my breath comes out like smoke. Lexi slides into the sleeping bag and lies flat on her back in a tent that was never meant for two people, especially not someone my height.

"I'll wait here," she says, smiling.

"Okay," I say, adjusting myself as I stand and take a mental picture of her.

Hot coals still glow from last night, and I sit in the chair and try to enjoy the sunrise even though it's cold.

The sky bursts into pinks and purples as fog floats in the valley below. I search the area for early morning wildlife, but don't see anything. I'm sure the sound of the engine revving up the mountain scared them away.

Fifteen minutes later, a lifted truck on off-roading tires comes into view and parks behind the Jeep. Philip gets out and walks over to me.

He's my height, and he's known as the playboy cowboy. We met at Harvard, and his family owns cattle ranches in Wyoming. After graduating, he moved back to help with operations. We've kept in touch over the years, and sometimes, we catch up when I'm in town.

Philip greets me with a cocky grin, giving me a firm handshake. "Decided to camp?"

"No, the battery is dead, and I didn't have cell service," I tell him. "I should kick your ass."

"You should be saying *thank you*. After staring at conference room walls all year, being outside is good for ya." He looks around. "I thought you brought someone with you?"

I point at the tent.

He bursts into laughter. "Did you sleep in there … *together?*"

I'm not amused.

"Yes, we did," Lexi says from inside the tent. The flap unzips, and she checks her shoes before putting them on. She stands and smiles as she smooths her dark hair down.

He places his hand over his heart. "Um, *hello*."

"Hi," she says. "Morning."

"Good morning, gorgeous. One question: why are you with him? Blink three times if you need me to rescue you."

She stares him down. "Oh, I *chose* Easton."

No words come out of his mouth.

"Well, Lexi, you've officially stunned him speechless, which *never* happens."

"Did it hurt?" he asks.

She tilts her head at him.

"When you fell from Heaven?"

"Okay, stop flirting with my future wife," I say, patting him on the shoulder.

He grins. "I don't see a ring on that finger yet."

"Keyword is *yet*," Lexi says, wiggling her ring finger, then glances over at me. "But very soon."

She's not acting. She's aware of the timeline and how things will move fast. Getting to know her on a personal level before we make it official is necessary.

Alexis clears her throat. "Anyone have a she-wee handy?"

I glance at her. "A what?"

"You know what? Never mind. Can I have the bear spray, please?" she asks.

"That's expired," Philip says.

"It's better than nothing," I tell him, grabbing it from the camping chair and handing it to her.

Lexi heads into the woods.

"Hey, bear!" she yells, her voice echoing as she claps.

Philip turns back to me. "Some of us have all the luck in life. I wish I knew how you do it," he says. "Speaking of, how's your sister?"

"Still off-limits to you," I say, crossing my arms over my chest.

Philip smirks as Lexi rejoins us.

He glances between us, grinning. "Let's try to jump this thing so you two lovebirds can be on your way."

I don't have to pretend in front of people. Wanting her close to me comes naturally; wanting everyone to know she's mine is instinct.

After last night and this morning, we're in a weird limbo; some might even call it purgatory. But I'll be patient, and I can wait until day fifteen to make sure I'm not going to fuck this up.

"Let's pick everything up," Lexi says, pulling the sleeping bag from the tent.

She rolls the mattress pad, and it only takes a few minutes to take down the tent. We load everything in the back as Philip douses the coals. It doesn't take long for the Jeep to start, and we climb inside.

"I'll follow you down," Philip says, removing his jacket and handing it to Lexi.

"Oh my God. Thank you," she says, sliding her arms into it with a smile.

"Thanks, man. See you at the bottom," I tell him, flipping the heat on high and clicking on the seat warmers. Even though the top is off, it helps some.

Lexi leans her head back against the seat, smiling. "I have a hangover."

"I do too. It's why I don't drink shit like that," I admit, keeping my grip on the steering wheel, taking it at a steady speed.

By the time we make it down, the sun is up and the temperature has risen, but it's still below fifty. It looks like it will be another beautiful day. Lexi returns Philip's jacket and I give him a handshake.

"I hope to see you two again," he says.

"You will," Lexi confirms, grabbing my hand.

"Hot damn," Philip says, grinning.

I give him a wave as we turn to the helicopter.

When we're back at my place, I brew coffee, and my phone rings.

Lexis sits at the breakfast nook, and I answer.

"I've been trying to call you since yesterday," Weston snaps.

"I'm on vacation," I remind him.

"I understand, but this is important. Remember how I told you I would review the contracts again?"

"Yes," I say. "Did you find something useful?"

"No other loopholes." He releases a breath.

"Okay. What's the fucking point of this call?" I pull two mugs from the cabinet.

"I found another clause. In a roundabout way, without all the legal jargon, it states that if fraud has been committed to take control of the business, the party responsible will lose all stakes in the company and inheritances."

"Of course," I whisper. "Somehow, I knew it wouldn't be this easy. I think it will be okay."

"Oh, I'm not concerned. I've seen the two of you together, but I know Derrick is up to something. I'm watching him, so be prepared for anything. I'll talk to you soon."

"Okay. Thanks for the warning," I say, and he ends the call.

I shove my phone back into my pocket. After filling two mugs, I set one in front of Lexi and take the stool next to her.

"I need a shower." She lifts her hair and smells it.

"Fuck, me too," I say while my coffee cools down.

When I glance at her, she's picture-perfect with her hand on the mug, blowing to cool off the steaming hot liquid. A small smile touches my lips as I pull the notebook and pen from my pocket and set it on the counter.

"Shall I pose?"

When I turn to the next blank page, she holds her fingers under her chin.

"I could draw you from memory, darling." I smile, and she looks at me over the mug's rim.

She reaches for her phone and turns it on as I start my sketch. Nonstop messages feed through, and I watch her expression change from happy to frustrated as I draw her.

"Everything okay?"

Her nostrils flare.

"Alexis," I say, grabbing her attention.

"It's begun." She flips her phone around and shows me the headline of an article.

ALEXIS MATTHEWS AND EASTON CALLOWAY.

NEW HOT COUPLE OR FAKE RELATIONSHIP?

"Who sent you this?"

"Carlee," she whispers. "She keeps up with it."

"Let me guess. They wrote about your upbringing, where you went to college, and how we met?"

Her eyes scan over it. "And they interviewed my ex."

"And what did he have to say?" My jaw clenches.

She already has trust issues because of him. *Fuck him.*

"He gave a *shit sandwich* comment. He started by saying I was a loving and caring partner. And anyone would be lucky to have me."

"That's true."

"And then ..." She shakes her head, her jaw clenching.

I unlock my phone, find the article, and wait for it to load. I don't typically scout this shit out. Weston tells me what I need to know because our image is essential. That's why it was so devastating when his divorce was announced to the world because he wanted it to stay private.

I read the headline and continue down the page. When Lexi

finishes reading it, she locks her phone and puts it on the counter. She's mad. Hell, I am too.

Alexis is a kind and caring partner. We've known each other since we were thirteen, and we often discussed marriage. I don't see her ever being with a man like Easton Calloway. He's not her type.

At the bottom, it ends with:

People who have known Alexis Matthews since she was a child aren't convinced this relationship is legitimate.

"I'm sorry."

"I can't believe he said we'd planned to get married. He failed to mention he was a cheating bastard. He has no idea what he's talking about." She scoffs.

"Do you agree with him?"

"Not what he said about *you*," she says, her green eyes meeting mine. "Ten out of five," she whispers the rating that she gave me before any of this was released.

It's music to my fucking ears.

She picks up her phone and texts someone.

I focus back on my drawing as she flips her hair over to one side with frustration.

"I cannot believe these people went all the way to Valentine and all they could dig up was my shitty, cheating ex who lives in the next town over. People in my hometown are like one big family, and they'll protect me from outside gossip. But outside of town, I'm fair game." She shakes her head. "It's a blessing and a curse."

I smile. "We should visit."

She searches my face. "Have you lost your mind?"

"Do you trust me?"

She nods. "You never *welcome* a vampire inside. Ever heard that? They'll meddle."

"We'll leave tomorrow."

She takes a drink of her coffee. Steam still rises from the top. "Do you think it's necessary?"

"Yes. Weston reviewed the contracts again. If committee members suspect I'm committing fraud, I will lose my promotion *and* inheritance," I explain. "We need to squash doubts. Control the narrative."

She glances at me. "You could lose it all, Easton."

"I'm betting on us with everything I have. It's a gamble, but my intuition about situations or people is always right. When it comes to us, I have no doubts."

Something is sizzling between us; it might take her a year to see that, but I have time. And in the end, maybe I'll have everything I want.

The silence drags on.

"Your confidence about visiting does it for me," she says. "We'll leave tomorrow then."

I pull my wallet from my pocket, pluck out a black aluminum credit card, and slide it across the counter toward her. "This is yours."

"Really?" She looks down at it in her hand. Her name is etched across the front in a shiny gold font.

"Buy whatever you want. There's no limit," I explain.

"On the card or for me?"

"Both. I have more money than you could spend in five lifetimes. Purchase whatever you want, darling."

She taps it against the counter and flips it around. "A month ago, I'd have said this would fix everything. I realize that's not true."

"Over the years, many people have said they'd be happy if they had my money. It doesn't solve the problems here." I pat my heart.

She sighs. "I'm learning that."

"What can I do to help?" I ask, smoothing my hand over the page and placing the ball of my pen where I left off.

"Help me repair a broken heart." She finishes the rest of her coffee.

"Ahh, only *time* can do that." I meet her gaze. "But I'm working on it. Trying to convince someone they're worthy first."

"Well. *Good luck,*" she tells me with a smile.

It's the anti-love coming out to play, the self-doubt her past relationships have created.

"Thanks. I'll fucking need it."

25

LEXI

As the plane touches down on the private runway, I feel sick.

"Are you okay?" Easton asks, interlocking his fingers with mine and kissing my knuckles.

"I'm nervous. It's not something I experience often."

"It's home though. Your stomping grounds."

"It is. But I left for a reason, and I had something to prove. Now, I'm back to flaunt my man?" I shake my head. "It seems *ridiculous*."

"You're not flaunting anything. I'm meeting your family before I propose. I'll ask your mother and brothers for permission and get to know those closest to you."

I search his face. "Do you have a death wish?"

"Some would say I do. But also, it's Southern tradition, isn't it?" He chuckles.

"Yes. Of course."

"I want to give you a full *ten out of five* experience, considering you're providing that for me."

I shake my head, but I'm smiling. I think about my dad, how he'd have adored Easton and his love for vintage cars. Dad probably would've threatened him to treat his little girl right. Not that Easton even needs the warning. He's been the perfect gentleman—other than him getting me fired, but I've forgiven him for that.

"I just want people to like you. What if this makes things worse?"

"They'll *love* me. Believe it or not, I can be charming. Together, we're unstoppable, babe." He laughs. "Oh, I almost forgot to mention that Weston has set up a private meeting with Mayor Martinez at the end of the week."

"Why?" My mouth falls open.

"I've decided to make a generous donation to Valentine for you, my darling. We're discussing where the funds will be assigned. I'd love for you to help with the decision-making, unless you'd prefer not to be involved."

I blink at him in disbelief. "Easton, that's amazing, but you don't have to do that."

"I know. However, it's being done anonymously, so no unwanted attention is brought to us or you."

"Right." I chuckle. "They'll know it was you after we visit."

"Speculation."

We deplane, and our luggage is loaded into the limo waiting for us.

I stop walking. "We're showing up in that? Shall we call the chief of police to give us an escort into town?"

"Too much?" he asks, watching me.

"Yes," I whisper. "I'd like *no* attention. We'll have enough to deal with already."

The driver stares at us, holding the door open, waiting for me to climb inside.

Easton doesn't move. Instead, he turns to the driver. "I'd like a different vehicle, please. No limo. Nothing extravagant."

He snaps the professional on. "Yes, Mr. Calloway. I'll send

another driver. Will an SUV be sufficient, or would you prefer something else?"

Easton waits for me to speak, letting me answer.

"That would be great," I say, smiling at the man.

He gives me a nod and unloads our luggage. Easton tips him, and the car drives away.

"I'm sorry," I whisper, knowing this will slow us down.

We're led to the private hangar as the crew scrambles around us.

"I've inconvenienced everyone."

"Please don't apologize." His voice is silky smooth. He places his strong hand on the small of my back and meets my eyes. "You are *never* an inconvenience, Lexi. I want you to be comfortable. Your boundaries, wants, and needs are important to me. At times, I'm out of touch. You bringing me back to reality is welcome and appreciated at any time of the day."

His phone vibrates in his pocket, but he doesn't answer. He's focused on me and our conversation. I like being the center of his attention.

"I mean it."

"Thank you," I say, relaxing. "Thanks for caring and not being upset. Most men—"

"I'm *not* most men." He tilts his head, giving me a half smile. "Also, I'd *never* be upset with you over something so … *trivial. You* being *you* is what I want and appreciate. Honesty is the best policy, consequences be damned. Speak up if it happens again, okay?"

I nod and wrap my arms around him. He pulls me into a hug, breathing in my hair as I inhale him. We stay like this for a few minutes, and I don't want to let him go, not when it comes so easily. Many don't make eye contact with us, but I know they're watching, but I'm not doing it for them.

Fifteen minutes later, a dark SUV with blacked-out windows arrives.

Easton leans close. "Is this okay? If not, say the word. I can do this with you all night. No fucks given."

"It's perfect," I say with a laugh, relaxing.

Then, we force ourselves away from one another.

Easton walks to the door and opens it for me. When I'm settled, he joins me on the other side. Once I'm buckled, I reach for Easton's hand, and he takes mine. I like how his thumb rubs across mine; it's a simple reminder that he's there and we're doing this together.

The front passenger door opens and closes and my eyes widen when I see Brody in his typical garb.

"There you are." I smile, leaning forward. "I kind of missed seeing you. What have you been up to over the past few days?"

Brody shakes his head but ignores me, per usual. It's to be expected.

Easton clears his throat. "Are you two friends now?"

"Yeah, he hung out with Carlee and me in our apartment. Even offered him a beer while he was hanging out." I smirk, knowing he made me lose a hundred bucks.

"Excuse me?" Easton's brows furrow.

"Oh, yeah. He didn't tell you?" I squeeze Easton's hand. "I also learned he's your cousin and a dickwad, like you."

Laughter falls from Easton's perfect lips and he grins. "And what else did he share with you?"

Brody chuckles, but doesn't say anything.

"That was about it."

I don't mention anything else we discussed. It will be our secret.

The driver climbs in, and we exit the airport.

I glance at Easton as we leave.

"I still expect the answer to my question in two days. I haven't forgotten, my little heartbreaker," he says.

I'm brought back to being in the tent, when he asked me if I was genuinely anti-love.

Right now, I don't know.

The answer should be *yes*, without hesitation.

However, this man has somehow burrowed himself under my skin and is swimming through my blood like poison, destroying all my opinions about love.

"Kinda feels like we're counting down to the new year," I say.

"In a way, we are."

"So, today is your lucky number day?"

He nods. "Yep. Thirteen."

"Should I expect a cheeseburger and a breakup text soon?"

Brody coughs to cover up his laughter.

Of course he knows.

He's probably witnessed each time Easton ate alone at Frankie's.

"Still to be determined," Easton says, smirking.

I playfully roll my eyes.

We drive several hours to Valentine, and Easton is on his phone the entire time.

It's late afternoon, and most shops on Main Street are still open. In the summer, they usually stay open later, thanks to the tourists who frequent Big Bend National Park and the observatory on Mount Locke. Things slow down in the winter, except in December, when the town transforms into a place one would find in a snow globe.

As we pass the bookstore, newspaper office, diner, and grocery store, heads turn. Maybe the SUV is too much.

"Fuck," Easton whispers, focusing out the front windshield. "Paps are already here."

Only then do I see them with the long-lens cameras, like they were waiting for us. I dip down in my seat, not allowing them to take a photo of me from the front windshield.

"I'm sorry," Easton whispers.

"It comes with the territory," I say, smiling. "No worries."

He nods as we continue out of town and travel down the

long, winding road, where most of the family ranches are in the area.

"Are we going to my parents' place now?" I ask, unsure if I'm prepared to face my mother so soon.

I haven't asked about our plans since it happened so fast, which might have been a mistake.

"We're staying at the bed-and-breakfast at Horseshoe Creek Ranch. I booked it for four nights. We'll fly back to New York on Sunday."

My mouth falls open. "My best friend growing up works there."

"Remi? Why are you making that face?"

It's shock.

"Because she knows me *better than* Carlee."

"This will be very interesting. I look forward to speaking with her."

"I already told her about you."

He smirks. "Even better."

Remi is three years younger than me, but we became fast friends when we were kids, after I spilled purple juice on her favorite T-shirt. Bad first impressions have followed me since I was a kid. She was the valedictorian of her class, intelligent beyond her years, and loved to read too. Not to mention, her family founded the town, which is their namesake. Everyone knows the Valentine family. They're small-town royalty.

I laugh. "Actually, I think she's having a barn birthday party this weekend. It's on the same property as the B & B."

"A barn party?" He's confused.

"It's better than a pasture party, especially if it starts raining. That way, there's shelter." I try to hide laughter because he has no idea what I'm talking about.

"You're bluffing," he states.

"I'm not. We should attend though. Her brothers, Beckett and Harrison, always host unforgettable parties. You might get the full Southern experience while you're here. By the end, maybe you'll be wearing Wranglers and saying *y'all* and *yeehaw*."

"And maybe you'll be saying *I do*."

"Still waiting for that ring," I say, shooting him a wink as my heart beats harder when he tries to hold back a smile.

Eventually, the SUV slows and turns into Horseshoe Creek Ranch's long rock driveway.

The farmhouse sits in the distance against the backsplash of the fading sun on hundreds of acres of land. Summer Jones and Beckett Valentine renovated the house last year and transformed it into a bed-and-breakfast. Summer is my age and Beckett is a few years older. They fell madly in love after nearly fist fighting one another for this property. In the end, they both won, because they fell in love, are engaged, and now share the ranch.

It's still light enough outside to see all the new structures on the ranch, mainly Valentine Veterinary Clinic and the stables and the horse training facility that's set far behind the house.

When the SUV parks in front of the house, I become more nervous than I was when we landed.

I didn't tell anyone I was visiting Valentine, not even my family. I'm working on my surprise skills, but considering I'm here to prove my temporary marriage is legitimate, this could be a mistake.

Easton opens my door and holds out his hand for me. We walk up the wide steps together, and my eyes wander over the flowers. I'm impressed.

Summer, the owner of the B & B and a friend, must've hired someone to keep them alive in this heat. It's known around town that she has a brown thumb and can't keep a plant alive to save her life. Seeing the purple and pink wildflowers makes me happy.

Easton opens the screen door and steps aside, allowing me to enter first. It smells like homemade chocolate chip cookies and freshly brewed coffee. We move through the common area toward the front desk that's set off to the side.

The last time I was inside was during the grand opening almost a year ago. The place is typically booked, especially during this time, so I'm curious how Easton pulled it off. I guess money talks.

I move toward the registration counter and don't see anyone around, so I ring the bell. I'm not sure if it will be Summer here or Remi.

DING. The noise is piercing.

I turn to look at Easton, and he shrugs, glancing around.

It's eerily quiet inside.

A few seconds later, Remi comes from the kitchen, carrying a plate of cookies, and her eyes widen. "Oh my goodness! What're you doin' here?"

"Surprise!" I say, and she hugs me tight. "Happy early birthday!"

She laughs and takes a step back, noticing Easton. Her eyes wander from his shoes to his suit pants; stark white button-up shirt, rolled to his elbows; over his tattoos; and up to his blue eyes and messy hair.

"Damn, you're *intimidating*," she says. "Wow."

I snicker because it's true, especially when he shows all the beautiful tattoos on his forearms.

"I've been told that on more than one occasion. I'm Easton Calloway. And you are?"

"Remington Valentine." She holds out her hand to give him a shake, and he takes it. She continues, "But call me Remi. Anyone who uses my full name gets punched in the dick." She gives him a sweet smile but holds up her fist.

"Noted. Well, it's very nice to meet you, Remi." He chuckles. "We'd like to check in, please."

She shakes her head; her ponytail swooshes. "I'm sorry, but I don't have a reservation in either of your names and we're currently booked until Sunday."

"It should be under Andrew Callo. It's an alias I use when I travel," he explains.

I turn to him. I didn't know he used aliases.

"Wow, you're the guy who rented the entire B & B through the weekend?" she continues.

Easton nods. "I like my privacy."

Remi lifts a brow, impressed. She moves behind the desk and types on the laptop. "I've got a note about that right here. No one will bother you, guaranteed. I'll pretend like you don't exist."

"That's appreciated," he states.

I'm brought back to being at the W and how everyone on the property knew not to disturb Mr. Calloway while he was there. Some things don't change.

Easton's cell rings, and he pulls it out of his pocket. He looks down at it before meeting my eyes. "I need to take this."

"Sure," I say, and he strolls to the sitting area and answers. His voice is low, so I can't hear what he's saying.

Remi leans across the desk, wearing a grin. "He's the one you texted me about, isn't he?"

"Yep. That's him, in the flesh."

I glance over my shoulder at all six foot two of him. He checks his watch and meets my eyes, as if I summoned his attention. A smile meets his lips, and he nods but continues his conversation. Electricity streams between us.

I'm doomed.

"You didn't say he looked like *that. My God.* I'm moving to New York."

"I know," I whisper, shaking my head. "I'm so screwed."

"I can tell." She waggles her brows at me as Brody enters through the front door. "Oh, who's he?"

"Brody, the bodyguard," I tell her, and she snickers.

She turns and grabs every key from a locked cabinet. "He rented all the rooms. Do you need all of these?"

"How did he pull it off?" I ask, looking down at ten physical keys on the counter.

She tilts her head. "He made an offer Summer couldn't refuse."

I shake my head. "I bet he did."

"But now that she and Beckett are expecting—"

"What? I didn't know. I bet she's so happy." Summer has always wanted a family. "Oh goodness, that means you're going to be an aunt. Congrats!"

She smiles. "Thanks. I'm excited about it, but Kinsley has already claimed the favorite aunt title."

It doesn't surprise me. Kinsley—Remi's older sister—is best friends with Summer.

She stops typing and her smile falters. "There are other things that have been going on though. Recently, I've noticed a lot of outsiders visiting."

"It's my fault," I whisper.

"I know. They offered me a hundred bucks to talk about you. I told them to get fucked though. So did Kinsley. Pretty much everyone has."

"Beau didn't," I admit.

Her eyes narrow. "What the fuck?"

Before I can say anything else, Easton and Brody join us.

I turn to him. "Here are our keys."

"Which goes to the suite?" Easton asks.

Remi sorts through them and holds the key up. "This one."

"And which room is farthest away from that one?" He meets her eyes and takes it.

She offers it to him, and Easton hands it to Brody, who places it in his pocket.

"Thank you. We don't need any others."

Remi chuckles. "I already like you."

This makes me beam. If Easton is Remi-approved, this will be easy.

In a way, she's a lot like Easton—introverted, very private, intelligent, and zero bullshit.

"And do we contact you if we need anything else?"

"I'll be here during the night shift today, tomorrow, and Friday. Summer will arrive in the morning around seven, and breakfast will be served at eight. She loves to make pancakes. Just eat them, okay? She's pregnant, and she'll cry at the drop of a hat if you refuse."

"I don't like pancakes," Easton states, and I elbow him in the stomach. "I'll learn to love them. Thank you, Remi." Then, he turns to me. "Ready to go to our room, darling?"

"Yes," I say and grab his hand.

"Thank you," I whisper to her over my shoulder.

She gives me a thumbs-up as we make our way to the narrow staircase, and he goes first.

The house is over a hundred years old, and some stairs squeak as we take them. Easton glances at me over his shoulder and grins. It's then I wish I could draw this moment.

As soon as we're on the top floor, he leads us to the room at the end of the hallway and unlocks the door. Easton steps inside and pulls me with him. Within one step, my back presses against the cool wood as he stands close.

One of his palms rests flat against the door, and his other lifts my chin, and I meet his eyes.

"So, was all the eye-fucking you did today real or fake?"

I smirk and lift my brows. "What do you think?"

He bends his head down closer to my ear. "I don't think I could handle it if I was wrong."

My breath hitches, and I grab his shirt, tugging him closer to me.

Mere inches from his mouth, I whisper, *"Real."*

26

EASTON

Birthday countdown: 33 days
Since meeting her: 13 days
Company takeover: 40 days

"Fuck, Lexi," I growl in her ear, knowing we're on a path of destruction together. "This wasn't supposed to happen."

"I know." Her soft lips trace the outside of mine as she holds on to my shirt. It's tight in her fists, but she doesn't have to force me, not when every fucking cell in my body pulls me toward her. "Are you going to kiss me?" she whispers, and it's desperate.

I smile against her lips. "Do you want me to?"

"Please."

Our lips crash together, and a hurricane of emotions floods through me. Her arms wrap around my neck, and the kiss deepens. Her tongue is greedy and tastes like the fruity champagne we drank on the way here. We're desperate, dangerous, and drunk on each other's touch.

"Are you just going to tease me every fucking day?" she asks, unbuttoning the top button of my shirt and quickly working on the next one. "I don't think I can take this for a year."

"Lexi," I whisper. I want to ask her if she's changed her mind about giving love a chance.

"I can't make any promises, Easton," she says, reading my thoughts. "That's my truth."

"All I need is confirmation that *we* have a chance," I say. It might be cocky as fuck, but I know if there's a possibility for us, I could have her.

She continues working on my buttons, but those angel eyes lock in on mine.

She nods and smirks. "Yes."

"That's all I fucking need, my little heartbreaker."

I gently grab her wrists, holding them above her head, pinning her to the door as my mouth memorizes the soft skin of her neck. I slide my lips across her jaw and to her hot, greedy mouth.

"We haven't made it to day fifteen yet," she mutters, her breasts rising and falling with each ragged breath.

I love the way her sweet skin tastes. "It won't change the way I feel."

She laughs, her stance straightening. "You're sure?"

"Positive." I let her loose, my fingers trailing down her arms. I gently cup her gorgeous face, hoping she knows how raw I'm being. This is *real* to me. The need, the want, and the fire burning between us are almost too much.

"I don't know how I'll get over you," she admits, wrapping her arms around my neck and pulling me in for another kiss.

"Then, don't," I say. "Go with the goddamn flow."

She places her hands on my stomach, guiding me toward the bed. Instead of falling back, I sit on the edge, pulling her toward me. My cock is so fucking hard; it might bust the seams of my pants. She glances down at it and swallows hard.

"Scared?" I lift a brow.

"Fuck no. I'm ready," she admits, wrapping my tie around her hand, pulling me toward her. She breathes into my ear, "Do you beg?"

I smirk. "*Never.*"

"Mmm. German shepherd energy," she mutters, capturing my lips. "My favorite."

Lexi removes my tie and finishes taking off my shirt. Her fingers run down my shoulders and she peppers kisses across my skin, climbing onto my lap and straddling me. She rocks against me, her ass tightening as I hold her steady against my chest.

"Worshipable," I whisper, meeting her gaze. "You drive me insane."

"You're just as guilty," she admits, pushing me back on the bed.

"So beautiful."

"When you say things like that …"

"I mean it," I confirm.

My hands slide under her shirt, holding her waist, and she pulls her T-shirt over her head.

She tosses it to the floor before reaching behind her back and unsnapping her bra.

The sun sets in the distance, and the room glows golden as I memorize how her hair and eyes shine. Timeless beauty. This woman quickly stumbled into my life and grabbed my heart before she fell.

Lexi leans forward, unbuckling my belt, watching me.

"You feel so good," she whispers, grinding harder against me.

The only thing between us right now is our clothes. I groan, licking my lips. She bends down, kissing me, running her fingers through my hair.

"Please tell me you packed condoms," she whispers.

I sigh. "*No.*"

She groans, chewing on the edge of her lip. "*Why not?*"

"Because that would have been presumptuous."

"It's called being prepared, Easton. But I guess there are other ways," she says, kissing down my chest.

Then, she unzips my suit pants, reaching inside my boxers to grab me.

Her breath hitches when her small hand wraps around my girth. "Okay, *now*, I'm scared."

I laugh out loud and she smiles, keeping her grip on me, stroking.

"Fuck," I growl, not wanting to take my gaze from her.

"May I?" She licks her lips and I place my hands behind my head, watching her.

"Mmm. Using manners like a *good girl*," I say, and she holds back a grin.

As she pulls my cock out, ready to take me in her hot mouth, a hard knock at the door rings out.

"You've got to be fucking kidding me," I hiss, frustrated.

It scares the shit out of Lexi, and she looks at me with wide eyes before placing her finger over her mouth. We're desperate for each other, breathing heavily, needy, and whoever that is needs to go the fuck away.

"*Open up*!" I hear in a deep voice that sounds oddly like my brother.

"Weston?" Lexi whispers, studying me.

"Hello?" my brother asks. "I know you're in there."

The haze we were in quickly vanishes.

"Excuse me?" I say, fucking livid as I tuck my cock back into my boxers and pull up my pants.

"I came to say surprise!" he says, leaning closer to the crack of the door. "What are you two *doing* in there?"

"Fuck off!" I yell as Lexi slides off the bed and grabs her bra and shirt.

She quickly dresses, walks toward the door, and unlocks it.

I can't say the word *don't* before she's cracking it. I adjust myself and stand as my brother pushes it open, looking around the place, wearing a shit-eating grin.

"I told you I wouldn't let you visit Texas without me," he says, smirking with his brow arched. He shoves his hands in his pockets, glancing between us. "*Oh,* did I interrupt something?"

Lexi glares at him like she might murder him. Her hair is messy on her head and her lips are swollen. There are no doubts about what was happening.

Guilt covers us.

"*Get. The. Fuck. Out,*" I bark, crossing my arms over my bare chest, jaw locked, ready to fight.

"Just know, I bet on you two," he says, and I remember he placed wagers.

"Weston," I growl.

"Okay, well, before I go …" he says, pulling something from his pocket and tossing it toward me. When I catch it, I glance down at the keys, noticing the snake on it. "Thought you might need this."

The door shuts.

Lexi looks down at my hand. "What is that?"

I hold them up. "Keys."

She tilts her head, rushing to the window. I join her and see outside sits the white Mustang Shelby Cobra, and Remi stares at it with amazement. Alexis opens the window.

"Are you kidding me?" Remi yells. "This is … oh my God!"

Lexi laughs, and I place my hand on her ass as she leans over to chat. "I drove it."

"No way. Let me, *please.*"

I shake my head and speak loud enough for Remi to hear. "Absolutely not."

"You'll have to ask his brother. He's the only one who gives the keys away."

"He's a dick," I mutter.

"Brother?" Remi asks as Weston steps off the porch, walking toward her. "Twins. I knew it. You seemed … *different*."

"She has a twin brother," Lexi says.

"Ahh, she's lucky he can't pose as her."

As Weston chats with Remi, Lexi turns to me. "You gonna tell me what it means now?"

I move forward, place my palm against her cheek, and brush my thumb across it. "That I'm falling in love."

Her lips turn into a smile, as if she knows my truth. It's like nothing else in the world fucking matters.

All consequences be damned.

I'm not reckless, but I'm willingly risking it all for a chance with this woman.

27

LEXI

I shut the window and turn to Easton. My eyes slide up and down his body. He looks like a daydream, a wild fantasy of mine.

He sighs heavily, pulls me toward him, and rests his hand around my waist. "I'm sorry."

"Not your fault." I slide my lips across his because it feels so right.

"I blame *you* for this." He chuckles.

"Why?" I pull away.

"Because your timing is always *shit*," he says.

My head falls back on my shoulders and I can't hide the laughter. "That's true. But it's about the chase, isn't it? Guess you'll have to be patient."

He leans forward, capturing my earlobe in his mouth. Then he whispers, "I'd wait a lifetime for you."

"Are you even real?" I ask.

My fingers thread through his hair as his teeth nibble against my skin, and goose bumps trail over my body as he kisses me.

Butterflies swarm inside my belly and I desperately gasp. I can't believe this man could be mine.

"As far as I know," he says. "Do I feel real?"

"Yes."

I'm not sure if my heart is ready for this. It's still shattered and not fully repaired, and I'm afraid Easton will be the one to break it, especially with that smile.

My stomach growls and he tilts his head. "Are you hungry?"

"Starving." I laugh. "Lost track of time, I guess."

"Seems to happen a lot. First food … then *dessert*."

Before he walks away, I grab his hand, pulling him back to me, my eyes trailing over his tattoos. I reach forward, tracing the outlines of the clouds on his shoulder. "Easton, wait. Did you draw these?"

His blue eyes sparkle. "You noticed?"

"It's your specific style," I say, walking around him, gazing at his left shoulder, noticing his ink tells a story across his chest and down his arms and back. "It's the big *life-changing* moments."

"Yes," he says breathlessly.

I steal a glance, my eyes trailing over him like he's living artwork, a gorgeous canvas of a man. As I study him, he doesn't take his gaze from me.

I move in front of him. "You're hiding your talent in plain sight."

"You're the *only* person who knows."

I paint my lips across his. "All your secrets are safe with me. Now, let's go eat some biscuits and gravy."

"Pass," he says. "Do they deliver?"

Laughter bursts out of me. "You're not in the city anymore, Dorothy."

"You'll learn everything is deliverable for the right price, my little heartbreaker."

"I guess. So, why is Weston here?" I ask curiously as I slide on my shoes.

"As a distraction. For us."

I smirk. "So, he'll pretend to be you?"

"No, but people will assume. And he won't let them think otherwise."

"He's your decoy?"

Easton nods. "When necessary."

I wake to an empty bed. For a brief moment, disappointment covers me like a warm blanket. I grab my phone and check the time. When I see it's nine a.m., I realize I slept in and missed breakfast.

I pull a pair of faded jeans with ripped knees and a Nirvana T-shirt from my suitcase, then slide on my Converse. After I brush my teeth and get dressed, I go downstairs.

I immediately run into Summer.

"Good morning," she says, pulling me into a tight hug. We're the same age, and we graduated high school together. "It's so good to see you. You're glowing."

"You too! Congrats on the pregnancy, ma'am. Remi told me. I'm happy for you."

She smiles. "Thank you. We're excited about it. Just praying it's *not* twins."

"Oh goodness, for your sake, I hope so too," I say, looking around, seeing if Easton is anywhere inside.

She lifts a brow. "He's on the back porch. Oh, and I think they ate all the pancakes, but I can make more if you'd like."

"No, no, it's fine. Thank you for everything."

She smiles. "I was relieved when Remi texted me yesterday and told me you were staying. I thought I would be dealing with an asshole through the weekend," she admits.

"Ah, yeah. You still are," I tell her with a laugh. "But he's calmed down. I think."

"Okay, well, I'll let you get to it." She shoos me away.

I open the back door and see the Calloway brothers sitting in rocking chairs next to one another. I move in front of them, crossing my arms over my chest, looking between them. They're wearing the same thing. Both of them smirking, mirror images of one another.

I take a step forward.

"Ah. Are you choosing correctly?" he asks with a clenched jaw.

"Don't want to embarrass anyone," the other says, sipping from a mug with a brow raised.

The fact that they are each wearing jeans, a black T-shirt, and a light-blue jacket that makes their eyes look like the sky doesn't help me any.

"Did you *plan* the twin thing today?"

Neither says a word, and this feels like a test, one I don't want to fail. Maybe I'm too confident in my decision, but I take a step forward, lean over, and place my lips inches from who I believe is Easton.

The real one *wouldn't* be able to handle this if I got it wrong, and when I don't hear any protest, I kiss him. Immediately, he kisses me back. His hand threads into my hair as he pulls me onto his lap.

"Please tell me I guessed right, or this is going to be embarrassing," I whisper with a laugh.

"You did," he says, brushing his fingers through my strands. "Did you sleep okay?"

I nod, knowing he held me until I fell asleep last night. By the time we ate, we were too tired to do anything but sleep. I felt safe with his strong arms wrapped around me.

Weston bursts into laughter. "Oh, so you know, for future reference, I'd stick my tongue in your mouth."

Easton's jaw clenches. "No, he wouldn't."

"He has no idea what I'd do." Weston sips his coffee, grinning as he stares forward at the pasture, where a few training horses are grazing.

I can tell he enjoys pushing Easton's buttons, but I know he has his brother's best interests in mind.

Always. That's indisputable.

I focus back on Easton. "How were your pancakes this morning?"

"I was polite," he tells me, grumbling. "*For you.*"

"Thank you," I say. "It's called Southern hospitality. You accept food, eat it, and say *thank you* with a smile."

"This will take some adjusting," he admits. "I'm accustomed to saying no and meaning it."

"Not while you're here," I say.

"Not when I'm with *you,*" he corrects.

"I like seeing you two like this," Weston says. "Don't even have to pretend."

Our heads snap toward him.

"So, when is the wedding?" he asks casually, rocking back and forth.

"Sometime within the next thirty-one days," Easton confirms. "Don't ask me again. I know you're keeping count."

Brody comes from around the house, steps onto the porch, and stretches. Sweat covers his shirt, and he's wearing athletic gear and running shoes. His muscles bulge out of his clothes, and I can't help but notice that his legs are covered in tattoos too.

"Okay, you're scary as hell," I say. "I think I do like having you as my bulky shadow."

I turn my focus back to Easton. "If we want to visit my mother today, we should probably get going. I believe she has a book club meeting tonight at five. Also, can we go alone?"

Easton tucks loose strands of hair behind my ear. "If that's what you want."

Weston snickers, and we ignore him.

"Brody, have fun hanging out with that one today," I say, pointing at Weston.

He shrugs, then grabs the handle of the screen door. "I'll be upstairs, showering."

I stand and pull Easton with me. "I'd like to take you around town first. Grab a mocha. Maybe we can visit the bookstore?"

"If it will make you happy."

"*Very* much."

"Consider it done. When would you like to leave?" He checks his watch.

"Now," I say. "I'd love to get the family stuff over with right after lunch."

"Let's do it," he tells me.

"Remember, the world is watching," Weston reminds us.

Easton shakes his head as we walk through the B & B. Summer is on the phone and gives us a wave as we exit out the front door.

I stand on the porch, looking at the car. "I can't believe it's here."

"I don't believe in serendipitous events, but—"

"So, you're letting me drive?"

He meets my eyes, taking a pause. When he lifts the keys and places them in my outstretched palm, I clamp my fingers around them and pause.

"Seriously? This isn't a cruel joke?"

"What do you think?" He smirks.

I jump into his arms, wrapping my arms around him. He holds me against him, lifting me with his strong hands under my ass as I kiss him. Carefully, he walks us toward the car.

"Thank you," I say.

He carefully sets me on the ground and opens the door for me. "Please don't make me regret this."

I place my hand on his shoulder. "I'll drive it like I stole it."

"I'd expect nothing less."

Then, I slide inside, sitting behind the red steering wheel with the cobra in the middle. I'm in the twilight zone, driving this car in Valentine. It's more like a dream come true.

Easton climbs into the passenger side, opens the glove compartment, and pulls out a pair of Ray-Bans.

"I think I'm having déjà vu," I tell him as he buckles.

He leans over, captures my lips with his, and smiles against my mouth. "I don't even fucking think so. Unless my brother kissed you."

"No, he didn't. He knew better."

I crank the engine, and it roars to life. I press the clutch, putting it into reverse. Rocks kick up when I give it gas, peeling out. The power beneath my hands is like nothing I've ever felt, and knowing what this car represents makes me smile. Weston chose it because he knows Easton better than anyone.

"She's a beast," I say, patting the red dashboard as dust trails in our wake.

We pass the veterinary clinic, and Cash Johnson—the owner and doctor—unloads bags from the back of his truck. He stops to watch the car in action. Hell, I would too.

"Already turning heads," Easton says, rolling down the window.

I do the same and hang my arm out the side.

We stop at the end of the driveway; I look both ways, and we take off down the winding mountain road. The smell of fresh air fills the car, and Easton's messy hair blows in the wind.

"Woohoo!" I scream out the window to nothing. No buildings. Just open land. And cows. And us.

I floor it, and soon, we're hugging curves, driving eighty miles per hour to town. The power under my hands, combined with the mean growl of the engine, puts a smile on my face. The only regret I have is not being able to show my father.

He'd have been as impressed as me, especially considering the significance of this model in muscle car history. The thought nearly takes hold of me, and I push the sadness away.

"Everything okay?" Easton asks, reaching over and squeezing my shoulder.

He *sees* me, and I appreciate how he notices me when most don't.

"Yeah. I was thinking about my dad. He'd have loved this car. Though I think he would've wanted to drive it."

"I'd have let him."

The thought warms my heart, considering I know how protective he is of his vehicles. Easton's eyes scan over the mountains. They're not as big and impressive as Grand Teton, but they are still beautiful. I steal glances as he removes his jacket and tosses it in the back seat.

"That should be illegal."

"Hmm?"

"You, dressed like that. No wonder you have a fan club."

He shakes his head.

"To think, until two weeks ago, I didn't know or care who *Easton Calloway* was."

"And now?"

I lick my lips. "I kinda don't want to share you with the world anymore."

He gives me a sly grin. "Relatable."

When we roll into town, people stare.

I park at the grocery store and glance at him. "You coming?"

"Sure," he tells me, and we get out. "What do you need?"

"It's not what *I* need; it's what *we* need," I whisper, walking to the pharmacy section in the back. I stand in front of the limited choices of condoms with my arms crossed. "What size?"

Easton's glasses cover his eyes, but I notice the ghost of a smile on his lips.

This amuses him.

"What would you guess?" He stands confidently.

I grab the extra-large ones, ribbed for *her* pleasure.

"Megapack," I say. "Think we can blow through thirty?"

"In a night?" he quips with a half grin.

We walk to the front. His hand rests on my hip as we wait at the end of the line.

"Self-checkout isn't an option?" he whispers.

"No one would be in your business if it were," I tell him over my shoulder as I set the box on the conveyor belt.

"Well, hello, Alexis," Mrs. Ballard, the clerk, says. Then, she glances down at the massive box of condoms and scans them. Her brows lift. "This all?"

"Oh, one more thing," I say, grabbing a few candy bars. "In case I get hungry."

When she gives the total, Easton steps forward, sliding his card. He gives her a smile and a nod, and I think I see her have heart palpitations. As I look around the small space, I realize *all* eyes are on us. We are center stage right now.

"We don't need a bag," I say, and she hands me my goods and the receipt.

"Have a *nice* day," she offers.

"Thanks. I think I might," I tell her with a wink, tossing the box in the air as Easton follows me to the car.

We get inside and he glances my way. "You almost gave that woman a heart attack."

"No, Easton, you did." I place the key in the ignition and crank the engine.

"You realize there was a man with a camera across the street."

I grin. "Just giving them *all* something to talk about. They can report on that. Everyone in Valentine will know before lunch that I bought a box of extra-large condoms and two candy bars."

"And tomorrow, the world will know," he says.

"Are you embarrassed?" I ask, glancing at him before I reverse.

"Fuck no." He shakes his head like he's offended.

We drive the short distance and park in front of the coffee shop. We order two iced mochas while, once again, every single person stares at Easton. Then, we take a stroll to Main Street Books. Easton interlocks his fingers with mine and smiles at me.

"I like it here," he admits as we pass a beauty parlor and a real estate office. "It has charm."

"It's home. I miss it when I'm away. But I miss the city too."

"I get that," he tells me, pushing open the door to the bookstore.

The bell rings above, and moments later, Hayden Shaw, the owner's son, greets us. He's several years older than me, and he's engaged to Kinsley Valentine. He moved back to town last year and proposed to her on New Year's Eve.

"Hey, Alexis. You're popular around here these days," he says.

Easton flips his glasses on his head and Hayden smiles at him.

"Hayden Shaw," he says, holding out his hand.

"Easton Calloway."

They give each other a firm handshake.

"It's Lexi," I correct as Easton places his hand on my shoulder, rubbing his thumb across my back. I love having him close. "Call me Alexis again, and I will kick your ass, Shaw," I threaten.

Hayden chuckles. "Right. Apologies, *Lexi*. What brings you two in here today?"

"Do you have any Kama Sutra books in stock?" I ask.

Easton chuckles and shakes his head.

Hayden walks past me, leads us down a long aisle, then points at the shelf. "Here ya go."

"Thanks," I say, examining the small selection.

"I know what you're doing," Easton says, leaning against one of the shelves.

I trail my finger across the titles. "And?"

"You're feeding the beast. Pregnancy rumors will spread next."

"That's going to happen anyway," I admit, pulling a few from the shelves. "What other reasons do people have to get married so quickly?"

He dips down, kissing me. "You're right. But you're fanning the fire."

"Let it burn," I tell him. "I think these should do."

"Beginner, intermediate, and advanced Kama books. Anything else?" he asks.

I nod. "Actually, yes. I want to browse the romance books."

"Lead the way," he says, following me across the store, carrying all three sex books in his hands.

When I was younger, I'd save my allowance to buy books I probably shouldn't have read. I always found Kinsley in here too.

Easton gives me space, watching me as my eyes scan the bright-colored covers that draw attention. I pull a few from the shelves, read each back cover, and slide them back in place.

Easton pulls the ones I picked up and adds them to the stack in his arms. "Any others?"

"What if I wanted them all?" I say, my hand running from the top of the shelf to the bottom.

"Done," he says.

"No, no, I'm kidding, Easton. You'll never see me again if you buy these books. Seriously."

I pluck a few others and add them to the growing stack he's holding in his arms. "Anything you want?"

"Just you," he mutters.

"You've got me," I tell him.

"For one year," he whispers.

When our eyes meet, I can almost imagine the life we could share. I try to push the thoughts away, but they take hold, digging roots deep into my soul. My dad always told me when I found the man I was supposed to be with, I'd know. I thought that man was Beau. But as I look at Easton, the feeling is different. It's intense, beautiful, dangerous, overwhelming … and I want to be irrational with him.

I swallow down the lump in my throat and take a mental snapshot of him like that—tattoos on display, holding a stack of sex and romance books. I understand why so many have turned him into a thirst trap. It's too easy.

I smile, hoping I never forget this image of him, exactly like this, with the sunlight shining through the store's front windows, his eyes softly watching me.

"What?" he asks.

"About the year thing? That's still to be determined."

He reaches forward and places the back of his hand on my head. "No fever. Sure you're not sick?"

I roll my eyes. "I'll take it back then."

He wraps his free arm around me. "We'll see what happens."

After Easton pays, we make it to the car. He carries my bag of books with one hand and slides his other in the pocket of my jeans, holding me against him. I can't help but glance at him.

"The eye-fucking, *Alexis*," he says, but it comes out like a low growl.

He's the master at keeping his head on straight. But I can see behind his glasses that he's side-eyeing me.

I burst into laughter, tucking my hand into his back pocket. "For show."

"Bullshit," he mutters, smirking, pressing his fingertips into my ass, and those butterflies tingle. "I know better now."

I can't hold back my smile as we walk the few blocks to the car.

Easton sets the books in the back seat and opens the passenger door for me. "I'm driving now."

I hand him the keys with a laugh and get inside. "Only because I want you to have the experience."

He grabs my hand and places a kiss on the knuckles. "I'm in charge here."

"That's what you think." I give him a wink and grab the door handle, closing it.

He taps the roof before he runs around to the driver's side. After cranking it, he gently revs the engine before we take off.

"Do you know where you're going?" I ask.

"Yes," he says, shifting the car into fourth gear, hauling ass.

I look up at the clouds and the blue sky, floating my hand out the window. Fifteen minutes later, he's turning into my parents' driveway.

"You know, if you file for divorce, you'll have to deal with my mother," I warn.

"*If.* Nice word choice," he says, parking and turning off the car. "And I'll be happy to."

As Easton opens my door and I step out, I hear my mother saying my name.

"Alexis?" my mother says again.

I give her a warm smile as my nerves get the best of me.

"Hey, Mom! Surprise!"

She walks to the edge of the porch. The shock on her face is evident.

"I want you to meet someone, Mama. This is Easton Calloway. My boyfriend and the man I'm marrying," I say with Calloway confidence.

He grabs my hand and interlocks his fingers with mine. My mother notices, and I think I see her smile.

"Well, you two come inside and catch us all up," she says, leading the way.

"Us?"

"Your brothers and I were about to eat lunch."

"They're here?" I glance at the time on my phone. It's almost one. I thought they ate lunch each day at eleven.

"Yeah," she says. "They got caught up in the field today and arrived late. It's lucky timing that you're here."

Easton glances my way. He knows my timing is awful, which can only mean one thing—this might be a total disaster.

28

EASTON

Birthday countdown: 32 days
Since meeting her: 14 days
Company takeover: 39 days

Lexi's palm grows sweaty as we walk down the hallway that leads to the kitchen in the two-story farmhouse. It feels like home, a place that was full of love, growing up. I envy this.

She leads me toward the kitchen, and I stop to glance over the pictures on the wall, all hanging in different-sized frames. It's a collage of Lexi's life.

"Is this you?" I ask, pointing to one of the photos.

There's a little girl dressed in a red wig, center stage, with her arms spread wide. By the positioning of her mouth, she's singing.

She laughs. "Yes, I played Annie in the community theater's summer show. I guess the billionaire thing has been going on for a while."

Laughter escapes me. "You're terrible."

There are countless photos of Lexi performing throughout the year, along with high school and college graduation photos. I notice the sparkle in her eye and the happiness on her face, which is the same one I witness when she looks at me. Her brothers have just as many photos hung too. I can tell their parents are very proud.

"Come on. Let's get this over with, please," she urges, pulling me away.

When we enter the dining room, connected to the kitchen, her brothers put their forks down and stare at me. Then, they stand, and I realize they're both an inch taller and stacked with muscles. I'm not sure why I expected anything else.

Lexi instantly smiles and gives them both tight hugs.

"You stink," she tells one.

"What're you doing here?" the other asks.

"Surprise! I wanted you to meet my boyfriend," she says. "This is Easton Calloway."

Immediately, her brothers grin. I slightly relax.

"Must be serious if you both came all this way. I'm Brett," the one with dark hair says.

I take his hand, and we exchange an aggressive, firm handshake.

"I'm Chris," the blond says, nearly crushing my hand next.

I give him the same pressure but with a straight face. I'm immune to intimidation; however, the message is heard.

They return to their seats and their plates.

Lexi's mother tells us to sit. "Oh, and my name is Melissa, but everyone calls me Mom, especially the man my daughter will marry."

Both of her brothers stop chewing and glance at each other.

"What the fuck?" Brett asks.

Lexi holds up her hands as she pulls out her chair. "Don't."

"Are you pregnant?" Chris asks.

"No. Now, stop. Seriously. I'm nearly thirty years old, and I don't need this bullshit."

"Can we watch our language?" Her mother's voice is stern, but it softens. "Are you two hungry?"

"No thanks," Lexi says as her brothers continue arguing.

An ear-piercing whistle fills the room and everyone stops.

"I am getting married to this man, eventually. So, for once, can you please be happy for me and not ruin this? It's a moment I've been looking forward to since I was a little girl. I don't care about your opinions because this is what *I* want. You should be thrilled I even came here to introduce you. If it wasn't for Easton insisting we visit Valentine, you'd have gotten a FaceTime call."

It's silent for a few seconds.

I know how much truth is intertwined in her words.

"I miss Dad. He's the only one who would understand," she says, her voice cracking.

I grab her hand and squeeze it.

"We all miss your father." Her mother clears her throat, then moves to the fridge. She grabs two glasses from the cabinet and fills them with tea. "I'm happy you're here, sweetie. I knew this day would come, and I can tell you two care about each other."

She sets the glasses before us and gives her sons a stern look. "*Behave and remember your manners.*"

I can feel the tension building in the room, but it doesn't bother me.

"So, how did you two meet?" Brett asks as he takes a bite of potatoes.

"I stole his watch." Lexi laughs. "Then, he got me fired."

"I felt awful," I admit. "It was a misunderstanding."

Chris laughs. "Sounds like she deserved it."

"I didn't do it on purpose," Lexi stresses. "But it's neither here nor there. Afterward, we ran into each other randomly. It was a lot of serendipitous events, and I quickly realized how good we could be together."

"Sounds like love at first sight," her mother says.

"It was," Lexi agrees, squeezing my hand. "Which is also very weird."

"No," Chris offers. "Dad said he fell in love with Mom the first time he saw her. I don't think it's that unbelievable. It happens to some people."

Lexi smiles and sucks in a deep breath.

"So, you want to marry my sister?" Brett focuses on me.

I notice the tattoos on his arm. It's a Western theme with a cactus, mountains, and night sky.

"Yes," I say without any hesitation. "It would be my greatest honor to have Lexi as my wife. She makes me a better person," I say, meeting her eyes. "I wanted this conversation to be more private without her here, but—"

"My timing is shit," Lexi says. "It is what it is."

"If you're asking for my blessing, Easton, you have it," her mother says.

"Thank you, I appreciate that."

"Don't have ours though. Come back before dark, and we'll discuss it," Chris says. "Beside the house is a long dirt road leading to our horse barn."

"Can we not do this?" Lexi asks.

"I'll be there," I say, not intimidated.

Maybe Lexi's right though, and I should be. I don't know their capabilities, but I won't back down.

"We'll see you then," Brett tells me as they finish eating.

"Well, this was a *great* talk," Lexi says. I can hear the sarcasm in her voice. "Love you, Mom. I think we're gonna let y'all finish up and head out."

Lexi stands and pulls me with her.

"So soon?" her mother asks.

Lexi kisses her on the head. "Yeah. I won't be a stranger though."

"It was an honor meeting you all," I say, then glance at her brothers. "I'll see you soon."

Lexi drags me away.

When we're outside, she places her hands on top of her head and breathes out as she looks at the sky. A butterfly skirts by and she shakes her head. "That went terribly. They're going to haze you."

"Whatever it takes."

She turns to me with seriousness written on her face. "They won't play by any rules, Easton."

"I have a little sister. I understand how this works. I'm not concerned."

"You keep saying that," she says.

"Don't worry about me, okay?" I grab her cheeks in my hands. "Promise."

"I hope I don't have to say I told you so." She sighs.

I squeeze her shoulder. "Let's get out of here."

We take the long drive back to the bed-and-breakfast, not saying much to one another.

When I park, I turn to her. "You know I have to meet up with them tonight. I can't skip that."

"I know."

After we eat dinner at the B & B, I grab the keys to the car. "I'll be back."

Brody stands to go with me.

"No. I have to do this alone."

Weston meets my eyes. "Try to protect your face, for my sake."

"Oh, sure, I'll try to remember that," I say, shaking my head. "Like I'm concerned about our face."

Lexi walks with me outside, smelling like a fresh shower. We look up at the dark purple sky, and she hooks one of her fingers with mine.

I open the door, leaning against the car. "Any words of advice?"

"Stay quick on your toes," she says, sliding her mouth across mine. "And good luck."

I take the driveway onto her family ranch, then turn onto the dirt road her brother mentioned. My headlights lead the way. After I park, I get out of the car, cracking my knuckles. The lights are on in the barn, and I walk inside.

"Hello?" I yell.

"Out back," a deep voice says.

I make my way toward their laughter. A small fire is built, and five guys are sitting around it.

Brett and Chris stand, each giving me another bone-crushing handshake.

"Easton, this is Beckett and Harrison Valentine, and Hayden Shaw. They're some of our best friends. We planned a small get-together tonight and thought you'd like to join us," Brett says.

"I'm staying at Horseshoe Creek Ranch," I say to Beckett, knowing Summer mentioned they'd recently gotten married when she made us one hundred pancakes for breakfast.

"Ahh, yes." He smiles. "Harrison is my brother, and he works with me at the training facility behind the B & B. Hayden is supposed to marry my sister at some fucking point, but we're still waiting for that to happen."

"You were in the bookstore earlier today with Lexi, right?" Hayden asks.

"Yeah," I tell him, and they offer me a seat and a bottle of moonshine. I can't help but laugh. I'm sure this isn't what Lexi expected.

Harrison points to the bottle. "Be careful with that shit. You won't be able to drive if you have too much."

"Noted," I say, passing it to Hayden.

Another guy enters from inside the barn. "Hey," he says.

"This is Cash. He's a vet. Runs the clinic," Brett tells me.

"Ah, yes." I give him a nod, stand, and greet him. "I'm Easton. I'm dating Lexi."

"Oh yeah. I saw your car at the B & B. Nice ride."

"Thanks," I tell him.

Chris turns his attention back to me. "So, what do you do?"

Now I *wish* I had the booze, because if they're asking, they haven't researched me, which can be a good or bad thing, depending. "I'm in diamond sales."

"Damn," Harrison hisses. "Are you sure you want to marry their sister? I have a few you can choose from."

Beckett gives him a dirty look. I could see myself hanging out with them regularly—even if the cowboy hats and Wranglers are a culture shock.

"We have some business to take care of," Chris says, picking up two sets of boxing gloves.

"You don't want to do that," I explain, knowing I trained for ten years with a professional. It's not fair.

Harrison claps his hands together. "Oh, yeah, they do. I can't wait to watch you beat the fuck out of them though. They need their egos brought down to reality. I've got a hundred on Easton," he says, pulling cash out of his wallet and slamming it down on his leg.

Beckett shakes his head. "Hogties and threats work so much better."

"It's friendly sparring," Brett says as Chris hands me the extra gloves.

I remove my jacket and watch, rolling my wrists and neck before putting my hands inside the gloves.

Turning my head, I notice the large area roped off with twine.

The last thing I'll do is back down from this.

If I have to fight her brothers for permission, then let's fucking go.

We move to the area, and Chris slams his gloves together.

"Rules?" I ask.

He takes a swing, and I easily avoid it.

"No dick shots. All else is fair game. It's over when one of us falls or knocks the other out."

"Street rules, then?" I ask as he punches his fist forward again, missing.

"Are you fucking my little sister?" he growls, and that's when I see the anger behind his eyes.

"Not yet," I answer truthfully.

This time, he rushes at me, wearing his emotions on his sleeve. His fists fly, but I take two steps, avoiding his sloppy attack. The fact that Lexi was worried is comical.

"I'm serious about marrying her," I explain.

He removes his gloves, throwing them to the ground. His fists lift back into position.

"Street rules," he confirms, his chest rising and falling.

I take mine off too. "We can stop this right now. Seriously."

"Look, he's fucking scared," Chris boasts.

"I'm not," I say, my tone even as I shake my head.

All the guys surround our makeshift arena. I look over at Brett and he shrugs.

As I'm about to say something else, Chris's fist flies forward.

I quickly step, and my fist slams into his jaw. His head bounces back on his shoulders and he wavers.

"Just go down," I say.

"Fuck you, pretty boy."

I pop my knuckles, protecting my face and staying light on my feet. I study him, watch him, and predict his next move. I give a fake right swing and let out a left hook.

"Shit," Hayden whispers as I deliver one blow that a professional couldn't withstand.

Chris stumbles backward until he loses his balance and crashes to the ground.

Cash rushes to him to make sure he's okay.

"If you hurt my sister," he says, spitting blood as I look down at him.

"I'll give you permission to fuck me up if I do," I say.

Beckett pushes Brett forward. "Your turn to fight him."

Brett shakes his head. "I'm good. But I do have one question for you, Easton."

He stands in front of me, all muscle, as I look down at my swollen knuckles.

"Anything."

"Why Alexis?"

I meet his eyes. "Because I'm in love with her."

A grin fills his face, and he pats me on the back. "Right answer."

Chris moans and I offer my hand to pull him up. I think he might go for my face, but he pulls me into a hug instead.

"Treat her right."

"You have my word."

Cash hands me the moonshine and I take a swig as we sit by the fire and then pass it on. They talk about Valentine and their work on the ranch and even chat about their significant others.

Realizing my watch is still in my pocket, I pull it out and put it on. It's barely past nine thirty.

"I should probably make my way back," I say, standing.

"You're one of us now," Brett says, and I go around the group and give strong hugs. "Don't fuck this up."

"Don't plan on it," I tell him with a wave as I walk through the barn and back to the Mustang.

I drive back to the B & B with the windows down.

As soon as I enter, I go upstairs for Alexis, but our room is empty. So, I walk through the house, searching.

"I know where she is," Remi says with her feet kicked up on the counter.

She's reading a book, but I can't quite make out the title.

"Where?"

She sets the book down. "There's a trail that leads behind the B & B. Take the single track to the end and you'll arrive at a clearing. You'll find her there."

I smile. "She's alone?"

"Your clone and friend went to town for dinner."

"How?"

She smiles, pulling a wad of cash from her pocket. "I rented them my car."

"And what do you drive?"

"A Mustang GT."

I laugh. "That was a mistake."

"Why?" she asks as I walk toward the back door.

"My brother will drive the fuck out of it."

Her jaw clenches. "I made him promise he wouldn't."

"Trusting him was your first mistake. The second was not charging him more."

Her mouth transforms into a line. "I might kick his ass."

"I think you should." I give her a nod and make my way outside to find Lexi.

29

LEXI

I lie out on the blanket, looking up at the billions of stars that fill the night sky. I hear footsteps behind me and turn to see a figure stalking toward me, but I know that gait.

"Easton?" I whisper, and he stops at the edge of the blanket, looking down at me. "You survived my brothers."

"I did," he says. "However, Chris might have a concussion."

I shake my head. "What?"

He sits down next to me. The hint of a campfire and alcohol mixes with his cologne. "I told them I didn't want to fight. *They* insisted."

"Are you unscathed?"

"Other than my knuckles. I boxed professionally for over a decade. I explained it wasn't a fair fight. Violence is never the answer, but if I'm fighting for *you*, for *us* … well, they gave me no other options."

I fall back laughing. "This is *too* good. I've been telling them for years that they need to stop threatening people I go out with, that, one day, they'd get their asses kicked. I can't wait to give my brothers a *told ya so*."

Easton lies back and looks up at the stars with me. I grab his hand in mine, and our fingers interlock.

He turns his head toward me. "What are you doing out here, alone?"

The breeze blows slightly. It's magical under the sea of stars as fireflies dance in the distance. An orchestra of crickets accompanies the fluttering of the butterflies inside my stomach.

I smile, keeping my eyes upward, recalling the summer constellations twinkling in the diamond sky. "My dad always told me that if I was lost, the stars would guide me." I point up. "Polaris."

"True north," he says.

"Like the compass and star field on your arm and shoulder," I tell him.

"Of course you paid attention." He smiles, brushing his thumb over mine.

"Why that tattoo?"

"My true north is my intuition. It always leads me in the direction I should go. No matter what happens in my life, no one will ever be able to take that away from me. My fortunes and my position at the company might disappear, but I will always be me. It's why I'm not scared, because if I lose it all, I'll get it back."

"You won't lose it," I confirm.

"No one knows what will happen."

"All we have is now," I whisper.

"When I'm with you, I just want to live in the *right now,* Lexi. Not tomorrow. Not six months from now. Not next year. Right now. It's all we have. The future isn't guaranteed, and your life can change in in instant." He snaps his other fingers, and it rings out in the silence. "You're fucking proof of that. Two weeks ago … I could've never predicted I'd be here with you right now."

I think about everything that's happened. Two weeks ago, I

was sleeping on Carlee's couch and scrubbing porcelain toilets, wishing for a callback on a show I'd auditioned for. Now, I'm jet-setting across the country with this man, lying on a blanket at the Horseshoe Creek Ranch, viewing the stars.

"I've never thought about it like that."

"I never predicted you," he says, but a silent conversation takes place as we stare up.

"I didn't either," I admit. "Two weeks ago, had you asked me where I'd be, I would've never guessed this. So, point taken."

We don't say anything for a few seconds. I sit up, reaching for the bottle of Fireball Remi gave me when I told her I was coming out here. I take a big swig of it, then offer the bottle to Easton.

He shakes his head. "Not that shit again."

Laughter escapes me. "It's never done me wrong. The Milky Way will rise around midnight; I was going to stay here and wait for it. If you'd like to join me," I say.

"I'm not going anywhere. We'll ring in the new year together."

"Day fifteen," I whisper, placing my arm under my head. "So, about that breakup text in the morning?"

Easton rolls over onto his side, props himself up on his elbow, and focuses on me. "Would you like me to send one so you can have the full experience?"

"If you didn't *need* this marriage, would your decision be different?"

"You're not my last resort, Lexi. You're my first choice. Someone I'd marry and *not* divorce a year later."

I reach up and run my fingers through my hair. "It's the confidence for me."

"Sometimes, when you know, you fucking know. I'm waiting for you to catch up."

"I know." I pull his mouth close to mine.

"I've already told you once that I'd wait a lifetime. I meant it."

His hands run through my hair, and he tastes like spearmint and moonshine.

A whimper escapes me as his tongue massages against mine. We're greedy and desperate.

"Don't break my heart," he says, and it's more of a demand than a plea.

I lightly paint my lips against his. "I don't want to. But broken people break people. I know that," I whisper.

"I'll glue your heart together, piece by piece." He brushes his thumb across my cheek as he searches my face. "This is real for me."

"It's real for me too," I say, knowing it's just us. No cameras, no friends, no family, only the two of us, alone. And when it's us like this, it's when the line is blurred. "Please tell me you brought a condom," I say.

His forehead leans against mine. "*Fuck.*"

I laugh against his lips and lift my hips, pulling one from my back pocket. He gives me a shit-eating grin.

"Prepared," I say.

Our mouths gravitate toward one another and I run my hands up his black T-shirt, lifting it over his head.

"Or presumptuous," he mutters.

"You can't deny me," I say as I guide him onto his back, kissing down his strong jaw and his neck, tasting the salty sweat from today on his tattooed skin.

"You're right," he admits with a strangled breath as I continue down his muscular stomach.

A sexy smirk touches my lips as I reach for the button of his jeans and unzip them. He's bulging against the material, and I enjoy knowing I'm the reason.

I meet his eyes, capturing every second of his attention as he intensely watches me.

"You're a fucking masterpiece," he says, his hand on my jaw.

His thumb brushes across my bottom lip, and goosebumps trail across my body.

"Then, together, we'll be a collection." I hook my fingers in his jeans, tugging them down. After I rip open the condom, I slowly sheathe him, admiring the thick vein that trails up the side. "Mmm. Extra-large was a good guess."

He lifts a brow as I desperately wiggle out of my jeans and panties. Easton helps me with my T-shirt, and I reach behind me, removing my bra. I straddle him, not allowing him inside yet. He sits upright as I grab his face.

"I want you so fucking bad," I whisper, searching his eyes, knowing there is only forward motion from here.

"You're in control, Lexi," he says. "You have been since the beginning."

I lean my forehead against his. "No promises."

"Just chances," he confirms.

I realize we're both searching for the same thing—a chance. I close my eyes, slowly inching down on him. He grabs my hips as I thread my fingers through his messy hair, kissing him as our worlds collide together. A sigh escapes me when he fills me full, like we were made for each other.

We stay connected, allowing my body to adjust to how big he is as I let out several ragged breaths.

"Fuck," he hisses, cupping my ass with his strong palms as I gently rock my hips.

"It's not supposed to feel like this," I whisper, feeling as if Cupid struck me right in the heart with an arrow. Sex has never been like this; no, it's a deeper connection, something I can't explain.

"Maybe it is," he desperately says.

Easton wraps his arms around me, and he traces my collarbone with his lips, sucking and kissing between my breasts.

My pants fill the space, and I sigh into his mouth. Our kisses are needy, and he growls against me as I take him from tip to base, pushing him onto his back. He's thick and hard inside of me, and if we continue down this greedy path, I will spill over and lose myself with this man.

It's never felt this way with anyone, and it scares me that it's already this good. Perfect pleasure.

Every inch of my body aches for him when we're as close as we can possibly be. I nearly beg for more of him. His thumb brushes against my needy clit, and my eyes squeeze tight as a whimper releases. With my hands on his chest, I pick up my pace.

"Shit," I whisper, my muscles trembling.

"Take what you need," he urges, pressing his thumbs against my hip bones, creating more friction, allowing him to go deeper than I thought was possible.

I hover above him, capturing his mouth.

"I want more," I beg, already completely full, but not able to get enough.

A devious grin meets his lips as he tugs on my bottom lip with his teeth. "Lie down."

"Mmm," I say as he rolls me onto my back, pulling out, teasing me with the tip of his cock. I look up at him, smiling. "This is real?"

"I sure as fuck hope so." He slowly slides inside of me, allowing me to readjust my thighs to take more of him.

"Are you okay?" he asks in my ear.

"I have a confession to make," I tell him as he kisses the softness of my neck.

"No one, other than myself, has ever been able to make me …" I lift my brows.

His eyes narrow on me. "That ends tonight," he confirms, trailing kisses between my breasts, above and below my belly button, until he has a front-row seat to my pussy.

I push up onto my elbows.

"*Easton,*" I whisper, his name like a prayer in the quiet night, knowing no man has ever gone down on me before, but he doesn't hesitate. He wants this as much as I do.

His warm mouth is on my clit, sucking as his tongue flicks against the bundle of nerves. I gasp, falling back onto my back as he devours me like I'm his last meal. The scruff of his facial hair between my thighs drives me wild as it continues on.

An electrifying hum shoots through me, and I can't help but rock against him as he slides one finger inside. Words … I know they exist, but I can't seem to form a single one as the orgasm slowly builds.

"More," I beg, nearly in a puddle for him as he smiles against my pussy.

"Enjoy it, darling," he whispers, kissing my inner thigh.

I breathe heavily, knowing how fucking close I was. I sit up on my elbows. "I was close."

A smirk meets his perfect lips. "I recall you saying you loved to be edged."

My mouth falls open as I gasp for my release. "You're an asshole."

"I know," he says, kissing my opposite leg, randomly giving my swollen clit a tease with his warm tongue.

I reach down, taking his hair in my hands, knowing this man is making me spiral from the inside out.

I don't know how much of this I can take as he teases me to oblivion. I'm so fucking close, and I think if he breathed on me, I might come.

"Mmm, I can taste how close you are," he says, sliding his tongue inside of me.

"Oh my God," I say, my entire body trembling.

"You want it so fucking bad, don't you?" Easton mutters.

"Yes," I grit out between my teeth, my breasts rising and

falling as I grab the blanket with my fists. "You're driving me crazy."

"How's it feel?"

I give him an evil smile. "Payback will be a *bitch*."

"I look forward to it, my little heartbreaker," he says, his tongue back at my clit, a flick every few seconds.

I'm so damn close that my heart might burst out of my chest. Every muscle tenses as I hang by a thread with this beautiful man buried between my legs.

"Don't make me beg," I barely get out.

"A good girl would."

I meet his eyes, fully willing to submit. "*Now.*"

"Deviant to the core," he says, sliding his hands under my ass, lifting me to his mouth as he licks from my cunt to my clit.

Five seconds later, the orgasm crashes through me, and I scream out, my voice echoing through the surrounding trees.

Easton positions himself between me, his arms on either side of my head.

"I need you more than anything," I whisper.

"Say it again," he demands, giving me a little more of him as he kisses me.

I taste myself on him as his movement grows slow, more intense. I open my thighs as wide as I can.

"I need *you* more than *anything*," I repeat, meaning it with every cell in my body. "*My truth*."

Easton gives me every long inch of him, and I love how good he feels, buried deep inside me, like he belongs there and only there.

Is this how it was always supposed to be?

"I feel the same," he whispers. "I'm addicted to you."

I thread my fingers through his messy hair, and behind his head, I see a meteor skirt across the sky.

I gasp. "Shooting star."

Easton looks over his shoulder, catching the tail end of it, before turning back to me.

"Make a wish," I say.

"I already did," he says, grinding deeper into me, and I feel the impossible—another orgasm building.

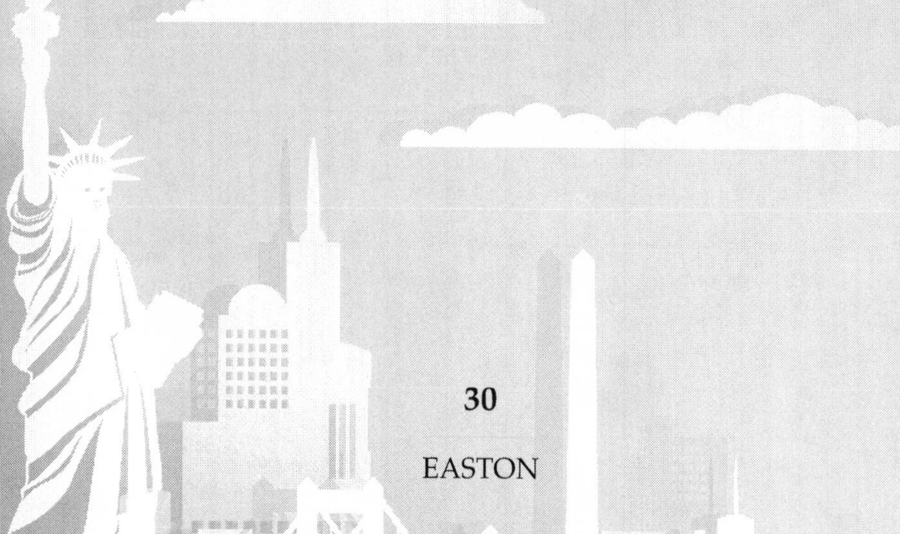

30

EASTON

Same day

Lexi's mouth falls open and she closes her eyes as deep, guttural groans release from her.

I trace the shell of her ear with my mouth. "Is my deviant girl gonna come again?"

"*Yes*," she breathlessly whispers. It's barely audible as her body tenses. "You feel *so* good."

"Mmm. You're mine." I suck on her earlobe, pumping harder inside of her.

She pants, and her back lifts off the ground as she lets go. The orgasm rips through her and her pussy contracts so tight around me that I nearly see stars.

A growl releases from her chest as I slam into her. I'm so damn close as I capture her lips, so I slow my pace. My eyes slam shut as I sink myself deep, letting the orgasm take control. I am nothing and everything with Lexi, and I don't know how I'll be able to let her go. I roll over onto my back and pull her close to me, kissing her hair as she rests her head on my chest. Our breathing is ragged, and our hearts race.

I pull out to take the condom off and notice it's not there. "Fuck," I whisper, making sure I'm not imagining it.

Alexis sits up with hooded eyes. "What is it?"

"The condom." I shake my head.

"Where is it?"

I remove the rubber ring from my cock. The bottom half is missing.

"Oh," she whispers, putting two and two together. "I'm not on birth control, Easton. I had no reason to be, but I think it will be fine. I can't get pregnant; I've tried before. For years. And I was tested for every STD after I was cheated on."

"I'm so sorry, darling."

She stands up, revealing the broken condom on the blanket.

Lexi dresses and I do the same.

I move in front of her and grab her cheeks, noticing she's upset. "Babe, I'm not marrying you to give me an heir. I don't care about that." I drop to my knees in front of her, peeling her shirt up and kissing her stomach. "You're *perfect,* just the way you are."

She wraps her arms around my head, pressing me against her as I inhale the sweetness of her sweaty skin. Her fingers twirl in my hair.

"You said you wanted kids with the right person," she mutters. "That's on repeat in my head."

"When that time comes, there are ways. But if you think that makes me want you less, you're fucking mistaken. It changes *nothing* for me."

She drops to the ground so she's in front of me. "You promise?"

"Yes," I say without hesitation, sliding my hand behind her neck and pulling her in for a kiss. "Raw truths, Lexi."

"Okay," she whispers, painting her lips across mine. Her

fingers press into my cheek as the kiss deepens. "I don't deserve you."

"That's where you're wrong," I say, nuzzling my nose against hers.

Her phone buzzes on the blanket, and she presses the button on the side. "The alarm I set for midnight. Happy day fifteen."

I chuckle as we stand.

Lexi looks up and points. "The Milky Way."

I shove my hand in her back pocket, holding her against me. "Incredible. I guess we can mark under the star love-making off our bucket list." I smirk.

She gasps. "Oh, you're right. But we might have to replace it with another."

"Fuck, I love the sound of that. What do you have in mind?"

"Your office."

I shake my head. "You're searching for trouble."

She wraps her arms around me. "I've already found him."

When the Milky Way is high above, we make our way back to the B & B with swollen lips and smiles on our faces as fireflies surround us.

"So, it's officially day fifteen, and you survived like a warrior princess. However, I still need the answer to my question. Are you anti-love?"

She glances over at me, smirking. "I was until I met you."

Thirty minutes later, we're stepping onto the back porch of the B & B.

"Is this the walk of shame?" Weston asks, sitting in the dark with Brody next to him.

"Kindly fuck off," I snap as I reach for Lexi's hand, leading her to the door.

"Heard you beat the shit out of her brother," Weston says, and Brody chuckles. "I got questioned about it at the diner."

I turn to Lexi. "You weren't kidding about news spreading around town fast, were you?"

"No," she admits. "By morning, everyone will know."

"Thanks for not getting punched in the goddamn face. You still owe me for the last time I had to wear a black eye for your ass," Weston says.

Lexi walks over to him, gives him the bottle of Fireball, and pats him on the shoulder. "You should really get laid," she says.

"Holy shit. Was that a burn?" Weston asks, bursting into laughter.

I open the door and lead my woman upstairs. When we walk into our room, I lock the door. After I quickly peel off her shirt, I kiss her shoulder. "Shower with me."

"I'd love to," she whispers, looking down at my hands. Her fingers brush across my bruised knuckles. "I can't believe you exist."

"Every time I look at you, I think the same."

I lead her into the bathroom that's inside our room and finish undressing her. My fingers memorize her naked body as I help her step into the shower. I join her, allowing her to stand under the warm stream as I grab the soap and take my time washing every beautiful inch of her.

"Easton," she softly says, eyes closed as I massage the shampoo into her scalp. "What happens if I fall in love?"

A ghost of a smile plays on my lips. "With whom?"

"With *you*," she whispers, playfully pursing her lips.

I dip her head back under the water, washing the soap from her scalp. "Tell me when it happens, and we'll go from there."

"You said *when*."

A smirk touches my lips. "I did. I'm waiting for you."

Birthday countdown: 31 days

Since meeting her: 15 days
Company takeover: 38 days

I wake to my cock in Lexi's hot mouth and warm hand.

"I'm dreaming," I whisper, hard and horny, as I lift the sheet, meeting her green eyes.

Starting at the bottom of my balls, she licks up my shaft before twirling her tongue across the tip, licking away the pre-cum. "You started it."

I laugh. "No, I didn't."

"You did. You pressed your cock into my ass and woke me up." She wraps her hand around me, stroking while her mouth sucks me.

"Fuck," I whisper with a grunt.

The early sunrise barely lights the room, but it's enough. Lexi is relentless, increasing her pace before slowing. My balls tighten and I don't know how much longer I'll be able to hold back as she continues to work me so damn good. I throw the blankets off of us as she tries to take me all the way down her throat. Her fingers dig into my thighs and my muscles tense.

"Lexi," I say.

"Please," she begs, tracing her lips with my cock, and, fuck, it's a sight to see. "I want to taste you."

I grab the sheets with my fists as I empty inside her mouth. She drinks me down, swallowing every drop, then swirls her finger on the tip, not wasting any of me.

"I think I'm addicted too."

I grin, pulling her up to me and allowing her to rest on my chest. "My turn."

"You know you're the only man who's ever done that?"

I lick my lips. "I love knowing I'll be the last too."

"Too cocky," she says.

I grab her wrist, gently tugging her toward me so I can kiss her lips.

"Deny it," I dare her. "You and I both know the avalanche can't be stopped, Lexi. Enjoy yourself."

I slide down the bed, staying on my back. She's wearing *my* T-shirt and a paper-thin pair of panties—if they can even be called that. They're mesh, and they leave nothing to the imagination.

She sits on my face, missionary-style, her thighs on each side of my head.

I peel the panties to the side and my tongue parts her pussy until my mouth is fully on her clit. Lexi sinks into me as I grip her ass with my hands. I hum against her, encouraging her to find sexual freedom with me. Her hands tug at my hair as her mouth falls open. High-pitched moans release from her, and with the house being so quiet, I wouldn't be surprised if they echo. I pat her ass and she looks down at me, realizing she lost control. *We* lost control.

She bites the corner of her lip and tweaks her nipple. Another moan releases and she places her hand over her mouth, rocking against me. I slow my pace, knowing she'll come at any second by how her body shakes with anticipation. I keep her on the edge until she nearly crumbles to dust. Gliding two fingers deep inside of her wet cunt, I wage war against her clit. Moments later, she quickly loses herself on my mouth.

"Easton," she screams out, and I laugh against her pussy as she fucks my face, fully riding out her orgasm.

She falls next to me in bed, and we stay in each other's arms until we've both come down from our high.

I kiss her forehead. "Would you like to join me for breakfast?" I ask.

"I'd love to," she says, but we don't move.

I don't know how much time passes as we hold each other, but I'm not counting.

"Great. We need to discuss our game plan for our meeting with the mayor tomorrow," I say, kissing her forehead.

"You're too good to me," she says with fire in her eyes, and I kiss the tip of her nose.

After we're dressed, we make our way downstairs and find Weston in the living room, reading a magazine with a longhorn on the cover.

"Now, *this* is the walk of shame."

"Who's ashamed?" Lexi turns to me. "Are you?"

"Fuck no," I say, twirling the Mustang keys around my finger. "We'll be back later."

When we're on the porch, I take the steps with Lexi. "Do you want to drive?"

"You're after my heart, aren't you?" she playfully asks as she scoops the keys from my hand.

I open the driver's door. "You know it."

We make our way inside the tiny diner, and when we enter, a gray haired woman greets us with a big smile.

"You're back again? Seems like you're gonna be a regular in here with how many times I've seen you in the past twelve hours."

Lexi giggles as we're sat at a table by the windows.

"Coffee, black?" the server asks.

"Yes, that would be great," I tell her with a grin, and then I turn to Lexi, who's sitting beside me.

"I'll take the same," she says.

When we're alone, she laughs while scanning over the menu, but I'm sure she has it memorized.

"No telling how flirty Weston was with everyone in here last night, considering how he acted with me."

"Sometimes, it has its perks," I tell her. "Like when we're at business events and I disappear."

"Do you do that often?" she asks.

"I can only pretend for so long," I tell her, but she already knows that.

31

LEXI

Yesterday, Easton and I spent the entire day at city hall, speaking with Mayor Martinez about the two million dollars Easton is donating to Valentine. We've decided that a portion of it will go toward repairing the historical library, renovating the high school football stadium, and building a new theater at the park. All places where human experiences can happen.

When we left, I couldn't stop stealing glances at Easton. How he walks, talks, and presents himself is impressive. Experiencing him be businesslike was hot as fuck. I don't think I fully understood how much he cares about people in general.

After I get out of the shower, I slip on some ankle boots, a pair of jeans I made into shorts, and a black tank top. My hair is straightened and my makeup is on point with a sassy red lip. Easton freezes when I leave the bathroom; his eyes slide up and down me.

"Wow," he whispers, grinning.

"Are you ready?" I ask, moving to him.

My eyes glide over the polo shirt and jeans. He's a mixture of naughty and nice and everything right.

How is it possible to be this attracted to him?

Easton pulls me against him. "You smell incredible," he whispers, nuzzling into my neck. His fingers run through my hair as he massages my scalp.

My eyes roll into the back of my head. "You do too."

He takes a step back, keeping his hands gently on my elbows, taking another look. "This is what you're wearing tonight?"

"Yes," I say, turning around and giving him the front and back, knowing these denim cutoffs are short. The pockets are longer than the material that covers my thighs.

"What if I don't want anyone enjoying how fucking gorgeous you are?" he asks with a brow raised. "I've already warned you that I'm a *very* jealous man, Lexi."

I place my hands on his stomach, pushing him back toward the bed, then sit on his lap, straddling him. Our hot breaths mix together. He's completely submissive—or he has me believing he is. I know better though. This man bows to no one, not even me.

"You don't have to worry," I say, feeling him grow hard beneath me. "You're the only person who wants me."

He laughs against my mouth, tugging on my lip and sucking. "Feed that *bullshit* to someone else. You can have anyone you want. If anything, I'm proof of that."

My hair surrounds him as I lean over him. "It's *you* who can have anyone you want."

"Really? Are you included on that list?" he asks with a brow popped, his fingers hooking into the belt loops of my shorts.

I brush my nose against his, then move to his ear. "Maybe."

He smirks. "Mmhmm. And who do *you* want?"

My phone buzzes on the bathroom counter, and I steal a kiss from Easton before rushing for it, leaving him splayed on the bed. He runs his fingers through his hair and sits up as I answer a FaceTime call from Carlee.

"Hi!" I say with a smile.

Had she not called, things might have started between us and not stopped. Though, if we don't leave this room tonight, I won't be upset. I look forward to spending time with Easton.

"Holy shit." She moves the screen closer to her face. She has a towel on her head and she's wearing her candy-heart house robe. "You look hot!"

"Are you drunk?"

She holds up a bottle of wine. "I'm really mad at my vagina for consistently wanting the wrong men who fall in love too fast. Keep the I LOVE YOUs to yourself, please."

Laughter slips out. Yes, she's drunk.

"I'm sorry," I say. "But also, that's hilarious."

"Tell me something good. Please let me live vicariously through you."

"Um … Easton beat the shit out of my brother. And we're about to go to a barn party." I set my phone down on the counter and take a step back. "Wearing these bad boys," I say, lifting my leg and showing her one of the leather boots I got on sale earlier this summer.

"Those are the *I'm getting fucked tonight* boots," she says. "Ah man!"

Easton chuckles in the next room.

She moves the phone closer to her mouth, like it makes a difference. "How are things?"

"Amazing," I whisper. "I have so much to catch you up on when I return to the city tomorrow. Let's plan something."

"Like a wedding?" she asks with a laugh.

"Hush!" I playfully roll my eyes, but I smile. "*Maybe.*"

She squeals. "Oh my fucking God, Lexi. You're in the stupid in-love phase."

"Shh," I say, putting my finger over my mouth, my cheeks heating. "Don't be so loud."

"You don't think he knows? Look at you! You're practically glowing," she says. "Love looks good on you."

"Okay, okay, I gotta go now," I tell her. The facts are truthing too hard. "I'll text you tomorrow."

"Tell your brother to call me."

"Which one?" I ask.

"Either."

As I shake my head, I end the call and glance at myself in the mirror.

Shit, she's *right*. I am glowing.

"You didn't hear any of that," I say, knowing he can still hear me because the space isn't that large.

"Hear what?" he states.

"That's what I thought. Now, back to your question."

He turns to me.

"You. You're the person I want."

He smiles, leaning against the wall, and looks out the window toward the barn. "When you're ready, we'll go there."

I tuck my hair behind my ears and stand beside him. Cars fill the pasture; if I had to guess, at least fifty people are at Remi's party.

Easton smiles. "I think we should build a home here. That way, you can visit your family and friends when you please."

I meet his eyes, unsure how this man can be more perfect. "That would be *incredible*."

"And if you decide to sign the divorce papers, you can keep it," he says. "A gift from me to you."

"Easton," I whisper, knowing, right now, there's an expiration date on this—on us. "We'll worry about that when the time comes."

"Yeah. Ready to go?" he asks, looking at his watch. I notice the abrupt subject change. "I think the party started forty-five minutes ago."

A laugh escapes me. Might be able to take the man out of the corporate office, but can't take the corporate office out of the man.

"That means we're right on time. Now, let's go drink some shitty beer and dance the night away."

"The things I do for you," he says.

"You *love* it," I tell him, grabbing his hand and leading him down the stairs of the bed-and-breakfast so we can take the trail that leads to the barn.

When I look back at him, he lifts a brow. "No fucking lies detected."

32

EASTON

Birthday countdown: 30 days
Since meeting her: 16 days
Company takeover: 37 days

We take the trail that leads from the house to the barn, so neither of us has to worry about driving. Lexi hooks her fingers with mine as we walk down the path.

"We should've pregamed," she says.

"I only do that when I plan on fucking around and finding out," I tell her with a smirk, and she laughs.

"Exactly," she says.

I shake my head. "What am I going to do with you?"

"Apparently, you're gonna make me your wife," she quips.

"Damn straight."

"Sooner rather than later, okay?"

"I'd marry you tomorrow," I admit, meaning every fucking word.

I think I hear her breath hitch.

"*Soon*, soon then."

"Twenty-nine days. So, yeah."

In the distance, the barn is lit bright and light leaks out from both sides. Chatter and laughter echo as we look up at the stars. Someone says something inaudible over a loudspeaker. Not long after, country music spills out into the pasture. Neither of us says a word as we move toward the party, but we don't have to. There's no other place I'd rather be right now.

"Ready?" she asks with a smile as I wrap my arm around her shoulders.

She fully interlocks her fingers with mine, and I'm so damn tempted to kiss her.

"As ever," I say, and we walk in through the large entrance.

All heads turn in our direction. Lexi glances at me, leading us toward the birthday girl. Everyone returns to their red cups full of beer as country music blares through the sound system.

When we're close, Lexi gives her a hug. "Happy birthday. I'm going to send you something when I get back to New York."

"Don't. You're enough," Remi says, nodding her head at me as I stand to the side.

My eyes wander around the room with all the smiling faces. Couples are dancing, friends are chatting, and everyone seems like they're living life to the fullest.

Moments later, the lights are lowered and someone turns on a colored disco light to set the mood. It smells like leather and fresh hay. There's a beer-pong table in the corner, and Lexi leads us over to it.

"We're next," she tells the table as the last ball sinks into the cup.

Beckett and Harrison give each other high fives.

"You're both goin' down," Harrison screams, pointing at us, grabbing the woman next to him to kiss her.

"His wife," Lexi says. "Took a lot for them to get together."

"It's usually *not* easy." I meet her eyes. *This easy.*

"Apologies in advance for kicking your ass," Beckett offers with a nod.

Lexi turns to me with the ball in her hand and clanks it against mine. "You know how to play? Keep your elbow behind the table and don't bounce—only bitches do that."

"Are you fucking kidding me?"

"Sorry, I thought you would've been busy playing croquet or something." She can't fully get the words out of her mouth before she snorts, tossing a ball and sinking it into a cup.

"I was more into polo," I admit as we toss again.

"You ride?" She gives an overhead throw and makes it.

"Yes." I make mine too.

She turns to me. "Okay, so you *are* perfect."

"For you," I say.

Six more cups, and we'll win.

A small smile plays over her lips as she throws again and misses.

I make mine, but it's not enough.

Beckett and Harrison both make balls in our cups and rethrow them. Lexi and I tap the red plastic together and drink the warm beer.

She makes a face, and so do I.

"That was awful," she hisses.

Beckett and Harrison don't seem to notice or care, but I have a feeling this isn't the first round they've played because of how much shit they're talking. They clear out all but two cups.

"We're gonna skunk your asses," Harrison says, giving Beckett another high five.

"You suck," Lexi says when Harrison flicks the ball and it lands in the last one. She begrudgingly drinks it, doing a little wiggle, like it helps it go down easier. It doesn't.

"Boo-hoo," Beckett mocks. "You lost, Lexi. I bet that stings."

She laughs and flips them off. "I *hate* losing to them. They rub it in."

"Aww, you're cute when you don't win," I say, brushing my thumb against her cheek. "Want a drink?"

"Not if it's hot, shitty beer."

I pull a flask from my pocket and hand it to her.

"Gotta love a man who comes prepared."

She takes a long drink, hands it to me, and I do the same. We stand off to the side, people-watching, laughing about nothing as we get buzzed like we're teenagers.

"I'm glad you're here," she whispers.

"I am too," I say.

She takes my hand, leading me toward the back of the barn and down a dark hallway. She twists a knob. We're inside a small office. After she closes the door, Lexi pushes me against it.

Her mouth is on mine as I rest my hands inside her pockets. We're a speeding bullet, soaring through the wind. The person I was before meeting her no longer exists.

"I need you," she whispers, palming my cock, which is hard for her.

I reach behind me, locking the door. I slide my hand inside her shorts and panties, my fingers sliding down her slit.

"You're already so wet for me," I growl in her ear, rolling circles against her clit.

"I wanted you before we left," she admits.

Pleading moans release from her as I slide one finger, then two deep inside of her. She sinks down to my knuckles, grabbing my biceps to steady herself as I move back to her bundle of nerves.

"So greedy."

"Easton," she says, her head falling back on her shoulders. It releases from her mouth like a prayer.

"I love hearing you say my name," I say into her ear, knowing she's already hanging by a string.

Lexi peels her shirt up above her perfect breasts. *No bra.* Her nipples are hard as pebbles.

"Did you hear me that night?"

She gasps as I dip down. I take her hard peak into my mouth, continuing to give her pussy what it begs for.

"Yes," I admit, and her breathing increases.

She likes that I heard her. She wanted me to.

"I'm so close," she says.

"Come for me," I whisper.

She nods, tucking her bottom lip into her mouth as she chases the orgasm to the very end. I give her clit just enough pressure with my thumb as I slowly finger-fuck her.

"Yes, yes," she whimpers, and when she finally spills over the edge, she screams out into my chest. Her breathing is ragged as she keeps her body resting against mine. I pull my hand from her panties and she laughs. "I can never get enough of you."

I place my fingers into my mouth. "Fuck, you taste so goddamn good."

She smiles like she's pleased. "Let me take care of you."

I kiss her hair. "I can wait, darling."

She tucks her hands inside my jeans, tugging me closer to her. "Don't you want me?"

"I want you every fucking second of every day, Lexi."

"Then, please let me have you when I want you. I insist, Mr. Calloway," she mutters, dropping down to her knees, taking full control.

My hands are fisted through her hair, and she works me so damn well that my knees nearly buckle. Guttural groans release from my throat when she cups my balls.

"This cock is mine."

She kisses up and down the shaft. Her emerald eyes meet mine as I lean against the door, knowing if she keeps up this pace, I'll lose it. She takes me to the back of her throat, her hand twisting as she licks and sucks me to oblivion.

"Fuck," I groan when she slides her hands up my body, under my shirt, and tweaks my nipples.

"Lexi," I growl, my muscles tensing.

One of her brows quirks up as I shoot warm cum in the back of her throat. She creates space, allowing me the pleasure of watching silver strands land on her perfect tongue. She swallows me down, licking up every drop as my heart nearly pounds out of my chest.

I feel like I've transcended realities as I look down into her bright eyes.

"Mmm. Thank you," she breathlessly says, standing up.

I tilt my head at her, readjusting my clothes and myself.

"Thank *you*," I whisper as she slides her mouth against mine.

"You're like a drug."

"Hate to break it to you, babe, but there's no rehab," I say.

"Good," she whispers. "We should probably get out there before people start wondering where we are."

I check my watch. We've only been gone for thirty minutes. "They probably haven't noticed."

"How do I look?" she asks.

I trace her bottom lip with my thumb. "Guilty."

"Always."

She smirks and grabs my hand, leading me down the dark hallway and back to the main area, where nothing has changed. People are still dancing. There's a beer line at the keg. Beckett and Harrison are still ruling the beer-pong table. I wrap my arm around her as we enter and hand her the flask.

"Will you dance with me?"

"Lead the way," I say, following her into the crowd of people.

I can still taste her on my lips, and I smile. My hands rest on her hips as she twists her fingers behind my neck. It's like everyone and everything in the room disappears, and it's only us, slowly spinning together.

When I meet her eyes again, her lips part and I dip down to devour her mouth. The taste of pleasure mixes on our tongues.

The sound of a deep voice calling her name over the music pulls us away.

Lexi turns her head. "Beau?"

"I heard you were in town and rushed over here," he says, moving closer. "Can I talk to you?"

"No," Lexi says, placing her hands on her hips. "I have *nothing* to say to you."

I can hear the anger in her voice.

He tries to reach for her hand, and I grab him, wanting to break his fucking wrist.

"*Don't. Touch. Her.* And if I were you, I'd take a step back."

He looks into my eyes and recognition flashes. I let him go as Brett and Chris step to my side, and they're more feral than me. Didn't think that was possible.

I cross my arms over my chest as a crowd forms around us.

"Why are you fucking him?" Beau screams at her, pointing at me.

I stay calm, knowing I'll beat his ass if I have to.

Lexi's mouth falls open. "You cheated on me!"

"Are you in love with him?" Beau questions. "Tell me that, Lexi."

She glances over at me, and it's like no one else in the goddamn room exists. We hold a silent conversation, and I see the sparkle in her eye, the one I said I'd never miss again after the first time we saw one another in the park.

She glares back at him.

"Yes," she states. "I am. But that's none of your goddamn business."

"Liar." He seethes.

"You have the audacity to call *me* a liar after everything you put me through? You're a cheating bastard!"

She's angry. I've never seen her this mad. Lexi takes a step forward and whispers something in his ear before returning to my side. He looks like she slapped the shit out of him, and I give her a smirk, curious as to what she said.

My grandfather once said that a person shouldn't fight with violence, but with words, because it's the only weapon that can cut so deep. Lexi proved that for me.

Quiet chatter fills the space and I glance around, knowing this is getting out of hand. The last thing either of us needs is this spreading around town or to the gossip columns.

The crowd parts, and Remi stands in front of Beau, her birthday crown on her head and hands on her tiny waist. Cash follows behind her, and so do Harrison and Beckett. She's brought her own personal army.

"You won't be ruining my birthday, Beau. Please leave."

Beau's mouth falls open like he wants to say something, but Lexi stunned him silent.

"Out you go," Beckett says, putting his hand on Beau's shoulder. Harrison grabs his other one, and they lead him outside.

I take Lexi's hand and we walk outside. There were too many eyes on her, and I could see that she was lost in her head.

We're on the opposite side of the barn, the one that faces the open land. Without the music playing, we can hear every word Beau says to the Valentine brothers.

Lexi sits on the ground with her back resting against the barn wall and leans her head on her knees. I place my hand on her back as they argue with one another.

Harrison raises his voice. "She's moved on. She's fucking *happy*. Sometimes, you win, and sometimes, you lose. You lost, Beau. Should've married her when you had the chance and not been a cheating cunt."

I'll have to tell him *thank you* for that later.

"She doesn't love him," Beau tries to reason.

"She doesn't love you either," Beckett says. "Now, leave."

"I dated an idiot," Lexi whispers, shaking her head.

"Leave," Beckett yells, and I can hear how agitated he is. "I'm gonna call the sheriff. I didn't want any trouble tonight from anyone. And here you are, fucking up my beer-pong record!"

I hold back my laughter.

More mumbles fill the space, an engine cranks, and gravel kicks up. Five minutes later, the microphone comes on, and it sounds like Harrison has it shoved halfway down his throat.

"Sorry about that, ladies and gentlemen; I thought we said pricks weren't invited! Let the good times roll," he says.

Everyone laughs, then the music continues like nothing happened.

"Are you okay?" I finally ask, rubbing her back.

She sits up and turns to me. "You know, for months, I asked myself how I'd react if Beau confronted me. I replayed the scenario a few times and didn't know how I'd feel when I saw him again. But ... when I looked at him, it was like staring at a blank page. There was *nothing* there."

"I've been there. It's freeing. And awkward."

"It is," she says. "I told him I've never had to *fake it* with you and that you give the best orgasms I've *ever* had."

A howl of laughter releases from me. "I was curious, but wasn't going to ask."

"Nothing I said to him was a lie." Her eyes soften.

I think back to her saying she was falling in love with me. Could that even be possible? I hope it is.

She crawls onto my lap and I hold her. I want to stay like this for a lifetime.

"Lexi," I whisper "There's no other woman I want to do this with. I can't imagine my life without you in it, and while it scares the fuck out of me, I'm ready."

She smiles and kisses me. "This will be the adventure of a lifetime."

"*Guaranteed*."

I think Lexi needs more time to realize the kind of life we

can have together, but time is something we're running out of. I hate the invisible clock that's hanging over us, but I wonder if we'd have taken the risk without it. There's no way of knowing.

She studies me. "I think I want our ceremony to be intimate —our special moment."

I smile and tuck loose strands of hair behind her ear, studying every feature so I can draw this moment later. "And what about the vows?"

"Still written," she says. "Convince me you're worth staying with forever."

"That sounds like a challenge," I tell her, enjoying the idea of telling her exactly how I feel.

She laughs against my mouth. "I don't think you'll have a problem."

"Honeymoon preference?"

"Surprise me," she says. "You're the only person on the planet who can, apparently."

"Oh, almost forgot." I dig into my pocket and pull out the black velvet box with the Calloway Diamonds logo.

"Please marry me. You really do make me a better man, and I'd be honored to call you my wife," I say when I open it.

An audible gasp whispers through the still night air between us. "Easton, I—I didn't expect this."

"My *fiancée* needs a ring," I mutter close to her, where only she can hear. "I designed every detail specifically for you."

She gives me her left hand and I kiss every single knuckle before sliding the pink emerald-shaped diamond onto her finger.

She covers her mouth, staring down at it. "This is too much."

"Not for my *fiancée,*" I say, moving her hair from her face.

Lexi grabs my cheeks and softly paints her lips against mine. I wrap my arms around her, our tongues twisting together, and my body is on fire.

"You'll be my wife," I whisper, and it's an admission.

"I like the thought of it," she says.

Movement happens in my peripheral vision as two people come around the barn. The girl pushes the guy against the wall and her hands run through his hair. They're desperate. Greedy.

"Remi? Cash?" Lexi says on my lap with swollen lips.

They turn to us with eyes wide.

"You didn't see us," Remi says, walking away.

Cash shrugs and shakes his head, then follows her.

Lexi turns to me, smiling. "She's always had a thing for him."

It makes me wonder if anyone else knows about them. I meet her eyes. "Do you want to get out of here?"

"Yes," she says, standing.

"Would you like to tell everyone goodbye?"

She smiles at me. "Nah, *we'll* visit again."

"Anytime you want."

Lexi grabs my hand and we take the trail that leads back to the B & B.

"So, before we get married, I'd like you to meet my parents," I say.

She stops walking. "I just got super nervous."

"Billie already likes you, so you'll do fine. She has never approved of anyone I was into."

"Really?" She laughs.

"Only *you*." I smile. "Are you free tomorrow?"

"You know I am."

"Great. I have a dinner planned for us. It will be a big family get-together."

She lets out a ragged breath and I wrap my arm around her.

"They'll love you," I say, kissing her hair.

"How can you be so sure?"

"Because everyone else already does."

"Everyone?" she insinuates with hooded eyes.

"*Everyone*," I confirm, knowing she understands I'm included.

33

LEXI

Easton carries our luggage down the stairs. Brody and Weston wait for us at the bottom, playing on their phones.

"The delivery company picked up your car, it should be in New York tomorrow," Weston says, glancing at the ring on my finger. "I take it you two had fun last night?"

I glance over at Easton, a blush hitting my cheeks. "Tons."

I hear footsteps from behind me, and at the top of the stairs, I see Remi.

"Hi, what are you . . ."

She smiles and walks over to me. "I heard the news. And on my birthday. I'll never forget the day. I'm so happy for you," she says, and I show her the ring.

"It's perfectly you, Lexi."

"Thank you." I can't stop smiling.

It feels too good to be true. It is.

This whole thing is fake, I remind myself.

Easton tucks his hands into his pockets. He knows Remi knows me better than Carlee. Her words hold weight.

"You two are fire."

He smiles at her.

"I played matchmaker," Weston says. "Kinda made this whole thing happen."

Brody rolls his eyes. "No, you didn't."

I turn my attention back to Remi. "Why are you working the day after your birthday?"

She holds back a smile. "I'm not."

I glance over my shoulder, up the stairs, where she came from. "Are you alone?"

Weston laughs, and Remi turns to him. "Shut up."

"Feisty little Texas girls," Weston states, lifting his leather duffel over his shoulder.

Brody does the same and they make their way toward the door.

"Don't be a stranger, either of you," she says to Easton and me. "But that one can stay in New York."

Weston laughs as he grabs the knob. "Oh, come on. I didn't give you *that* hard of a time."

"Worse than my brothers," she says.

"Damn," I quip. "That's pretty bad."

Easton chuckles. "We should leave if we're going to make dinner tonight."

Remi moves to him. He holds out his hand to give her a handshake, and she pulls him into a hug.

"I'm sure it's known, but if you hurt my friend, I will chop off your balls."

"Great," he tells her. "Her other friend has my cock. So, you two can have a party."

I snort. "It was Carlee," I say.

Remi nods. "I knew I liked her."

When I glance toward the front door, I see the SUV waiting in the driveway. "I'll see you soon."

She pulls me into another hug and whispers, "He's mad about you."

All I can do is smile as I pass Easton. When we step off the porch, our suitcases are taken from his hand, and we climb into the vehicle. Brody sits in the front, and Weston is in the back. We take the middle row.

A few minutes later, we're heading down the long, twisty road that leads to town, and then we're passing through it. I look out the window at the park in the middle of the town square and smile when we pass the library.

Easton grabs my hand, butterflies dance, and endless possibilities of us and the future fill my mind. Nothing about the way I feel is fake, and the sooner I'm willing to admit that, the better. However, I have my doubts that I could ever be enough for the man who can have anything he wants.

"My mother texted me this morning and I promised that we'd come back and visit soon."

"I'd like that a lot," he says with a wink.

Two hours later, we arrive at the private hangar, and outside, the jet waits for us with the stairs down. I must've fallen asleep, but I dreamed about nothing.

My door opens and Easton greets me with a smile. "Sleeping Beauty is awake."

"Did I snore?" I whisper, feeling exhaustion creep in.

"A little," he whispers with a smirk. "Tomorrow, we'll sleep in, I promise."

He follows behind me as we board. When we walk inside, we're greeted by the same flight attendant who's accompanied us on each trip.

"We'd like to be left alone for the duration, please." Easton's polite but also stern as he places his hand on the small of my back, leading me to the back area.

"Yes, sir," she says.

As I turn to look over my shoulder, I see Weston and Brody board, but they take the executive seats toward the front of the plane.

Easton slides the door closed, and I realize we're in a small room with a couch, television, and an executive chair and table.

"My private estate room," he says. "For long flights."

I take a step forward. "You're telling me you have a bedroom on your plane, and you've not christened it?"

His eyes flutter closed as I kiss him. It's slow and intentional.

"That ends today. But first, we buckle until we're at a safe altitude."

"And then?"

"Let your imagination wander."

When the plane is soaring in the air, Easton unbuckles himself, then me. I turn to face him, our mouths desperate and hands needy.

"Did you wear this tiny fucking skirt for me?"

"Yes," I admit, aching for this man so damn much that it hurts.

He lays me back and his hands graze over my hard nipples. He whispers, "We'll have to be quiet."

"I'll try," I say breathlessly.

I tuck my lips into my mouth when his hand gently slides between my thighs. I inch the material upward, showing him the black silk panties I wore.

He adds more pressure to my clit on top of the material. My eyes slam closed; the sensation of him is almost too much.

"Mmm. You're already so wet for me," he growls into my ear.

"I can't help it," I admit as he slides the material from my body, tucking it into his pocket. "A souvenir?"

"You fucking know it."

My head is spinning.

Earlier, I was on a plane, biting my fist as I came, and now, I'm wearing a designer dress and Jimmy Choos, carrying a purse that fits nothing more than my phone. I was sent for a massage, a blowout, and makeup done by a celebrity artist. How is this my life?

Easton opens the door to the limo, and we're parked in front of a contemporary Italian restaurant. It screams elegance, and a person obviously doesn't enter without a reservation.

As soon as we step out of the car, the shutters of the cameras snap. I cover my face with my left hand. The beautiful ring Easton designed for me is on full display. I want the world to know this man is mine—even if it's only for a year.

Easton wraps his arm around me, dressed in a black suit tailored for his muscular body. His red tie matches my dress. He leans in and whispers, "If you see a celebrity or someone you might recognize, pretend they don't exist."

"Easy," I tell him. "My eyes will be locked on you all night."

"Mmm," he says with approval as two men in suits open the door for us.

As soon as Easton enters the dimly lit room, the woman at the door leads us into the dining area with crisp tablecloths and long, lit candles. I keep my eyes forward as Easton glides across the room like he owns the place.

He glances over at me and smiles, and I return the gesture. We're led to a table where his family is sitting. Weston stands when he sees me, giving me a smile and a bow.

"Lexi," he says, taking my hand and kissing it. "So lovely to see you again."

I hold back a laugh because I saw him eight hours ago, when we landed.

Easton pulls out my chair, and once I'm settled, he sits beside me. His strong hand is on my thigh, and I enjoy the dominance of it.

A waiter immediately steps forward, filling our glasses with water and pouring a quarter of a glass of white wine.

"Hello all," Easton says. "Thank you for joining me tonight."

"You're late," his mother interrupts, giving me Meryl Streep vibes. But she's gorgeous, with white-blonde hair.

Every person sitting at this table is beautiful. Easton and Weston are the perfect combination of their parents.

I glance at Easton and he smirks. "I got tied up," he says.

The reality is, he bent me over the bed before we left the diamond in the sky. I had no idea we were late, and he didn't mention it.

"Anyway, I'm thrilled to introduce you to Lexi Matthews, my fiancée, the love of my life," he announces, then goes around the table, giving me introductions.

I smile and nod.

"This is my mother and her husband, Ralph."

Weston snickers.

"Actually, I'm Scott," he says.

Easton's lips slightly part, but he quickly recovers. "Scott, yes. Apologies. This is my father, Frederick, and his wife, Katrina."

"Hi," I say.

"And, of course, you know Billie. And Weston."

His sister leans forward and gives me a wink. "Great to see you again, Alexis 'Lexi' Matthews."

"You too," I tell her with a smile.

"And what day are we on?" she asks.

"Seventeen," I whisper, glancing at Easton.

His mouth quirks upward, but he tries to keep his badass public persona in check. I know better though. The man is a softy—at least when it comes to me.

"I hope he gave you a trophy," she whispers.

"He did," I say, showing her the ring.

A grin spreads into a wide smile. "Grandmother's diamond?"

The table grows quiet.

"Yes," Easton says. "You all seem *surprised*."

"I'm not," Weston quips with a chuckle, sipping his wine. "You *always* said when you found *the one*, you'd propose with Grandmother's stone. I expected it. Everyone else should have as well."

I swallow hard, feeling blindsided by this revelation. "*Easton*."

"Lexi." He smiles at me, and my heart nearly bursts out of my chest.

It's more than *just* a ring for him; it's *the* ring. I'm not sure I can accept something so precious and meaningful; however, if he's always said that, then he was forced to continue with the plan. Any cracks, and it could shatter.

The moment passes quickly, but we will discuss it.

We glance at the menus that are bound in soft leather. Everything is foreign to me—from the amount of silverware on the table to the names of dishes printed on the vellum paper.

"What are you having?" he asks as he leans in, and his eyes pierce through me.

"What you're having," I say with a nervous smile. I'm too in my head.

"Good choice." He orders for us both.

As our wine is refilled, Billie talks about her fashion line and how far ahead they are on designs and production. She's beautiful and elegant, and she has an air of *don't fuck with me* that surrounds her. Actually, all of the Calloways do.

"So, Lexi," his mother says. "Do you two plan on having children?"

It's not a question that should make my anxiety spike, but it does. I place my hand on top of Easton's, which hasn't left my thigh since we sat.

"Maybe one day," I explain. "Who knows what the future holds?"

"Well, I'd love grandchildren before my kids are given another brother or sister."

His mother is *ruthless*.

"You sound like my mama," I admit. "In the South, popping babies out right after a wedding is almost like a custom. But after meeting Connor and seeing how great Easton was with him …" I meet Easton's gaze, and for a moment, it's me and him, lost in one another. "He'll make an incredible dad."

She gives me the hint of a smile. It's good enough for me.

"Well, you two can borrow him when you'd like. He's a little terror and he drives his nanny wild. The kid is thirty months old, and I've already gone through three different people. The Calloway tantrums are awful," Katrina says, sipping her wine. "Actually, he's been screaming *Lexi* since he visited Easton. I suppose you're the reason why."

"Aww," I say, but the smile that was on Easton's mother's face transforms into a scowl.

Billie snickers.

"And, Weston, how's the divorce?" his mother asks.

"I'm having the best time, Mother. You know how that is. Marrying and divorcing, then doing it all over again," he says with the utmost disrespect in his tone.

Easton sucks in a deep breath. "Don't," he tells Weston between gritted teeth.

I don't feel bad about how dysfunctional my family was. Actually, the Calloways are pretty normal with all their inner drama.

His father speaks up. "I heard you're into the theater, Lexi. Easton told me you act and sing."

I smile. "I do. I graduated from NYU years ago. My dream was to perform on Broadway."

"Easton's invested in one of the theaters. I'm sure he could make some phone calls."

"I'm sure he could, but I prefer to earn it and not have it handed to me. Lately, I've been thinking about writing a screenplay. A love story," I say.

"You should," his father says.

Billie nods, and Easton glances at me.

"Really?" he whispers.

"Yeah," I admit. It's not something I've shared with anyone other than Carlee, but it was originally a tragedy.

Another bottle of wine is being opened and poured, and Easton excuses himself.

"I'll be right back," he mutters into my ear.

I nod, bringing my attention back to his mom, who's sitting directly across from me.

Billie asks a few questions, and I watch Easton cross the dark room. Before he turns down a hallway, he's stopped by a woman in a black dress that hugs her slim body. He takes a step back, his hand touching her elbow as she smiles. The woman leans in and whispers something in his ear, her hand on his chest.

I suck in a ragged breath and Weston glances at me. I grab my glass of wine and take a gulp as he excuses himself.

"Where's everyone going?" his mother asks, searching around.

I give her a smile and shrug, hating watching Easton with someone else. Weston interrupts the conversation, stealing the attention. Easton looks in my direction, then disappears down the hallway.

Five minutes later, Easton returns to me just as our first course is being served. I follow his lead, choosing the utensils he uses. And for the rest of the night, I float through the conversations as a well-rehearsed actress.

When it's time to leave, we say our goodbyes with loose hugs and kisses on each cheek. The limo arrives, and we're rushed outside, avoiding the cameras as we climb in.

Easton turns to me, his mouth positioned in that devilish smirk that I both love and hate. And right now, I'm not sure what he's going to say.

34

EASTON

Birthday countdown: 29 days
Since meeting her: 17 days
Company takeover: 36 days

The limo pulls away. It's quiet; the streetlights light her face briefly as we pass under them.

"Everything okay?"

"*Perfect,*" she says with a smile, but I can see *her*. The real her.

"You're a *terrible* liar." I shake my head and chuckle.

"I'm a *great* liar. You're better at reading me than most of the population."

I swipe my thumb across her cheek and meet her eyes. "Raw truths, Lexi. What's going on?"

She sucks in a breath. "I didn't like seeing you with someone else."

I understand what she's going through. I felt the same way last night, when I saw her ex, knowing his mouth had been on hers.

"Says the woman who encouraged me to date others while our arrangement was in order. Am I understanding this correctly?"

"That was before ..." she whispers.

"Mmm?" I want her to continue that statement.

"Before I cared," she says confidently.

"There's only you, babe. You're it." I give her a half grin, moving close to her mouth.

Our lips crash together and I fist my hand through her hair.

"Who was she?"

This makes me chuckle. "She thought I was Weston. I don't recall her name. I warned you about this. It happens frequently."

"Now, I feel stupid." A blush hits her cheeks.

"Don't." I shake my head. "I couldn't handle watching another man touch you, Lexi. If you think I'd have sat there and watched that ..." I shake my head. "The moment he approached you, I'd have been by your side."

She smiles. "Helicopter boyfriend."

"Oh, you thought that was acting?" A laugh releases from me. "I've never had to with you."

The car rolls to a stop and the door opens. We step out and Lexi looks up at the building.

She laughs, covering her mouth. "Empire State?"

"After you," I say as we walk through the doors.

We're led to the elevators, and we take one to our first stop, then another to the very top. One of the security guards nods at me, and our private guide stands over to the side.

Lexi turns to me. "You did this?"

"For *us*," I say. "Want to go outside?"

"Yes," she tells me, and I push open the door.

The summer wind surrounds us and she smiles so fucking wide that the whole city sparkles.

She shakes her head. "I can't believe this."

I press my hand on the small of her back. "Are you happy?"

Her eyes look up into mine, then down to my lips.

"Yes. Are you going to kiss me?" she whispers.

I take a step forward, tracing her mouth with mine. "Do you want me to?"

"Yes," she desperately says.

Her hands fist my shirt and I slide my tongue against hers. My name is breathless on her lips as our worlds collapse and crumble together. We will destroy one another.

"Fuck, Lexi," I mutter.

She takes a step back, glancing down at the ring. "Why didn't you tell me this was your grandmother's?"

"I knew you'd find out when it mattered."

"Easton"—her voice is quiet—"I can't accept this."

"You're being humble." I tilt my head at her, wishing she knew how priceless time was with her.

"*No.*" She twists it around on her finger. "I heard what Weston said. This should've been reserved for *her*."

"It was," I say without hesitation, knowing damn well the person who's meant to have it is wearing it.

She shakes her head and laughs.

"Why do you think it's impossible for me to want you? I don't understand."

"Because we're not the same," she says.

"Ah. Explain it to me," I urge with a smile. "Tell me how we're different. Without the bullshit, Lexi. List the differences that matter."

Her mouth opens and closes like she understands.

"Last time I checked, we were equals."

She laughs. "I'm not your equal."

"You are," I say. "So, start acting like my queen if that makes you believe it's true. Act like the woman you think I should be with. Because I'm not sure if you've noticed, but I just want *you*. That's it. No one else. Lexi Matthews, the girl who wears graphic tees in public and politely tells people to fuck off. Lexi

Matthews, the woman who snores like a princess when she's exhausted. Lexi Matthews, the smut queen who also has a weird fucking obsession with billionaire books. I think that's who I'm supposed to be with, but I don't know; you're convinced there's someone else who's more deserving of my attention."

"I'm insecure when it comes to you. I feel like an imposter. That's the truth."

"And you think I'm not? Babe, I know you don't give two fucks about materialistic things. So, tell me, how do I give a woman everything who doesn't *need* anything, not even love? That's what I'm trying to figure out."

"You're right. *Things* aren't my love language, but experiences are. You know that. Otherwise, I doubt we'd be here. You've already got me figured out, and you know exactly what I need and want."

"There's the truth I've been searching for," I say. "Welcome to the party. It's fun here, where we don't give a fuck and we can be truthful about what's going on."

She shakes her head.

I check my watch, then meet her eyes. "I'm waiting for you to finish."

"You know I'm falling for you, Easton."

"Oh, I know; I wanted to hear you say it."

I tilt her chin upward and meet her eyes.

"In a crowded room, the only person I'm looking at is *you*. You're the last thing on my mind when I close my eyes at night and the first person I think about when I wake up in the morning. I thought we'd cross the line and I'd get you *out* of my system, and things would go back to how they were before I met you, but that didn't happen. Every time you touch or kiss or fucking glance at me, it makes me think about our future."

She looks out at the city as I steal glances at her. I wish I could read her mind.

"This wasn't supposed to happen," she whispers.

"Let me guess … bad timing?" I ask with a laugh.

"Always. I just … I had aspirations. And it wasn't to be Mrs. Calloway."

"So, make your dreams come true. I'm not stopping you whether you have my name or not." I shrug. "I believe in *you* and your dreams, whatever they are."

Our mouths magnetize toward one another again and I tuck her hair behind her ears.

"I'm serious."

"I know," she whispers. "God, I need you," she says desperately, and it almost comes out in a plea.

I laugh against her hair. "I kinda like it when you call me God."

As I drop to my knees, I look up into her eyes.

"This was written in invisible ink on my bucket list." She chews on the corner of her lips.

I flip the red skirt of her designer dress over my head. When I see her bare pussy, I rub my face across her.

No panties.

"I was *prepared*," she whispers.

"Mmm. My bad fucking girl."

I rub my hand against her thigh, lifting her opposite leg over my shoulder. She willingly gives me access to her beautiful cunt that's dripping wet for me. Lexi leans against the wall, and I take my time, worshiping her the way she deserves, exactly how she likes.

My greedy fiancée rocks her hips against my mouth, riding the scruff on my chin.

It doesn't take long before whimpers release from her, and it's like music to my goddamn ears. I can tell by how she tastes and how her muscles shake with anticipation.

"I'm insatiable for you," she whispers.

"Enjoy it, darling," I say, giving her a finger.

Time stops as she teeters on the edge.

"Easton," she softly cries out, the orgasm bolting through her.

I laugh against her, not stopping until her pussy quits throbbing.

When I pull away, I reposition her dress but stay on one knee. As I look into her eyes, I place my fingers in my mouth. "I fucking love the way you taste."

She pulls me up toward her and our lips crush together.

"Can we get married tomorrow?" she asks. "Just me and you. Our moment. No one else's."

"Are you serious?" I search her face, needing and wanting confirmation.

She nods. *"Yes."*

I smile against her lips. "I'd burn the world down for you, Lexi."

She grabs the lapel of my suit coat. "That's what scares me the most."

"With great power comes great responsibility."

"We're *so fucked*."

I kiss her forehead, and then we finish the circular path around the top before going inside. We hold hands as we ride the elevator down.

A small smile plays on her swollen lips when I meet her hooded eyes. And I realize I've *never* been in love before.

Not until now.

35

LEXI

The plane touches down in Fiji.

Neither of us told a soul that we were flying halfway across the world to whisper our vows to one another. It's deviant; it's everything that no one will expect. And that's why I love it so much. It's the ultimate surprise to everyone, but it also gives us the opportunity to be alone. Just us.

Easton hasn't stopped smiling, and, fuck, neither have I.

We depart the private jet and a limo picks us up and drives us to the mansion he rented. We get out and stumble to the door, laughing, barely able to keep our mouths and hands off one another. We've been stupidly giddy since we left the States. We're like teenagers in love, completely unpredictable and unapologetic.

"One hour," he says, pressing me against the wooden door. "Are you ready to be *my wife*?" he growls against my lips.

"Yes." I laugh as he wraps his arm around my waist. "Do you mind being late to our wedding?"

"That would be tragic." He chuckles. "They'd wait all night for us though."

There's a knock on the door and it's the only thing that breaks us from our trance.

"Shit, our luggage. We need that," Easton mutters against my lips.

I step aside, smoothing my hair down on my head as the driver sets our suitcases by the door. Easton generously tips our driver, and soon, we're alone again.

I take a few steps toward him, wrapping my arms around his neck. "I'm happy we're doing this."

"I wouldn't have it any other way," he says after I steal another kiss.

If we get started, we really will be late.

When we walk farther into the house, I notice all the walls are windows, and the blue ocean goes on for miles. There's a pool back there too.

I gasp.

"Surprise," he says, grinning. "I knew you'd react like that. Totally worth it."

"You *always* have the best views."

A small smile meets his lips. "Only when you're in the frame."

"You're very good at that," I tell him, playfully poking him in the side as I walk back to my suitcase and dress. Even he, all muscle and tattoos, wiggles away from me.

"At what?" He walks toward his suitcase.

"Saying the right thing at the right time."

"Oh, *that*," he says, but that grin tells me he knew what I was referring to. "I'll see you on the beach in forty-five minutes?"

"I'll be there," I tell him, wheeling my suitcase to the largest bedroom in the house.

The bathroom is connected, and I can't take my eyes off the beach. It looks like a calendar picture, all of it. I hang my dress on the hook in the bathroom and take it from its travel bag. I'm not sure how I managed to get this dress delivered to me before we left, but I did. It's white with a keyhole neck, an open back, and a slit that goes to my middle thigh. The skirt is flowy and I feel like a goddess as I walk. I slide on some strappy silver sandals. As I sit on the edge of the bed, I replay it all.

Deep in my heart, I know this is the right thing to do. Easton wants to be mine, and I'd be lying if I said I didn't want to be his. If it's wrong, I don't ever want to be right.

After I'm dressed, there's a knock on my door.

"Please don't be late."

I can tell he's grinning and can imagine the expression on his perfect face.

"We'll see," I say. After one last look, I take a selfie with the ring, and the fading sunlight leaks through the windows.

As the smile touches my lips, I grab Easton's ring and the handwritten vows I started this morning. The butterflies go wild. I take another deep breath, then I follow the walking path that leads directly to the beach. The wind blows, and when I look up, I don't see anything I recognize in the night sky, but the stars are still there.

Two torches are lit and shoved into the sand because the sun should fully set right after we finish our vows. When my toes are in the sand, Easton's gaze is on mine. His hair blows in the breeze as the waves crash behind him. His khaki pants are rolled to his calves, and a white button-up shirt is rolled to his elbows. A smile fills his face as I walk toward him. It's like a magnet pulls me directly to him.

"Hi, Lexi," the officiant says as I stare at Easton.

"Hello," I offer.

"Easton stated you'd be starting, so when you're ready," he says.

I give him a smile and nod, bringing my attention back to the man I'm about to marry. He lifts his hand to my cheek and I lean into his touch.

"So *fucking* gorgeous."

"You are," I whisper, feeling like I'm drowning in his blue eyes.

It's then that he fully captures me. All of me. And I think he knows it too.

"*Easton.*" I laugh, holding the paper and swallowing down my excitement. "Honest truths with you, always. I considered not spilling my heart out and writing something generic, but I'm all about the adventure, and my daddy always told me to let the truth set me free. I know I suck at first impressions, and I have the worst timing in the world."

His head falls back with laughter, messy curls bounce, and his blue eyes meet mine.

"But," I continue, smiling. "Somehow, you find that adorable."

"Because it is."

"That's how I knew you accepted me, my humor, and who I am at my core. My essence. I was nervous about what I'd say, worried I'd say too much or too little, and then I remembered that you want me for *me*."

I meet his eyes with a smile, then return to the page.

"I'm so happy to be *your* person. I want to be the one who will join you on crazy life adventures, like getting married on a whim in Fiji because we can. Or sleeping in a one-person tent with a child-sized sleeping bag when in forty-degree weather. Or watching the Milky Way rise as the crickets surround us." I pause, remembering what else happened. I think he's reliving it too.

"Next up is dancing at Stonehenge and ice-skating at Rockefeller Center. And I know this is happening so fast, like a whirlwind, but they say love happens when you least expect it. I wasn't expecting you, Easton. I was avoiding you, avoiding love, avoiding living. But here you are, and I'm so grateful we found each other. I wouldn't want to do this with anyone else. I *know* you're the man I'm supposed to marry. I care about you so deeply," I whisper. "I'm honored to be your friend, lover, and soon, your wife."

He moves forward, and the officiant doesn't say anything as Easton grabs my cheeks and kisses me.

"I couldn't wait. I'm sorry. I needed to kiss you so desperately."

I laugh against his mouth. "I needed it too."

"That was perfect," he says, touching my forehead before pulling away and sliding his notebook from his pocket. He removes the lid from his pen.

"Alexis Lexi Matthews, my fiancée, my biggest inspiration, and my soon-to-be wife. When I look at you, I see a life that I didn't think would ever be possible for me. A life full of laughs, love, and experiences that I couldn't have with anyone else." He meets my eyes, glancing back at the page.

"The moment I looked into your eyes, I knew I'd found what I'd been searching for my entire life—you. Everything changed for me that day. And I know we joke that your timing is shit, but what if it's just right? Because those tiny little mistakes led up to this very moment, the one we're living right now. You are the woman who's taught me what love truly is because I know you can't be bought. I'm in love with you, Lexi. And I already know that I'll love you until I take my last dying breath." He smiles at me, continuing with his pen on paper.

"One second, love," he whispers, grinning. His voice is husky, mixed with his intense gaze that sends goose bumps flying over my skin. "Stay like that for me a little longer. You're so fucking beautiful."

I laugh and a few tears spill down my cheeks because I know he's drawing this moment, right now, in his book, and everything he said was straight from his heart. He finishes, shoving the notebook into his pocket, removing the space to kiss away the happy tears. I told him to prove he's worth spending forever with, and somehow, he has.

"Before me and yourselves, you've proclaimed your love. Do you have the rings?"

We nod, meeting one another's eyes, and slide the symbols onto our fingers.

The officiant smiles. "Please seal it with a kiss from now to eternity."

My mouth crashes against Easton's, and I'm lost in his touch as he slowly kisses me.

"*My wife*," he whispers.

"*My husband*," I say. The word feels foreign on my tongue, but it also feels right, like this is how it was always supposed to be.

When we pull away, Easton takes my hand, and we turn and watch the dark red sun hang lazily on the horizon. The sky bursts in rays of orange and pink as the fading light reflects across the water. It dips below the Earth, and we hold on to one another.

As I turn around, I realize we're alone, just the two of us, exactly how I wanted. "I don't ever want to forget this," I admit.

Easton smiles, pulls his notebook from his pocket, and flips it to the last page. He turns it to show me the sketch. Me, with my hair blowing in the wind, smiling with the beach and sun behind me.

"This is how you see me?"

"Yes," he says, smiling and kissing my forehead. "Gorgeous and deviant."

I wrap my arm around his waist, tugging him against me. "Now what?"

"We're going out," he tells me, taking my hand and leading me back to the house.

When we're inside, he changes shoes. I run my fingers through my hair. "Ready?"

"Yes, hubby," I say, and when we walk outside, the Mustang is waiting for us in the driveway.

"How?"

He shrugs. "I've got ways."

Easton and I climb in. We drive across town, elated, and Easton parks in front of a rustic bar.

"They only play oldies," he says. "Tonight, we're boomers."

"No way," I tell him.

"Adventures."

Easton grabs my hand and we walk inside, our fingers interlocked.

It's like stepping back in time with the decor and jukebox.

People are dressed in costumes and dancing in the middle of the room.

Some are playing pool in the corner, and I turn to him. We're transported in time as I lead him to the dance floor.

Even though we're not dressed for the occasion, neither of us has any fucks to give it as we dance and make out on the dance floor. Here, no one is watching us, no one cares, and I love seeing him like this, so free and careless, laughing and smiling. Giving him my heart is too easy.

"I'm drunk on you," he says, wrapping his arm around me and lifting me in the air, spinning me around.

"My husband," I say, grabbing his face to bring his lips down to mine. "*Thank you.*"

"For?"

"Showing me the *real* you. I know you don't share that version of yourself with anyone."

His eyes darken and he smirks against my mouth. "Just you, Lexi. *Only you.*"

36

EASTON

Birthday countdown: 28 days
Since meeting her: 18 days
Company takeover: 35 days

When we arrive back at the house after a night of dancing, I carry Lexi from the Mustang to the inside. She laughs against my chest and inhales me as I open the door.

"Do you think everyone will be mad at us for getting married without them?"

"Fucking *livid,*" I tell her, kicking the door behind me.

"You didn't have to carry me," she says, still in my arms.

"Fuck yes, I did," I tell her, keeping her in my arms. "Maybe this will be your mode of transportation going forward."

She places the back of her hand against her forehead. "Like a damsel in distress."

"Like a queen who can't be bothered with a menial task like walking."

"I hope, one day, I can be the woman you believe I am," she says as I set her down.

She steadies, then interlocks her fingers behind my neck as I rest my hands on her waist. We sway to a silent song.

"See, the funny thing is, you already are. I'm thrilled you don't know though. I can't have you knowing you can control any man you lay eyes on. That'd make my life even more fucking difficult than it already is," I say into her ear.

"It's never been like this with *anyone*," she admits.

"How many times do I have to tell you that I'm not *anyone*?" I say, spinning us around. "I think I was made for *you*."

She's giddy, drunk on life, on *me*, and I fucking love to see it.

"That's the truest thing you've ever said," she says.

"I hope so. You recklessly fucking married me, darling."

She pulls away, meeting my eyes. The moment grows serious. "And that's why this scares me. When I'm with you, I don't care about anything. Only you and us. You make me reckless. I want to throw all inhibitions out the goddamn door. I just hope … I hope we don't destroy each other in the end," she whispers against my mouth.

She wants confirmation that this will be easy, that we'll be together forever, that it can always be like this. Until I know we feel the same, it's not something I can promise. I don't want a year with Lexi. I want forever. And I'll wait as long as it takes for her to realize and not be afraid to vocalize what she wants, even if her body gives her away.

"Whatever happens, I'll have no fucking regrets," I say.

"I trust you know what you're doing." Lexi takes my hand and leads me outside through the sliding glass door.

The moon rises over the horizon and the lights in the pool cast a neon glow. Lexi's fingers work on the bottom buttons of my shirt until she reaches the top. Her hands trail down my chest and over my torso with light fingertips.

This woman's torturous touch has my heart fluttering and

my breathing uneven. She's everything, all I've ever wanted, and now that I've found her, I'm not letting her go. No woman has ever been able to grab hold of me so quickly, and Lexi has me in a fucking choke hold. And knows it.

She pushes the material over my back and the shirt falls to my feet. My eyes close as her hands glide over my tattoos, and she stops at my heart.

"I never noticed there's space here."

"That's where your name will go."

"Easton, that's permanent," she says.

I meet her gaze and tuck strands of dark hair behind her ear. "So are you. No matter what happens, you'll always live here for what you've given me."

"Your family's company?"

I shake my head. "*Hope*."

She sighs against my mouth, running her hand through my hair, pulling me toward her. "Are you going to kiss me?"

"Do you want me to?" I ask like I did the first time *I* crossed the line with her. I brush my nose against hers and anticipate her answer.

"*Fuck yes*," she nearly begs, and we're a mixture of teeth and tongues and desperate pants.

She tucks her hands into my pants and unbuttons and unzips them before pushing them down to my ankles. I growl against her skin, lifting the pretty dress she wore for me over her body. I trace her collarbone with my lips, tasting her sweet skin, mixed with the salty air. A ragged breath releases from her as I inch her panties down, my palm adding slight pressure between her legs. My finger slides between her slick slit, and she's so fucking wet for me. Considering my cock is at full attention, there's no hiding what she does to me.

Lexi glances down at how hard she makes me with desire behind her green eyes. She takes my hand and leads me into the warm water with her.

"Oh, this feels so good," she moans, swimming to the deep end. The pool is heated; it was a requirement when I booked.

And when her mouth is back on mine, it's exactly how I envisioned it.

The waves of the ocean crash in the distance, and the moonlight reflects over the water. We have the perfect view of it from our vantage point.

"I'll never forget today," I say, wishing I could draw this moment. I bank it to my memory, studying the angles of Lexi's face.

"I won't either," she mutters, wrapping her legs around my waist as I keep us afloat. Leaning in, she tastes my lips.

"Was this part written in invisible ink too?" I ask.

"Yes." She reaches down, stroking my cock.

"Fuck," I groan in her ear as she goes at an agonizingly slow pace.

Our breaths are strangled as our tongues wrestle together. I ache for more of her.

"Please touch me, *Easton*," she says between pants.

"You never have to beg," I whisper. "I just want to enjoy every second like it might be our last."

She melts under my touch as soon as my fingers rub against her needy clit. A sigh escapes her as I place my hands under her ass, lifting her onto the side of the pool. She widens her thighs, giving me full access to devour her perfect pussy.

"More," she pleads, but it comes out like a demand.

Lexi is insatiable, greedy, and addicted to me. I slowly dip my finger into her cunt, until I'm at the knuckle, smiling against her skin. A small cry escapes as her hips buck forward.

"So goddamn beautiful," I say between licks and sucks, giving her wet hole another digit to the knuckle.

"That feels so goddamn good," she whimpers, rocking her hips against me as I return to her swollen bundle of nerves.

She's racing to the edge, like it's a sprint, greedily chasing her orgasm as she takes what she needs from me while I slowly finger-fuck her, tickling that G-spot.

I love the way she tastes, lapping up her sweetness. Gently, I push her thighs wider, sliding my tongue into her cunt and continuing down to her cute ass.

Her needy pants and breathing quicken as I lick around her puckered hole before adding pressure with my tongue.

"East—" she whimpers as she sinks into me, allowing me to eat her from front to back until her body trembles.

When her mouth falls open, I continue, but I slow to a crawl.

"Easton," she hisses.

I kiss her pussy, smirking against her slick folds. "Don't want you to forget who's in control here."

"Asshole," she pants, grabbing and tweaking her own nipple.

My cock aches for her, all of her.

"You know I'm … so fucking … *close.*"

Her back arches off the ground. I work her clit in large circles, giving her flicks, before I suck her to oblivion.

"Oh. Oh. Yes. Yes. My God."

Her pussy tightly clenches around me as I continue giving her my mouth and tongue, and she convulses, screaming out my name, gasping for air, with her heart rate ticking fast in her throat. She stares up at the sky, trying to catch her breath, her pussy still on display.

"I need you, Easton."

She crawls on her hands and knees to the Bermuda grass of the putting green that's beside the pool. Her ass and dripping wet pussy are on full display. I lift myself over the side of the pool and then join her on the grass. She pulls me down to her until I slide the tip between her wet folds.

Her long lashes flutter closed. "I want to feel you." She pulls me to her mouth. "All of you. Nothing between us."

I nuzzle into her neck, smelling her skin, and glide myself deep inside of her. She adjusts to me, a sigh on her lips.

"You were made for me," she groans when I trace her jaw with my mouth.

"I was," I say as we make love under the stars with the waves crashing in the background.

It starts off gentle and grows intense as Lexi's cunt tightens around me.

"Fuck," she hisses, not able to say anything as she comes again.

I position myself on my knees and grab her ass with my hands and fuck her deep and hard, loving how she pulses with each pump.

"Lexi," I groan. My voice comes out in a deep husk.

When I'm close, she rolls me over onto my back.

"Can't let you forget who's in control." She smirks, riding me, popping her pussy up and down my length.

Satisfying sighs release from her, a glisten of sweat forms on her body, and I sit forward, capturing the hard peak of her nipple into my mouth.

"I'm close," I whisper, knowing I'll tip over the edge at any moment as my heart nearly bursts from my chest.

My eyes slam closed as Lexi continues to fuck me into oblivion, and I think I see stars when the orgasm rips through me. She continues her assault on my cock until my groan releases and I stop pumping into her. Then, she collapses on my chest.

We lie, connected, with her on my chest as I pet and kiss her hair, holding her in my strong arms.

The euphoria of being with her still has its hold on me and my mind as I stare up at a sky I don't recognize.

"During our vows, you said you knew you'd love me until you take your last breath."

I nod, kissing her shoulder. "I did. I meant it."

"I can't say those three words yet, Easton," she admits, holding me tight.

"I know," I whisper.

"Don't give up on me." She tilts her chin so she can look into my eyes.

"*Fucking never,*" I whisper, taking her chin between my fingers before kissing her.

37

LEXI

It's our last hour in Fiji, and sadness takes over as we load into the limo and drive to the airport. Yesterday, the Mustang was picked up for transport and will arrive in the city next week.

For twenty-four hours, we stayed inside, insatiable for one another. We slept, made love, and ate when hunger took over.

We walked the beach, swam in the ocean, and held each other under the southern hemisphere, studying a star-filled sky with constellations I didn't know. It felt like being on another planet, like I'd taken over someone else's life.

Still, I can't believe it.

These six days being married to Easton have passed like a dreamless blur and I don't want them to end, but we're not in fairy-tale land anymore; it's time to go *home*. The word feels foreign.

Something has changed.

Is this *love*? The four-letter word has plagued me for so long that I'm scared I'll lose it if I find it. I tell myself that if I shield my heart now, the fall won't be so destructive, and maybe if this does end one day, I can recover from my Easton Calloway addiction.

"What are you thinking about?" Easton wraps his arm around me and I lean into him as we breathe in the fresh beach air. The window is down, and the sunroof is open, allowing the early morning rays to leak in.

"You. *Us*," I admit. My words float in the air.

"I'm going to miss this," he mutters, placing soft kisses on my neck and against my hair.

I know he's not talking about the island or the beach. He's referring to the uninterrupted time we were given to spend together.

"You're my priority, pretty girl."

I don't want to get attached, but I know it's too late.

"Easton, your job is your priority. That doesn't change because of us. It's the reason there is even an *us*," I say, knowing that he'll return to work tomorrow and he needs to be prepared. In his world, a lot can happen in two weeks. If anything, I'm proof of it.

He smirks. "Don't do that."

I turn to him. "Do what?"

His dark, messy hair is pushed to the side. Deep blue eyes, which change color depending on what he's wearing, stare back at me. I glance at the light brush of freckles on his nose that are barely noticeable, but I've kissed and memorized every single one since we said *I do*.

Easton Calloway is a thirst trap, and he's quenched every one of mine.

"Don't act like something will be different between us when we return to New York."

"It will. How many days until you take over the company?" I ask, meeting his eyes.

"Twenty-six," he exhales.

I smile, knowing he's been counting. It's what he does. He

counts down everything—from his relationships to the seconds of his day.

I study him. "Don't lose sight of that, okay? That was important to you. I don't want it to change."

"Sorry, darling, you don't get to decide my priorities when your name is at the top of the list."

"But—"

His lips crash into mine; his hand gently rests on my cheek. "Nothing changes, Lexi," he whispers against my mouth. "Especially not how I feel about you."

And I want to believe him so fucking much that it hurts.

"Some days will be easy, and some days will be hard. That's what I signed up for when I agreed to marry you," I say, repeating what he told me. It was a *truth*.

"So, let's enjoy the good days while we're living them instead of missing them like they're already gone," he says, kissing me more slowly.

He tastes like *me*.

I inhale the tropical soap on his skin, wanting to remember this, us, just like this.

"How did you know that's what I was doing?"

"Because I see you, Lexi. I can feel what you're thinking by how your breathing changes or by the expression on your face," he admits. "I'm not letting you push me away. Each time you do, I'll purposely pull you in even harder. You do realize that, don't you?"

"Is that a threat?" I ask, wearing a devious grin.

"It's a *fucking* promise, *wifey*."

I laugh, shaking my head. "For a minute, I thought you were getting soft on me."

He whispers in my ear, "I'm never soft when you're around."

I glance down at his shorts, and he's hard; the outline of his thickness can't be missed in those khakis.

I rub my palm against his cock—*my cock,* the one that

belongs to me now—and his breathing increases. I follow the scruff down his jaw to his quickening pulse.

"You're beautiful," I whisper, in awe that I have this man.

"I was thinking the same about you," he says as I undo the top button and slowly bring the zipper down.

Easton lifts his hips and his cock flings out at full attention.

"That's a loaded weapon," I tell him, surrounding his tip with my lips, bobbing down.

I pull him out with a pop and lick down the vein that runs the length of him. He's so fucking thick that I have trouble fitting him in my mouth at certain angles. I reposition myself so I can take him to the back of my throat. Gently, I grab his balls, and he lets out a groan when my free hand slides up his stomach.

"Lexi," he whispers, fisting my hair, giving me little tugs that have me squeezing my thighs together.

I want to make him feel so fucking good that he never forgets who he belongs to, temporary or not.

"My bad girl," he growls out, his hips bucking upward.

I love watching him climb to the top, and I hold him there until he nearly begs, but he won't. He never does because he loves to watch me play. He enjoys giving me control.

I stroke and suck and lick until he's nearly trembling. I lift my maxi dress and straddle him. The only thing between us is my panties.

"I feel how wet you are," he groans and moves my panties to the side.

"Yes," I whisper. "I *need you*."

We had each other for breakfast; now, we're onto brunch.

I slide out of my panties, making it easier to take him all in. Whimpers release from me as my pussy devours every inch. I'm wet, needy, and when he grazes his thumb across my clit, my body *begs* for more. It doesn't take much when we're together.

Minutes pass like seconds, and our pace slows when Easton

is close, teetering on the edge. Our breathing increases, and with his lips and teeth on my neck, we tumble into the abyss together.

The orgasm rips through us and the warmth of him pools deep inside me as we lose ourselves in the moment. When I'm with him, the fog doesn't clear, and I hope it never does.

After we clean up, I slide my panties over my body.

He searches my face. "Are you happy?"

"You know I am. You can read me too well."

He smirks. "I can. Just testing you. Also, you must promise not to be mad at me when I tell you something."

"Uh, no," I say.

He pulls out his phone, takes a picture of me, and turns it for me to see. "Are those hickeys and teeth marks?"

I chew on the corner of my lip, touching where he was.

He tilts his head, watching my reaction, and fucking *smirks*. "You *like* that I marked you."

I can't deny it. "I like the world knowing that you chose me."

"They know," he says. "They all fucking know. And I'd choose you a hundred more times if I could."

Butterflies flutter and I ask myself if this was ever pretend. The silence draws on as I try to pinpoint the moment I felt the spark between us.

"What are you in your head about, darling?" he asks, sliding his sunglasses over his eyes.

I laugh, hating that he can do that so well. "*Stop* reading me."

"You make it too easy," he mutters as the car takes a turn.

It's the last stretch of road before we arrive. Soon after, we'll be on a private jet, flying to the city.

"I was trying to figure out when *this* happened, when I …"

"Fell for me?" He chuckles. "I knew you were *the one* the first time our eyes locked."

His admission has my pulse quickening. "I felt something too. Maybe we shifted timelines together."

"It feels like that," he says.

When we board, we're giddy smiles and desperate kisses. We move to the executive seats in the middle of the plane and I take the window, as always.

The only proof we have of what happened lives in our minds. It's sealed with truths and precious metals wrapped around our fingers.

"Did you know this would happen?" I ask, snuggled in his arms as the plane takes off.

"What's that?" He meets my eyes.

I close the window blind and turn to him. "That I'd be eating out of your palm by the end of your vacation."

He licks his fuckable lips. "Fourteen days is all it's ever taken for someone to fall in love with me."

My mouth falls open and I shake my head. "All of it was by design."

I think about the length of time he'd date people—fourteen days.

"Yes, and this trip was a Trojan horse." He laughs, kissing my forehead before brushing his nose against mine. "It's just, this time, I fell too."

"No." I shake my head. "The difference is, you fell *first*. And *harder*."

"Fuck yes, I did," he whispers, capturing my mouth. "And I'd do it again. Ten out of five."

Could we *really* have fallen in *love* so quickly? When I look into his eyes, the answer is yes. Easton's tough as nails, and even though he hides his vulnerabilities under his suit, they exist alongside mine.

When the outside factors are stripped away, we're two humans who care, crave adventure, and want to be loved and loved in return.

Together, we're safe. Apart, we're dangerous.

And I find comfort in knowing I've finally met my match.

When we're back in the States, a car awaits us to take us to the diamond in the sky. Our bags are loaded as we slide inside. Easton has his phone in his hand, and I've got mine. Neither of us has powered them on.

I glance down at it like it's a curse. "I don't want to deal with this until tomorrow, after I've slept."

The flight was long. We left early this morning and hadn't gotten much sleep the night before. Easton has to be at the office in a handful of hours. Our time together is slipping through my fingers like sand.

He returns it to his pocket. "You're right. It can wait."

The car slows before the high-rise and we exit. Easton wraps his arm around me and holds me close as the doors to the building slide open. When we're on the elevator, he kisses my forehead and wraps his arms around me.

When we finally enter the diamond in the sky, the lights are low. The golden city surrounds us, the buildings shining bright.

Easton smiles, capturing my attention in a snap. In moments like this, I have a hard time remembering who I was before I unapologetically barged into this man's life.

"Home sweet home," I say, seeing my new books we bought in Texas stacked high on the counter.

Easton yawns, and I can see how tired he is.

"Shall we go to bed?" I ask, and he loops his finger into mine as we climb the stairs.

"Do you want to pick a room?"

I laugh and he tilts his head.

"Yours."

He grabs my elbow, brushing his thumb against my skin, and

smiles. "*Ours. Only* confirming you haven't changed your mind about us."

"I'm not leaving the center of whatever mattress you're sleeping on unless you want me to," I admit.

"So, never. Got it." He gives me a boyish grin and I nearly melt right there.

Easton takes a quick shower and I jump in with him as we rinse the day off our bodies. Then, we climb between his silk sheets and he holds me against his chest. I fall asleep to the calm sound of his beating heart.

My eyes flutter open with Easton's cock pressed into my back. His breathing is smooth and even and I know he's still sleeping. I glance out at the twinkling lights of the surrounding buildings and let out a content sigh, wishing I knew what the future held.

"Go to sleep," Easton whispers in my ear. His voice is a sexy gruff.

I suck in a deep breath and smile on an exhale.

I want my thoughts to let me go so I can drift off to dreamland with him again, but my mind races. "I'm going to miss you."

"I know," he says. "Meet me for lunch tomorrow."

"Burgers?"

"I'd love that," he tells me, his chin on my shoulder.

His breath floats against the nape of my neck, his chest against my bare back. His hand slides into my panties and I sigh heavily when he touches me.

"*Fuck*," he growls as my hips buck forward, giving him access to my wet slit.

It doesn't matter how much of him I have; I always ache for more.

I bite on my bottom lip, knowing it won't take much to get me off. My breathing turns into pants, and soon, I'm sliding out of my panties. Easton is on top of me, burying himself deep inside. I grab on to the sheets with my fists as he pumps into me.

"Easton," I groan, opening my thighs, wanting him to break me in half. "I want to feel where you've been tomorrow."

"Mmm, you will," he says as I cry out, the pleasure too much to bear.

"I'm so in love with you," he whispers. "So fucking in love."

And like a summer breeze, we're whisked away, chasing total ecstasy and finding it together. The two of us collapse after only temporarily satisfying an insatiable hunger.

The next time I wake, I reach over to an empty California king. Where he was is cold to the touch. Based on how high the bright sun is, Easton's been gone for hours.

I notice a small sheet of paper on the nightstand.

The outside reads, *One Week Married to You.*

I open it, and there's a drawing of me sleeping in bed *this morning*. I glance at the vantage point, knowing exactly where he was standing as he drew this, and I can imagine him there with the intense expression on his beautiful face as he sketched everything, down to the knobs on the drawers of the nightstand. The detail of my hair, the crumpled blankets, and the curve of my back are impressive.

When I unlock my phone, I see it's ten minutes until ten. It's the latest I've slept in since I crashed into Easton at the W. I needed sleep after gallivanting around the world with a man I'd only dreamed existed.

I go downstairs, wearing one of Easton's T-shirts, and move to the kitchen. I stand on my tiptoes and grab my mug from the cabinet, pulling it down and sliding it under the espresso machine. After looking around the gadget, I press a button on top. A song plays, the beans grind, and seconds later, a beautiful, dark espresso drips into my cup.

"No way," I say, glancing down at the crema floating at the top. I swirl it around, inhaling it.

"Good morning, beautiful," Easton says from a speaker on the counter. His face pops up on the screen.

I lean over and rest my chin on my hand. "*Good morning, hubby.*"

"How'd you sleep?"

"Better with you," I mutter, not fully awake.

"Those panties," he says. "Mmm. My only regret is not being there right now."

I look over my shoulder and notice the cameras in the corners of the rooms. Having cameras inside your house is a *rich people* thing. "Lunch still?"

"Yes," he says, checking his watch. "A car will be there for you in forty minutes."

"Forty?"

He nods. "Please don't be late."

"I'll be ready, just for you," I tell him, blowing on the hot liquid.

He smirks and the screen goes black.

"I know you're still watching," I say, glancing around at the cameras as I sit on one of the eight stools that line his long marble counter. "Oh, wow, this coffee is great. Kudos. Guess you do have good taste." I snicker and lift the mug.

"Alexis," Easton says from the monitor on the counter.

I glance over my shoulder at him, and it's almost like he's here.

"You're *distracting* me."

"Stop making it so easy," I say. "I'm sitting here, minding my business, drinking espresso."

"Looking like a cocktease." He chuckles. "I have to be in a meeting in two minutes. I'm sure everyone is waiting for me."

He stands, showing me his pants and how his cock is nearly bursting the seams. The outline of him in his suit pants is a fucking sight to see. But I know how it feels to want someone so damn bad that it hurts—him specifically.

He shakes his head and sits back in his chair. "But I'm so fucking hungry for you."

A mischievous grin sweeps across my face and I flip my hair over to one side as I move closer to the screen, like it will give us privacy.

"Why don't you have *me* for lunch instead?"

His eyes flutter closed as he scoots further back in his chair. He's contemplating it.

"I might be bad for business," I whisper.

"But fucking fantastic for *me*, darling. Tempting, but I have to go. Have a wonderful day, and I'll see you soon." He blows me a kiss.

I catch it, wanting to steal his attention a little longer, but refuse to be his greatest distraction. "You too."

The video chat ends, for real this time, and I lean against the counter. Neither of us is wrapped around the other's finger; we're handcuffed together, and there is no key.

I glance at the pink diamond, the stone he reserved for *the one*. And it's on my finger.

I walk to the windows and view the park below. It's busy with people enjoying the summer weather.

I finish my coffee, and rinse out the mug, then I glance at my cell phone. It's like a poisonous snake waiting to strike.

I know what Easton and I did—secretly eloped. We robbed everyone of the experience of attending the wedding of the century.

I avoid reality a little longer and go upstairs. When I enter

Easton's closet, I stand in shock. It's the size of Carlee's apartment. It's essentially a department store. Every color—blue, black, gray—is available in ties, suits, and shirts. And I imagine Easton wearing every single one. Polo shirts, khaki, and sailing shoes. Shorts, vintage band T-shirts, and tennis shoes galore. At least he has style.

On the other side are beautiful ball gowns, pantsuits, and dresses. One section has graphic tees and ripped jeans from black to blue to white. Converses, in every shade, all my size. I glance at one of the T-shirts, and it says, *Billionaire Obsessed,* in cursive.

I burst into laughter and slide it on. "Smart-ass."

I grab a pair of jeans, noting that the tag reads *Gucci.* Another pair is Balenciaga. These are *designer* clothes. My eyes scan over everything he purchased, and it's well over six figures. I want to know how he pulled it off without me knowing.

A small dresser with a mirror on top sits between summer and winter wear. There's a card folded in half with my name scribbled across it. I smile when I notice Easton's handwriting.

Surprise, darling. I knew you'd find this eventually.

"He's so good at this," I say, bending over to put on shoes.

As I straighten to stand, I glance into the full-length mirror. My fingers trail across my neck, where Easton lost control. Light bruises pepper my delicate skin. I decide to wear my hair up so no one misses it. If we're giving *us* a real chance, everyone needs to understand he's mine—at least for now.

When I'm downstairs, I grab my phone, and it feels foreign in my hand. I haven't turned it on in a week because we were lost together. I press the button and wait.

The headlines quickly load after I type his name into the search bar.

EASTON CALLOWAY IS OFF THE MARKET.

EASTON CALLOWAY IS MARRIED!

EASTON CALLOWAY FOUND HIS FOREVER WOMAN!

EASTON CALLOWAY AND HIS WIFE!

EASTON CALLOWAY MARRIES DOWN!

EASTON CALLOWAY'S FAKE MARRIAGE

THE DIAMOND PRINCE HAS WED.

I see countless pictures of us together in Fiji. When we were there, everything disappeared. It felt like it was just us. We were foolish.

The text messages flood in, along with missed call notifications from Carlee, Remi, my mom, and my brothers. It's too much.

I sit back on the cushion, wishing it would swallow me as my phone buzzes.

The front door swings open and I make eye contact with Easton. I can barely speak as he bolts toward me with fire in his eyes. I stand up to greet him and his hand finds its way behind my neck, pulling me closer.

I laugh against his lips. "What are you doing here?"

"I canceled the meeting," he said. "I didn't give a fuck. I *needed* you." He lays me back on the couch. "I *chose* you."

"Reckless," I say, running my fingers through his hair, wanting him closer.

"You're right. You might be bad for business."

He stands, removing his suit jacket and tie. I join him, pushing his shirt from his shoulders, then remove his belt and slide his pants down.

When he reads my shirt, a howl of laughter escapes him. "Surprised?"

"You're too good to me," I tell him as he quickly removes my shoes, pants, and panties like a magician.

"You make me want to be better. I'm a better man because of

you."

He parts my thighs and sinks deep inside me. We're desperate, like the six hours we were separated was too much.

Deep grunts release from him as I nearly gasp for air. We greedily chase our high, pushing one another to climax, as if we were running a marathon. He pumps inside of me hard; our moans mix, creating a symphony of passion. I don't ever want this to get old. I don't want anything to change.

My muscles seize and I base-jump off the cliff as I come, the orgasm rocking through me. It's so intense that it nearly shatters me to pieces as guttural groans come from my throat.

"Fuck," he growls, continuing to slam into my cunt until he loses himself.

We're breathless, but we still find enough air to slowly kiss one another.

"When I left the office, I felt like an addict. Nothing else mattered but you."

"I know. You do that to me too," I whisper. "It's what makes us dangerous for one another."

He brushes his nose against mine. "Fuck, I know."

"I always wished someone would look at me like you do."

"Relatable."

He places a soft kiss on my lips, and we lie in each other's arms until Easton's phone buzzes, pulling us away. We clean up and redress.

Easton checks his watch once he straightens his tie. "I can't do lunch, not with the traffic being as bad as it is. I'm sorry, darling."

"Don't apologize unless you regret what we did instead," I say.

He smirks. "Zero fucking regrets *anytime* I choose you."

I grab his tie, tugging him toward me. His lips brush against mine.

"Same."

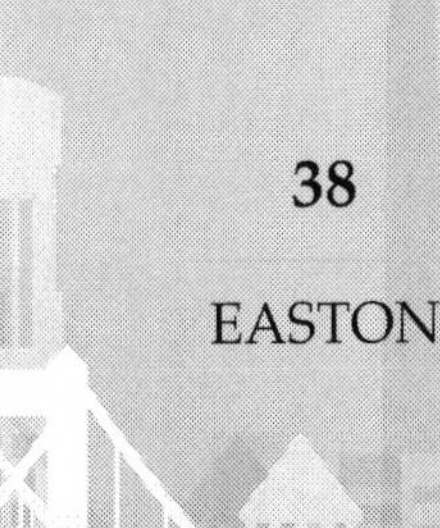

38

EASTON

Birthday countdown: 20 days
Since meeting her: 26 days
Company takeover: 27 days
Married: 7 days

When I walk into my office, Weston enters. He had a meeting in Los Angeles this morning and arrived in the city while I was having Lexi *for* lunch.

He sits in front of my desk, wearing a shit-eating grin, and then he glances down at the wedding ring on my finger.

"I heard you were given an applause that rocked the building when you entered the office this morning."

I smirk. "Ah, yeah. Sad you missed it."

"I knew you were going," he tells me. "As soon as I got notification of your flight plan, I tipped off the paps."

My smile fades. "*Weston*."

"I apologize. And whether you believe this or not, the photos of you two in Fiji were essential."

My anger level climbs. "What *photos?*"

From the moment I walked into the office this morning until now, I've been bombarded. After being on vacation without interruptions, that was to be expected. I've set no personal time aside to look up anything, and I was on a call during the drive to and from seeing Lexi.

He shakes his head, but his smile doesn't falter. However, I can see how fucking serious he is. "Before you get too pissed, I'm protecting what's *ours*. Know that. I'm as invested in this as you. Accept my apology because you know you'd have done it if the roles were reversed."

"You're right. I *would* have," I admit.

The fog I was in from being with Lexi fades away.

"Now, it's time to polish your crown, brother. Let's fucking rule this." Weston stands and gives me a handshake. "Congratulations. I'm happy for you."

"Thank you," I tell him. "You know it's *real*, right?"

"Oh, I'm aware. No one on the planet can deny how you feel about one another. It's obvious. It's *been* obvious."

Weston leaves me to my thoughts.

After three consecutive afternoon meetings, where my stomach growls through each one, my father calls me into his office.

I sit before him at the desk that will be mine. The wedding ring on my finger confirms it.

The Calloway logo is eloquently carved into a dark wood that's so precious that it can't be exported out of the United States. This is the same desk my grandfather and my father have sat behind, and soon, I will too.

My dad glances down at my hands, and I didn't notice I was twisting the ring. It feels foreign on my finger, but I enjoy it. I enjoy knowing Lexi picked this out for me and that I won't take it off anytime soon.

"Congratulations," he says. "I like her. You two seem like a perfect match."

"Thank you. I believe we are."

He stares at me like he's waiting for a confession.

"Are you happy?" he finally asks.

"Very. I didn't imagine it could be like this." A smile threatens to take over.

"And the promise you made to yourself?"

I know what he's asking—if I married for *love*. He's allowing me the opportunity to reveal my lies. I don't have any.

Memories of our adventures play through my mind like a motion picture. There is no one else I could've ever imagined marrying. Lexi is it—the endgame.

"Fulfilled," I confirm.

My father stands and gives me a tight hug. "Love is always on time," he tells me.

"It is," I say, releasing him. "I understand the marriage clause now. Grandfather knew that if we were married, we'd force ourselves to have work-life balance."

My father grins and nods. "Yes. Something only a man in love would say."

I clear my throat. "When you married Mom, did you love her?"

It's not a conversation the two of us have ever had, but it's something I've always wondered. After becoming an adult and knowing how difficult it's been to navigate my personal life, I wonder if my father was in the same predicament as me—needing to fulfill a contract.

"I did at one time," he says. "Your mother was my everything until she wasn't. Son, it wasn't anything either of us did. Sometimes, you wake up and realize you're living a lie and going through the motions of life. We both agreed to see other people, but to stay married. It didn't work out, so we divorced."

I contemplate that for a few seconds. "You had an open marriage? I thought that was a rumor."

"All rumors begin from a spark of truth. Don't forget that. Now, I want to discuss something else, but we might need five minutes."

He glances at his watch, and as if he summoned Weston, he enters.

My brother takes the chair next to me. We look at each other, trying to read each other's mind. Neither of us knows why we're here. It's been a while since we were randomly called to my father's office. All meetings, even *personal* ones regarding family, must be on his calendar.

I don't want to turn into him.

"I need you both to fly to South Africa in the morning. You'll be there for two weeks. A few mines are being sold and we've been offered acquisition before the sale goes public," he explains. "It's an incredible opportunity for us. I'm sending a team of geologists and surveyors to join you. Purchase it cheaper than the original offer by at least twenty percent. Oh, and, Easton, leave your wife at home. I need your head in the game without *any* distraction."

My jaw clenches tight and Weston glances at me. The two of us hold a silent conversation.

"What time is the flight tomorrow?" Weston asks.

"Be at the airport at four in the morning," he confirms.

Both of us stand, and neither of us says anything else.

When we're in the hallway, Weston meets my gaze.

"I'm fucking *livid*."

"They say distance makes the heart grow fonder." He pats my shoulder, but I brush him off.

"I'm going home," I say, not caring what time it is or what else is on my agenda. If I'm leaving in twelve hours, I will spend every spare second I have with my wife.

"See ya bright and early." Weston turns and walks in the opposite direction.

My driver waits for me outside and so does Brody. The drive to the Park Tower takes too long.

When I finally arrive at the diamond in the sky, Lexi is on the couch, reading a book: *Screenwriting for Dummies.*

"You're home early." She sits up, grinning.

She meets me at the door, wrapping her arms around my waist.

"What's wrong?"

She *does* see me.

"I have to leave in the morning. I'm being sent to South Africa for two weeks for a mine acquisition. I'm sorry, darling, but you can't join me. My father … made it a goddamn point to say so."

Her brows furrow, but she forces a smile. "It's fine. Not a big deal. I have a lot of shit I need to take care of anyway, like changing my name."

I hold her tighter against me. "Alexis Calloway. Love the sound of it."

"Maybe I'll be your cam girl while you're gone. Give you something to look forward to."

I capture her mouth. "I'll miss you."

"What did you say to me … enjoy the moments while we have them? Let's do that because I can see that you're counting down the hours in your head."

"You're right, and we have less than twelve hours before I have to leave."

Of course I'm counting.

She wraps her arms around my neck and I rest my hands on her waist. "I guess you'll sleep on the plane because I'm not wasting another second."

"It's like you're reading my mind, Lexi."

"I am," she confirms.

It's nearly three in the morning, and we're lying on our backs, staring at the ceiling, our bodies covered in sweat from rolling with each other all night.

This woman is my weakness.

My alarm will sound in ten minutes, then I'll leave for the airport. My body begs for sleep, and I'll find it as soon as I board.

"I'll call you every day, and we'll FaceTime."

She holds me tighter. "Deal. I'll make it worth your while."

"Music to my goddamn ears," I say.

Her breathing calms as her arm hangs over my stomach. I draw circles on her arm as her eyes close. She lets out a sigh, and I love us like this.

Lexi's the calm in my storm, and I don't know how I'll survive two weeks *without* her.

"I'm going to miss you," she admits. "In case I haven't told you."

"I know, darling. I can tell. This feels like goodbye, and I fucking hate it."

She smiles. "Good news is when you come home to me, we'll know if we were temporarily under each other's spell. It's a great experiment."

"Doesn't mean I have to like it," I tell her, tucking hair behind her ear.

The alarm goes off, informing us that it's time for me to leave. She grabs me tight before releasing me. I slide out of bed, slip on my boxers, bend over, and kiss her sweetly before getting dressed.

"It's not goodbye," she whispers.

"There will never be a goodbye, Lexi. That's a promise."

39

LEXI

The first day without Easton was odd.

The second day was rough.

The rest is a blur; I no longer know what day we're on because they've all bled together.

My phone rings and I roll over in bed to answer the FaceTime call.

"Good morning, my pretty girl," he says, smiling. "How'd you sleep?"

I'm on my side, barely awake. "Morning. Better when you're pressed against me. How's your day?"

He seems tired and I wish I could hold him through the phone. That perfect smile returns.

"You're so beautiful," he whispers, and I see he has a pen in his other hand.

"Are you drawing me?" I ask.

"Yes, you're the highlight of my day." His eyes sparkle. "Every fucking day since I met you."

I stretch in bed. "I feel special."

"Because you are." He continues to sketch.

The worry I saw seconds earlier has already faded. His jaw is no longer clenched.

Easton's voice falls to a whisper. "I miss you so fucking much; it hurts."

"Two weeks should be easy," I say. "It's not."

"It's been the hardest nine days I've had in recent years."

Nine days. Of course he's keeping track.

After a few minutes, he shows me the drawing. The pillow is squished under my head, and I'm smiling like I am now.

"Doesn't do you justice," he says.

A few minutes later, I blow him kisses bye.

"I'll call you as soon as possible," he promises.

We study one another and the continuous silence lingers for a few extra seconds. It's the *I love you* silence, where I know he wants to say it, but doesn't because he's waiting for me. But I refuse to say something so significant over the phone.

He smirks. "Have a wonderful day, darling."

"You too," I say.

The call ends.

I roll over, pulling the comforter over my head, and somehow fall back asleep.

When my eyes flutter open again, it's just past nine. I take a shower and go downstairs. Each morning, I make a shot of espresso, then enjoy the sunshine on the balcony. Today is no different.

The doorbell rings as I'm about to gulp down the rest of my coffee. I jog through the living room and check the peephole. A delivery person holds a box wrapped in white paper with a red bow tied around it and a bouquet of white roses.

I open the door.

"Lexi Calloway?" the person asks.

His words have my face breaking into a smile.

"Yes."

I sign for it and the goodies are handed over.

Once I close the door, I glance at the camera in the corner of the room. "Easton, what have you done?"

I've been chatting with him throughout the day like he's here, knowing he'll go back and watch the video like I'm vlogging for him. He mentioned it's his entertainment before bed, so I've tried to make it fun.

I've even worked in some corny jokes, hoping they'll make him laugh. It's the least I can do because I know he's stressed. I can see it on his face and hear it in his tone.

"The flowers are gorgeous," I say, setting them in the middle of the breakfast nook. I pull the edge of the silk red ribbon tied around the box, and it falls to the floor. Carefully, I peel off the paper. "Gotta give it to you; you're the king of surprises."

I glance inside, and it's a bunch of individually wrapped gifts. On top is a card with my name on it, and it's in his handwriting.

This man.

"You're so sneaky," I say, smiling at the camera. "How do you continue to pull it off?"

It's not hard to imagine that sexy smirk on his lips.

I read the note.

Dear Wife,

Our marriage has officially outlasted every relationship I have had in nearly twenty years. Happy day fifteen.

—Your Already-Obsessed Husband

I place each gift on the counter, picking up the largest one first. I unwrap the paper and see a laptop. A note is taped to the front.

For your screenplay writing. I can't wait to read it, darling.

—Your Biggest Fan

I slide open the box, and my name is etched on the front—Lexi Calloway. The smile on my lips is undeniable.

"Thank you. I'll let you read it first. I can't wait to get started." I rub my finger across my name. "I'm so lucky."

The next one is smaller. I squish it, then peel off the note.

Because it's the truth.

—Better than every Book Boyfriend

I tear open the paper and lift a black shirt with white text—*Belongs to Easton Calloway.*

Laughter escapes me. "If this didn't give it away, I don't know what will." I point to my neck, where the faded marks of his lips and teeth are still visible.

The tabloids *loved* it.

The very last one is a ... *sex toy.*

I continue reading.

My very bad girl,
It's a long-distance vibrator. Text me an eggplant emoji once it's connected to the app and you're wearing it.

—Your Lover, Near or Far

I stare at the camera and shake my head. "I'll play. I look forward to it."

I study the bright pink toy and read the instruction manual. *"Clit pleasure. To bridge the intimacy gap."*

I go upstairs, and minutes later, I text him.

LEXI

ASSHOLE

Three hours later, I leave to meet Carlee at our little hole-in-the-wall a few blocks away. They still have the best salmon bagels in the city.

The vibrator randomly clicks on and off at varied speeds. Easton has brought me to the edge at least once an hour since I texted him earlier, and I don't see that stopping *anytime* soon.

When I walk in, I smell freshly baked bread and spices.

Carlee glances at my shirt. "Do you have any idea how many people are going to make those?"

"I know." I chuckle. "It wasn't my idea."

Her brow pops up. "Mmm. Really? He really does have a sense of humor."

I snort. "You have *no* idea."

We order and sit at a dirty table by the window with our food in hand. Neither of us cares because the place is full, so we take what we can get. Chatter fills the area, and I see a man with a camera across the way.

"Thanks for this," she says, taking a bite. "It's amazing."

"I always told you that if one of us found a sugar daddy, we all win," I say, giggling. "I honestly thought you would first though."

"Girl, me too." Carlee holds up her hand, and we exchange a high five. "The difference is, you're not with him for the money."

"You're right," I admit. "I wouldn't care if he was broke. We'd make it work."

She nods and laughs. "I'm such a good matchmaker."

"You know, Weston also says that. You two will have to fight it out when you officially meet." As I open my mouth to speak, the toy vibrates inside of me. My eyes widen and I grab my iced coffee and drink.

"You okay?" she asks, studying me.

I nod. "Mmhmm."

The toy slowly pulses, and I regain my composure as the agonizing pleasure begins to take over.

"I'm still kinda pissed at you for not inviting me to your wedding. You robbed me of the only opportunity I will *ever* have of being a maid of honor," she says. "Always the bridesmaid."

"Oh, hush, you'll find someone who doesn't say *I love you* within the first thirty days," I tell her.

"Have you and Easton?"

I study her, wanting to share this truth with her. "Not yet."

She knows I'm weird about it as well. Every man I've ever said those three words to has left *me*.

She glares at me like I have a nipple on my head. "You do though."

"You're right," I whisper. "So damn much. I was planning to tell him after thirty days because I didn't want it to be cursed. You're so vehemently against it, and there's a reason for that."

She bursts into laughter, but she nods. "It's different when you say it first to someone who you know loves you. These fuck boys just toss it around."

I place my hand on my upper thigh and squeeze as the

vibrator continues to pulse. I imagine him in another country, pressing random buttons on an app.

Carlee meets my eyes. "Have you been reading what the gossip blogs have been saying?"

"Not really," I say as the droning inside of my pussy continues.

"Well, the pregnancy rumors have started," she admits, knowing my past, knowing it's nearly impossible for me to get pregnant.

I groan. "I think they'll be disappointed in nine months."

My muscles tense and I swallow hard. If Easton keeps this up, I'll be melting under his control in this dining room full of people trying to enjoy their bagels.

My phone buzzes on the table and I see it's Easton FaceTiming me. He usually does when he leaves for the day, and it's around six p.m. there, so he's right on time.

"Answer it," she says, seeing ASSHOLE displayed on the screen.

"I'll be right back," I whisper, happy for the temporary escape.

I rush to the one-person restroom down the hallway and answer. I lean against the cool wood door, knowing I'll lose myself in less than a minute if this continues. I'm so fucking close.

"My *wife*," he mischievously says, wearing that delicious smirk.

I tuck my lips into my mouth as my heart rate increases.

"Easton," I whisper, and a whimper escapes me.

"Seems I called at the right time. Where are you, darling?"

My eyes slam shut as the world fades away. "Eating lunch with ..."

A deep rumble of sexy laughter releases from his lips. He's still dressed in business attire.

"Are you going to come for me?" His voice dips down to a gravelly tone.

I nod, knowing my panties are dripping wet for this man.

The locked door handle jiggles, followed by a knock.

I clear my throat. "Almost done," I say.

"No, you're not," Easton tells me, and the vibrations stop.

My eyes bolt open.

"Easton. I *need* to," I whisper. "*Please.*"

"Not yet," he tells me. "And you said you loved being edged."

"Not all damn day."

I'm so sexually frustrated, and he knows it. He also knows exactly how much to give me before pulling away.

"I'm in control, babe. FaceTime me when you're lying in our bed, naked. Until then, have a fucking *incredible* day. It'll be worth it. Trust me."

The call ends.

"He's an asshole," I say with a huff. By the smirk on his face when he ended the call, he knew it too.

The knock on the door startles me back to reality. I flush the toilet and wash my hands so that it seems like I was in here for a reason other than the toy buzzing against my pleasure button.

The vibrating stops, but I know it's only temporary. Easton's like a tiger. He waits, knowing when my body has calmed before he restarts his long-distance war on my pussy.

I take another minute, and the guy gives me a dirty look when I open the door, but I ignore him. When I return to Carlee, we chat about life and I fill her in with everything that happened from the Grand Teton to Fiji. She listens with a proud smile, gobbling up all the details, and doesn't pressure me to share anything besides what I give.

We grab our coffees and walk our usual route to the subway through Central Park.

I hug her. "Let's do this again."

"Sooner rather than later," she says, and I agree.

As I head toward the diamond in the sky, the vibrating kicks on and I drop my coffee. It spills across the ground.

"Alexis, are you okay?" Moments later, I hear my name from behind.

I turn to see Brody.

"Have you been following me all day?"

"All *week*."

"Shit," I hiss. "Okay. I gotta go. Tell your boss to *calm down,* and I'll be fine."

Unable to stand there any longer, I rush down the sidewalk and enter our high-rise. As I step onto the elevator, the buzzing begins every twenty seconds and lasts for three. There's no escaping the pleasure that builds.

When I walk inside the penthouse, I close the door, the buzzing erratic, and I know he won't let me come until I'm home and naked in *our* bed.

I peel off my shirt as I walk toward the stairs, and the moment my foot touches the first step, a guttural groan releases from my throat.

It's more intense as I unhook my bra and drop it on the floor. As I take the second flight of stairs to our bedroom, I kick off my shoes, then slide off my jeans and wiggle out of my soaked panties.

With my phone in my hand, I push open the door, ready to FaceTime him, but I stop. Easton's standing in front of me, freshly showered, wearing a pair of black joggers. His cock is hard and I nearly fall to my knees when I meet his eyes.

"Surprise, darling."

40

EASTON

Birthday countdown: 12 days
Since meeting her: 34 days
Company takeover: 19 days
Married: 15 days

"Easton," she whimpers, nearly collapsing from the orgasm that's threatening to take over.

I hold her in my arms, kissing her like tomorrow will never come.

"Am I dreaming? How? *It's a fifteen-hour flight.*"

She dips down and kisses me; it's desperate and so goddamn intense that I can't get enough of her already. Nothing in the world matters except for this moment.

"I left yesterday after I got off the phone with you. I just … I couldn't be away from you any longer. So, I hopped on a private jet to see you. I've been traveling all night for this moment. But I've got good and bad news." My hands glide over her naked body, wanting to memorize every curve of her.

"Bad news first," she whispers, writhing under my touch.

"My little pessimist," I say, my teeth grazing her salty, sweet skin, and I lead her to the bed. I drop to my knees in front of her and place soft kisses along her inner thighs.

Her fingers thread through my hair, setting my body on fire. I meet her eyes before getting too lost in the moment.

"Our trip has been extended. I won't be home until my birthday. Me or Weston."

"*No,*" she whispers. "That's … I don't even know how many more days that is."

"*Twelve.*"

"And the good news?" she asks.

"I'm here with you until the morning. I'm sorry," I whisper. "Leaving caused a major shitstorm, but I don't give a fuck, not when it comes to you."

I kneel before her, my queen, and remove the toy from her beautifully wet pussy and devour her pre-cum.

"Mmm, fuck. You taste so damn good," I say, gently sucking on her swollen bud.

She immediately rocks against my mouth. And I can't deny her this, not when I've denied her for *hours*. Not when I haven't seen her for seven torturous days.

"I want you to come for me, darling."

"I *need* to," she pleads. "You've teased me all day."

I laugh against her. "For this *very* moment. I told you it'd be worth it."

I give my girl two fingers, slowly sliding them inside to tickle her G-spot as she rides my mouth.

When her back arches, Lexi freezes for what feels like an eternity before her body collapses around me; the groans that release from her nearly rock me at my core.

"Let me have you," she begs.

I don't wait before I'm sliding down my joggers and slamming deep inside of her as her wet cunt pulses around me. I give it to her hard and slow as she pulls me down to her.

"I missed you," I whisper into her greedy mouth.

She pants in my ear, "I missed you so much."

Her mouth is against the softness of my neck, peppering kisses before pinching my skin between her teeth. "Mmm. Maybe I'll mark *you*."

With my fingers through her hair, I slightly tighten my grip as she sucks and licks my neck up to my ear. "I want everyone to see I belong to you," I say.

"They know," she says.

I give her every deep inch of my cock, and she moans out. I love hearing her pleasure, knowing I do *that* to her.

No matter what happens, if she's happy, I'm fucking delighted. I was made to worship her and will do so until I take my last breath. That's a goddamn promise.

"I finally found you," I say as her body falls to pieces in my arms, under my *touch*. We fall over the edge together, spiraling and tumbling.

A few more pumps has me emptying myself deep inside her. It's something we discussed in Fiji. She's not convinced pregnancy is in her future but wants it to be. Giving her my baby would be the second happiest day of my life after marrying her. But even if it doesn't happen, I'd be truly happy with our life like this, just us.

"About time." She chuckles, kissing me.

I rub my thumb across her face and kiss her.

"I love you, Easton," she whispers against my lips. "I love you so much."

I lift upward, studying her eyes, still deeply connected. "Fuck, I love you too, Lexi. More than you'll ever know. I'd have waited a lifetime for you."

"Thankfully, love is always on time," she whispers.

I smile, not able to wipe it from my lips.

"I'm so glad I left and came here. You're my sunshine," I tell her.

She lies across my chest and I run my fingers through her hair. When I look into her green eyes, I can't believe this woman is mine. How is this possible? The odds were stacked against me.

I feel her smile against my chest, and she's happy; I know that much is true. And, fuck, that makes me ecstatic.

"I'll burn down the world for you. I'll burn it to the goddamn ground without apology. Consequences be damned."

"I hope you never change," she says, kissing up my chest until she's at my lips. "Husband."

"I'm not sending divorce papers," I confirm.

"I wouldn't have signed them anyway," she says, kissing me.

"Want to take a bath with me?" I ask. "Get you cleaned up."

"Yes," she says with a laugh. "Book boyfriend aftercare."

"Sometimes, *real* boyfriends—scratch that, husbands—are better than book boyfriends."

I stand, sliding my arms under her, and carry her to the bathroom. I set her on the tub's edge as I turn on the water. When it's half full, I slide in, and so does she. With her back against my chest, I wash every part of her from behind and kiss her as she tells me how much she missed me.

She turns to me. "I think, going forward, when you're away from me and you decide to …" Her eyes slide down to my cock. "You have to let me watch."

"Mmm. I'd fucking love that," I tell her. "And it goes both ways?"

"Yes," she says, popping her brow before she kisses me again.

"I'm thinking about you anyway," I say.

"I love that for me," she mutters.

I can see she's grinning as her head rests back on me. My hand slides between her legs, and I wash her.

"I love that for you too," I say as she sighs, grabbing my forearm. "So fucking needy all the time."

"Only for *you*," she whispers, her breathing already ragged.

Leaving her was one of the hardest things I've ever done, but I had no choice.

After being in the air for sixteen hours, I made it to the morning meeting. While I had been in New York, nothing had changed; contracts continued to be negotiated, and no agreements had been made.

I do not wish my life away, but I want the days to pass quicker. It feels like a repetitive nightmare that never ends.

Each day, I'm forced to be "on" in a crowded room of a hundred people for eight to ten hours. Weston does most of the talking; he's articulate, and he clearly communicates, and I welcome it because he's the master of schmoozing. My magic happens when we go in for the deal.

While I'm here, I'm quiet; the only person I want to speak to is on the other side of the world. We have a six-hour time difference, and we've made it work, even if we're both exhausted, counting down the minutes until we'll see each other again.

This time away has made me realize how enamored I am with my *wife*.

Maybe that was the point.

I text her as Weston and I drive to the mining site to conduct another walk-through with our inspectors and geologists.

It's almost nine in the morning in New York. She should just be waking up.

EASTON

Thinking about you, pretty girl. Have a beautiful day.

Her text bubble pops up before I lock the screen.

MY WIFE

Perfect timing. I was about to FaceTime you.

MY WIFE

EASTON

Give me ten minutes.

MY WIFE

Text me when you're ready for the show. But hurry.

I try not to smirk, but it's impossible when she sends me a picture of herself lying in bed, covering her perky nipples with her arm. Her eyes are closed, and she's smiling, almost shy. I know better. She's as cute as a tiger and ferocious as one too.

My brother shakes his head and rolls his eyes. I'm sure I'm as annoying to be around as he was when he first met Lena. He's intolerable when he's in love. Apparently, I am too.

"What's up with you?" I finally ask.

Since we arrived, he's been in a mood. You'd think we traded places, which is unusual. There is no good cop or bad cop in this acquisition. We're both bad, and we take no shit from anyone.

"I'm ready to return to the city," he admits, checking his watch before he moves his attention outside.

The sun is out, and giant clouds float in the light-blue sky.

"Not enjoying my company?"

My brother has always had fun during our travels, for work or not.

"No, I've missed meeting up with someone."

"A woman?"

"No one," he says, meeting my eyes, which is a mistake. I can read him better than anyone.

"You're *lying,*" I say nonchalantly.

"I see a lot of women, Easton."

"You're the one who said you missed someone. It's not the meeting you miss; it's the person," I tell him. "So, who is it?"

I lock my phone and shove it in my pocket, interlocking my fingers as I give him my attention.

"Drop it," he states, keeping his focus out the window.

I chuckle. *"Interesting."*

The silence draws on for a few minutes.

"I'll eventually find out who it is," I confirm. "But I'll let it be your secret for now."

41

LEXI

It's officially been twelve days since I saw Easton after he recklessly flew home to see me. While he's been away, our days have been full of random, missed phone calls, FaceTime, and sex-toy play, where he's at the controls.

At any minute, Easton will walk through that door to me after what feels like an eternity.

I'm holding a chocolate cupcake with a candle I haven't lit yet. I'm wearing a black party dress, which he picked out, along with the black pendant necklace and earrings Easton gave me on our first date. With the room semi-dark, I feel like I'm center stage, and in a way, I am.

"He's late," I whisper, glancing down at my phone, then tuck it inside the pocket of my dress.

He's *never* late, so while I'm tempted to text him, I won't. This is another one of my *bad timing* things—or at least that's what my subconscious says.

As the knob turns, I light the candle. When his blue eyes meet mine, I see the fire burning behind them. That smirk I love so damn much finds his lips and he drops his briefcase on the floor and moves toward me in four long strides.

"Fuck, you're beautiful," he says, his face being lit by the cupcake.

"Make a wish." I hold it up for him.

"It came true just now. I'm home, and you're here," he says, kissing me first.

Easton closes his eyes and grins before blowing it out.

"Did you make it a good one?" I ask.

"Fuck yes. The *best* one," he says, wrapping his arms around me.

I keep the cupcake in my grip as I hold on to him with my other arm. I laugh as the kiss deepens, and moments later, Weston enters.

Easton turns and glares at him with a huff. "We just spent three weeks of fun together. What do you need?"

"*Your* wife texted *me*," Weston says, turning to me. I did text him because I needed them both in the same room at the same time. "What's the emergency, Lexi?"

I give him a cheeky grin.

"*SURPRISE*!" All their friends and family members jump out from behind the couch and the kitchen, and several walk down the stairs.

They both roll their eyes, a perfect mirror image.

I wrap my arms around Easton. "Surprise! Maybe my timing isn't as shitty as I thought."

"Oh, it still very much sucks. You were lucky this time," he says, swinging me around as I laugh. He takes a bite from the cupcake. "I missed you."

"I missed you so much," I say, whispering in his ear. "This will only last for two hours."

"Good. But thank you for this. No one has ever been able to surprise us," he admits.

This makes me smile. "A rule breaker. A heartbreaker. And now a record breaker? Who'd have thought it was possible?"

He laughs against my mouth, and it's hard to pull away from him, but somehow, we do.

The only time he's not touching me is when he hugs his sister. Billie squeezes me the tightest though.

"Glad you're keeping this one," she tells Easton, and he gives me a warm smile.

"Me too," he says, but his eyes don't leave mine.

The intense eye contact nearly brings me to my knees. I love it when he looks at me that way.

It's now that I wish I hadn't thrown this party. I'm greedy, and I don't want to share him with anyone, not with how much I missed him. But he needed this. My heart lurches forward and I swallow hard as the silent conversation streams between us.

The room fills with chatter and he says hello to those who make it a point to give best wishes for his birthday and our wedding.

There were a few moments when I didn't think I could pull this off. Carlee helped with cakes and decorations, and Brody gave me a list of who he believed should be invited. Without their help, I'm not sure it would've been possible. Surprisingly, every person I'd invited showed up.

I glance around and find Carlee chatting with Philip, the guy whose Jeep we borrowed. She's laughing her ass off, and I wave her over. After a minute, she excuses herself.

When close, she lowers her voice. "He's more *country* than us."

She's from a small town in Texas too. It's called Merryville, and they celebrate Christmas year-round.

"I know. Oh, I want to introduce you to someone," I tell her, then turn toward Weston.

Immediately, he stops his conversation with Easton.

"This is my best friend, Carlee. She helped me plan this," I say.

He gives her a smirk as their eyes meet. It's like *magic*. And I finally understand what everyone sees. I witness it on Weston's face.

"Hi, *Carlee*. Weston Calloway."

He holds out his hand, which she takes. He kisses her knuckles and she laughs.

"It's so lovely to meet you *finally*. You're *iconic*."

Weston chuckles and smirks. "That's what they say."

"Oh, please tell me more," Carlee says, watching him over her champagne glass.

I notice the sparks, and I think maybe I'll play matchmaker for once.

Just as I'm about to say something, Easton grabs my hand and pulls me through the living room, saying hello and smiling at those we pass. I see the desperation in his eyes as he leads me outside to the balcony. There's no one out here but us as he crashes his lips against mine. My eyes flutter closed as our tongues swipe together. I taste the chocolate cupcake on his lips and get lost in him, in us.

"Fuck, I missed you." He pulls me into a hug, and I breathe him in. "Thank you," he continues.

"For what?"

"For giving me something to look forward to. The light at the end of the tunnel."

"You realize you were late to your party." I hug him, kissing his chin.

"Ah, you're right." He smirks.

I run my fingers through his messy hair, admiring how fucking beautiful he is. "I can't wait to see what you drew while you were gone."

A chuckle releases from him. "They're all of you."

Billie opens the door and steps out. "Want to come in and blow out the candles so we can leave you two alone?"

"Yes," he says, grabbing my hand and practically dragging me inside.

On the counter, there's a chocolate cake with an elegant *E* and a vanilla one with a *W*.

"Stand behind the cakes so we can take pictures," Billie says, pulling out her phone.

I'm thankful she speaks up and snaps some photos because I'm too caught up in the moment, seeing everyone around with smiles. Every single person in the room is someone. Every single person has a want, a wish, and a dream. And at the end of the day, at our core, many of us are the same.

I fold my arms in front of my body, watching Weston try to dunk Easton's head in the tall cake. Carlee stands beside me.

"Are they always like this?" she asks.

"Yes," I say. "*Always*."

"Ahh, that's cute," she says as Weston meets her eyes with a smile playing on his lips.

We sing "Happy Birthday" to them as they wrap their arms around one another and sway to everyone singing off-key but me.

Easton clears his throat. "So many people I appreciate are in this room. Wow. Thank you for attending this surprise party and welcoming us into the next decade of our lives. I hope it's better than the last," he says, meeting my gaze. "I'm certain it will be."

"Yeah, thanks, Lexi. No one has ever surprised us together before, so kudos."

"I threatened everyone who RSVP'd," Billie says from the back of the crowd.

Laughter fills the room.

Afterward, Easton helps me cut slices for our guests, and everyone gets a piece of both. An hour later, we're telling everyone goodbye until the only people left in the penthouse are me, Easton, Carlee, and Weston.

"I hope you have a great birthday," I tell Weston.

He pulls me into a tight hug. "So, what was the emergency?"

I playfully smack him as Easton peels his brother's arms off of me.

"Don't like that," he says.

I laugh, taking a step back. "Don't want to make him jealous."

"Fuck no, we don't," Weston says. "Thanks again for everything."

"Carlee gets a lot of the praise," I say. I think I see her blush.

Weston turns his attention to her. "Would you like to be walked out?"

"Sure," she says. Then, she turns and gives me a hug and Easton a handshake. "She's jealous too."

"Don't tell him my secrets," I say.

"Not a secret," Weston adds. "I've witnessed it."

"Goodbye, you two," I singsong, gently guiding them toward the door.

Then, Carlee and Weston leave together. Easton locks up, his mouth on mine the moment the deadbolt slides into place.

"That's the first time I've seen my brother genuinely smile in twenty-one days."

"Really? Shall we play matchmaker?"

He chuckles. "Hmm. Maybe. But I think he's secretly seeing someone."

"Oh," I say. "I didn't realize. Maybe I'll calm down on that then."

Seconds later, Easton's arms are under my body, lifting me in his arms and carrying me upstairs.

"You smell so damn good."

"You do too," he says as he nudges open the door and sets me on the bed.

"Are you ready for your birthday present?" I ask.

He nods, unzipping my dress, and I stand before him in the tiniest set of lace lingerie, something I picked up for him.

"What I've always wanted," he says, his eyes drifting down my body. "*Best gift ever.*"

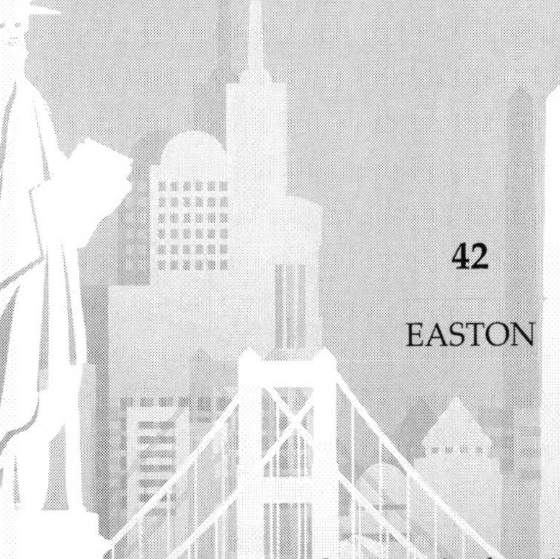

42

EASTON

Since meeting her: 47 days
Company takeover: 6 days
Married: 28 days

The next morning, I have Lexi *for* breakfast, and afterward, I meet Weston in the Park Tower lobby.

While we were in South Africa, he told me he was returning to the penthouse he purchased in the same building a few years ago, so we agreed to ride to the office together each morning.

It selfishly allows me to confirm if we're twinning by coincidence or if he's been playing a fucking joke.

He smiles when he steps off the elevator, running his hand down his black tie and navy suit.

I shake my head, wearing the same thing. "How? Do you have cameras in my closet?"

He shrugs, then slams his hand onto my shoulder. "I've told you, little brother, I can read your mind."

After the car arrives, we head to Calloway headquarters. I

laugh because it's always been my brother and me, just like this, planning world domination.

While we were away, I noticed something had changed inside him. Or maybe he'd been like that for a while. The day I returned from traveling for six months, I met Lexi, and she's been my focus ever since. I feel like a shitty brother, like I haven't been there for him as he navigates through this messy divorce.

"I'm going to try to hang out more," I say, not wanting him to lose himself.

Over the decades, Weston has never let me spiral when things didn't go as I had planned. My brother is always there for me; I haven't given him the same kindness.

His face softens and he grins. "I'd like that."

I won't pry again until he's ready to talk, but I know something is happening in his private life. However, he's been guarding himself after dealing with his toxic ex. She tried to strip him of everything he was—confidence and heart. It's one reason I was shocked he coaxed Lexi into joining him the night he had her meet me at The Garage. Feels like forever ago.

Weston dates often, but he's been off his game since Lena.

He pretended for me. He knew Lexi was my match.

As soon as Weston and I enter the building, Taelor stops us. She notices the twinning immediately. Everyone *always* does.

"Your father is searching for both of you," she says, not meeting our eyes. "He instructed you to wait for him in his office—right now."

"What's going on?" I ask.

"I'm not permitted to say."

Her words don't give me hope.

I glance at Weston and we walk to the opposite side of the building. I'm exhausted from being away from home and traveling, then the party last night, which I appreciated so damn much.

Afterward, I stayed up most of the night with Lexi, making love, then I held her in my arms until we fell asleep. No regrets, and the smile on my face says as much. I might be tired, but I feel like I'm on top of the world.

"Did we miss a memo?" I ask, noticing how no one glances in our direction when we make eye contact.

Weston walks beside me, just as confused.

He can also feel the vibes are off. I don't need this during the final days of the transition.

This week, I am scheduled to spend time with my father as he ties up loose ends. Saturday, we're supposed to throw a company party, a farewell, on his last official day.

Monday, I will be CEO, and I'm fucking ready. For over a decade I've followed in my father's footsteps, assuming I'd take this position. But so has Derrick.

However, I fulfilled my contractual duties just in time. It's proof that love conquers all.

"Maybe Dad wants to congratulate us for doing what the board wanted, but *better*," Weston offers.

It's a nice thought, but I know better.

"I doubt that," I say, knowing we don't get thank-yous.

Being Calloways, the heirs to a multibillion-dollar business, comes with the expectation of being unstoppable. Thank-yous aren't given for doing what should've been done. We were sent because we could make impossible deals happen. Call it charisma, call it luck, but it comes with being a Calloway.

I allow Weston to enter first. We sit next to one another in seats in front of the famous Calloway desk. I want to run my fingers across the intricacies of the carved logo, but I don't.

After a few more minutes pass, I glance down at my watch; it's barely past seven.

This feels off, but I blame my tiredness. We've worked nonstop, and maybe that's by design; the last test my father set up for us to see if we can handle it.

At fifteen past seven, he enters with wild hair on his head. The door slams as he rushes to his desk. My father resembles a goddamn supervillain as he interlocks his fingers, looking between us. I watch him, wondering if I'm like him—cold at times and charming when he needs to be.

The same blue eyes that Weston and I have glare back at us. He's undeniably mad. I haven't seen him like this in years.

"Do you know how long we have until I retire?" my father asks. He's being stern.

"Six days until Easton takes over," Weston answers. His jaw clenches.

"You're right. *Six days.* So, why the fuck am I dealing with this?" He seethes, flipping his computer screen and clicking on a video file.

The screen pops up, and it's a still frame of me and Weston chatting in my office. My brother glances at me, and I realize we're both wearing gray suits. Fuck, I remember this day like it was yesterday.

"What is this?" Weston asks.

I don't need to watch this. I don't want to.

"This is a PR and contractual nightmare. It was sent company-wide and to every major media outlet," he says with flared nostrils as he presses play.

Weston's voice lowers. "All you have to do is get married and make it believable. That's it."

"Okay, so what if I meet the love of my life while I'm fake married?" I asked.

"Oh, it should be a real marriage on paper and in public. Scandals are wonderful for business too."

I groaned. "This is fucking ridiculous."

"You only have to stay married for one year. Pretend to be the happiest, in-love couple in the world, and no one will question

anything. And if you find the one, wait to pursue her until you've divorced your temporary wife. After three hundred sixty-five days, you'll be free to do the same thing you're doing right now, and you can continue your toxic affair with the company."

The screen goes black, and my father glares at us.

"Why were there cameras in my fucking office?" I ask, livid. "Did you do this? And where are the other conversations we had?"

He shakes his head. "Can you imagine how disappointed I was to learn that my sons, the men given the golden keys to this empire, had set out to *defraud* it? Your grandfather ... thank God he isn't here to witness this atrocity."

"I can explain," I say, not knowing where to start. "It's not fake. I —"

"Not right now, Easton. It was your *intentions* that disgust me. Both of you. The board is questioning if you should take the position because they're not sure they can trust you."

"That video doesn't prove anything," I say.

He doesn't listen.

"It proves that neither of you respect the terms. If you'll lie about this, what else are you capable of? I should be thinking about my goddamn retirement right now, not this."

My father inhales a breath.

"Effective immediately, you're both on temporary leave, and all assets are frozen until stated otherwise. I need to speak to legal and the board to decide what this company's future is. Oh, and, Easton, you don't have to wait a year for your divorce. You can do us all a favor and stop pretending with your actress 'wife.' " He puts the word *wife* in air quotes. "And don't ever lie to me again."

My jaw clenches tight as I glare at my father.

"Respectfully, *go fuck yourself*." I seethe.

"The act ... *still*?" His demeanor is threatening.

"When I don't get divorced, I'll enjoy watching you choke on your fucking words." I stand up, pushing my chair under the table.

There is nothing I can say to make him believe it's real. Nothing.

The disappointment in the room is so thick; it nearly chokes me.

Weston stands, buttoning his coat jacket.

"We're a package deal. You get us both, or you get neither," Weston says. It's the gamble my father took knowing the clock was ticking.

"Get out of my sight until I figure out what to do. You've made a goddamn mess out of this. Knowing you could take something so damn sacred and make a spectacle out of it."

Weston tries to say something more, but my father pounds his fist on the desk. "Leave!"

On my way out, I close the door, and it slams shut. The building grows quiet as we head toward the elevator. We've been ostracized. Proof that life can change in a snap, as if I needed it.

We walk into the elevator and take it down to the bottom floor.

When we step out, my brother shakes his head, shoving his hands into his pockets. "That fucking sucked."

"It's *over,* Weston. You and I both know that. Unless we can find out who's responsible and take control of the narrative."

Our car arrives and we ride across town.

"This is my fuckup," he tells me. "I'm sorry. I thought we were safe in your office."

I don't say anything as I try to determine what else this person might have on me.

"This has Derrick's name written all over it," he says.

I nod. "I know. But we need to prove it. How could he have gotten into my office? The door stays locked unless I'm inside."

"That's where we start."

"I can't imagine what the headlines say," I mutter and unlock my phone to type in my name.

EASTON CALLOWAY & HIS PRETTY WOMAN

EASTON CALLOWAY: NEVER IN LOVE

EASTON CALLOWAY'S MARRIAGE OF CONVENIENCE

EASTON CALLOWAY'S HEART IS STILL AVAILABLE

EASTON CALLOWAY BACK ON THE MARKET

THE CALLOWAY WEDDING WAS AN ACT

ALEXIS MATTHEWS CALLOWAY: ACTRESS OF THE YEAR

ALEXIS MATTHEWS: THE STAR OF THE SHOW

WESTON CALLOWAY IS THE PROBLEM

WESTON CALLOWAY DIVORCED FOR A REASON

THE CALLOWAY BROTHERS: MASTER MANIPULATORS

THE CALLOWAY BROTHERS: UNABLE TO LOVE

DOUBLE TROUBLE AND FRAUD

The articles go on for pages about how Lexi and I aren't in love, how Weston was the real problem in a past relationship, and how the two of us don't respect relationships or family. The blatant lies are the most frustrating.

My father is right. This is a public relations nightmare.

I click on the images and see hundreds of photos of Lexi and me together, and I can't help but scroll through them. From the beginning, she's always looked at me the same—with hope in her eyes.

A devious smile touches my brother's lips. "I've got a plan. You and Lexi should disappear together."

He's more calculated when it comes to navigating the social aspect of our job. With his charm, he can get anyone to do whatever he wants, even eat out of his palm.

"How long?" I ask.

"However long it takes. I'll find you. But don't make it too easy."

We exit the car and walk through the foyer of our building. We step into the elevator together and ride up.

As it stops on his floor, he turns to me. "Trust me, little brother."

"I do," I say before the doors slide closed. "Don't make me regret this."

"I won't."

If anyone can make this right, Weston *will*. He's reckless, a fucking kamikaze by nature, and has my back like my shadow.

43

LEXI

I'm typing away on my laptop, staring at a blank cursor and screen. I took a few screenwriting classes in college, but it was so long ago that I'm reading books to help me refresh.

As I place my fingers on the keys, Easton enters. When I see his expression, I know something is wrong.

"Hey, what's going on?"

His jaw is clenched tight. "Would you stay with me if all of this disappeared tomorrow?"

"Yes," I say without hesitation, moving to him. When I'm close enough to wrap my arm around him, I do. "I'd love you more than I do now because *things* don't matter. The amount of time we spend together is what's important. We could move to Texas and live in the loft apartment above the hair studio downtown. I'd get a job at the bookstore and you could open up an art gallery and fill it with your drawings. I'd be just as happy because it's me and you, Easton. I choose *you*. Not the materialistic *things* that come with being with you."

"Thanks," he says, smiling, pressing his lips against my forehead. "I'm so fucking *lucky*. I love you, Lexi."

"I love you. Please, tell me what happened?" I ask. This is the first time I've seen him like this.

"Everyone believes Weston and I tried to defraud the company, so we've been suspended until further notice."

I search his face, not fully understanding what's going on. "Defraud?"

"They know about the original intentions of our marriage arrangement, darling," he whispers, and I pull him into my arms. "Recordings of my conversations with Weston regarding faking a relationship with you were leaked to the public. It's a runaway train, and I can't stop it."

I kiss him sweetly, holding his cheeks in my palms. "It's okay. It doesn't matter."

"I love you so fucking much; it hurts." He kisses me like I'll disappear if he closes his eyes.

"Hey, I'm not going anywhere. We know our truth, and that's all that matters," I confirm.

"Let's go on a road trip. Me and you," he says, pulling me into his arms. "Weston said we need to disappear. And there's no other person I'd rather get lost with."

"Really?" I ask. "Route 66. That's a bucket list item. We could drive from Chicago to California. How much time do we have?"

"However long it takes. We'll sleep under the stars, take dumb roadside photos, and go on an adventure. Let the road guide us."

"This sounds ... fun." I nod, chewing on my bottom lip and laughing. "I'll go wherever you want. When do we leave?"

"Now." He smiles against my mouth.

I pull away and tug his suit jacket. "*You're* the magic, Easton. Whatever you lose, you'll get back."

He nods, his gaze so intense that it nearly steals my breath. His confidence returns in a snap. "You're right."

"You told me that," I say. "So, *you're* right."

Easton and I pack a suitcase each. He grabs money from his safe and shoves it into a leather duffel bag.

"Uhh, how much is that?"

"A hundred thousand," he says.

My eyes widen. "No, we are not traveling with a bag of money like criminals."

"It will be fine."

He zips up the bag and I finally notice what he's wearing—jeans, a T-shirt, a baseball cap, and sunglasses. I can't help but admire him.

"You're eye-fucking me again, Lexi."

"It's too easy."

He walks over to me. My hand slides behind his back and I hold him tight, not knowing how he's keeping it together so damn coolly. I can tell he's working scenarios out in his head, because he's calculative in everything he does.

"Do you want to talk about it?" I ask.

"No. Weston's taking care of it."

He grabs my hand and we leave like we robbed the place.

When we make it downstairs to the cars, Easton goes to the keys, and when he unlocks the door to the Charger, I shake my head.

"You're searching for trouble," I say, sliding across the seat.

"We've found it," he says, walking to the driver's side. After he cranks the car, he grabs my hand and kisses it. "Ready?"

"Hell yeah," I say, squeezing his thigh.

"To Chicago we go. Then, it's two thousand four hundred forty-eight miles of pure fucking fun with my wife."

I smile. "Just me and you, babe. Bonnie and Clyde. Running away from it all."

He chuckles, leaning over and brushing his lips against mine. *"No fucking regrets."*

When we exit the garage, Easton turns on the radio and blasts some oldies from the '90s—*his* teenage years.

The sidewalks are full of paparazzi waiting for us—more blatant than usual. The number of flashes nearly blinds me, and I cover my eyes, trying to shield them from the brightness.

Easton lifts his middle finger out the window and flips them off as he burns out. Not long after, we're leaving the city and worries behind us.

I glance in the side-view mirror, seeing the buildings and blue skies fade into the distance as he opens the engine up on the highway.

As we cross the bridge, I do a quick Google search, and I see the Internet is out of control with articles and photos about our *fake* relationship. I click on the video of him and Weston and watch it. Easton glances at me, keeping his hand on my shoulder as we cruise.

"Meh," I say. "How does this prove that we're not together? Shouldn't matter."

"My father knows the true intention behind our relationship, and it makes me seem untrustworthy. In a fucked-up way, I understand, but I also expected grace after things changed."

EASTON CALLOWAY IS A SCAMMER.

FAKE MARRIAGE CONFIRMED.

EASTON CALLOWAY IS STILL ON THE MARKET.

THE GREATEST ACT OF ALL TIME.

GIVE THIS FAKE COUPLE AN OSCAR.

They used pictures from our time in Fiji and called it overacting.

I suck in a deep breath, then turn off my phone. I place it in the glove box. Easton hands me his hand, and I do the same. We have a GPS guiding us to the hotel we're stopping at for the night.

"Just us," he says. "No devices for the rest of the time."

"I can do that," I tell him, smiling.

"Want to join me in my *fuck it* era?"

"I thought I already had," I tell him, shooting a wink, and he gives me that smirk.

The engine revs, and soon, we're soaring down the highway without a care in the goddamn world. *Together.* The way it was always supposed to be.

Ten hours later, we're pulling off into a roadside motel parking lot. The M is crooked, and the curtains look like they were hung over thirty years ago. Easton glances at this place, which looks like it was dropped straight from a Hollywood set.

"You're sure about this?" he asks, glancing at me. I can sense his unease.

I tilt my head at him. "Are you scared?"

"Scared?" His voice lowers. "Darling, I'll fuck you on the ground. I don't care."

"Adventure," I tell him with a nod, and he shakes his head.

He opens my door and we make our way to the office. The bell rings on top of the door. A coil of cigarette smoke twirls upward from the ashtray on the counter. A woman with blue eyeshadow and bright pink lipstick studies the two of us.

"Where'd you two come from, Hollywood?" She glances between us.

I can't help but snort. "I thought the same thing when we pulled into the parking lot."

The world melts away when he glances at me and then turns back to her. "We'd like a room for the night."

She glances at our rings, inhales her cigarette, then blows the smoke toward the cracked-open window. "I need you to fill out this paperwork and gimme your driver's license. Then, it's one hundred dollars a night, plus a two-hundred-dollar deposit."

Easton sets five hundred dollars down on the counter. "You can keep the change if you don't make me fill that out," he says.

She gives us a physical key, and we walk outside.

"It's going to be fine," I say, trying to stay positive as we walk to our motel room.

He places the key inside the door, then swings it open, flicking on the orange-tinted lights. There's a huge stain on the carpet in the middle of the floor.

"Nope," he tells me. "I can't do this."

"A dingy motel is your limit?" I laugh.

"You found it," he tells me, turning around. He returns the key to the office, grabs my hand, and leads me to the car without glancing over his shoulder.

"You paid five hundred dollars for that room."

He laughs. "Oh fucking well. In the car we go. I'll figure it out," he says, opening the door. He shuts it, shaking his head.

Easton climbs in and taps the GPS, programming in a different location. It would be easier to turn on our phones, but it's best if we don't.

Twenty-five minutes later, we're pulling into the parking lot of a camping store. Easton and I go inside and grab the gear we might need for the night.

An hour later, we turn into a roadside campground. We're assigned our campsite and given the code to the bathroom doors.

Easton and I quickly pitch the tent before it grows any darker. He purchased a box of wood, and we use a Quick Start block to get the fire going.

When our base camp is set up, he sits in a chair and I take his lap, like we did all those weeks ago.

With his arms wrapped around me, he kisses my neck right below my ear before he whispers, "I'll never take us for granted."

"Me neither, babe."

Gently, Easton kisses me. "No matter what happens, I'll always love you."

"Easy days and hard days, remember? This is one of the hard ones," I whisper. "And that's okay. We're traveling the country, camping under the stars, and we'll have the time of our lives."

He holds me tighter. "I already am. Weston will fix this. I saw it in his eyes; nothing can stop him when he gets like that. It's the only time I back away and let him take full control of situations."

"I trust him," I say. "He's done so much for us already."

"I have a feeling it's *more* than we know." He twists my hair in his finger and smiles at me.

I lean back on him, smiling as we stare at the fire. His finger traces circles on my stomach as he slowly breathes in my ear.

Right now, it might feel like the world is burning around us, but in the end, we'll still be standing stronger than *ever*.

44

EASTON

Since meeting her: 51 days
Company takeover: ?
Married: 32 days

It's been four days since we left New York, and I have yet to turn my phone on once. However, I know my father postponed the passing of the torch considering the event was supposed to happen today.

Weston will find me. He *always* does.

Lexi and I have eaten in dives and diners and stopped at so many roadside attractions that I've lost count.

We decided against anything luxury. We go nowhere where we might be recognized. We travel the Mother Road as it was always intended—off the grid in an old hot rod in the middle of July with a Polaroid Instant camera and film so we don't miss a single fucking moment.

I've taken the time to sketch every stop—from a Route 66 museum to the Gemini Giant to the drive-in theater, where we made love in the back seat. If we come up on an old gas station, we pull over to admire the architecture. We've taken countless selfies at murals painted across the sides of buildings. And each second I'm with her, I fall harder. Not sure how that's even fucking possible.

I've never been happier than I am right now, even considering the shitstorm I left behind. I'm not concerned, either.

When fat drops hit the windshield, I click on the wipers, sliding them away. We've driven four to five hours daily, and we haven't rushed at a single attraction.

Time doesn't matter. Lexi taught me what it means to be lost without wanting to be found. *It's freeing.*

We've driven through Illinois, Missouri, and Kansas and christened every state. Now, we've added visiting all fifty to the bucket list.

Right now, we're driving sixty-five in the desolate part of Oklahoma on roads without shoulders. We're an hour from the Texas state line, and it's just an open road and land.

The sky in the distance is the color of a bruise as we drive straight into the storm. The engine growls, and I keep my hand tight on Lexi's thigh as she snaps a photo of me.

I've driven more miles since we left the city than I ever have at one time. More firsts with Lexi than not. She grins when she sees the giant sign that says *Welcome to the Lone Star State.*

"Home sweet home," she says, breathing in the air, smiling. "We have to go to the Big Texan. It's in Amarillo, where the old Route 66 used to be. Best steak of your life, guaranteed."

I laugh. "That wasn't on the bucket list."

She nods. "It is now! It's the home of the seventy-two-ounce steak!"

"Fuck, everything *is* bigger in Texas," I mutter, not able to mentally picture how much meat that is.

"Yep, there's a whole challenge around eating it all too.

Everyone in the room watches as this huge clock hangs over your head."

"Oh, we're going," I tell her. "But that means we must add something else to our list to replace it."

"*Our* list." She smiles. "I like how you said that."

It rains harder, and on either side of us are pastures. It's difficult to see outside as the car gets pounded. We come across a rest stop that's an empty parking lot, so I pull over and park. We're in no rush.

Leaning forward, I study the angry clouds, wanting to check the radar, but refusing to let my cell phone blip my location.

"Dance with me," she says, pulling my thoughts away.

I don't hesitate before I leave the car and walk to her side. She joins me and kisses me as the rain falls against our skin. It fucking hurts, but we're alive and together. I twirl her around and dip her down. We're laughs and smiles and memories and adventure, and it's moments like this that I'll never regret falling in love with my little adventure-taker. *My wife.*

Drops of water fall off my hair and splash across her cheeks, and I pull her closer to me. "Dancing in the rain was added?"

"Yes, just now," she says.

Her nipples press through her T-shirt, and it grows heated between us. Her cheeks are between palms as I desperately kiss her. The water from the summer storm falls around us.

I press her against the car and she reaches down, grabbing my cock that's strained against my jeans, feeling exactly what she does to me.

"Fuck," she says, chewing on her lip.

"Back seat?"

"Yes."

We're like teenagers, tripping and giggling, falling into the back seat, soaked. Our hands and lips are full of want and need and everything in between as we struggle to remove wet clothes from our bodies.

"I love this." She giggles.

"Me too," I say, slamming my lips against hers as I sink my cock deep inside of her.

She hisses out, opening her thighs wide as I pump into her. She rocks her hips and her teeth slide down my neck as her strained pants fill the space.

"I'll never get enough of you," she whispers.

"I hope you don't," I say, knowing we're never satisfied, even when we lose ourselves together.

"Are you doing okay?" she asks, knowing today was supposed to be the day.

"With you by my side, nothing matters, Lexi."

The pressure of the world should destroy us, but it only makes us stronger, just *like a diamond.*

After we check in to the motel next door to the Big Texan and change into clothes that aren't wet, we walk across the parking lot and put our names on the waiting list. The two of us stroll around, playing a few arcade games, then enter the gift shop and buy shot glasses and magnets. People glance our way, but I don't think it's because they recognize us.

We're beautiful together.

Lexi signs us up for the challenge, and we pay before trying our luck. We'd lose even if we were sharing.

Lexi and I step up on the platform at the Big Texan, smiling. The announcer gives us the rules and points at the clock, and a room full of people, from the bottom floor to the upstairs area, is staring at us.

"Wait, this is live-streamed?" I ask, glancing at Lexi. Then, I see the camera pointed at us.

"Shit, I forgot about that," she says, getting up and going to the announcer. The live stream is cut a few moments later and the cameras are turned off. She returns. "Fixed it."

"Thanks. Now I guess we're eating four and a half pounds of fucking steak each."

I pull my hat down farther. If Weston is searching for me … *here's a crumb.*

She leans over, placing her palm on my cheek, forcing me to see *her.* When I look into her green eyes, it's almost like the whole room quiets as I focus on her, even though it doesn't.

A minute later, our big-ass steaks, the size of a plate, are set in front of us. We're allowed to make sure it was prepared correctly before we begin eating this comically large amount of food.

"We're losing," I say, glancing at her, not rushing as I take a bite of steak because it's allowed to test the temperature.

She's right; it is fucking good.

"I know," she says, raising her eyebrows with a smirk. "I didn't think it was this big."

"Not the first time I've heard you say that," I mutter into her ear.

The timer starts, but neither of us rushes. When the timer runs out, it's obvious neither of us tried.

Afterward, we walk outside and take selfies next to the historic sign that talks about the old Route 66 road and how it traveled by the restaurant before the interstates were built.

The parking lot is full, and people shuffle in and out. It's a tourist attraction.

Lexi and I walk across the parking lot with enough leftover steak in to-go boxes to feed a family of ten.

"That was a mistake," she says, holding her stomach. "But it's been on my list since I was a teenager. Dad and I said we'd always take the drive, but we never got around to it."

"Did you make him proud?"

She shakes her head. "No way. He'd have at least expected me to get halfway."

When we enter our home for the night, Lexi and I fall onto the bed and stare at the ceiling.

"I don't think I'm eating meat for a year."

"Me neither," she says, turning toward me.

I glance at her. "Are you happy?"

"*So* damn happy," she says in a whisper. "Are *you*?"

"I've never been happier," I say as she kisses my scruffy chin. I haven't shaved once since we left. "That's a truth."

"I know," she says, wrapping her arm around me and lying on my chest.

I could stay like this all night. Forever, even.

A knock wakes us from sleep. At first, I'm unsure where I am, but I see it says it's four in the morning on the bedside clock.

"Easton," I hear a voice say outside.

Lexi rolls over. "Who is that? Brody?"

"I think," I say, moving to the door and glancing outside.

My cousin is agitated.

I open the door and he glares at me like I'm an inconvenience.

"What the fuck is wrong with you?" he asks, and I step aside, allowing him in.

"I've been expecting you," I say, but not *this* quickly.

I thought we'd have at least made it to Arizona before they caught up with us. I guess Brody is worth every penny. If, by some miracle, I get my job back, he's getting a raise.

Lexi sits up and smooths her hair down.

"There are missing persons reports out for both of you. Do you know how many people are worried? People believe you're …" He doesn't finish.

Dead.

I glance over at Lexi, and she understands what he's inferring.

Brody turns to me. "You need to return to New York immediately."

I shake my head. "No."

"Does my mom think—" Lexi tries to ask.

"Yes, *everyone* does. The conspiracy theories have gone from fake relationship to misunderstood couple who wanted love to conquer all. Not to mention what Carlee did."

Lexi pulls her hair up into a high bun. "Oh no, what did she do?"

"She released everything from text message conversations to pictures she took of you two together. It's all anyone is talking about right now. It's a tribute to your love; since you've been gone, she's interviewed everyone who has seen you two together—from the flight attendant to the random drivers to the man who married you in Fiji. Handfuls of people. Her journalistic research is top-notch. You both need to leave."

I suck in a breath as he hands me plane tickets. "I'm not fucking going."

He laughs and shakes his head. "I knew you'd say that. Weston told me to tell you it's time."

45

LEXI

It's the first time I've flown first class. The plane is empty, considering it's so early in the morning.

Easton always allows me to have the window seat, and as we lift into the sky, I take his hand in mine. His thumb rubbing across mine comforts me. I suck in a deep breath, not knowing what we expect when we land. We still haven't turned on our phones.

"What're you thinking about?" I ask, seeing *him*, knowing he's tumbling in his head.

We might have started as a lie, but our reality changed before we were married.

"You. *Us*," he says, leaning in, his voice low. "I don't remember what life was like before you."

"Based on your tiny moments, *boring*." I smile, thinking about his drawings and how much they've changed since we've been together. "I agree though. I wasn't living until you."

He chuckles. "You're the adventure I'd take a million times over."

I squeeze his hand tight as he leans in and paints his soft lips against mine.

"I'm sorry for our trip getting cut short. I promise to make it up to you."

I smile. "Gives me something to look forward to."

I must've fallen asleep because when the plane touches down, I wake up. Easton squeezes behind my neck, gently massaging me.

We deboard and walk through the airport, holding hands. His Ray-Bans are on and he's wearing his baseball cap, sporting a beard. I love how he can still change his appearance like a chameleon.

He grins at me as we walk past the dancing fountain with lights toward the pickup area.

"Stop it," he says, wearing *that* smirk.

"I can't help it," I admit, openly eye-fucking him.

Anytime we're together, we're explosive, like glittery fireworks in the summer night sky.

He wraps his tattooed arm around me, not giving a fuck if people are watching. I love seeing him like this, carefree and not as guarded in public. Going away did us some good.

When we're in the car, Easton turns on his phone, and I do the same. It's worse than when we returned from Fiji. Countless text messages from friends and many missed calls from my brothers fill the screen. When I see my mom's name, the guilt of disappearing weighs on me.

Easton pats my thigh. "Call her."

"Okay." I suck in a deep breath.

He texts Weston, and soon, his phone rings, so I take the opportunity to chat with my mother.

"Alexis?" she says, and I can tell she's in tears. "Are you okay?"

"Yes, Mom. I'm sorry. We were driving Route 66 and turned off our phones," I explain. "I didn't mean to worry you."

"Don't you ever do that to me again," she sobs. "I was

devastated. It was on national news. Photos of the two of you have been posted everywhere."

"Next time I leave like this, I'll tell you. I promise. I'm fine. I'm happy. Just enjoying life with Easton and doing the touristy things Dad and I planned to do." When the words leave my mouth, I feel my emotions bubble.

Easton notices, grabbing my free hand.

She's crying now.

"Okay," she whispers. "Okay, sweetie. Thank you for calling me. I'm so glad you're safe. Everyone is worried sick. I need to make phone calls to let them know you've been found and you're safe. Thank you."

"I love you, Mom."

"I love you too. You're grounded." She laughs, letting out a relieved sigh. "Come home and see me soon."

"I will, I promise." I apologize one more time before hanging up.

I text everyone that I'm okay with an apology. It takes an hour's ride from the airport to catch up.

I turn to Easton. "How did everything get so out of hand?"

He chuckles. "You know how you have bad timing?"

"Yes," I say.

"Weston's plans always go to the extreme."

"Oh." I contemplate that. "So, you expected this?"

"Not this, but something dramatic. It always works out," he explains.

I nod. "And if it doesn't?"

A smile touches his lips. "We'll move to Texas and rent the apartment above the salon. You'll work at the bookstore, and I'll open an art gallery. It sounds like a dream life I could fall in love with."

"You're telling the truth," I say, not needing confirmation.

Easton smiles. "The outcome is out of my control. I'm along for the ride with you."

I suck in a deep breath, not knowing if I'm ready to read anything the Internet has to offer.

Then, I realize I don't care. I don't care what anyone has to say about us. The dramatics, the back-and-forth of it all. They can think whatever they want. So, with my fingers over the keys, I lock my phone and shove it in my pocket.

"Not even curious?" Easton asks, and I glance at his phone, seeing he's texting Weston.

"Not an iota," I tell him. "If Carlee wrote something for us, we're golden. I know my best friend. Her words are her weapon, and she uses them for good in a world of lies."

Easton shoves his phone into his pocket when the car slows outside the diamond in the sky. "We need to be at the office in two hours."

"We?" I ask.

"I'd love for you to join me, darling, considering it involves you."

46

EASTON

Since meeting her: 52 days
Company takeover: ?
Married: 33 days

After showering and dressing, the two of us take a car to the office in Manhattan. It's afternoon, and the buildings shine and sparkle. We don't say much on the way there, and it's ominous.

Weston instructed me to arrive at fifteen until two in the large boardroom with Alexis in hand. The boardroom can easily accommodate fifty people when needed. While we could walk directly into the lion's den, Weston would *never* do that to me.

As soon as we step out of the elevator, Taelor approaches us. My brother must have called everyone in today. "I'm glad to see you two are back from the dead. Weston's waiting for you."

Lexi and I walk through that building like I fucking own it. I *should*.

Before we enter, I stop, giving her my attention. "No matter what happens today, I choose you."

"Same," she whispers.

The uneasiness in the air is thick.

"Ready?" I ask.

She grabs my hand. "Yes."

I suck in a deep breath and push open the door. When we walk inside, Weston is sitting at the head of the table. Thankfully, it's only us. He checks his watch and stands.

"Wonderful to see you both alive and healthy," he says with a smile. "Did you have fun?"

"Actually, yeah," I tell him. "Wasn't ready to cut it short."

Moments later, the door bursts open and my father enters. I see the stress on his face. Two steps, and he's wrapping me in his arms, hugging me tight.

"What is wrong with you? We thought …" He glances at Lexi. "We thought the both of you were gone." His voice falls an octave lower, and I can see the guilt and shame written on his face.

Good. He deserves to feel that way after how he treated me the last time we spoke.

"It's almost like you care," I say, and it comes out heartless.

He acts hurt, but I have no more fucks to give.

Before the conversation can continue, the board of directors floods in behind him. Derrick enters and stops when he sees me with Lexi, and I don't like how he lingers on her. She leans into me as if I'll protect her from his beady fucking eyes. I will.

When everyone is in their usual places, Weston smooths his hand over his suit jacket and stares at the door.

Moments later, Taelor walks in with a cart stacked with paper. Then, she slams a packet in front of each of the eighteen people around the table, even Lexi.

Weston clears his throat and sits. "Thank you all for attending this emergency meeting, especially on a random

Sunday afternoon. Appreciate that. I guess we should get started. Nice to see you, Lexi and Easton. I'm so glad you're both here and well. I'm sure everyone else is too."

He glares at our father. Weston used emotional warfare without apology.

"Exhibit one: the video," Weston says. The screen lowers from behind him, and he plays it. "You've all seen it. But I have another one for you to watch." He double clicks, and it's a long-lens view of Lexi and me in Fiji, laughing and kissing on the beach.

We thought we were alone, but we weren't. It's not moments I wanted to share with the world, but as I watch us together, it's hard to deny anything.

"And this one," Weston says, playing another from us eating together in the diner in Texas. I was feeding her French fries. "There are countless interviews, accompanied with affidavits. Maybe we did have a stupid conversation, but look at the date. That night, Easton picked her up at her apartment and let her drive to The Garage, where they got to know each other better."

I glance at my brother, knowing damn well that's a lie, but he gives me a smirk.

"The future of this company hangs by a thread because you don't believe their genuine marriage is real? Look at them," Weston says. "*Look*. It's not an act. They're like this all the time. And it's not up to you to decide if it's real. Easton married, as he was supposed to, and kept his word to himself to marry for love. What else do you want?"

Weston makes eye contact with each person, ending with Derrick.

"Before I forget, Derrick should be fired for breaking into my brother's office. I recovered some mysteriously deleted footage."

"What?" my father exclaims. "Explain."

"I did not," Derrick denies.

"Thought you'd say that," Weston says, pressing play on the following video.

It's Derrick, after hours, sneaking into my office three weeks before I returned from overseas for the first time. And Taelor is helping him.

"What the fuck?" I hiss.

Taelor stands by the door and I glare at her. My nostrils flare and Lexi squeezes my hand three times to remind me she's right there.

Weston seems disappointed. She was a great secretary, so I can only imagine what Derrick bribed her with if he became CEO. Probably a promotion.

My father is seething. "You sabotaged my son?"

"Before we get into that, please look at the packet before you. This was always a joke between them because their communication has been honest from the beginning. This fake-as-fuck contract is proof of that. Three hundred pages, poking fun at the ridiculous arrangement. Flip to the back page and read the fine print."

Lexi reads it for the first time. She bursts into laughter, and then I do too.

By signing this contract, you recognize that this is a farce, and we should give each other a chance.

"Lexi, is that your signature at the bottom?"

"Yes," she says, "it is."

"Does everyone see the date and time of it?"

My father breathes in. "The day after the video. It was after their first date."

"It was blown out of proportion. So, can we stop meddling in my brother's personal life and get back to business? I'm growing exhausted by the dramatics," Weston states.

A few board members mumble to one another.

"Derrick, you're fired," my father says, standing and opening the door to the room. "Leave."

"You can't do this," he grinds out. "You can't fire me. The position was supposed to be mine."

"Leave," I say as Weston calls security.

The tension grows as Derrick rushes toward my father, and I stand up. Something shiny and metal is in Derrick's hand, reflecting light.

A knife, I think, and my adrenaline rushes when I look into Derrick's dead eyes. The scene unfolds in slow motion, but Weston is fast. He kicks out his leg, slamming his heel into Derrick's knee. A crack rings out, and then I move forward, wrestling him to the ground. All of my pent-up anger that I have toward this man releases from my fist into his face.

He fights back, but doesn't land a single blow as I shove my free hand into his jaw.

Over the years, he's tried to discredit me, wanted to set me up to look like the bad guy, and even fed the media false information to catch me off guard. He has always been the problem.

Security enters and Weston pulls me away, backing me up against the wall. It's pure fucking chaos.

"Look at me," Weston says, placing his hands on my shoulders, forcing me to focus on him and only him.

Moments later, arms are being wrapped around my waist. *Lexi.* Fuck, I almost forgot she was here.

"I'm sorry." I pull her close to me. "I'm so sorry."

"Are you okay?" she whispers, studying me like I'm a miracle.

I made it out unscathed, other than my bloody knuckles, where I broke skin.

Once Derrick has been escorted out, along with Taelor, my father clears his throat, and the room quiets. We take our seats.

"When I was a young boy, my father always told me the truth should be regarded above everything. I taught my boys to tell the truth, even when it hurts, because, in a world full of lies, it's all we have." My father meets the eyes of every person in the room. "If you say this marriage is real, Easton, I trust you're being truthful."

"I am," I confirm, taking Lexi's hand in mine, and I graze my thumb along the outside of hers. "This woman is my everything, and I'm willing to lose it all for her."

"You shouldn't have to," Weston says. "Easton always said he wouldn't get married for any reason other than love. He kept that promise to himself and met our grandfather's requirements. Yes, that conversation happened, but it was a push in the right direction. I'd like everyone here to raise their hands, especially those who had a private wedding ceremony with just you and your partner." Weston looks around. No one moves. "They did it for themselves, not for a spectacle. Otherwise, you'd all have received an invitation."

Lexi laughs and I glance at her, holding back a smile. It was the original plan when we were unsure of how we felt. Our desires quickly changed; we cared less about everyone else and focused on us.

My father speaks. "I'd like to make a motion that we continue forward with the transition. Easton will fulfill his role as planned and the farewell party will be rescheduled for this Saturday."

"I'll second that," Weston says.

Votes are taken, and it's unanimous. Lexi smiles, and I know no matter what would've happened, we'd have had each other. Life still would've been amazing.

"I love you," she whispers, squeezing my fingers three times. "Congratulations."

"I love you too," I say back to her, feeling overwhelming pride.

Tomorrow, I'll finally take on the role I was born and trained to do.

I will *officially* become CEO.

47

EASTON

Since meeting her: 58 days
Married: 39 days

SIX DAYS LATER

The room is full of employees, investors, and industry leaders. We're gathered here to celebrate the Calloway brand, to send off my father, and to congratulate me. I look out into the crowd as I stand at a podium on the stage set up in the ballroom. It feels right as I give the speech that I wrote for this.

"I will continue to make my grandfather proud in everything I do, as I've always strived to do. As I stand here as your chief executive officer, I know this is how it was always supposed to be." I lean closer into the microphone. "Well, there are a few things we could've done without."

The room erupts into laughter and my eyes find Lexi sitting at a table in the front, looking so goddamn gorgeous as she eye-fucks me from across the room. It all disappears for a few seconds. She lifts her brow—a dare—and I give her a smirk, ready to leave to be alone with her. I snap back to my speech.

"I'm excited for the future and what difference we'll be able to make together as a work family. Before I wrap this up, I want to give a special thank-you to the love of my life, my other half, my wife. Thank you for standing beside me when no one else did and for always giving me hope. I love you, darling," I say, meeting her eyes.

She blows me a kiss, and I catch it, shoving it into my pocket.

The ballroom erupts into applause as the who's who of business give a standing ovation. Tonight, we ate incredible food, danced, and celebrated Calloway Diamonds. Somehow, with everything that's happened, we stayed on schedule with the transition. My first week was incredible.

Right now, as I look around the room, I'm pleased, happier than I thought was possible. I have everything I've *ever* dreamed of.

I had faith it would work out even when everything was falling apart. Somehow, there was always a silver lining—a window opened when a door was closed.

As I walk off the stage, random people shake my hand, and I'm polite, but I make my way to Lexi. She's my safety net, and she calms me in a room full of strangers.

"Charming. Charismatic. All Calloway," she says, standing to meet me.

I smile against her mouth, then move to her ear. "Can we escape?"

"Yes, please," she says, breathing out. "*Love* the way you think."

I make eye contact with Weston; he grins and knows I'm leaving. I said my speech, so the spotlight is back on my father, where it should be. While he's decided to stay as an adviser to the company until he's no longer needed, for the most part, he's hands off after tonight.

Before we leave, I take one last glance around the room. My

father sees me, and I nod at him. He returns the gesture, and then Lexi and I exit. There will be plenty of ballroom parties for us to attend.

When we step outside, the valet is waiting with the Mustang. I slide into the passenger side, and she pumps her fist in the air.

Lexi climbs inside, removes her high heels, and hands them to me. Then, she shifts into first gear, taking it easy until we're on the road.

"Damn. Sexy Lexi," I say, reaching over to run my fingers through her hair as I massage the back of her scalp. "There's something hot about a woman who can drive a stick."

She laughs, giving it more gas, burning rubber as we take a turn. "Sorry," she singsongs, but I know she did it intentionally —my little rule breaker.

"The contract really said all that shit?" she asks.

I chuckle. "I banked on you not reading it."

She shakes her head. "I'm kinda sad I didn't. It was comedic gold in a nerdy way."

When we arrive at the diamond in the sky, our mouths and hands are on one another.

"I'm so proud of you," she says between kisses and nibbles.

"Thank you," I whisper.

"You're welcome," she says, taking my hand and leading me upstairs.

Lexi sits me on the edge of the bed, and my arms wrap around her waist as she stands between my legs.

"Close your eyes," she whispers. "I have a surprise for you."

I smirk up at her and do as she asks. Lexi walks away from me and then returns.

"Give me your hand," she says, placing something in my palm. "You can look now," she says.

I glance down and see a white stick. A pregnancy test. I bring it closer and read a plus sign in the tiny window.

"Lexi," I whisper, looking up at her. "Are you—"

"Pregnant. Yes." She beams.

I drop to the floor, wrapping my arms around her, kissing her belly and holding her tight against me. I inhale her; the moment is everything. Elation fills me, and I feel tears—*my tears*—as emotion takes over. "This is the happiest day of my life."

She laughs, and I stand, noticing happy tears streaming down her cheeks too. I kiss her so desperately.

"We're going to have a family," she confirms as I pull her into my arms, wanting to dance, feeling like I'll fly.

I'm on a high as I twirl her around our bedroom, and we laugh, giddy and excited.

"Remember that night we wished upon stars?" I ask, and the smile on my face hurts.

"Yes," she says, meeting my eyes, capturing my mouth.

"I wished for this life with you," I whisper.

She chuckles. "I did too."

EPILOGUE

WESTON

TWO WEEKS LATER

We sit in a dark and dingy dive bar located at the bottom of a basement with shitty lighting and sticky floors. Oldies lightly float from the overhead speakers, and the baseball game plays on the ancient televisions hanging on the wall. No one has ever bothered me here because they don't give a shit who I am. It's been my refuge since the divorce began, my secret escape.

"I knew she'd be the one for him," I say to Carlee as I sip my whiskey.

She's sitting next to me, wearing a pair of ripped jeans and a shirt that shows the perfect amount of cleavage to leave anyone wondering. The woman dresses like she's looking for revenge.

"You were right," she mutters. "Now, what do I get for playing matchmaker?"

I roll my eyes. "Pfft. You *helped* play matchmaker. Let's not forget, I nearly *died* for this." It's an overexaggeration.

However, there was a knife involved. Thankfully, we stayed

safe, and all those boxing lessons Easton took years ago came in handy.

She tilts her head. Her arm brushes against mine, and I notice how our legs touch. We're sitting close. Our stools are butted next to each other, and it's like this every week. But I know Carlee is great at the game, *a master of flirting.* My match in every way. She's pretty, like a rose—and as vicious as the thorns on the stem. Her confidence makes her as dangerous as dynamite. She's my best-kept secret—has been for months.

"Don't be dramatic," she says, knowing what happened.

I do not doubt that Lexi told her in detail what happened in that boardroom.

I pull my gaze from her and focus on the TV.

"But I made sure Lexi was at the right place *every single time* for you. The hotel. The park. And what about that date, when you let her drive your brother's coveted car? I helped with your *scheme* from the very beginning, Weston. Somehow, you lived to tell the tale."

"I'm like a cat. I've got nine lives." I laugh. "But let's not forget, the hotel room was a goddamn *disaster*. That went too far."

"He wasn't supposed to be in the shower," she says, reminding me that we've talked about this several times since it happened. "You guaranteed that Lexi would walk in on him reading a book in bed. Let's not mention how you got them stranded on top of a mountain when it was forty degrees outside in bear country, of all places!"

I shake my head. "My brother is very protective. He'd have fought a bear with his fists for her. Ultimately, it all worked out exactly how it should've."

She lightly bumps me with her shoulder.

Flirt.

But I can't deny how it makes me feel, especially after playing dating roulette for the past six months.

"Come on. Give credit where credit is due," she pleads, and it's so goddamn cute.

"Regarding *our* matchmaking, we will always *share* the trophy."

"And what about our agreement?" she asks, glancing at the game's score.

I turn my attention back to her. "When you're ready, I'll give you an exclusive interview."

"*And*?"

"*And* a photo shoot," I add.

An adorable grin slides over her lips. "Thank you. I'll ensure your story is told the way it should be told. Your truth."

"Thanks," I offer.

I'm doing this because I gave her my word and she was an integral part of the puzzle.

Not to mention, when it comes to my brother, I genuinely want the absolute fucking best for him. Sometimes, lovebirds must be *pushed* from the nest to see if they'll fly together. We were lucky they did; otherwise, they would've destroyed each other. I was willing to risk it. Easton and Lexi were their worst enemy, and it took finding one another to realize that. Divine timing might have brought Carlee and me together for several reasons; the first was to help two people we care about. The second … *well …*

"We should start a business together," I say when a beer commercial fills the screen.

"The two of us? And do what?" she asks.

"Matchmaking. Could be *extremely* lucrative, considering how good we are at it."

She laughs, meeting my eyes. I see how the corners soften. "You're *not* serious."

"We're *one for one*. Have a perfect record to date. It's painfully easy to see when two people would be perfect for one another,"

I say, glancing over at her, wondering if she's catching any hints I'm throwing her way.

She narrows her eyes. "Weston, you *married* an *actual* snake. Hell, she might even be Satan."

After she opened up, Carlee explained why she wasn't a fan of my ex and how she knew Lena was a narcissistic bitch. Her words, not mine, but I agree. I've never publicly discussed why I asked for a divorce. Easton knows, but that's it. The rest is speculation, rumors spread to discredit me and my image. Eventually, I'll tell Carlee everything, as I promised, because I'll never lie to this woman. Based on what she's shared, she's dealt with enough of that from men.

"You and I know some people are incredible at masking their true selves."

"Or maybe you're too busy looking for the good in people when they're clearly showing you they're a monster." She shrugs. "There were signs. You lacked boundaries."

"Damn," I tell her. "How much do I owe you for my therapy session?"

Carlee bursts into laughter before it slightly fades. "I think that's the first time I've laughed all week."

"With all the clowns you deal with?" I shake my head. "That's a *shame*."

The bartender stops by, and I order a round of tequila. It's our tradition, the last shot of the night before we say our goodbyes.

"We don't base our expertise on *our* track records, just the people we hook up," I explain.

"Hmm. What if we created a *very* specific survey and paired people together like it's a virtual wine tasting?"

I nod. "Or we could host a speed-dating meetup where all the same *flavors* are in attendance. It's different, chatting with someone online than in person. In person, you can feel when sparks fly."

When I'm with her, we talk about life without judgment, and it feels like a genuine relationship. She's not afraid to be honest, and she isn't trying to impress me, and it feels like a friend zone.

We're two lonely people who meet once a week to drink and talk about nothing. It sounds depressing.

Our weekly meetup started on a random Monday night two months *before* Easton and Lexi crashed into one another. The only time I've ever missed was when I was in South Africa. I realized, thanks to my brother pointing it out, I'd desperately looked forward to seeing *her* every week.

While I wait for the bartender to return, I scroll on my phone, glancing over pictures of my brother and Lexi. "They are good together."

She leans over and glances at the screen. "They are. I can't believe they have so much in common. They're like the *same* person."

"I didn't think it was possible, but yeah. They're a match made in a Brooklyn dive bar after a drunk night and an almost hookup," I say with a chuckle.

"I wasn't going to hook up with you," she states. "I stupidly tried to kiss you, but then realized you were a fuckboy."

"You're more of a fuckboy than me," I say.

We've discussed it. As soon as anyone says *I love you*, she's out.

I learned this place, Sluggers, is one of Carlee's hideouts after she breaks it off with someone. It's a tradition she started in college, and every time she ends it with someone, she visits to drink tequila.

Over the year, I'd seen her there a lot, and she'd seen me too.

She spoke first and even bought me a drink, which I found fucking cute. Our meeting was happenstance.

One random night, we chatted about our best friends—Easton and Lexi—and realized they'd be the perfect couple. My brother was conveniently booked to stay at the hotel where they both worked. So, we devised an elaborate plan to have them be at the right places at the right time. I know my brother's habits better than anyone and can predict his every move, so I used that information to my advantage. But that's my and Carlee's deep, dark secret, one we'll keep until death. We are the true masterminds behind it all.

Her voice pulls me away from my thoughts. "So, now that we've officially played Cupid and our duties are over, what does that mean for us?"

I've been thinking about the *now what* all week. "What if we became real friends?"

"Me and you?" she asks, her golden-brown eyes sparkling. Her pouty red lips quirk up into the corner. "You're trouble," she says.

"At least you know what you're getting yourself into," I say, knowing she's aware of my baggage. "But I'm serious."

She smirks, not taking her gaze from mine. She hesitates before holding out her hand. "Okay then. *Friends.*"

I take it and kiss her knuckles.

She lifts a brow and pulls her hand away from me, knowing I'm the master of flirting as well. "I'll have some rules with this arrangement. I don't befriend *anyone.*"

"Luckily for you, I'm not just *anyone.*"

"Calloways." She slowly shakes her head, but I see the smile threatening to take over.

I check my watch, knowing I need to leave if I'm going to make my dinner date. The two hours we spent together passed by too quickly.

The bartender sets down our tequila shots with salt and lime. We lift them, tap the edges together, then lick the rim, shoot it back, and bite the lime.

After I pay for our drinks, I meet her gaze, readjusting my tie. "Same time, same place?"

"Yep. I'll see you next week. Thanks for the drinks," she says.

"My pleasure," I say, standing.

She turns to me. "I'm glad our meetups are continuing."

"Me too," I admit. "So, is this staying our secret?"

"Yeah, it would probably be best," she says.

I push the mismatched stool under the bar, then move close to her ear and lower my voice. "I have a car waiting for you outside when you're ready to go home."

"You don't have to do that," she says.

"I know." I squeeze her shoulder before I leave.

I don't like the thought of her drinking and traveling alone at night in the city. So, I make sure she's safe anytime I'm around.

As I make my way up the stairs of the back exit, I wonder how long Carlee will stay, wishing she knew what she *already* does to me. Being friends *is* a start, an opportunity I won't waste.

So, let's fucking go.

Continue Weston & Carlee's story in
THE FRIEND SITUATION
https://books2read.com/thefriendsituation

Want more of Easton & Lexi?
Download an exclusive bonus scene featuring them here:
https://bit.ly/thewifesituationbonus

AUTHOR'S NOTE

Easton Calloway is a neurodivergent character who is dear to my heart. While I did not blatantly write *he's on the spectrum,* I'm including this note so it's understood.

It was mentioned that Easton dealt with speech issues and began sketching because communicating was difficult. Art was his escape, something he could control when the words would not come. This was inspired by someone who was very close to me growing up. They have high-functioning autism and discovered their voice through sketching when words weren't available. They also continued with this hobby through adulthood. This character is deeply personal, and I hope he is worthy of being on your book boyfriend list.

As a neurodivergent author, I'm very grateful to be able to tell this story. I appreciate you reading *The Wife Situation* and giving me and my words a chance. Thank you so much!

KEEP IN TOUCH

Want to stay up to date with all things Lyra Parish? Join her newsletter! You'll get special access to cover reveals, teasers, and giveaways.

lyraparish.com/newsletter

Let's be friends on social media:
TikTok ♥ Instagram ♥ Facebook
@lyraparish everywhere

Searching for the Lyra Parish hangout?
Join Lyra Parish's Reader Lounge on Facebook:
https://bit.ly/lyrareadergroup

ACKNOWLEDGMENTS

Thank you to everyone who was there for me during this book release. I will forever be grateful for your support, willingness to keep my secrets as I planned surprise releases, and for pushing me to be better. I've written some of my best words recently because of it, and I'll forever be grateful.

To my readers, I love you. You're the best a girl could ever have, and I'm grateful that you keep showing up for me, supporting me, and my words, and loving my characters with so much passion and enthusiasm. I'm so happy you're on this adventure with me. *Let's goooooo!* I have so much more to come; most haven't been announced yet. Eek. (Hiding secrets in plain sight like Taylor Swift these days.)

Have to give a shoutout to my editor Jovana Shirley and my bomb ass proofer David Michael. You made this book shine like a diamond. Thank you to The Author Agency PR for helping spread the word about this book and being a part of the surprise!

Special thanks to my hubby, Will (Deepskydude), who lets me spend a lot of time with the fictional characters who live rent-free in my head. One day, it will all be worth it. I love you. I wouldn't want to go on this wild adventure with anyone else. To the stars…

ABOUT LYRA PARISH

Lyra Parish is a hopeless romantic who is obsessed with writing spicy Hallmark-like romances. When she isn't immersed in fictional worlds, you can find her pretending to be a Vanlifer with her hubby. Lyra's a Virgo who loves coffee, the great outdoors, authentic people, and living her best life. You may know her from when she co-wrote under the USA Today Bestselling pen name Kennedy Fox.

Made in the USA
Columbia, SC
08 June 2024

36866795R00267